DARK DUETS

DARK DUETS

ALL-NEW TALES OF HORROR AND DARK FANTASY

Edited by

CHRISTOPHER GOLDEN

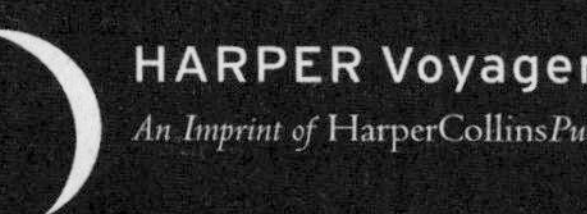

HARPER Voyager
An Imprint of HarperCollins*Publishers*

This book is a work of fiction. The characters, incidents, and dialogue are drawn from the author's imagination and are not to be construed as real. Any resemblance to actual events or persons, living or dead, is entirely coincidental.

A continuation of the copyright page appears on page 423.

HarperCollins books may be purchased for educational, business, or sales promotional use. For information please e-mail the Special Markets Department at SPsales@harpercollins.com.

FIRST EDITION

Library of Congress Cataloging-in-Publication Data has been applied for.

ISBN 978-0-06-224028-6

14 15 16 17 18 OV/RRD 10 9 8 7 6 5 4 3 2 1

CONTENTS

DARK DUETS

AN INTRODUCTION

Christopher Golden

Writing, I often say, is a solitary occupation, but I am not a solitary person. What I am is someone who shares his enthusiasms. I've never been able to help it. If you talked to my classmates from elementary school, some of them may recollect my embarrassing lunchtime habit of erupting with an impromptu survey: "Whoever likes peanut butter," I might blurt, "raise your hand!"

And, of course, my hand would be waving.

When I love a book or a movie or a television series, I want everyone else to love it just as much. One rewarding element of working in one of what I quite proudly consider "the geek trades" is that I will, in all likelihood, find myself in a room in which, were I to shoot up my hand and shout "Whoever likes stories about grave robbers, haunted zeppelins, and evil children with their heads on backward, raise your hand," there are likely to be others with their hands waving. I'm going to go out on a limb here and suggest that you, dear reader, might actually be one of those.

This enthusiasm can be contagious, and when you are a storyteller and many of your friends share the same occupation (compulsion), sometimes a strange, alchemical reaction takes place. Over the years, I have had far more than my share of moments when I have been chatting with a writer friend and the lightning bolt of inspiration strikes us both at the same time. A joke or a crazy idea has led to a sudden shared recognition that something very cool has just been born, and that it is up to us to make it grow.

Not all collaborations begin this way, of course. More often than not, they are purposeful, the result of two authors who admire each other's work and set out to find something they want to write together. Perhaps one has a concept that she can't quite figure out the shape of on her own, and a fresh perspective is desired.

No matter how it comes about, I've always been a fan of the team-up. The results are always fascinating, truly entertaining, and sometimes even magical. I can still remember when I first learned that Stephen King and Peter Straub were writing *The Talisman*. And yet, despite the fact that so many of us wish to share our enthusiasms, collaboration is actually fairly rare. Writing fiction is usually a very personal, intimate process, and finding someone with whom you'd like to share that process is more difficult than you might imagine. In fact, collaboration in general is harder than you'd think. Logic would suggest that since you are halving the number of pages that you, yourself, are responsible for, you are halving the work involved. In truth, collaborative fiction is more work than writing something by yourself. But the work, and the relationships that may spring from it, and the magic that sometimes results, are their own rewards.

As a lifelong fan of the team-up, I've often wished and hoped to see two of my favorite writers pool their abilities on a piece of fiction. As an editor, I decided to see if I could make that happen. The book you hold in your hands is the result.

The pitch for *Dark Duets* was simple: an anthology of stories written by pairs of writers—and in one case a trio—who have *never* collaborated before. Just as the individual stories meld the talents of authors for the first time, the authors themselves are a combination of elements and genres. While the stories all fall beneath the umbrella of dark fiction, within these pages you will find the darkest of horrors and the most twisted tales of suspense, noir oddities and urban fantasy, paranormal romance and darkly comedic speculative fiction.

The best part of editing this anthology came from not knowing what to expect. As each new story arrived, I found myself delighted with the variety and inventiveness—and sometimes the total lunacy—of these collaborations. The authors, it seemed, were having a blast, so much so that more than one story grew to novella length and I suspect will soon spawn further adventures of their central characters.

So many of the best and most interesting conversations of my life have begun with the phrase "Wouldn't it be cool if . . ."

And it is. Oh, it is.

I couldn't be happier with the results of this mad experiment.

Take your seats; the orchestra is warming up and the performers are taking the stage. There will be many strange songs sung this evening, all of them dark duets.

TRIP TRAP

Sherrilyn Kenyon and Kevin J. Anderson

He huddled under the bridge and hid from the world outside, as he had done for as long as he could remember. . . . No, he could *remember* a time before that, but he didn't like those thoughts, and he buried them away whenever they appeared.

The bridge was old and unimpressive, long ago marred by spray-painted graffiti, mostly faded now. The county road extended from an Alabama state highway and crossed over a creek that was more of a drainage ditch, overrun with weeds and populated with garbage tossed out from the occasional passing car. Brambles, dogwoods, and milkweed grew tall enough to provide some shelter for his lair.

Skari lurked in the shadows next to piled cans, mud-encrusted debris he had hauled out of the noisome drainage ditch, a bent and discarded child's bicycle (struck by a car). A stained blanket provided very little warmth and no softness, but he clung to it nevertheless. It was *his*. All the comforts of home.

He had a shopping cart with a broken wheel, piled high with the few possessions he had bothered to keep over . . . over a long time. He hunched his back against the rough concrete abutment, shifting position. The dirt and gravel beneath him was a far cry from the grassy, flower-strewn meadow he sometimes saw in his dreams. He didn't belong in meadows anymore—just here in the shadows, standing watch at the nightmare gate. He had to guard it. Skari wouldn't leave his post.

The tall milkweed rustled aside, and he looked up at the freckled face of a skinny little girl. "I see you there," she said. "Are you a troll?"

Skari tensed, half rose from his crouch. Many layers of tattered and filthy clothing covered his skin, masked his monstrous features. The girl just blinked at him.

"What are you doing here?" When he inhaled a quick breath, through the humidity and the odors of the drainage ditch, he could smell the little girl. The tender little girl.

"My brother says you're a troll, 'cause trolls live under bridges. You're living under a bridge," the girl said. "So, are you a troll?"

Yes, he was, but she didn't know that. In fact, no one was allowed to know that. "No. Not a troll," he lied.

She smelled tender, savory, juicy.

"Come closer."

The girl was intrigued by him, but she hesitated. She was smart enough for that at least.

Skari squeezed his eyes shut and drove his head back against the concrete abutment of the bridge. Again. The pain was like a gunshot through his skull, but at least it drove away the dark thoughts. Sometimes it just got so lonely, and he got so hungry here. He'd been thinking about eating children, tasty children . . . thinking about it altogether too much.

With a crash through the underbrush, a boy came down the embankment. Her brother. He looked about nine, a year or two older than the girl. Both were scrawny, their clothes hand-me-downs but still in much better condition than Skari's. The children did have a raggedness about them, though, a touch of loss that had not yet grown into desperation. That would come in time, Skari knew . . . unless he ate them first.

Next to his sister, the boy made a grimace and said with a taunting bravery that only fools and children could manage, "I think you're a troll. You smell like a troll!"

Skari leaned forward, lurched closer to the edge of the shadow, and the children drew back, but remained close, staring. "Methinks you smell yourself, boy."

Rather than hearing the threat, the boy giggled. "*Methinks?* What kind of word is *methinks*?" He added in a singsong voice, "Methinks 'methinks' is a stupid word."

Skari grumbled, ground his teeth together. His gums were sore. He picked at them with a yellowed fingernail. No wonder witches ate children. It was sounding like a better and better idea to him. His stomach rumbled.

He wanted to lunge out from the gloom, but he knew the nightmare gate was there somewhere behind him, just waiting for him to let down his guard. Skari had been assigned here to stand watch, *sentenced* to stay here.

For many centuries, evil had bubbled up from the depths of the world, and the nightmare gates through which demons traveled always appeared underneath bridges. Skari couldn't leave his post, had to stay here and protect against anything that might come out. It made no sense to him why a vulnerable spot might appear under this small county-road bridge in northern Alabama, but it was not for Skari to understand. He hadn't felt the evil gate in some time, although there was plenty of evil in *him*.

"How long have you been there, mister?" asked the girl.

"Longer than you've been alive."

A car peeled off the highway and drove along the county road. Its engine was loud and dyspeptic, one tire mostly flat so that as the car crossed the bridge overhead, it made a staccato *trip-trap-trip-trap-trip-trap*.

"What's your name?" the boy asked, as if it were his turn to dare.

His name. Yes, he had a name. Other people had called him by name, laughed with him, even a beautiful maiden who had once whispered it in his ear. But not anymore. He had no friends, no home, just what he clung to under this bridge where he stood guard.

But he did have a name. "Skari."

"Scary Skari!" the boy shouted, and the girl laughed with him.

"Come closer!" He was so hungry for those children, so anxious to emerge into the sunlight again, even though it would cause him pain, make him twist and writhe. Skari grew ill from the very thought. It might be worth the pain, though, just for a bit of freedom . . . or maybe just for a taste of fresh meat.

"Billy! Kenna! Leave the poor man alone."

The two children whirled, startled. They looked as if they'd been caught at something.

Their mother came up, a woman on the edge of thirty, her brown hair pulled back into a ponytail. She wore no makeup, but her face was washed clean. Her clothes also had that worn look to them.

"He's a troll, Ma—he lives under a bridge," said the girl, Kenna.

"He smells," said Billy.

The mother looked mortally embarrassed, rounded up the two as she peered under the bridge where Skari huddled with all his possessions. "I am so incredibly sorry they disturbed you. What can I say?" She hauled the children out of the weeds, maybe to keep them safe from him. "They both flunked home training, but it wasn't from lack of effort on my part."

She sounded conversational, a forced friendliness, as if she felt they had something in common.

"Why does he live under a bridge, Ma?" Kenna asked.

Skari was startled to see the woman hesitate. A bright sheen of tears suddenly appeared in her eyes. "Just be thankful we don't live there."

He heard the unspoken *Yet* in her voice.

"It's all right," Skari said. "They weren't bothering me." His stomach growled, but not loudly enough for anyone else to hear. "I've been called worse than smelly . . . and that by my own family."

"Well, I appreciate your understanding. I'm Johanna. It was nice meeting you."

She seemed uncomfortable, backing down the embankment, protecting her children—and good thing. She didn't want them talking to strangers, especially ones who hid under bridges. Especially trolls.

The air was full of the whine of insects, laden with ozone. Overhead, dark thunderheads clotted. If a downpour came, it would make the humidity more tolerable for a while.

"We need to get back to the car, kids," Johanna said. "It's the only shelter we've got."

"I don't want to go back and sit in the car, Ma! It's hot."

"Been there for days. There's nothing to do," Billy added. "When are we gonna keep driving?"

"As soon as we get gas money. Somebody'll come by."

Whenever Skari saw people, they were from the cars that stopped at the rest area on the highway next to the bridge. It had beige metal picnic tables, trash cans, running water, restrooms, and not much else. Not even traffic. Skari had seen vehicles come and go, and most of them didn't stay long, but now he remembered a rusted station wagon piled with belongings. It had been there a while. He thought he'd heard a loud muffler, a struggling engine, tires crunching gravel, doors slamming—two nights ago? Johanna and her children probably had a handwritten sign on a scrap of cardboard asking for help with gas money or food.

Skari tried to remember how to make conversation. Some part of him didn't want the family to go away . . . not yet. "Are you having trouble, ma'am?"

"No . . . yes . . . maybe."

"Which is it?"

"All of the above. But it's my problem. Don't trouble yourself."

Skari glanced behind him, sensed the nightmare gate. But the barrier was strong, stable—as it had been for many years. Nothing was trying to get through right now. He ambled closer to her, taking comfort in the thunderclouds that muted the afternoon sunlight.

"We don't got a home no more," Kenna said. "The mean man made us leave."

"What mean man?"

Their mother let out a heavy sigh. "We were evicted. I lost my job a year ago and haven't been able to find another one. I used up my savings, and we're trying to make it to Michigan where my cousin lives."

"Michigan?" He didn't have much familiarity with maps anymore, but he did understand that Michigan was a long way from northern Alabama.

"We'll manage somehow," the mother said. Fat raindrops started to strike the ground. "We just need a little to get by, step by step. If we make it to Michigan, we can have a fresh start." Her expression tightened, as if she had forgotten about him entirely. "We'll find a way to survive."

Before he could stop himself, Skari blurted out, "It's not so bad. You and the girl could live off the fat of the boy for at least three days."

Johanna's eyes widened and she drew back, startled. Billy thought it was a joke and he nudged his sister. "They wouldn't want me anyway. Girls are the ones made out of sugar and spice and everything nice."

Skari's stomach rumbled. "Don't believe too many fairy tales."

The rain began falling in earnest, thick drops pattering and hissing all around them like whispered laughter. Johanna grabbed the two children. "Come on, back to the car!" She flashed a glance over her shoulder, then ran with a squealing Kenna and Billy off to the rest area.

Skari went back under his bridge, took up his post at the long-sealed nightmare gate, and watched the world as the rain washed the scent of children from the air.

Water ran down the side of the bridge, trickles turning his dank and gloomy lair into a soupy mess. Skari just huddled there. The bugs seemed to enjoy it, though. Even after the storm stopped, leaving only leftover droplets wrung out from the sky, he heard frogs wake up in the creek. Something splashed in a puddle farther downstream. It wasn't yet full dark, but the clouds hadn't cleared.

All the burbling background noise masked the sound of stealthy footsteps, and the fresh rain covered the girl's scent until she appeared. "Mister Skari, are you hungry?"

He was startled. The appetite became ravenous within him. Was she taunting him? He could lunge out right now, grab her before she could run, use his dagger to break her up into delectable pieces, roast her meat over a fire and have a feast. But after the rain, he'd never be able to build a fire. No matter, he was hungry enough to eat her raw.

Skari slammed his head against the abutment again to drive away the thoughts. No, *no*! The hungers, the dark desires had always been gnawing in him, but he could fight them back. He could . . . he *could*!

Kenna extended a rumpled white paper sack. "I brought hamburgers. Do you like fast food?"

No, I don't like fast food. I want something slow enough I can catch!

"Hamburgers?" he asked, his voice a croak.

"Somebody gave them to us at the rest area. They're leftovers. Mostly good, but the fries are cold and soggy. I wanted to offer you the last one. Ma doesn't know I'm here." She extended the sack closer, and with a quick movement he might have been able to snatch her wrist. "It's still fine. Only a bite taken out of it."

With a sense of wonder, Skari took the sack and pulled it open. An explosion of wondrous smells struck him in the face. His mouth watered. He was so hungry!

He stuffed the burger into his mouth, fished around with his paws in the bottom of the bag to grab every small, withered french fry. "Thank you," he said, his words muffled around the food. Tears stung his eyes.

He remembered feasting with some of the other warriors, a delicious banquet thrown by the victorious lord after a particularly long and bloody battle. They had slain countless scaly demons that day, driven them back through the nightmare gate and barricaded it under a stone bridge. Skari remembered how much blood there was in the air on the battlefield, how the smoking black demon blood had a sour acid smell, unlike the vibrant freshness of the roasted boar in the lord's fire pit, unseasoned meat shimmering with grease. He and his fellow foot soldiers had eaten the celebratory feast, drinking the lord's best wine and his cheapest ale. It was all so delicious!

That was before Skari had failed, before he had been cursed . . . before he'd been given this sacred duty.

He finished the food now, licked his crusted lips, and straightened, searching for his scraps of pride and memory as desperately as he looked for more fries.

"Is this your stuff?" Kenna was rummaging in his shopping cart, moving aside the piled possessions he had gathered over the years, decades . . . centuries.

He sucked in his breath. He didn't dare let her find his weapons, the spell-sealed dagger. "Get away from there!" The girl jerked back. "You shouldn't be here. Go back to your mother, your family." He raised himself up, and Kenna looked awed and terrified as Skari grew and swelled, an ominous lurching shape under the bridge. She backed away, stumbling in the weeds. Skari lowered his voice, speaking more to himself than to her. "You have a family. Don't forget that."

She ran back to their forlorn station wagon, and he heard her crying, which made his heart heavy. Another stone of guilt, another failure, another thing to atone for. But Kenna had her brother, her mother . . . a mother who actually cared for her children.

Skari's mother hadn't been like that. When he'd run away to fight in the demon wars, he'd been cocky, full of false bravado, sure that no nightmare monster breaking out of hell could be worse than the shrewish woman who had beaten him, starved him at home.

He'd been so wrong about that.

For a while, his comrades had become his family. The clerics had blessed them all, the noblemen had armed them, the wizards provided magical talismans with blades dipped in bloodsilver that could strike down demons.

In the first two engagements, Skari had been out of the fray, far from where the monsters boiled out from beneath the bridge. Warlords and armed warriors had fought the slavering demons, while clerics and wizards struggled to seal and barricade the nightmare gate. Skari was terrified, but uninjured—and the war went on.

In the third battle, though, when the fanged and clawed monsters turned, charging into the pathetic group of Skari and his friends, he watched his best comrade, Torin, die. Torin was a baker's boy from the same village—they'd run off together—and Skari saw the demons tear him apart, twisting Torin's arms and legs from his torso like the bones from a well-roasted quail carcass. Another demon had bitten off Hurn's head. The long-haired tanner's apprentice had feminine features and a cocky smile, and the fanged monster had opened its hinged jaws, engulfed the boy's entire head, bit down, then spat it out amid a gout of foul breath. Hurn's head had struck Skari right in the chest.

He didn't remember dropping his sword or running screaming past all the other soldiers. Many hundreds of human soldiers had died that day, but the demons were driven back at an incredible cost of brave blood. Skari, though, was captured by the lord's men, found to be a coward, sentenced to be executed by a headsman's ax. But he was given a choice—a choice that he hadn't known was so terrible. The wizards offered him the opportunity to become the guardian of a sealed gate, to be made immortal, to stand watch in case the nightmare hordes ever tried to break free again.

Babbling, Skari had agreed. He dropped to his knees weeping, begging them to make him a guardian. He had not known that choice would be worse than simply dying.

Skari had lost his family, his friends, everyone and everything. He had been alone for centuries, moved from bridge to bridge when it was deemed necessary, when a new vulnerable spot appeared anywhere in the world.

"Your job is to protect mankind," the wizard had said.

The lord who stood before him had a grim, heartless face. He had lost a hand in the last battle. He had seen Skari run in terror from the monsters, and Skari knew he had earned his isolated eternity. His crime was not so great that he deserved hell itself, but bad enough for him to be sentenced to this purgatory. His fate, his *job,* was to protect humans against evil . . . even though his close proximity to the nightmare gates had twisted him, too.

He could never let the evil escape again. He couldn't let it get to Johanna and her two children.

He turned to the bridge wall behind him where he could sense the simmering gate. It had been quiet, silent, but he dare not let his guard down. Dare not leave . . . dare not have hope. He clenched his filthy, scabbed fist and hammered against the hard wall. "I hate you!" Nothing was worse than to be trapped alone where you didn't want to be.

While he kept the nightmare gate guarded, he thought of Kenna and Billy, homeless, penniless, cast out by a "mean man," vulnerable to human predators and unkind fate. Even if the demon wars were over, the darkness of human society was heartless, too. At least the demons were obvious enemies, and they could be defeated.

His thoughts kept going to the woman and her children. How could he defend against the troubles Johanna faced? The family was like the one he'd never had. Maybe that was another part of his punishment: to feel such helplessness after he'd begun to sense a connection. But what could he do?

We just need a little to get by, step by step, Johanna had said. *If we make it to Michigan, we can have a fresh start.*

As he thought of them, he sighed. They were the ones he fought for. But if he simply ignored their very real, though not supernatural, plight, he might as well let the evil behind the nightmare gate eat them. It would be like running away from the battlefield, a coward again.

He went to his cart and dug through his cluttered possessions, the detritus and treasures piled and packed there . . . until he found the last few things he had from his original life in another time, another world: a thick gold medallion, one small ring, and a handful of silver coins, spoils from his first battlefields. The trinkets had amounted to a fortune even then, an even greater one today.

For centuries, he'd kept them safe. Now, they would help a young mother and her children reach safety.

It was full night, and the nightmare gate seemed strong, stable. He sensed no whispers of evil back there, only emptiness. But he did feel the pain and the need of Johanna and her children.

Halfhearted rain began to fall as he trudged to the parking lot of the rest area. The station wagon was dark, closed up for the night as the family huddled there for shelter, safer and warmer than under a bridge. It was the only vehicle there. A single white mercury light shed a pool of illumination over the picnic tables. A metal sign peppered with divots from shotgun pellets said NO OVERNIGHT PARKING—STRICTLY ENFORCED. But no one had bothered to enforce it for days.

Shambling forward, a looming shadow surrounded by deeper shadows, Skari approached the driver's-side window and thumped on it. He heard a startled gasp from behind the glass, the children stirring. He saw the glint of the mother's eyes; she was concerned, ready to fight. In the darkness, they would be able to discern his gargantuan size, but unable to see his ugly twisted features, his scabrous skin.

He held up the pouch. "Didn't mean to scare you, ma'am. I just thought this would help you get on your way."

Johanna rolled down the window just enough for him to push the pouch through. She took it, and he turned, not wanting to speak with her, not waiting for her to see what he had given them.

Skari ambled back into the night, hurrying before any demons could discover the unguarded nightmare gate, before he would have to endure the mother telling him thank you.

No more than an hour later, as he sat in the damp gloom of his lair, Johanna, Billy, and Kenna appeared under the bridge, walking closer. They weren't afraid of him. The mother held the sack with the medallion, the ring, the old coins. "I can't take this."

"Yes, you can. Those things do me no good, but for you they can make the difference. Buy yourself a new chance." He tried to remember how to soften his words with humor. "It should keep you from having to eat the boy for at least a week."

She laughed, and her brow furrowed. "It'll keep us from living under a bridge." The boy and girl gathered closer, and they all looked at Skari. Johanna's face was tight, and he saw tears in her eyes. "This is the nicest thing anyone's ever done for us. Thank you."

The little girl burst forward, threw herself against him, and hugged him tight. "You're not a monster."

Billy nodded and said strangely, "You're saved. I'm glad we didn't have to kill you."

No sooner had the boy spoken than pain shot into Skari's body. He hissed as it burned through him, screaming through his muscle fibers. His skin began to boil and discolor. Underneath his layers of old, crusted clothing, his body twisted in a spasm. He bent over and threw himself against the bridge abutment, his mind ringing with terror.

Were these people escaped demons? Had they come here to attack him? He staggered to his shopping cart, grabbed it. He had to get the bloodsilver dagger, defend himself, defend the world—but the cart crashed to one side.

Unable to stand the pain, Skari doubled over, dropped to the muddy, garbage-strewn ground—

And shrank. Confused, Skari looked at hands that were no longer gnarled ugly paws. They were hands again. Human hands. He flexed his arms, pushed himself to his feet.

The mother and children stood before him, watching, but their eyes didn't look evil. In fact, they seemed glad . . . relieved.

"The demon wars were over long ago," said Johanna. "The nightmare gates are permanently sealed, but after all this time, the guardians themselves have become dangerous."

Billy added, "Not only were you immortal, you became inhuman, too—so close to the darkness that it found a home in you."

"We've been sent to find the last few remaining trolls, to test them," Kenna said in a voice that did not belong to a little girl. "To see if they need to be destroyed, or if they have remembered human decency and compassion. You, Skari, are one of the last. We were afraid for you."

Instead of the eyes of a little boy, Billy's eyes were hard and ancient. "But you convinced even me."

"You are free now," Johanna said. "The world is safe from demons . . . and it is safe from you."

Kenna grinned, and her eyes sparkled. "We release you from your post."

WELDED

Tom Piccirilli and T. M. Wright

It's a familiar story—

Kid and girl fall in love. Homicidal maniac kidnaps and butchers girl over a three-day period in an isolated cabin on the beach. Kid is left for dead at the shore with a partially crushed skull. Parents fail to identify girl's remains. Kid winds up with a couple of metal plates welded in his skull. Kid awakens from coma and has to learn to walk again, feed himself again, rediscover spatial geometry, et cetera. Kid is called down to the morgue. Kid identifies girl's bits based on a shred of a rose tattoo on a scrap of her left buttock. The parents, of course, didn't know. Seven months after her death girl is at last buried. Memorial service has five thousand mourners and is blitzed by the media. Helicopters, reporters crawl over kid. Kid spends twelve weeks under psychiatric care for consistent outbursts of rage and violence. He does harm to himself. He does harm to others. Shrinks claim explosions of frenzy and phantom auditory and visual phenomena are the result of lasting minor brain damage. He sees things and hears things. Cops cut him a break and don't stuff him in prison for bar brawls, for beating up pushy journalists, for drunk and disorderly.

Maniac racks up an additional nine kills before the feds shut him down. Maniac, like all the best murderers, terrorists, and assassins, has three names: Ricky Benjamin Price. Kid, like all the best heroes, has no name. Ricky likes writing letters. He writes his congressman, his president, the Associated Press, the *New York Times,* the ACLU, the pretty newscaster on Channel 4, the families of his victims, and he writes the kid. Nobody responds, except for the kid. Nobody visits, except for the kid.

The kid's there now, letting Ricky's soft and seductive voice work its magic on his nerves. He sits on a chair outside the cell while Ricky lies on his bunk, his arm thrown over his face, motionless except for his lips. The voice is like cold cream on sunburn. You take your kindnesses where you can, and Ricky's voice is just that, a kindness, a mercy. The shrinks, the cops, the protesters pro and con capital punishment screaming outside, they all grate and fray and scrape. The kid can't stand their gruffness, their know-it-all attitudes, their noise, their touch. Everything they do or say drives him up a fucking wall. He hates everybody.

The kid's been visiting the prison for five years. Ricky's been on death row nearly the whole time. His execution's set for tomorrow at nine P.M. You'd think it would be midnight, but no. Nine P.M.—who knows the reasoning behind it. Ricky seems to be looking forward to his impending death. The kid isn't so sure how he feels about it. The girl's parents are out there right now, grouped up with the yahoos and rednecks drinking beer and promising to keep their lights off so there's enough juice to fry Ricky good.

Of course, Ricky's getting the hot shot, and the kid's got a front-row seat.

Ricky wanted a firing squad. The kid thought that was still allowable in this state, but apparently not. They denied him. The kid knows what it's like to go to sleep almost forever, lying there paralyzed, struggling for breath, while the waves roll over your knees and try to drag you under and away. They've got a lot in common now, him and the guy who almost killed him.

Ricky whispers on. What he says doesn't really matter. Most of it is a play-by-play rundown of exactly what he did, and when, and to whom, and how they tried to run, or scream, or fight back. The girl was brave and very strong. She didn't go easy. Ricky points this out over and over. The girl scratched and bit and struggled. She did better than any of the others. The kid feels the same stirring of love and pride he's felt for her for years.

His skull aches and thrums and rattles full of locusts. He gets migraines that make the world tilt and send him into free fall. Ricky is used to the kid clenching his temples and crying out by now, and he calls for the bulls so somebody can drag the kid's ass off to the infirmary. Aspirin are considered contraband but Ricky's got a couple and offers them to the kid, who waves them off.

The bulls come. The setup is sort of funny. You can't mingle with the cons so the infirmary is kind of a secondary ward set off from the primary one, with a lot of reinforced glass between the two. But you're right here, and the cons are right there. The kid's vision is unfocused, he's seeing two, three, four of everything, looking beyond dimensions into parallel universes, the edges red and black and throbbing. The prison docs are aware of his condition. They treat him as a psych patient. They juice him with powerful sedatives, the stuff they give to the psycho killers who stabbed their mothers ninety-five times.

The cons stare at him through the glass. He stares back. He's in here with a little boy who skinned his knee while visiting his father, who still has nine years to go on a fifteen-year stretch. The mother of the boy stares off into a dream, seeing herself in another life, another time, with fulfilled expectations, no guilt, no humiliation. The boy sniffles. The mother gnaws her lip. A pregnant woman who started having false contractions is moaning in the corner. She's rattling in Spanish about how she wants to get the hell out of here so her child isn't born behind bars. The kid hopes they move her out soon too.

The doc comes over and touches the kid's head. His brain burns and sings. The metal feels white-hot. The doc pulls his fingers back quickly as the kid groans in agony. The doc hands him two horse pill pain meds and writes on a chart. The doc asks boring questions, not like Ricky. The doc asks about pain levels, about the consistency of stool, about sleeping habits, drug use, alcohol consumption, sexual function. The doc asks why the kid keeps coming back week after week. The doc asks about nightmares, about the violent outbursts, about anger management, psychosis.

Ricky's back on death row but his voice is still whispering under the kid's welded metal plates. The voice is malleable, mellifluous, slick, oily, like aloe. The girl is screaming under there too but Ricky shushes her, calms her, quiets her, the way he did in real life, or thought he did, before she worked a screw free from her cot and stabbed him in the guts with it. Ricky nearly croaked from peritonitis. The girl wishes that he would have. The girl stares at the cons too.

One Aryan with the face of Adolf covering his entire chest has got his tongue unfurled. He's bandaged with three seeping shiv wounds. He makes kissy faces at the kid, he makes kissy faces at the pregnant woman, he makes kissy faces at the little boy, and the girl says, "Before you go, you ought to kill him."

Maybe she's right. Maybe it's time for another brutal surge of rage. The kid isn't afraid of his capacity for ferocity anymore. It feels good to cut loose. It feels righteous. And how are you going to get in trouble kicking the ass of a guy who has Hitler's face on his chest? The only real problem is getting through the glass, getting to the other side of the glass.

Funny though, the girl's never come right out and asked the kid to kill

Ricky. She doesn't seem to hold too firm a grudge against Ricky, despite the horrors and the slicing and the chewing and the rest of it. The feds, even with their top forensic scientists working the evidence, only got about half the story right in the end. The girl has explained to the kid in excruciating detail exactly what happened to her and the others.

The kid stands and knocks gently on the glass, then shoots the Nazi the finger. The Aryan sneers, reaches under the mattress, and holds up a little triangular piece of glass with a taped handle.

"No wonder he got shanked," the girl says in his brain, pressed to the metal, sweating, beautiful as always. "That shit couldn't protect anybody."

The kid searches for a way past the glass. The doc is in his office area, chatting with a nurse, laughing, the doc reaching out to touch the nurse first on the shoulder, then the elbow, then the hip. The doc is oblivious to everyone in here. The doc is oblivious to the cons, to Adolf, to Ricky's voice still humming, almost cooing, making the kid's hands feel electrical, like there's lightning in his fingers, and there is. The door is locked, but the girl was observant and picked up on the keypad code. The kid doesn't even have to press the numbers, he just touches the pad and the lock pops and the door opens an inch. He slips inside.

Another door, another keypad, another code, another time that he doesn't have to do anything but let his fingers touch the pad. The other door pops.

The Aryan is watching him enter. Adolf is watching him enter. The girl says, "Use his own shiv. Gut him."

The Aryan tries to climb out of bed. There are other cons in the infirmary, some of them hurt bad, some just faking and keeping an eye out, like they're planning a crash-out. One opens his mouth and says, "Hey—" to the kid, and the kid spins and brings his elbow across and down into the con's collarbone.

The snap is so loud they hear it in hell. The girl tells him so.

The con hits the floor like a bag of wet sin. The kid continues on. The girl talks on. Ricky whispers on. The Aryan starts to mewl. Adolf starts to give a speech, his weird swipe of hair flopping across his forehead. The Aryan climbs out of the bed and holds his little piece of glass up in a defensive pose, jabbing at the air. He holds the weapon all wrong. Ricky knows the right way. He murmurs how you hold the blade out flat, low, so you can stab or slash or slice, forward or backhand. The Aryan hobbles forward and the kid leans in, blocks the shard of glass coming in toward his kidneys—these guys, they think the secret is to puncture the kidneys, forgetting it takes weeks to kill a guy that way—snaps his fist against the Nazi's wrist, slaps the blade from it, and then goes to work.

Adolf is smiling now, getting a kick out of all this. His speech has moved on to the Jews, to destroying the Allies, to purifying the nation, and a hundred thousand Germans are Sieg Heiling in the square, going fucking crazy. The girl points up. American planes are flying overhead. Who the fuck knows what year it is. It doesn't matter. Ricky says it's 1941. The girl says it's closer to '43. The kid has no idea and doesn't care. He jabs the Aryan's gut, especially the area where he'd been stabbed before. After three or four hard shots, his fists are covered with blood. It's a fine feeling. Ricky loves it. The kid doesn't mind it.

Everyone loves to talk about the smell of blood, but it has none, not at first. Blood has to oxidize first, and then it grows copper colored, dries into a powder like rust, and then it has that acrid scent the morbid poets sing about. The girl bled a lot. She was kept around dying by inches for a long time. Ricky used to talk to her endlessly. He did things to her that still make the kid tighten his arms across his belly. The girl doesn't care anymore. Why should she? She's dead.

So's the Aryan. The kid went too far, or maybe it was the girl, or Ricky, or Adolf, or all of them. In any case, there he is on the floor, his ribs shattered into splintered knives that have torn his organs to pieces. There's a deep blue tinge to his flesh beneath the ink. It looks like his lungs are punctured. It looks like his heart's impaled.

The other cons watch. The other cons take notice. The other cons do not fuck with the kid. The pregnant woman on the other side of the glass is staring wide-eyed. So is the little boy. The little boy's mother is still absorbed in her daydreams. Her eyes are full of handsome bankers with huge swimming pools who give her diamond necklaces. The doc is feeling up the nurse. The nurse is being felt up.

The girl's parents are chanting along with the other capital punishment fiends, trying to drown out the protesters who are singing some hymns that strike sparks off the metal in the kid's skull. All of it is starting to get to be too much. He backs away from the corpse and bumps into the footboard of another bed, pulls off the sheet covering the legs of another con, some guy faking a fever so he gets out of punching license plates or chain-gang roadwork or whatever it is they do here. Kid wipes his hands as clean as he can on the sheet and drops it.

Ricky hums along with the protesters. He was raised in a very religious household by deeply believing parents. He doesn't blame his upbringing for the way he turned out. His parents were nice, good people. It wasn't their fault. Neither was it his pastor's or the congregation's or his neighbors. He doesn't hold God accountable. He doesn't hold himself accountable either. He takes one of those views that say you are what you are, you are what you are meant to be, what you are fated to be. The girl says it's an excuse. Nobody was meant to be what Ricky is. Ricky counters with the fact that there are more like him every day. Maybe it's evolution. Maybe it's the natural order.

Time to move. The kid slips back through the door. The doc is going full blast on the nurse now, finger fucking her right there, practically out in the open. She's rubbing him through his trousers. Ricky's getting a little turned on, but not as turned on as he was when killing the girl or helping the kid kill the Aryan.

The kid makes it back to the waiting room, and the pregnant woman sees the dried streaks of blood on his hands and knows, knows in her pregnant heart, what is pregnant inside of him. She crosses herself. The gesture somehow soothes the kid a little, calms him, even while the girl snorts and scoffs in disgust. She hears her parents too. She hates them. She hates all the living now, but that's not her fault. All the dead hate the living. It's just the way it is, just like Ricky is the way he is, just like the kid is welded between them and to them.

The kid washes his hands in one of those old-fashioned shitty drinking fountains, the water arcing about a half inch. The boy has forgotten about his skinned knee now. The pregnant woman isn't about to give birth. The mother of the boy takes him by the elbow and calls for a guard. The guard shows and everyone moves off together. They're escorted down the corridors and out the front door, down the long sidewalk, past the main gates and the gatherers. The kid is recognized at once. There's an even louder buzz. People grab at him. They question him. The girl's parents smile at him. He smiles back. The girl doesn't. She's still slightly offended her parents couldn't ID her body, but the kid doesn't blame them for that, not at all.

"How are you?" her mother asks him.

He should answer fine. That's the only answer anybody really wants or expects. He should say fine. He should embrace them and share in their sorrow. He should let one of them or both of them pat his back and rub his shoulders and stroke the back of his head. It's what they did the last time he saw them. It made him feel better, a little, for a second. It took away a little of the lightning pain.

Reporters call him by name. Reporters jump in his face. Reporters jam microphones against his mouth; they jab at him with cameras. The protesters want him to sing with them. The yahoos want him to seethe and spit venom.

The kid walks past them all. Some follow. He doesn't run. He doesn't speak. He finds his car. He gets in and drives home slowly, Ricky's voice dulling the intense traffic noise. The girl is sitting in the passenger seat, looking out the window. She's got something to say about almost everything. The kid doesn't remember her being so chatty, but death is apparently very boring. He isn't looking forward to his own.

They cross a toll bridge and she says she misses the tollbooth guys who used to work there. Now you drive by and you catch a bill in the mail a couple of weeks later. She is nostalgic for the things that have changed since she's died. TV shows that have gone off the air, songs played by bands that are no longer together. She asks him about things he doesn't give a shit about.

"Are you listening to me?" she squawks.

He is and he isn't. He's really thinking about the ocean. He misses it. He hasn't gone swimming since Ricky caved his head in. Hasn't walked in the shallows, hasn't even dipped his feet in off a dock. He still remembers lying on the shore with the waves pushing him up into the sand and then pulling him out again while the girl screamed and Ricky chased her down. He remembers Ricky talking then too, endlessly talking, keeping up a steady stream of chatter that didn't make any sense, at first, not until it got in deep and festered and could be examined at length.

Ricky talking about his nightmares, his fears, his honest hopes, his games, his skills, his twists, his kinks. Explaining what he was going to do, and when, and how it would go down, and why it had to happen like that to one girl or another. He killed as many guys as he did girls but nobody focuses on them because they usually went quick. He brained most of them when stealing the girls. He left them dead in their beds, in the parks, at the beaches, at the drive-ins. Ricky was at the drive-in when they caught him, sitting there watching the end credits roll, with popcorn in his teeth.

The kid was the only one to survive. He doesn't know why. No one does, not even the dead. People made a lot of jokes about his hard head, but they should try it now. If anybody ever hit him with a rock in the back of the skull again the stone would crumble into dust. Ricky once asked him if he was bulletproof now. Some asshole comes up behind him with a .22, a .32, maybe even a .38, would it get through or would the bullet shatter the way it sometimes did off bone? The kid didn't know the answer. Ricky suggested he ask the doctors. He should know these things.

The girl harbors deep resentments. For Ricky and the kid, and her living friends, her sisters, her dog. She remembers the way Ricky pulled her away down along the beach, the kid's body lying there in the sand, not even struggling, not even fighting to get up. Not climbing to his knees, not getting to his feet, not screaming, not coming to save her. The kid half in the water like he was just body surfing. The kid thinks she's being unreasonable as hell, but she counters that it's her right to be irrational. She's dead.

You can't argue with logic like that. He lets her try to pry up the plates and worm guilt into his brain. It doesn't really matter. He's already as guilty as he can possibly be. She knows this but she can't help herself. She rages still. She cries still. She shrieks still, the way she did when she was Ricky's prisoner and he brought out the tools that first time. At the moment she thought she was all alone, but afterward she learned that many people heard her anguish. They all mistook it for something else. Cats fighting. Babies crying. Dogs prowling. The neighbor's TV too loud. Her screams echoed on the wind for miles and miles, up canyons, down the beaches, over distant fields.

When the kid gets back to his place, a new letter from Ricky is waiting for him. Ricky will never run out of things to say. The letter goes on and on, page after page, and Ricky, who often tells the same stories over and over, still finds a way to make his missives interesting, exceedingly readable. Ricky's voice reads Ricky's letter aloud in the kid's mind. He finishes the letter and puts it with the others in the box in his closet. It's the fourth box he's filled. The other three are sealed away in the crawl space.

The girl hisses at him, "Why do you keep that insanity so close at hand? Do you want to be crazy? Is that it?"

Maybe that's it. Maybe it's not. He hasn't figured it out yet. Maybe it's his nature, his fate. He doesn't expect to ever figure it out. He only expects that the letter writing will end with Ricky's hot shot. He knows Ricky's voice is with him forever.

It's a familiar story—

The kid lies on the couch and the girl crawls over him the way she did when she was alive. She liked being on top. She liked being close, as close as she could get, and would tell him to hold her tight, tighter, tighter than that, crush the breath from her lungs. He would grip her tightly and she'd yawp and go, "Not that hard! That hurts!" He'd ease up. They'd watch the news together. She'd comment on the ugliness of the world. He would watch quietly. She would ask him over and over again, "What's wrong? What's wrong?" He would stare at her and have no answer. He never had an answer to any of her questions, and still doesn't.

"What's wrong?" she asks.

He could respond at length. She has time. She has nothing but time.

He watches the news and sees her parents out in front of the prison and listens to the warden give a canned statement, and listens to the leader of the protesters discussing God and forgiveness, and he listens to the yahoos yahooing. He listens to a couple of cats fighting, a baby crying, and wonders if someone like Ricky has grabbed someone like the girl and someone like the kid is lying with his skull in fragments at a lakeside or on a beach or at the drive-in. He wonders if he should investigate. He gets to his feet. He starts for the door.

She asks, "Where are you going?"

Ricky's voice tells him it's nothing, it's nothing. It's nothing to worry about. And it isn't. He opens the door and sees the cats fighting near the trash cans where the apartment manager has left them.

He shuts the door, he sits again, she sits on his lap, he flips the station, he holds on to her tightly, he looks at the tattoo on her ass. He presses the side of his face to her back. She's in excellent shape, every muscle and tendon hard and well defined in her flesh that is only memory.

Sleep comes the way it has come since the attack. It comes like a rock to the head. It comes like a voice under the metal welded to the skull. It comes like murder. You can't prepare for it. You can't get comfortable first. You can't make room for it in your life. It descends and owns you.

THE KID WAKES up and it's morning. Reporters are at the door, calling his name. He goes to the window and pulls the curtains aside. The group is suddenly lively, active, like a gathering of pigeons that have spotted a cat. They call to him. They wave. They're like a mob of Japanese tourists. They aim cameras at the window. The prettiest journalists preen. They try to draw him out with their moist lips, their heated gazes, the arcs of their breasts and asses.

The kid knows he is only news because he is alive.

The girl is there with some of the other girls, girls just like her, that Ricky tortured and killed. Some of the boys have come along too, lost, mostly forgotten, unwanted, uninteresting. They all look the same, the same as the kid did five years ago. They're young, soft, without much character to their faces. No worry lines, no gray, cheeks buffed to a healthy, rosy glow, a golden hue, bursting with life and stupidity. They fill the room, smiling, laughing, like this is a frat house and they're preparing for a kegger.

The dead boys and dead girls reminisce. The kid wonders if any of them have any burning messages they want to pass on to friends or family. Or for the world to know before Ricky finally goes down. He turns and faces them but they're dancing now. They're playing a song that was popular a few years back. The girl moves up behind him, gets close, puts her lips to the back of his neck, reaches around him and grinds slowly. Ricky has things to say about dancing. Ricky has things to say about everything.

She reaches down. She tries to rouse the kid. The others are doing their thing. The song plays on and on. He wants to smash the CD player, the MP3 player, the iPod, but he doesn't own any of that. They've brought the music with them from the darkness, from the past, from the place where you go when you do not go all the way away. The pretty reporters bend their knees a little and sway. The girl becomes more grabby. She's not holding on to the kid so much as she's holding on to life. Whatever life she can still get her hands on.

The others moan. The others say what they need to say. They keep trying to make their peace but can't quite do it. There's no peace left to be made. They're angry that the kid is friendly with Ricky at all. They're angry he made it. They hound him the way they've hounded him for years. They cluster. They breathe his air. They try to peel up the metal plates and lie down under them, inside his blood and bone. They want him to give voice. They're keenly aware of the reporters out front. They have messages for their parents. They have messages for Ricky.

The reporters are getting a little more aggressive now. They press the doorbell. They knock. They call the kid's name. They peer in the windows. They shout out large amounts of money.

"Twenty thousand for an interview?" one of the dead boys says. It's an impressive number, even after you've been croaked. It only serves to infuriate the dead boys and girls. If they had lived, they would've taken the money. If they had lived, they would be eager to tell their stories. If they had lived, and it was the kid's ghost that was annoying them, they would listen, they would help him however they could, they would pay more attention.

"You do like having us around, don't you?" the girl asks.

The answer is no, but he can't tell them that, especially since they're already inside him, in his marrow, in the marrow of his mind. They're as welded to him as the plates to his skull, as Ricky. He wants them gone, but he doesn't know what he would do without them. The thought of losing Ricky fills him with a sense of dread he doesn't understand on any level. He doesn't know what the hell he's going to do when Ricky dies. He fears Ricky's voice will leave with his life, and the kid will be left with nothing but these other dead.

"Thirty thousand?" the dead boy says, repeating a number hurled from outside. "What would you do with thirty thousand bucks?"

The kid thinks of what he might have said six or seven years ago to that kind of offer. He would've done what with the cash? Sailed around the world? Visited exotic locales? Bought a cabin on the beach? He'd always wanted to travel, used to dream about it, plot it, graph it, chart it, map it with the girl. Indochina, Burma, Egypt, Brazil, Pago Pago. There's still time, he imagines, except there isn't, and there never was.

"He's going crazy again," a dead girl, not his dead girl, says. He can't handle the dreams and hopes he once found refuge in. They cause nothing but pain now. The metal plates are heating up as if someone is standing there with a blowtorch, burning him. He twists and writhes on the couch, the music still playing. The kid falls to the floor, manages to get to his knees, his feet, crosses the room, opens the front door. He's ready to scream at the mob to leave him alone.

Except only the prettiest of the pretty journalists is standing there now. Time has passed. He checks his watch. It's late. It's getting late. Ricky's due to take his shot soon. The kid has to move if he's going to get to the prison in time.

The girl says, "She isn't so pretty."

But the pretty reporter is. She's beautiful. She's lovely. She's alive. She holds herself in a way that exploits all her natural charms, all the curves and the brimming self-confidence. This is a woman who has handled herself well and overcome great odds. She's vanquished her foes and resorted to whatever tactics she needed to resort to for that moment. She carries her guilt perfectly, as if she's not carrying any guilt at all. She says another number.

"Fifty thousand."

Kid likes her voice. It's a mellifluous voice, but it has grit, substance, personality. He likes watching her lips. He likes the way she moves toward him, saying his name with some endearment, as if she's been waiting for him at the train station for a long time and has just spotted him. He imagines her there, on the platform, waving to him. He shuts his eyes. She's spurring his dreams again. The metal continues heating, red-hot, white-hot.

He tries to tell her to stop.

He tries to wave her away from him.

He tries to find Ricky's voice in his mind to calm him, center him. The pretty reporter is close, with a mike in her hand, a cameraman appearing from nowhere, from everywhere. The cameraman says, "We're rolling."

The reporter asks, "Concerning Ricky Benjamin Price, have you forgiven him for what he's done to you?"

The kid wants to say that at the moment he's not as angry with Ricky as he is with her. Ricky kills dreams; she's igniting them, she's burning him. The kid has to shut her up. He lunges and presses his mouth to hers while she lets out a squeal of surprise and maybe lust. Who knows. He can't tell. It doesn't matter. He tastes her. He smells her. He breathes her in. She's alive. That matters.

The cameraman goes maybe two-fifty, a big bruiser carrying big hardware, none of that compact machinery the small guys run around with when they're after a story. Nah, he's got the serious stuff, the old-school camera like a boulder on his shoulder. The bruiser catches a nice close-up of the kiss for maybe a three-count before he goes, "Heeyy—"

The kid wants to explain to her. You don't know what you've done. You don't know what you're doing. You need to run. You have to run. Go. Go.

The girl says, "She's not going to go."

And somehow the pretty lady senses what he's saying to her. Maybe he's saying it aloud although he can't hear himself. He can't hear all that much over what's going on in his head. He wants the fifty large now, in cash, thinking that maybe he can pay somebody off at the prison to stay the execution. It's late, it's too late, but he has to try.

The reporter slaps him. She tags him nicely. It's not exactly a slap, more of a punch, and it hurts, catches him flush under the left ear in the ganglia of nerves there. The plates clang together. His head lights up even more.

The girl, his girl, his dead girl, goes, "Whoa."

The dead boys and girls want to explain themselves. They're dictating laundry lists of people they want to say something to on camera. Mothers and fathers, little sisters, brothers, cousins, loved ones of every stripe. They've got advice to share, secrets that need to be revealed. They bark, they plead, they demand. They want their turn at saying last words. Making amends, giving confession.

The reporter says, "I'm sorry. I . . . I'm sorry . . . please . . . let's just—"

The kid launches himself, full of Ricky's whispers. He backhands the reporter, drops her hard. It's one of Ricky's signature moves. All the dead girls gasp, remembering. The cameraman says again, "Heeyy—"

The kid slips his hands in under the camera, eases it off the guy's shoulder, helping him, doing him a favor. The guy goes to one knee at the side of the pretty reporter. He's in love with her, he's got to be in love with her. Who could work beside her, stare at her, see her every day, and not be in love with her?

Cameraman asks, "Are you okay?"

"What happened?" she says, a dab of blood leaking from her lower lip.

"You didn't have to hit her!" the girl goes.

But of course he did. Everyone knows that. They realize what else is inside with them. They know the truth.

In the kid's hands the camera comes to life. The screen lights up. He sees himself in it even though the lens isn't pointed at him. His other self seems to be trying to get his attention, tell him something meaningful and necessary. He tries to figure it out but can't. He lifts the huge old camera over his head and brings it down on the sweet spot of the cameraman's skull with an enormous crunch. Glass shatters. Plastic shatters. Bone shatters. Metal shrieks. The guy's eyes bulge but stop short of popping out. The reporter screams. A few of the dead girls scream. Two dead boys scream. It's a hell of a chorus. The kid might be screaming too. So might the other version of himself, whoever and whatever that is. Ricky laughs.

It's a familiar story—

There's just a little left to do. He does it quickly, efficiently, the way Ricky used to when he was pressed for time. He cleans up. He stashes and dashes. He kills and chills. He checks for nosy neighbors. He hops in his car and floors it to the prison.

CROWD CONTROL IS nonexistent. Everybody's got a cause to preserve and Ricky's at the heart of it all. The girl's parents have been out here for days, unnecessarily. Their faces are badly sunburned. He can see that in the prison lights. Her father's bald head shines red as the asshole of the sun. Her mother's face is full of glee, as if finally there will be justice for their daughter, at last she'll be able to rest in peace.

The girl says, "Idiots."

That's not the worst thing she's ever called them. She hated them when she was alive and she feels even more anger toward them now.

More reporters are waiting in the wings. The witnesses of the execution are sequestered off to the side. They're penned in, like cattle. The protesters and protesters of the protesters all shout at one another. They don't consider this a solemn moment. They can't see the ritual of it all. The reporters shout out their questions and tug at sleeves and ask the most cloying questions. They should all be allowed to come along inside. They should all show the world what it's like for Ricky Benjamin Price to meet his doom. It's such an awful scenario that the kid groans just thinking about it. The father of one of the other dead girls stands shoulder to shoulder with the kid and sort of props him up. He's an ex-marine. He's very into showing the world that he will not be bowed. He stares straight ahead. The bulls unlock the gates and march the witnesses in.

They enter the little viewing room. They take their seats. The girl's parents sit on either side of him. Her mother murmurs and coos and *tsk*s. Her father does what the ex-marine did, puts a hard shoulder to him, presses him, holds him up.

The girl says, "He used to do that to me in church all the time."

There's curtains across the viewing window. They part slowly, like the curtains rising on a stage. Act I, Scene I. Ricky enters, in the middle of a seven-man procession. He's talking, of course he's talking. The priest is praying. The warden is giving the speech about how Ricky's been decreed to die at the appointed hour for the crimes he's committed. The bulls drag him to the X-table and strap him down. There's a doctor to stick the needle in. The machine that delivers the poison is practically transparent. You can see all the instrumentality within. You can see the lethal fluids. You can see the depressors. You can see the mechanics of the thing. It is, in its own way, a parallel to what Ricky did to the girls. The way he explained everything he was going to do, the way he showed them each instrument beforehand and displayed the function of their own organs. He left their eyes for last.

The mothers and fathers and other family members can't contain themselves. There are curses, prayers, vicious barking outcries of fury and pain. Some of them turn away from the window. Some of them angle in. Ricky turns his head and meets the kid's eyes.

The girl says, "He's ugly. He's always been ugly, but he's gotten uglier."

Kid knows the reason for Ricky's ugliness. It's his fault. Greater corruptions have been piled upon Ricky's flesh and soul because of the kid's actions. Ricky is uglier today than he was yesterday because there are more murders to add to his catalog of corruption. The kid is now Dorian Gray and Ricky is the portrait.

The dead boys and girls say, "It's getting hot in here."

And it is, inside the kid's head, where the fear and the frustration are building, and the migraine is buzzing and almost blinding him, his vision red and black, vibrating him into new universes. Sweat pours off his face and he keeps drawing the back of his hand under his chin, across his throat, the same way the girl would do to him when they were at the beach and he'd sweat this same way in the sun.

But they're not talking about the room, not talking about this room. They're talking about their room, in the room between the metal and the brain.

"You've waited a long time for this," the girl's father says. "Enjoy it."

Ricky tells him to kill the man. It's easily done. Sitting here, this close,

Ricky whispers how many ways he could do it. He ticks them off. One, two, three . . . he gets to nineteen. There are more, but he's made his point, and the point has calmed the kid down a bit. The dead boys and girls see their folks and their siblings and cry out for them, try to reach out to them. The kid has trouble holding his hands down on his knees.

The warden asks Ricky if he has anything to say. Ricky always has something to say. Ricky says and says and says. He says so much that the warden has to cut him off. The witnesses are all moaning and sobbing again. The ex-marine is cursing. The girl's father is sort of growling deep in his throat. Her mother tries to take the kid's hand and he shakes her off, gently. To touch him like that is to destroy yourself.

She tries again and receives an electric shock. The spark arcs like something out of Frankenstein's lab. It leaps. It's bright blue and buzzes. It snaps against her wrist like it wants to ride her bloodstream up to her heart. There's a small dot of black where the flesh is burned. She sucks wind through her teeth but that's all. The girl's father glances over and sniffs. The smell of burned flesh is pungent in the small viewing room. The kid imagines this is what the viewing room for the electric chair must smell like.

Ricky mouths words to the kid, specifically for him. They're words of love, which make it all the worse.

The girl says, "That disgusting freak."

The other dead boys and girls are offended too. Ricky never showed them any love or mercy, but that's because they didn't survive. Ricky doesn't have any use for the dying or the dead. He doesn't even have any use for himself anymore.

Originally, Ricky asked that he be dissected alive on television. It was a suggestion that made everybody go fucking nuts. The human rights groups, the prison boards, the anti-capital-punishment people, the pro-capital-punishment people, the cannibals, the sadists, the voyeurs, the other serial killers, fucking everybody.

The warden signals a go.

The first plunger depresses. It's supposed to paralyze Ricky. It doesn't. The contents of the needle make him smile even more broadly.

Someone in the viewing room goes, "My God."

Others echo the statement. "God. My God. Oh God."

The second plunger depresses. Ricky begins to laugh. He's still talking, of course, he's always talking. Kid flashes on the pregnant woman and wonders if she's in or out of labor yet. He wonders if Ricky's going to come back in some newborn. He wonders if Ricky is going to shake things up in hell.

The third plunger depresses and Ricky's body bucks a little, something that's supposed to be impossible. His muscles strain. He looks like he's trying to rise. The witnesses do the gasping thing again. They moan again. The women duck their heads like they don't want Ricky noticing them. The men stare on.

More sparks fly from the kid's fingers. Small arcs but they're traveling, moving from person to person, chair to chair, forward toward the window glass. The blue light bops and weaves along, touching them all. Maybe it belongs to Ricky. Maybe it belongs to God.

The ex-marine goes, "What the fuck?"

Ricky relaxes and shuts his eyes. His chin slowly lowers to the side. It's a pose of innocence, an awful caricature. He looks content, at peace. At last he shuts up. At least here he shuts up. In the kid's head he's still whispering, thankfully. Ricky croons while the doc puts a stethoscope to Ricky's chest, then moves it to his wrist, then moves it again to his throat. The doc says Ricky's dead. The warden repeats it. The witnesses give a sigh of relief, and there's a few chuckles and sobs of happiness. The dead boys' and girls' names are invoked. Parents claim their children will rest easier now. Parents claim justice has been served. Parents claim they will sleep better now that the monster is dead. Parents don't know what the fuck they're talking about.

The spark reaches the machine. The machine schitzes out and the depressors depress, repress, compress, unpress, drawing blood up through the needles and into the tubes that had contained the poisons. The IVs in Ricky's arm slurp his blood up. You can see it leaving his body and entering the machine. The pressure in the syringes goes haywire. The needles crack. The tubes burst. Ricky's blood jets against the window as powerfully as a cut throat spurting arterial spray.

There's something beautiful in the designs made by his painted blood. Everybody's screaming. The dead boys and girls are laughing. They find it exciting, and it is. They recognize art in the making. Their parents scramble. The bulls are going wild inside the chamber. The priest is praying. The warden is shouting. Ricky's dead body is dancing. Adolf is still adolfing. The machine is on fire.

The girl says, "You just had to ruin it for everybody."

Maybe she's right. The kid must've wanted this. The only reason things like this happen is because he wants them to happen, needs for them to happen, or else Ricky does. But Ricky's finished now, except for what he's saying, except for what he's going to be saying forever now from the other side of the endless spanless darkness of infinite dimensions.

"You're getting turned on," she says.

She paws at him. She feels him. She likes when he gets aroused, whether it's by her touch or her memory or her death or someone else's. The blood makes her hot. She's hot there beneath the heated metal. The next migraine hits and he thrusts his hands against the sides of his head and lets out a squeal of agony that brings the whole room to a silence. They all look at him. Some stare into his eyes. Some stare at his scars. Some show mercy. Some look at him pitifully. Some hate him because he seemed to be friends with Ricky. The girl's mother smooths the back of his hair down. It feels like she's hacking at him with a hatchet.

"Don't you dare murder my mother," the girl says, which surprises him, since before her death she'd been talking about how much she wanted to get away from this woman, how stupid she was, what a pain in the ass she was. Now she sounds protective, almost loving. Quite a switch after all this time. Even dead people can change.

He bolts. It's allowed. It's acceptable. What else are you going to do? Some of them talk about the future, some of them talk about the past. Some of them have become friends in their shared tragedy. Some of them discuss having dinner together. Some of them want to go get a drink.

The kid rushes for the door. A bull stops him like he's making a prison break. The screw's beefy arm is held out in front of him like a semaphore. The kid grabs hold of the wrist, whirls, and flips the guy over his back. The bull lets out a cry, then another. They're loud enough to get into the little room. The warden looks. The other bulls look. Ricky's corpse looks.

The kid makes his way out into the hall and vomits. The bulls sniff at him like it's their problem, like they'll have to mop it up now, not some lifer who's been wielding the same mop for the last thirty-five years. The kid begs, "Let me out," but it takes forever. They have to escort him, they have to call ahead to get all the gates and doors open. They drag him off like he's a condemned prisoner, which he is, sort of. These pricks, these people, they all have to put pressure on, they all have to squeeze him.

Outside he flails against a railing and gasps, sucking air. The crowd cheers, like it was him who'd pushed the button, pulled the lever, punched Ricky's ticket. He could've, perhaps he should've, and now he stumbles down the walk. He tries to read the signs that are being pushed his way. Passages from the Bible, literary quotes about the diminishment of mankind, pro-death-penalty vitriol, remember Sally, remember Robert, remember Timothy, remember Janet. He doesn't remember any of them. Someone hands him a baby, a real baby, a live baby, a goo-goo baby girl, like he's supposed to bless the child, or maybe murder it. Who hands a complete stranger a baby? The child goes, "Da da da da da da da da." Singsongy, kinda with a salsa beat to it.

The girl says, "That yours? You that fucking kid's da da? Were you cheating on me?"

He's not the kid's da da. He hands the baby back, not to the same person, but a different stranger. There he answered his own question. Who hands a complete stranger a baby? He does. Da da that.

Somebody gives him a full pint of Jameson's. The seal's not even broken. He twists the cap off and sucks deeply from the bottle. The liquor hurts his head even more. A couple of the dead kids drink deep, a couple of them go "phphooey, phoo . . . yuck" because they've never had a sip of the hard stuff. It brings things into focus for him, for a second. Which is Janet? Which is Timothy? He shoves his way through toward his car. The journalists are on him again. He wants to explain to them how dangerous it is, what they're doing, where they're standing, pushing him, touching him. He shoves his way past, makes it back to his car. He's no longer news, he should no longer be news. Ricky is dead.

THERE REALLY IS nowhere else for him to go, nothing for him to do, but return to the beach. It's clear and obvious. He walks alone on it. The waves crash, the waves reach. He scans the sand for the rest of his skull, his mind, his life. He lost it all somewhere around here. He sees footprints and thinks of the girl running for her life. The girl thinks of him lying there dying. Ricky thinks of them both, and the others, and a surge of pleasure fills him like a shot of adrenaline directly into the heart. You've got to wonder if he can still be saved, even after the mess with the machine. Some lab assistant in the morgue stealing Ricky's body out the back and injecting it with bright green liquid, some anti-death serum. Somebody's got to be working on it, some other maniac in some other basement.

A storm waits over the water. Perhaps it's been there since the day the kid died, or should've died. Perhaps it's come back to meet him, hovering here for years, waiting. The pain is so great now that the kid drops to his knees as the sand crabs rise and begin to make their way to him. Sparks flash from his fingertips, his eyes, his open mouth.

The girl says, "This is it. This is the end."

Maybe she's right, maybe not. The storm comes closer. Black clouds swirl overhead, vortexes, funnels, sweeping down and bringing up tens of thousands of gallons of water. It gushes around him in the wind. The dead boys are especially impressed. A couple of them liked fishing, dug boating, lived on the water. Lightning blasts down and leaves more strange patterns of bubbling molten clouded glass the size of Cadillac hoods across the beachfront all around him.

Ricky calls this the divine. Ricky calls this the infernal. Ricky believes in great mythic resonance. It's been there since his early religious upbringing. When he was alive, he was always walking along the beach hoping for tidal waves and hurricanes, as well as scoping victims. Ricky wants the world to burn, the world to drown. He wants to ride high on the next ark. Well, he did, when he was alive.

Ricky paws the dead. Ricky makes moves. He has no need to dismember but he still wants to fuck, still wants to have some fun. The kid turns and turns again as the lightning crashes down. The thunder is explosive but not as loud as Ricky's voice in his head, not as loud as the dead girls' disgust and the memories of their shrieks. The metal in his head draws the lightning to him. He's the tallest thing on the plain, and he's magnetized. His watch is going nuts. His fillings hurt. His mouth is full of fire.

Someone has got to be nearby. Ricky thinks his thoughts in the kid's dented skull. The kid searches strangers out. He looks for retirees, he scans for young lovers, fishermen, he watches for kids who've come out to drink beer on the beach in wild weather. His hands glow blue and white. His hands can do amazing things.

The sand crabs stare up at him, curious, expectant. He sits and waits for the ocean or the sky to kill him. It would be a proper ending. He thinks he deserves that, at least. Ricky got a proper ending. The girl, in her way, received one. And so did the rest of them. He stands and walks along, the tide rising, the waves swelling, breaking against his knees, the foam exploding against the side of his face. Lightning continues to shear down, thunder like thrown sticks of dynamite.

He moves around an outcropping of rock. He moves around fencing, up and down dunes, slipping past saw grass. Isolated beach houses come into view. The kid keeps going. He walks up to a gorgeous place, the kind of place he and the girl used to talk about buying one day, the kind of place that it's easy to talk about because everyone talks about places like this, and he knocks on the door with his burning fist.

Ricky enjoys the isolation, the deep loneliness out here, in the storm, on the water, away from the hateful population.

A girl very much like the girl, his girl, his dead girl, like all the dead girls, answers. Ricky's mouth waters. The kid's mouth waters.

She says, "Can I help you?"

The metal in his head clashes together and rings like the loudest church bell in twenty centuries.

It's a familiar story—

DARK WITNESS

Charlaine Harris and Rachel Caine

It seemed to Emma Saxon that she'd been driving forever when she saw the crosses. No—not the crosses. First, she saw the woman.

Mom, her daughter Laurel's voice was saying, in the blurry, distorted tempo of a slowed recording. We'll be late if we don't hurry up. So Laurel must have been in the passenger seat, but Emma couldn't seem to turn her head that way. The road was black, the headlights showing nothing, yet somehow there was a woman kneeling down under a single streetlight. Her image was broken into stark blacks and whites by the harsh light.

She was hammering crosses into the hard ground.

Two crosses: mere crooked boards, nailed together, painted white. Cheap tinsel streamers floated from them in an unseen, unfelt wind.

Emma was pressing the gas but the van was slowing down, slowing down, and to Emma's horror the woman turned to look at her. She had only a black hole for a face and a flash of pale, nauseatingly yellow eyes. The horrible woman inclined her head toward the crosses, and Emma had to look. The crosses read EMMA and LAUREL in crooked letters of blood, blood that dripped down the chilly white of the crosses, and her daughter was saying Mom, we're going to be late, late, late . . .

And then Emma turned her head, finally, away from the crosses and the light and the blood and the eyes, and he was sitting in the passenger seat, smiling at her with that sharply handsome face and those piss-yellow eyes and she opened her mouth to scream and the scream turned into a shrill electronic shriek that went on and on and on . . .

Emma opened her eyes and slapped at the snooze button on the alarm clock. She missed the first two times, got it the third. In the sudden, terribly thick silence she tried to get her breath, tried to blink the tears out of her eyes. The room felt very cold, and she turned on her side and wrapped the covers more tightly around her shaking body.

Not again, not again, I thought I was past this . . .

She'd stopped having dreams about the bastard years ago. Why was she thinking about him now? What had she done to deserve that new trip into hell?

The shower started up in the hall bathroom, and Emma groaned into her pillow. Laurel was already up. Although she was more than old enough to get up, fix her own breakfast, and be off to school, Emma had made it a rule to sit down with her daughter every morning, even if there was only time for a cup of coffee (for Emma, milk for Laurel) and a breakfast pastry apiece. Emma needed that touchstone of normal life.

Get up, Emma told herself, but part of her didn't want to obey. The bed was warm and safe, and the world out there . . . that was cold, and uncertain, and—with the dream lingering in her head—terrifying. *Get up for Laurel. You have to do it.*

That got her moving, though she felt frail and her skin was sensitive, as if she were recovering from a feverish illness. Everyday items seemed oddly juxtaposed, sinister, dangerous. Emma hesitated before thrusting her bare feet into her slippers, sure they hid scorpions or spiders, but when she stood she felt only the normal comfort of cotton-covered foam. She put on her bathrobe, brushed her hair, and was in the kitchen taking out the ingredients for scrambled eggs before Laurel came down the hall.

Her daughter was sixteen, and with the birthday had come attitude, tons of it. She was wearing eyeliner today. Emma didn't protest; they'd had a fight about last week's experimentation with eye shadow, which had been extremely overdone, so now she elected to pick the battles she was likely to win. The eyeliner looked good; it made Laurel's rich brown eyes seem larger and brought out the golden gleam in their depths.

Gold, not yellow. It isn't yellow. "Good morning, sweetheart," Emma said, her voice coming out in a croak. She cracked four eggs into a bowl while clearing her throat. "Sleep well?"

Laurel grunted. Yes or no? It didn't much matter. She was at that awkward stage where she could—and would—mutter secretively to her friends for hours on her cell phone, but you couldn't get three words in a row from her if you were her mother. Even now, Laurel pushed her long, straight hair back over her shoulders in an absent gesture and bent over her phone, fingers flying as she texted. Emma had tried to make a no-phone-before-breakfast rule, but that had been a battle she definitely couldn't win. She said, mildly, "No phone at the kitchen table, Laurel; you know that."

Laurel groaned dramatically, but she put the phone on the counter next to her backpack. She emphasized her instant boredom by drumming her fingers on the table, maintaining her silence.

Fine. Let her work for it. "Milk's in the fridge," Emma said.

"Where else would it be?" Laurel asked, and rolled her eyes, but she got up and poured herself a glass. Without being prodded, she loaded the coffeemaker and set it to brew, a hopeful sign of morning cooperation. Emma whisked eggs and loaded up the skillet, made toast, and plated the food. The two of them sat down to eat in (mostly) companionable silence. Emma made two attempts to find out what Laurel planned to do over the weekend. Laurel's response was a shrug that could mean anything.

Typical.

Laurel gulped down her eggs, toast, and milk, hastily dumped her dishes in the sink, and grabbed her backpack and phone as if they were life preservers in a shark-filled ocean. She headed for the door.

"Forget something?" Emma asked, standing. Laurel sighed—dramatically, of course—and came back to give her mom a quick kiss on the cheek. "That's better. Have a good day, honey. And call me when you're on the way home."

"I can walk three blocks, Mom; I'm not five."

"Just to be safe, okay?" Emma said quietly.

"Okay! You know, you have to let me grow up."

"Sure. But not today."

The put-upon look on Laurel's face was pricelessly funny, but Emma didn't laugh—at least, not until her daughter slammed the door and went jogging down the driveway to meet her friends for the walk to school. *Next year, she'll be driving,* she thought. *Dear God. How am I going to survive that?*

But next year's problems were just a dark cloud on the horizon. Emma felt better now, stronger, more in control of her life as she washed the breakfast things. She showered briskly, dressed for work, and headed off to the office. As she drove, she thought of her one o'clock meeting, and the presentation she had to prepare before then. Of course, accounting wouldn't have any of the figures ready until an hour before. It was a relief to occupy her mind with the mundane. How could she have let the dream spook her so badly? Why had she even had such a nightmare?

She had no idea what had brought it on until she stopped for a red light four blocks away from their house. Something fluttered at the edge of her vision. With dread, she turned her head to look. Two white crosses had been pounded into the hard ground, just at the base of a streetlight. Cheap tinsel streamers tangled and bounced in the morning breeze.

Emma's breath caught in her throat. She looked in the rearview mirror. Empty. Impulsively, Emma parked in the gas station lot on the corner. On unsteady legs, she walked over to take a look. The sun was still unbelievably fierce in late September, and the Dallas heat was unrelenting. Scorched grass crunched like tiny bones beneath her feet, and she felt the dream overlap into reality and bend it all out of shape, into the sharp angles of adrenaline and madness, until she saw the names.

JEREMY. AUDREY. And a faded picture stapled to the larger cross, Audrey's cross, that showed a middle-aged woman with a young boy next to her. There was no indication of what had happened. Weren't such crosses always erected for traffic accidents? She'd never stopped to look at one of these homemade roadside memorials before, and the faded picture brought home to her that the intersection she used every day was a place where someone else's dreams had died.

"Sorry," she said, and felt embarrassed when she heard her own voice. She hurried back to her van and started it up and felt the knot in her stomach slowly untie. The dream was just a dream. Not her name on the cross, and not Laurel's. It was just an ugly mash of truth and fiction, like all nightmares. Now she knew where it had come from. Nothing to worry about.

Accounting didn't have the figures ready when she got there. Typical.

By the time her presentation was over, she'd forgotten all about the dream.

LAUREL BROUGHT HOME friends for dinner. She texted first, though, which gave Emma time to evaluate the contents of her refrigerator. Luckily, there was enough steak and chicken to go around.

When they arrived, all together, Emma knew two of the guests: Laurel's best friend, Amy, she of the curly red hair and pale blue eyes, and Elena, who was dark haired and dark eyed and spoke with a faint Spanish accent. Elena had become a friend more recently, but her manners were good and she had a sweet smile.

This time, for the first time, Laurel had brought home a boy.

He was good-looking, too—a little taller than Laurel, with shaggy blondish hair that kept falling in his eyes. He was tanned and fit and broad shouldered. He didn't look up much, but when he did, Emma caught a glimpse of dark eyes. There was something familiar about him—maybe the cheekbones. Perhaps he'd gone to school with Laurel when they were much younger?

Laurel said, "This is Tyler." She didn't say anything else about him, which was unusual. Normally, she'd have been babbling out the details

(He's in my history class, He's on the tennis team, He wants to design video games). Tyler himself volunteered nothing. He seemed to be working hard at blending in with the furniture. He sat at the far end of the table, as far as he could get from Emma.

"So, Tyler, how do you know the girls?" Emma asked, as she passed the potatoes around to Elena. The girls all exchanged quick looks that Emma couldn't read, and Tyler didn't raise his head. He was spooning gravy over his potatoes with great concentration.

"I met Laurel at the library," he said. He spoke softly, and he definitely did not meet her eyes. "We both like biographies."

That was almost suspiciously nonthreatening—like something rehearsed. But she supposed it could be true. Laurel nudged the boy, and he said, "History, too."

"I didn't know you liked history," Emma said to her daughter, her tone bright and conversational. "I'm always trying to get you to read historical novels."

"Not novels, Mom. History. Real history. And myth and legend and all kinds of things. You're always trying to get me to read fiction. I don't like fiction."

That was news, because there were shelves of well-read novels in Laurel's room. The Harry Potter series. Tons of paranormal books for teens. All kinds of things that Laurel and her friends had been white-hot passionate about for the past few years. Suddenly, that was over.

"What are you all reading now?" Emma asked, and that got the conversation jump-started again, with the girls talking over each other excitedly. Amy was still on the fiction bandwagon. Apparently Elena was the driving force to move Laurel over to the nonfiction shelves.

Tyler stayed quiet, eating his steak as if his life depended on it. He seemed shy and awkward. Despite her native caution, Emma's heart went out to the boy. This wasn't easy for him. Though he ventured a comment every now and then, the girls' conversation flowed over him like a river. At least he was trying.

When dinner was over, Emma served cake and ice cream and put on a movie. She left them to have fun.

A couple of hours later, Emma could hear their voices in the hall and registered that they were saying good-bye. She wasn't listening with much attention: curled up in a chair in her office, she was engrossed in her own book. She didn't expect them to come thank her for the meal, though that would have been nice. She was surprised to hear a quiet knock on the open door. Slipping her bookmark in her place, she looked up to see Tyler standing there.

For a split second, she saw a glint of yellow in his eyes. Something inside her cringed. She scolded herself severely; her reading lamp had a lemon-yellow shade. She'd only seen its reflection. She forced a smile.

"I just wanted to say—" He licked his lips and started again as he shifted uncomfortably, one foot to the other. The boy was very neatly dressed, Emma noticed. He surely hadn't gone to school dressed in the stiff khaki pants, checked shirt, and clean sneakers. "I just wanted to say thanks. For having me in."

Emma smiled more genuinely. How nice! But from his grave face, she could see he wasn't finished.

"I—look, you're going to hate me, I know that, and I just wanted to say that—I'm doing this all wrong."

He looked so wretched that Emma put her book aside and stood up, feeling sorry for him. "It's okay," she said. "Tyler, why in the world would I hate you? If you and Laurel are going out together—"

"No!" he said, and looked up at her. Again, she caught that odd flare in his eyes, and she felt the answering sick kick in the pit of her stomach, but it was the lighting. Reflections. Tricks of memory. "No, that's not it. I—look, it's just that I wanted to meet you. I wanted to know why."

"Why . . . ?"

He looked down at his shoes and shook his head. "Why you gave me up," he said. It was almost a whisper. "Why you didn't care. Why you didn't want me."

She sucked in her breath, and it made a sound as sharp as a scream. She stepped back, until the wall stopped her, and she felt cold, unaccountably heavy, as if she might sink straight through the floor. "What—what are you talking about?"

Tyler met her gaze and held it. This time, she saw no glints of yellow, no reflections. Nothing but pain. "I'm your son," he said. "I'm the one you gave away."

And then he turned and started to walk away. She cried out then, a sound that ripped itself out of her soul, and reached out to him—not to hold him, not to hug him, but to push him.

Push him away. Far away.

He didn't stop. He didn't look back. She heard him saying good-bye to Laurel and Amy and Elena, and she heard the other girls leave after him.

But she sat in her chair, numbed, frozen, unable to think what to do or how to stop the destruction that was rushing at her, at her daughter, at this tight family unit she had built so carefully out of lies.

It was all coming apart.

Kill him, something in her said. Brutal and quiet and practical. *Kill him before worse happens.*

But she couldn't do it when he'd been born, and she couldn't do it now, not after having seen his pain.

Maybe I was wrong, she thought. It was a frantic thought, a child's desperate plea for mercy. *Maybe he's not like his father.*

But he was. She knew he was.

Because if he wasn't . . . what did that make her? What awful, terrible monster did that make her?

The next day passed in a nightmarish fugue. She didn't know how to find the boy, how to contact him; she couldn't ask Laurel. Her daughter would know something was wrong.

But when Laurel was late coming home, she couldn't stand to wait any longer. She started to call, but no, her voice would betray her.

Texting was safer: *Where are you? Who are you with?*

She imagined Laurel telling her phone, none of your business, but the text back was more polite. *Just Amy and some other ppl. All OK.*

Emma couldn't ask the deadly question, Are you with Tyler? She just couldn't. So she compromised. *Where are you?*

Mall. Emma could almost hear the *where else would we be?* at the end of that, and see the eye roll. *Home soon.*

He'd met her at the library. Maybe she wouldn't have invited him shopping. Maybe it might all go away, now that he'd been here, seen Emma, said what he had come to say.

Maybe it was over.

Emma tried to pretend it was, desperately. She made dinner—Laurel's favorite, beef stroganoff. She rehearsed answers to questions in her mind. *I don't know what he's talking about. Honey, you can't believe what strangers tell you.*

She was stirring in the noodles when she heard Laurel's keys in the door. Without turning, she said, "Hey, honey, thanks for being on time." Which, of course, Laurel wasn't; sarcasm was a nervous defense against the fear churning inside her.

Because she didn't turn, she missed whatever nonverbal cues Laurel might have been giving her, but she couldn't miss the tone in her daughter's voice. The hard, flat, angry tone. "Why didn't you tell me?" Laurel asked.

Emma put down the spoon and turned to look at her, and with one glance she knew, knew, that it was all going to fall apart. There was no rehearsal for this. No possible response that made any sense at all.

"Why didn't you tell me I had a brother?" Laurel said, and the sick feeling in Emma's stomach turned black and toxic, and she sank down in a chair at the kitchen table, staring blindly at her hands. On the stove, the stroganoff bubbled and hissed, and she ought to be stirring it, but she didn't care. Let it burn. "Mom? Mom! Answer me!"

That last rose to a shout, almost to a scream, and Emma raised her gaze to fix on her daughter's. The golden flecks in those eyes. The fury in her face. The betrayal.

For sixteen years, she'd kept secrets, and now . . . now they were out. But she tried anyway.

"I don't know what you're talking about," Emma said. Her lips felt numbed, as if someone had hit her. "Honey—"

"Tyler. I'm talking about Tyler!" Laurel spat. "He has all the papers, all the proof that we're twins. Twins. And you gave him up? Why did you give him up? How could you? Didn't you love him? Do you even love me? My God, what are you?"

It was all black with pain, all of this, and she hated hearing it in Laurel's voice, knowing that her daughter was infected with this horror too. She'd tried to shield her. Tried her very best to make it go away.

But like the dream, it came back.

Emma took in a deep breath, closed her eyes, and said, "I had to give him up. I couldn't keep him."

"Why?" It was a wail, and she heard the tears in her daughter's voice.

Against the black velvet backdrop of her closed lids, Emma saw a flash of yellow eyes. "Because . . . because I would have hurt him," she said. "It was the only way I could save him, Laurel. I kept you because I could. But he—he was—" She couldn't explain this, not in a way that her daughter would ever understand.

"He was what? He was just a baby!" That last rose to a scream of raw fury and hurt, and then it was too late; Laurel was gone, the door slammed loudly enough to rattle glass, and Emma opened her eyes and wiped away tears and realized, with a jolt of horror, that her daughter was running away from her.

Into the dark.

Toward an evil she knew nothing whatsoever about.

Still, Emma tried. She ran out the front door just in time to watch her daughter slam the passenger door of a sedan, catching a glimpse of Tyler behind the wheel as it sped away. *He's too young to drive,* she thought ridiculously, conventionally, knowing that was the least of her problems. She wheeled back into the house and flew into action.

Emma had sense enough to take dinner off the stove and dump it aside, and sense enough to open up the gun safe and take out the two things she'd sworn she would never need again: the silver-coated knife and the revolver filled with custom-cast silver bullets.

The other thing in the gun safe was a manila file folder. Emma hesitated, then grabbed it. The file. The whole story. Gruesomely illustrated. She didn't know if it would do any good at all, but she took it anyway. She changed into dark pants, dark shirt, black jacket: like an assassin, she told herself. In case sneaking was necessary.

And then she went out; not after her daughter, but after her son.

Finding Laurel wasn't that hard; though Emma had always tried very hard to be a normal soccer mom, she'd never been able to shake the habits she'd acquired when her life was ripped to shreds. For years, she'd lived in a state of caution, of paranoia, of fear so pervasive it was existential. So while she let Laurel have leeway, she kept a tether on her. The cell phone had a tracking feature, and if there was one thing Laurel would never, ever discard, it was her cell.

Tyler was definitely moving quickly. The signal that Emma locked in was on the freeway. Emma mounted her own cell phone into the console of her van, put the revolver under the seat where she could easily grab it, and set off in pursuit. She kept the speed reasonable until she was safely on the interstate; it was late enough that the traffic was lighter, and speeding cars were nothing new around here anyway. She weaved in and out of traffic, following the blinking light of her daughter's mortal danger as it sped west, and she felt absolutely sure that her life—the life she'd constructed—was over.

I'll take him with me, she thought. *One way or another, this stops here.*

She was gaining on the signal by the time they'd hit the outer borders of Fort Worth, out into what was officially the countryside . . . and that was dangerous, because the cell coverage would get spotty the farther out from population centers they ran. That might be the intent, she realized. She needed to catch them before the signal disappeared.

She floored it, blowing past slow-moving trucks and sedans and semi tractor-trailers, some whose drivers blew their horns in warning; she didn't heed them, didn't care about the consequences of what she was doing. She'd been waiting for this, she realized. Whether she'd been able to acknowledge it consciously or not, she'd been waiting for this to happen every moment since Laurel's birth.

There was a kind of freedom in knowing it was finally here.

She caught up to the signal.

It was a truck. A cattle truck, rattling along in the night, full of scared and shifting cows on their way to the end of their lives.

She could imagine Tyler, smirking, coming alongside the cattle truck, taking Laurel's cell, tossing it into the stinking hauler. Easy enough to do, especially if it was stopped at a light. His idea of a joke. That made sense, because his father would have found it hilarious.

The realization hit her like a bullet.

My daughter could be anywhere.

Emma pulled over to the shoulder in a spray of gravel; her tires skidded, and she almost went over the steep shoulder, but she didn't care. She couldn't get her breath, and her heart was pounding so hard and fast it filled her ears with a furious drumming. A desperate silent scream was locked inside her vocal cords.

And then she heard the cheerful sound of her cell phone's ringtone.

She put the van in park, shook her trembling hands to get feeling back into her fingers—that was how hard she'd been gripping the steering wheel—and then yanked the cell phone off the console. The screen read PRIVATE CALLER. No number visible.

She didn't say hello.

She didn't need to.

"Don't you just love modern technology?" the voice from her nightmares said. "I fucking love it. Makes everything so easy. Just—reach out and touch somebody."

Her phone made a little chirping sound; she had a text message. She opened it and saw a smiling photo of Laurel, taken with a flash. Laurel, inside Tyler's car.

"You know who this is, don't you, Emma?"

She couldn't answer, didn't want to answer, the way a child puts the covers over her head to hide from the monster in the bedroom. She could feel his attention fully on her, like the scorching heat of the sun in the desert.

"Do you want her back?"

She swallowed painfully, licked her lips, and said, "Yes." It took everything out of her, but she did it.

He laughed. She reached down under the seat and took hold of the gun; she put it in the seat next to her, as if its mere presence could protect her from that laughter.

But nothing stopped the sound from crawling inside her, touching her, taking her. That confident, utterly callous laugh—it told her he was certain he could repossess her.

"You've been watching us," she said; it came out more like a whisper than she wanted. "All these years."

"Nope. No point in wasting my time. You're predictable," he said. "One of your best qualities. Tyler's taken a liking to little Laurel, and good for him; a brother ought to care for his sister. He's bringing her to me for a proper introduction. If you want to be here for it, you'd better get back on the road."

"Where?" The fear had drained out of her, as if she just couldn't contain it anymore; it was too big, too vast. It had ruptured the skin of her and bled out, leaving her empty.

He gave her an address in Rockwall; at least an hour's drive east across the metroplex.

"Emma?" She'd thought that she couldn't be afraid anymore, but the sound of her name in his mouth made her shudder. "You be careful on the roads, now. Wouldn't want you to miss this."

She didn't wait for him to hang up. She put the phone back into its holder on the console, put the van in drive, and sped away, sliding into traffic just ahead of a Mustang. The young man in the passenger seat flipped her off as the smaller car whipped around her. She didn't care.

She took the next exit, U-turned, and floored the gas headed back the opposite direction.

He'll wait, she thought. *He'll want me to see. He'll want me to know.*

She had to pray that was true.

There was something eerily unsurprising in the utter middle-class normality of the subdivision. The brick wall at the entrance bore the words SERENE SHORES. To justify the "shores," there was a large pond right inside; it was probably charming in the daytime. Now, there were only the indistinct pale shapes of ducks dotting the bank and dark smooth water, and the trees looked frozen and twisted. She drove around the pond and then turned right. The streetlights lit up the front of a McMansion, built on the same pseudograndiose lines as its neighbors looming only a couple of feet away, maximum houses on minimum lots. There was something vile about this ultimate horror hiding here, in this neat, pretentious suburban neighborhood.

She pulled up to the closed garage door. Tyler must have put his car inside. She prayed Laurel was in the house. Emma shut the engine off, dropping the keys and her cell phone into one pocket of her leather jacket and jamming the revolver into the other. She picked up her purse with the file stuffed inside, took a deep breath, and opened the van door.

The front door was flanked by two Chinese temple dogs, staring off into the distance; there were leaves and spiderwebs and a wrinkled flyer for a tree-trimming service jammed in behind the one on her right. As she looked down, half crazy with fear, she suddenly had a premonition, a strong one. She'd learned not to ignore those; if she'd listened to the first one she'd ever had (*I really need to catch a ride home from school today, not walk home*), she wouldn't be in this fix now.

So she took the gun from her pocket and put it down in the shadow between the temple dog statue and the brick wall.

Then she rang the bell. A cheery little three-note chime sounded from within, and only a second or two went by before the door swung open.

Tyler was standing there.

He didn't say a word. He took a step back, avoiding her gaze. That was smart. If her stare were able to kill, he'd be writhing on the floor. She stepped inside. The door closed behind her with a soft, final click. She clenched her teeth and walked on.

The entry hall had striped wallpaper. The house smelled like lemon furniture polish and vanilla—air freshener, not the warm scent of things baking. The art was of the Thomas Kinkade school: cozy cottages bathed in sunshine.

"Sorry about this," Tyler said, his face turned away. "I really am."

She didn't speak. She couldn't. There must be something of her in him, but he was his father's puppet. She followed him down the hallway, past darkened doorways, to a brightly lit living room. The monster's lair.

The lair gave a good imitation of a homey den. The monster and her daughter were sitting on the sofa, having some flowery-smelling variety of hot tea. There was a muted TV program playing on the wide-screen television set. Tyler's influence could be seen in the room—gaming equipment, wireless controllers dumped on the coffee tables, empty soft drink cans on the pass-through bar to the kitchen. Everything about the room was . . . normal, and at the same time completely fake, as if the monster had ordered a room of furniture from some store ad and positioned the pieces exactly as they'd been in the photograph.

There was one personal touch: a single photograph, framed and centered under a spotlight on the wall . . . a posed image of her and Laurel, done years ago for a Christmas card. How did he get that? She couldn't think about it, couldn't worry about that now.

She said, calmly and firmly, "Laurel, please come here."

Laurel's father looked up at her and smiled. He wore the same skin she remembered. It sent a seismic shock through her . . . like the house, he was bland, nondescript, brown hair (dusted now with silver) and brown eyes. His skin tone was medium, too; a dozen witnesses would have given him a dozen different nationalities, depending on their preconceptions.

He couldn't be picked out of a crowd, and that was the point. The entire point.

"Emma," he said. He sounded pleased. "Have a seat, we were just talking about you."

"Laurel, please come here."

Laurel took a sip of her tea and settled in deeper on the couch. "I'm fine, Mom." Emma couldn't read her voice, and Laurel was looking at the creature in the man suit. Was she really oblivious to the danger?

Emma wanted nothing more than to launch herself across the coffee table, grab her daughter, and get out of that room, but she knew that was what he was waiting for. She focused on him. If she'd brought the gun inside, she would have tried to kill him now . . . but she realized that wouldn't have worked. He was expecting instant, unreasoning violence.

So she said, "What name are you using these days?"

His eyebrows raised, as if he was very mildly surprised. "The same one I've always used, Em. Charles Wilson. I noticed you changed your name, though. Laurel, did you know your mom used to have the last name Kazinski?"

"What?" Laurel blinked, and her bright, accusing eyes focused on Emma for the first time. "How much more haven't you told me? God, Mom. My real name is Kazinski?"

"Your legal name is Saxon," Emma said. "Everything he tells you is a lie, Laurel. Believe me."

"Why should I?" her daughter shot back. "You've lied to me my whole life. What about Tyler? Even if you couldn't keep him, why didn't you tell me I had a brother somewhere out there? And you told me my dad was dead!"

I hoped he was, Emma thought. Her breath caught in her throat as she saw Charles—this was the first time she'd ever known what he called himself—put an affectionate hand on her daughter's shoulder. "Don't be too hard on your mom, kid," he said. He patted gently. He left his hand there. Every nerve in Emma's body screamed at her to do something.

"Your mom went through a very hard time," he told Laurel. "Look, I was no prize; I admit, I left before you two were born. Your mom went into a tailspin, and she had to be treated for depression. She gave your brother up for adoption because she was so angry at me. I'm just happy that I came back to my senses after that. I was able to get him back."

"But—but you didn't look for us? For me?" Laurel looked up at him, and for the first time, she frowned a little. "Why not?"

"Well . . . I did talk to your mom. But she told me she didn't want me to be part of your lives. Then she moved away and changed her name. It took me a long time to track you guys down again, and once I did, I wasn't sure I ought to contact you. It was Tyler who made that decision. Right, son?"

Tyler, leaning against the wall, nodded. Could he really have grown up in this house, with this . . . thing? He was staring down at his feet, looking remote and almost disinterested . . . but that was a mask, Emma thought. He was scared.

Almost as scared as she was.

"Laurel," Emma said. She reached into her purse, and Charles's stare came to fix on hers. She saw the pulse of yellow fire in his gaze, but she was ready for it this time. Although it terrified her, she didn't let it stop her. She took out the file and handed it over to her daughter. "He's lying to you. This is the truth."

Laurel opened the folder and gasped. She clapped a hand over her mouth as she stared at the first photo of her mother's battered, misshapen face. She turned it over. The next one was of the damage to Emma's torso. Laurel gave a high-pitched noise of denial. When those pictures had been taken, Emma had been hardly older than Laurel was now.

Charles smiled. He didn't look away from Emma's face.

Laurel turned the pages with a trembling hand and looked up with horror in her eyes. Finally, something had gotten through. "Mom!" The word was soft, almost muffled, and Laurel closed the folder and tried to get up to come to her.

Charles's hand on her shoulder held her back.

"That wasn't me, sweetheart," he said, not even making an effort to sound concerned. "I was her boyfriend when that happened. She was already pregnant by me when she was raped. I freaked out; wasn't my finest hour, Laurel, I know that. But I came back. I came back."

"Mom?"

Emma held her hand out. Laurel slipped out from beneath Charles's hand and went to her, and as Emma put her arm around her, she felt a surge of strength.

"He's lying," she said flatly. "He attacked me on my way home from school when I was seventeen. I never knew his name, but I knew—I knew what he was."

"And what am I?" Charles asked, and tilted his head to one side. "Go on, Emma, tell our daughter what you think I am. Let her know just how insane her mother really is." When Emma didn't take the bait, he sighed. "Laurel, your mom is sick. I'm sorry, I wish I didn't have to tell you this, but she thinks I'm some kind of demon, and you and Tyler—she thinks you're both some kind of demons, too."

"Not Laurel," Emma said. "Just the boy. It's always the boy, isn't it?"

"You're insane," Charles said. "Laurel, do you hear what she's saying? How crazy that is?"

"Is it?" Emma backed up, toward the doorway. Charles, sitting calmly on the sofa, didn't move; he watched, still toying with her, still smiling that unsettling little smile. "Is it really? I'm not letting you have my daughter, you bastard. No way in hell."

"Hell," he repeated, and he moved his gaze from her to Tyler, who was between them and the hallway. "Funny you should say that, because I've got nothing to do with hell. That's a concept that came long after me. I'm not the devil, you know. I'm just . . . well. They call me a Witness."

Laurel took in a sharp, trembling breath, and Emma knew just what was happening—the ground was moving under her world. She'd thought it was all malls and boys and simple, though sometimes brutal things . . . but maybe her mom was crazy, and maybe her dad was, too. Her rapist dad.

Maybe it was something worse. Maybe neither one of them was crazy.

"Witness to what?" Emma asked.

"Witness to the end," he said. "I'm here to see it."

"See what?"

"Everything," he said. "I must watch the human race forever. I have to look like one of them to do this. But bodies wear out, and I have to make new ones. Only the most special women will do, Emma. Like you. Like our daughter." He laughed, then shook his head. "I know it sounds sick. It's just the way things work for Witnesses. Nothing personal."

Nothing personal. He'd said that—she remembered it as clearly as she did the feeling of the blood running down her cheeks, of her broken teeth grinding in her mouth. As she remembered the cruel, relentless weight of him on her, and the taste of her own desperate, muffled screams. She remembered that phrase, the dispassionate way he'd said it then. He'd made it almost a chant. Nothing personal, relax, nothing personal . . .

The memory made her lose control.

She still had the knife, and instead of doing what she should have done—lunging for Tyler with it, forcing him out of the way—she went for Charles. For the source of the evil, not its issue. She dove over the coffee table and right into him as he sat on the couch.

And he didn't even try to stop her.

She sank the blade deep in his guts and pulled up, muscles straining and twitching with the pulse of adrenaline, and something inside her that had been bottled up screamed and jumped and capered with delight.

He was smiling. He was still smiling, she had to make him stop smiling.

Then it was too late to think about what she was doing, there was blood gouting all over her, and he was falling sideways, so much red gushing out of him, all over her, and his eyes rolled back in his head but not before she saw that last guttering flash of poisoned yellow in them.

He never stopped smiling.

Over the roaring in her head, Laurel was screaming. *I killed him,* Emma thought as she staggered to her feet. It felt good, but it also felt strangely distant. *I killed the bastard, finally. He'll never touch me again.* It tasted like victory, but felt like a loss. It occurred to her, slowly, that she'd just killed her daughter's father in a particularly gruesome way, right in front of her.

But when she turned toward Laurel, she realized that Laurel was screaming for an entirely different reason.

Tyler had moved away from the wall. He was in front of his sister, staring at her, and his eyes were flickering, igniting into a bright, hot, poisonous yellow. Her son said, grinning, "Thanks, Mom. Knew I could count on you to do the hard part."

Her instinct was to rush blindly at him, to wrest Laurel away, but she knew better; that was what he was waiting for. Instead, Emma backed away, to the still-twitching corpse of the dead man, and pulled the knife free of his body.

Tyler's grin dialed down from glee to business.

He lunged forward to seize Laurel's wrist even as she tried to run. He pulled her into a tightly enveloping embrace. "You really should go, Mom. I don't think you're going to want to see what comes next, do you? You've kind of already been there. Wouldn't want you to get flashbacks and crack up again. . . . Hey, sis, did you know that dear old Mom spent six months before we were born scratching padded walls and mumbling to herself? And then spent another year after she gave me up getting high? Dear old Mom, the crackhead. They didn't even let her hold you until you were nearly two, after she detoxed."

"Stop," Emma said. She'd never, ever told her daughter about those dark, awful days; she'd tried to forget they ever existed. She took in a deep breath and took a step toward him. Her grip was too tense on the knife, and she deliberately relaxed. "Tyler, you're as much a victim as I was. You never asked for any of this, and now . . ."

"Sorry, were you talking to someone? Because I know you weren't talking to little Tyler, that squirming bundle of joy you almost killed when they tried to put him in your arms. If you'd had your way, little Tyler would have had his baby neck broken before he took his first breath. Right?"

"Yes," she said. She'd lied to Laurel for so long, but it was time for truth now, hard and scalding truth. "I knew what you were, even then."

"You knew because I told you," the thing inside Tyler said, and arched one of her son's eyebrows. "I told you everything, just like I've told each of them, for thousands of years. But nobody remembers, because if they did, they'd go mad—or worse, they'd go sane. You came the closest, I have to admit. You almost knew."

"Let her go," Emma said. "Let my daughter go. Take me instead."

"Nice try. But like I said, I'm a Witness. I see everything. I am the Many-Eyed, the Recorder, the All-Seeing. So I know that right after you got clean and sober, the first thing you did was get yourself fixed, like a stray dog. Too bad; I'd have taken you up on it, just to see the look on your face. But not to worry. Your genetic heritage lives on in this lovely young lady. Time to start the next incubation cycle."

"You can't do that," Emma said. "She's your sister."

"Do you think I care about stupid human genetics? I'm eternal, sweetheart, and she's just a temporary measure to keep me here in flesh. I'll find someone else for the next go-round." He shrugged. "Compatible women are always drawn near me. They can't help it. It's part of the gravitational structure of the universe."

And as if his words had unlocked some secret closet in her mind, she knew. She saw. She remembered the vision he'd shoved into her mind as he was planting his seed inside her . . . a vision of a universe so complex, so vast, so cold that it had driven her mad. And always, the Witnesses. Part of the world, waiting, with the keys to open the way to something she could only, incoherently, call the Apocalypse, because the vision of that bloody vista of death and despair couldn't be looked on directly.

To a Witness, she and Laurel were nothing, nothing at all, but vessels to ensure his perpetuity: broken bottles left empty on the road in the wake of his speeding car.

She also knew something else, something glimpsed in one blinding second—the one thing he'd given her that he didn't want her to know.

He could be stopped. Not with the silver knife; he'd let her kill his old shell as a sign of his arrogance. He'd done it for his own convenience. If she buried that knife in Tyler's chest, he'd laugh, spit blood in her face, and cut her to pieces with the same bloody blade.

That spark of hope steadied her in a way that all the fear in the world couldn't.

"If that's true, there's another compatible girl close by," Emma said. "Let me find her. Let me bring her here. And then you can let my daughter go."

That surprised him. Finally. She saw him stop and consider her, frowning just a little. "You'd do that? Bring another woman here, knowing what I'll do to her?"

"I'll do anything to save my daughter," she said, and she meant it. "I swear to you, on my soul, I will keep my word. But you have to swear you won't rape Laurel, seduce her, or harm her in any way while I'm gone. Swear it on your name."

A flicker of yellow danced in his eyes, and he smiled a little wider. "You have done your homework. All right. On my name, I swear that I will not rape, seduce, or harm your daughter while you are gone." She felt a little shiver through her bones, a kind of power rippling in the room.

"Mom?" Laurel whispered, shuddering. Tears gathered in her eyes. "Mom, you can't leave me. You can't."

"I'm sorry, sweetie," she said. "But he won't hurt you. He swore on his name. Try to stay calm. I'll be back soon." Emma took in a deep breath, turned to Tyler. "Tell me how to identify her."

The piss-yellow glare in her son's eyes flared almost red and then subsided almost to nothing . . . until she could see her human son beneath it. Or the shell that was left of him. Though this broke her heart, it forged it into steel at the same time.

"You'll know her when you see her," he said. "They've got a glow. Look at Laurel. Really look."

She turned her gaze on her daughter, and she saw it—maybe she'd always seen it, in some way, but now she recognized it consciously. An aura of gauzy light drifting behind her like mist.

Like wings.

Like angel wings.

"Blood of angels," the Witness whispered almost in her ear, and she shuddered. " 'The sons of God saw the daughters of men, that they were fair' . . . you carry that, Emma, you and Laurel. That's what makes you perfect."

She fought to keep her voice from shaking. "Get away from me."

He took a long step back, and his voice rose to a normal level. "If you go look, you'll find her. She'll be close. You won't have to go too far."

"Mom—" Laurel pleaded.

"I have to do it," she said to her daughter. She knew that if she looked in the mirror now, she'd see the same gauzy light behind her own body, but mutilated, dirty, broken. She couldn't allow that to happen to her own child.

No matter the cost.

Laurel was still calling her name when Emma walked out the door, retrieved the gun from the place she'd concealed it, and got into the car to search for their salvation.

EMMA SPOTTED THE girl less than two blocks away. It was easy. She was the only pedestrian in the quiet neighborhood. She was striding confidently down the dark sidewalk, a tall blond girl, maybe a few years older than Laurel. Under the streetlight, she looked tan. There was a backpack slung over her shoulder. She was wearing a red hoodie with a community college logo on the breast. A girl with her whole life ahead of her.

And those ghostly angel wings whispering through the air behind her.

Emma pulled the car to the curb, rolled down the window, and leaned over to wave at the girl. The girl hesitated, looking around (nighttime, stranger), but then she bent over to look into the car. She didn't come closer, which was smart; but that didn't matter, because as soon as the girl's eyes were level with hers, Emma brought up the pistol and pointed it right at her.

The girl froze.

"What's your name?" Emma asked her. The girl, terrified, suddenly looking like a child instead of a woman, just stared back at her with blank, shiny eyes. "What's your name?"

"Jenna," she finally whispered. "Please don't—"

"Jenna, shut up now and listen. This won't make any sense to you, but to save your own life, you better believe me. I want you to turn around and run, run back to campus. Then I want you to find another school on the other side of the world and go there. Get the hell out of here. Don't come back. Wherever it is you would naturally go? Now do the opposite. Save yourself."

"I—" The girl licked her pale lips. "Okay, okay, sure, I'll go."

"Tonight. I mean it. I'll be checking, Jenna. You get the hell out of town on the first plane you can find. Act like a psycho killer is after you, because he is. Understand?"

"Yes," Jenna faltered. She clearly believed she was talking to the psycho killer. Emma felt her attempt had only frightened the girl senseless.

But she sighted the pistol on Jenna's chest anyway. The girl gasped. "Tell me again what you're going to do."

"Transfer. Get out of town," Jenna said. "I will, I swear! Please—"

"I'm not going to hurt you," Emma said. "But I'm not the one you should be afraid of. If you ever see a man with yellow eyes, don't hesitate. Run."

Then she put the gun back on the seat, put the car in drive, and sped away, leaving Jenna bewildered and shaking on the sidewalk. In the rearview, she saw the girl start to run the opposite direction from the way she'd been going.

She'd done the best she could do.

She had no doubt that Jenna would be dialing 911 before she reached the end of the block, so she'd have very little time before the cops would be cruising Rockwall, looking for her van. Emma shook the bullets one-handed out of the revolver, then drove to the pond at the subdivision entrance. She got out and pitched the revolver as far as she could into the murky water, exciting some mallards, and then got back into her van and used her cell phone's browser to find the nearest church.

It happened to be a Methodist church, but the denomination didn't matter to her; she was compelled to be in a sacred space. She'd avoided churches most of her life, for her own reasons; she'd always felt presence in them, and it had frightened her.

Now, it didn't. She knew—because of what she'd glimpsed in the Witness's mind—that the church was where she should be. There was safety there, but it was more than that.

There was power. She just had to find it. It was Laurel's only hope.

No cars in the Methodist parking lot. The side door had an office hours sign in the window, but of course it was night. Emma expected the door to be locked . . . but when she tried it, the handle turned. She had the sense, strange but very real, that she was expected.

She made her way through the dark halls to the sanctuary, and she went inside; it was a neat, clean place, straight lines of pews with red velvet cushions and burgundy carpet. The arched windows were patterned stained glass, now black with night, and the whole place had a hushed, silent feeling to it. There was an area for the choir behind the pulpit, and a simple wooden cross hanging above the altar. No adornments.

She felt a sudden surge of electricity go through the air, and the bulbs in the fixtures overhead flared on, brightened to an almost unbearable intensity, then went out. The church was left bathed in moonlight, and the feeling of energy racing through it lifted the hairs on her arms. She saw the thin blue crackles of it between her fingers.

And then a voice whispered in her ear, "I've been waiting for you."

She spun, and saw—saw something that her brain refused to process, a raw spiraling tangle of light, bright as the heart of a star. She fell to her knees not out of piety, but out of awe. Even with her eyes tightly closed she could see it hovering before her.

"Do you know who I am?" the voice whispered. It didn't seem to come from the light; it seemed to be on her shoulder, always on her shoulder.

"Uriel," she said. She didn't know why she said it, but the name floated up from her, and she knew it was right. "You're Uriel."

"It is my honor to deliver to you your destiny," that whisper said. "Emma, child of angels, you have been chosen. Rise, and receive that which you seek."

She couldn't have refused even if she'd wished; there was so much strength and inevitability to what the angel Uriel was whispering. She stood, not even aware of the effort, of the muscles working, because the light that was blooming inside her was so warm, so sweet, so perfect that she felt utterly at peace.

And then the pain took hold. She felt her life burning away, the dross of it disappearing in an excruciating blaze of power. The darkness was coming, close enough to touch.

"Peace," Uriel's whisper said, and she caught her breath and felt tears break free to steam away from her cheeks. "I give you the kiss of peace. Your destiny is upon you, Emma."

She let out that held breath slowly, and as it trembled in the air, the beautiful, terrifying thing that had faced her was . . . gone. Just gone. Not a fading, not a slow withdrawal. Uriel was gone as thoroughly as if he'd stepped through a door and slammed it behind him.

The only evidence that he'd been there was steam rising from the carpet like morning mist and the burned-out bulbs in the ceiling lights.

Emma looked down at herself. She looked the same, though steam rose from her clothes, too. And even from her skin. The pain was gone, and so was the feeling of power.

But she knew that she was different.

She smiled and turned toward the altar, and said, softly, "Thank you."

Nothing. But she hadn't expected anything this time.

SHE WENT IN without knocking and found Tyler standing behind Laurel, holding her as a human shield. He'd expected Emma to come in shooting, she realized. She might have done that if she hadn't understood it wouldn't accomplish anything.

But she didn't need to. She knew that now.

"Where is she?" Tyler asked. "The girl?"

Emma said, "Outside. But I'm not bringing her in until you give me my daughter."

Tyler was smart, and he was powerful, and he was immortal—but he was not omniscient. He studied Emma, and he saw nothing except what she wanted him to see—the same tattered, ragged light trailing behind her like broken wings. The same beaten, degraded look in her eyes. "You're a weak little bitch, aren't you? Humans. No wonder the Apocalypse is coming for you. You deserve it." He thrust Laurel at her.

Emma held her daughter in her arms for one long, precious second, feeling the strength of desperation in Laurel's embrace, and then whispered, "You have to go now, baby. Get in the car and drive away."

"Not without you," Laurel whispered back. "Mom, please!"

Emma kissed her temple—just a bare brush of her lips—and felt her child go still and quiet. "Hush," she breathed. "Now go, baby. I love you."

That kiss had given Laurel more than words—it had given her knowledge. All the knowledge that Emma now possessed, of the Witnesses, of the angels, of what was past and what was to come. Not omniscience, but some portion of wisdom.

And that gave Laurel the strength to push back from Emma, look straight into her eyes, and for the first time in their relationship, Laurel saw her. Saw her for the girl she'd been, the broken thing she'd become, the woman she'd tried to be for her child.

Saw her for the bright-burning thing she was now.

"I love you, Mom," she said. "Thank you."

And then she took the keys from Emma's hand and walked out the door with no hesitation. Emma didn't turn to watch her go. She heard the car start, the tires hiss, and the engine roar as Laurel drove away.

Silence fell.

Tyler was still smiling. It looked less like a human expression now than a hole into darkness.

"Well," he said. "You owe me a girl. So let's have it."

"You don't think I really brought one, do you?" she asked. "Come on, Tyler. I wouldn't give you an innocent victim, and you know it."

He shrugged. "Well, it was worth a shot. Sorry, Mom, but your usefulness is pretty much over now. You got any weapons you want to try? Knife? Gun? Ballistic missile? Break it out and let's get it over with. I'm impatient. I want to start tracking Laurel, and your pain's getting boring."

"Is it?" She stepped forward, empty-handed, eyes locked on his shining yellow ones. "Is it really? Are you sure?"

"What are you doing?"

"You're my son," she said. "Tyler, you're my son. Maybe I didn't want you. Maybe I should have killed you. But I didn't. You're here. Whatever else you are, I still love you for being my son."

He frowned slightly and took a step back. "I'm not your son. I'm wearing your son, bitch. A slight difference."

She kept moving toward him, moving slowly, quietly, and Tyler finally took another step backward. She saw him recognize it, that energy crackling in the air. A lightbulb popped in a lamp. Another one, with the sound of a gunshot crack. The stereo, playing softly in the corner, let out a distorted squall and a puff of smoke. But Emma moved closer.

His next step put his heel into the blood of the body of his father, his last host. He had nowhere to go now.

Emma stepped forward, her chest almost against his. As he froze in confusion, she kissed him.

The kiss of peace.

Time stopped, and universes paused in their spinning. Heaven and hell took in breaths.

And then the Witness was cast out, screaming, into the abyss that was neither heaven nor hell, life nor death, but eternal darkness.

She felt him being unmade in the merciless emptiness—ripped apart. Lost forever, all his schemes, all his ambition, all his destiny, gone.

All his evil, cut off at the root.

And it hurt.

God, she was so glad it hurt.

Her son collapsed in her arms, and his heart beat on in faltering thuds once, twice, three times. For an instant, his dark eyes focused on hers, and she saw the gratitude there. The love. The peace she had given him.

"I'm so sorry," she said. "For everything. Go to God, Tyler."

He did. Without pain.

She lowered him back to the carpet, closed his eyes, and folded his hands neatly on his chest. What the coroner would make of this, Emma couldn't guess—death by heart attack or stroke, maybe. Or some kind of family death pact.

It no longer mattered to her.

Human bodies were as fragile as lightbulbs, and as prone to shattering. The power that Uriel had poured into her—the power that had opened a window to darkness and unmade a demon—was gone now, poured out like starlight into that void, and it had burned away everything else inside her

She was a dying bulb, and she felt the last flickers of light course through her veins. It felt sweet now, life. Sweet and clean and restored to the clarity it had possessed when she was a girl, full of promise and possibility.

Emma walked out into the dark and stood there for a moment, soaking in the late September warmth. All around her, as if it was broad daylight, the night-soaked grass flared green, the flowers shouted colors, and the world spoke.

She raised her face to the sky and laughed in delight.

And then she was gone.

JENNA SEARLES WALKED down a gray street in Portland. In the late fall chill, she wore layers of protection against the relentless drizzle. Despite the cold and rain, she had to admit she liked it here. Tall evergreens, mountains, coffee shops on every corner. And Portland liked her; she had friends who had come to her as if she'd always been meant to be here.

From time to time, she thought about the woman in the van, that desperate, crazy woman. As she'd been packing in the early morning, the cops had come to her parents' house to tell Jenna that they'd found her. The news reports had given Jenna the full story—the murdered dad, the dead son, the woman collapsed from a massive stroke on the front lawn. They'd never found the gun. But they'd found a fascinating file. The details were never in the papers.

For no good reason, Jenna had chosen to take the dead woman's advice. To her parents' consternation, she'd packed up and left for Oregon, which was as opposite to Texas as she could get. She liked the University of Portland and its funky students; she liked her new friends and her cool apartment. It felt like . . . destiny, somehow.

She stopped to get a cup of hot chocolate and sipped it as she hiked up the hill toward the university grounds. Cars whizzed by, stirring fallen leaves; there was a sharp smell of burning wood in the air. People were starting to put out Christmas lights.

She paused at the light to wait for the safe crossing, and a soft jingling of bells drew her attention a few yards down the side of the street, off her route. Normally, she wouldn't have glanced that way.

That was how she came to see the crosses. There were three of them clustered together—crude white-painted wood, black paint, faded silk flowers jammed in at the base. The jingling came from frayed ribbons with bells tied at the ends, tossed in the wind.

She could see the names from where she stood. EMMA. TYLER. The third cross was blank.

Jenna shivered, as if someone had just walked over her grave, and then the light changed, and she kept walking, and put it out of her mind.

REPLACING MAX

Stuart MacBride and Allan Guthrie

"God, Wesley, you're *such* a child." Angelina thumps back into the passenger seat, arms folded across her chest. Bottom lip sticking out. Eleven years old, going on forty.

Wesley tightens his grip on the steering wheel, skin tightening across his bruised knuckles as he peers through the windshield into the darkness. "I'm not the one sulking." Thick globs of snow swirl through the BMW's headlights. The road twists and turns, skeleton trees guarding either side, jagged branches a canopy of claws as the big four-by-four's tires bite through the snow. Would be good to know where the hell he's going. Bloody road isn't even on the sat nav. But then the thing's been sod-all use since two hours north of Oban. "And when did you get your hair cut? I liked it when it was long."

She runs a hand through the auburn pixie cut, then sticks on her headphones. "Supposed to be going out for pizza. Never think of anyone but yourself, do you?" She narrows her eyes: mean and green in the dashboard's glow. Just like her mother's. . . . "You know something? Hugh's *right*, you're—"

"Stop it!" Wesley pulls the nearest wire from her ear. "Will you please just . . . *stop,* Angelina? How many times do we have to do this?"

She leans forward, just enough to make slamming back into the seat look more dramatic. "It's not even your weekend."

He tries for a smile. Softens his voice. Tries to take out the gravel and knots. "Come on, you're too young to stay by yourself. You know that."

"Could have stayed at Susan's house. She's got a spare room."

"Well, Angel, you're with me."

A road sign pokes out of the snow on the passenger side: Cladh Ciorag 5. Where the hell is Cladh Ciorag?

"Why didn't Mum want me with her?"

Jesus Christ . . . "I don't know. It was a last-minute thing. They didn't tell me."

"She could have told *me*." Angelina clenches her mobile, the display screen haloing her lime-green fingernails. When did she start wearing nail polish? "It's so *unfair*."

"I'm not the bad guy here, okay?"

Silence.

She just crosses her arms again, jerks her chin up. "I need a piss."

"A piss? Is that how we brought you up? A *piss*?"

"Gosh, *Wesley,* you're right." Her eyes go wide, one hand pressed against her cheek. "Swearing is horrible. *Much* worse than kidnapping someone."

"Picking someone up from orchestra practice isn't kidnapping. For God's sake, Angel, you can be such a . . ." Wesley works his hands around the steering wheel. Flexing his fingers. Taking deep breaths. "Look, it's late. We're both tired. We just need—I don't know—to find somewhere to stay. Get something to eat. Then we'll have a fun couple of days together. You'll like that, won't you?"

"No. I hate you."

"Come on, a trip up north, like we used to when you were little. Remember? You and me, a nice fire going, marshmallows, hot chocolate, and ghost stories?"

"Yeah, *Wesley*. Way to be desperate." Her thumbs peck at the phone.

"Stop calling me Wesley."

"Your name, isn't it?" One more poke and the phone gives a two-tone chime. She holds the handset against her chest. "Anyway, Hugh lets me call him Hugh."

"I don't care what Bloody Hugh lets you call him: I'm your father!" Bloody Hugh. Good old bastarding, vicious, devious, little, shitty Bloody Hugh. Bloody Hugh who destroyed everything.

More silence.

"Look, I'm sorry. I . . . I'm just tired. Been a long day."

A big wooden sign looms out of the gloom, fixed to the trunk of a crippled oak. The picture of an old-fashioned Scottish house, with a pond or something behind it, sits above the words LOINNREACH HOUSE B&B picked out in cheery letters. A rectangle of plastic hangs beneath it: VACANCIES.

Angelina turns in her seat to watch it go past. "What are you doing? I told you I need to pee!"

The brake pedal judders beneath his foot as the BMW slithers to a halt.

Angelina stares at him. "Jesus, Dad!"

Dad, not Wesley. So that's what it takes.

He sticks the car in reverse and backs toward the turn, brake lights painting the snow blood red between the shadows.

Wesley reaches back into the car and grabs Angelina's bag. "Do you want your clarinet, too?" The words come out in a cloud of fog. The freezing air sandpapers his ears and cheeks. Every inward breath makes his fillings ache.

"Yeah, because I'm *totally* going to trust some slack-jawed banjo-picking tosser who runs an ancient B&B in the middle of nowhere not to steal it. Leave it locked in the car." She hauls on a big woolly hat, tucks her hair in out of the way, sticks her hands in her pockets, and stomps toward the front door. "God, you're such a loser."

Bathed in the warm glow of half a dozen floodlights, Loinnreach House looks a lot grander than it did on the sign—a two-story slab of white with broad gable ends and a couple of dormer windows poking up from the white-covered roof: black eyes beneath startled eyebrows. The lights catch the falling snow, making it shine like flakes of gold. Over to one side, what looks like the edge of an agricultural building stretches away into the shadows, beyond the floodlights' reach. No sign of the pond.

The house door opens just as Angelina's reaching for the knocker, and a frumpy-looking elderly woman wearing a red-spotted white apron smiles at them. She wipes her hands on a tartan tea towel, leaving smears of white flour on the fabric. "You must be freezing."

Angelina shrugs one shoulder. A mannered, too-cool-for-school gesture. Well, that's what comes of private education. A very *expensive* private education, and who was paying for it? Bloody Hugh? Fat chance.

"Yeah, we're thinking of staying. You got an inside toilet?"

"Angelina!" Wesley closes the car door and thumbs the remote. The locks *clunk* and the indicators flash, but he goes around and checks the handle on the boot anyway. Just in case. "I'm sorry, it's been a long day. She didn't mean to be rude." Wesley hurries toward the house. "Beautiful place you've got."

Mrs. Apron's smile grows wider, punching a couple of dimples into her cheeks. She squats down until she's eye to eye with Angelina. "We've got eight inside toilets, three bathrooms, a billiard room, six guest bedrooms, and broadband Wi-Fi. How does that sound, princess?"

Angelina shifts from foot to foot, knees together. "I *really* need a pee."

"Down the hall, second door on the left."

Angelina pushes past, into the house, disappearing from view.

Mrs. Apron turns, watching her go. "And don't mind Buttons: he's a big softy." She faces Wesley again. Wrinkles pucker her lips. Loose skin puffs her eyes. She smells warm, though. Comforting, like fresh-baked bread. "Lovely girl. Pretty, too. You must be proud."

"Yeah. I am . . . usually."

"Honestly, don't worry about it. Me and George have a teenager of our own. I know what they're like." She holds out a hand. "Jeanette Constable."

He takes his glove off and grips her hand in his. The skin's dry to the touch, dusty from the flour. "Wesley. Wesley . . . Smith."

"Welcome to Loinnreach House, Wesley. And please, call me Jeanette." She keeps hold of his hand, looking up at him. "I just *know* you're going to be very happy here."

The floorboards creak beneath the dusty purple carpet as Wesley and Angelina follow Jeanette's broad back along a corridor lined with heavy oak doors, each one with a brass plaque bearing a name like TABBY, TORTOISESHELL, or SMOKE. Baby portraits in gold frames cover the walls, black-and-white, color, and a couple of sepia prints too. Not a single adult to be seen.

Wesley stops outside one of the rooms and runs his fingers across the metal rectangle screwed to the wood. "Mackerel? Cats and fish? Kind of a random naming system . . ."

Stomping up ahead, Angelina puffs out an exaggerated sigh and shakes her head from side to side, making the bobble on her hat wobble. "Don't you know anything? They're all kinds of cat markings."

"Oh, you know your cats! I'm impressed." Jeanette pulls out a long wooden fob and slips the attached key into the door at the end of the corridor. The one marked CLASSIC. She pushes the door open. "Angelina, you're in here." She steps back and ushers them into a small room with a single bed along one wall. A pine wardrobe in the corner. A small desk underneath a sash-and-case window. "We breed Maine Coons."

"Like Buttons? He's *huge*."

"And that's why he's a grand champion." She reaches an arm around Angelina's shoulders and steers her to the window. "Look down there."

Angelina presses her nose against the glass. "Are those cages?"

"Cat runs."

Wesley dumps the bag on the bed and joins them. The room overlooks a courtyard lit by a row of spotlights. Snow covers the roof of a single-story building running perpendicular to the house. Clumps of ice cling in patches to the long floor-to-ceiling wire-meshed enclosure along the front of it. Inside, climbing frames and ramps cast shadows on the ground. Something that looks like a small lynx perches on a plank, looking up at the window. It stretches. Yawns.

"Wow. Can I go see them? Do you have any kittens?"

"Not just now. But . . ." Jeanette holds up a finger. "We've got two pregnant queens. One's due in a couple of weeks. It'll be her first litter. We're very excited."

Angelina's eyes go wide. Like she's six again and it's Christmas morning. "Is Buttons the daddy?"

"No, he's retired. Ah, but in his day . . ." A sigh. "We have three other boys now. I'll get Ellie to give you a tour later if you like? Show you our little family?"

"Wait till I tell Mum." Angelina bites her bottom lip, bouncing up and down on the balls of her feet. "She'll be *so* jealous. We can't have a cat because Hugh's allergic."

Wesley sits on the edge of his room's double bed. Dark-wood paneling on the walls, dark carpet on the floor, wine-red bedspread, curtains the color of dried blood. It'll be like sleeping inside a tumor. Two deep breaths, then he stands again.

A handwritten note lies on the old oak dressing table: "Honesty Bar—help yourself to a dram or two, and let us know how many you've had when you check out!" It sits next to a bottle of Dalwhinnie and two crystal tumblers. Wesley pours himself a large one, the bottle skittering against the rim of the glass. Shaking.

He downs half of it in one, then pulls the curtain open an inch. The BMW's outline is softening beneath a blanket of snow.

Bloody Hugh who never put his hand in his pocket. Bloody Hugh, stealing other people's wives. Bloody Hugh, kicking and biting and swearing.

Wesley yanks the curtains shut again. Throws back the rest of his whisky.

Takes a deep breath. Checks his phone for messages.

Nothing. Good.

He rests his head against the curtain's dry, musty fabric. No one's looking for him. Yet.

The phone bleeps as he switches it off, then he slides it back into his pocket, checks his face in the mirror above the yawning fireplace, and heads downstairs. The stairwell's lined with yet more photos of babies and children. All happy and smiling.

The door at the bottom is off the latch, faint voices on the other side. Sounds like Angelina and Jeanette and a third voice he doesn't recognize. He opens the door and steps out into a blast of freezing air.

WHITE FLAKES DRIFT down, shining in the spotlights outside the row of cages. There's a whiff of something sour: rotting onions and rough vinegar, with the creosotey undertone of industrial disinfectant.

Two huge cats prowl the concrete floor behind the wire mesh. One's a silver-and-black-striped thing with tufty ears. The other's peaches and cream, with a ridiculously fluffy tail almost as big as its body, waddling as its swollen belly swings from side to side. A third cat, massive and ginger, sits on one of the platforms, motionless, like an oversize owl, with a crinkly white ruff.

Wesley steps out into the snow.

A thin dusting sticks to Angelina's woolly hat, giving her head a festive look that dies when it hits her scowling face. "You don't even like cats, *Wesley*."

Great: back to calling him Wesley again.

Don't rise to it. Be an adult. No point kicking off a domestic in front of strangers.

Jeanette raises an eyebrow at a scruffy-looking teenage girl in a thick padded jacket and Wellington boots who's carrying a mop and bucket. "I'm sure he just hasn't met the right one yet, has he, Ellie?"

A pair of striking eyes—one blue, one green—stare out at him from underneath the hood of Ellie's coat. There's something . . . feline about the way they tilt up at the corners. She's a head taller than Angelina. A heart-shaped face framed by straggles of long blond hair, a straight nose that's a little too long. Not conventionally pretty, but she'll probably be a heartbreaker in a couple of years.

She beams a set of perfect teeth at him. "I like your hair." Her voice has that lilting west-coast Highlands-and-Islands warmth to it. "I wish I was a redhead, but Mum says I'm not allowed to dye it. Why don't you like cats?"

He leans back against the door frame. "It's not that I don't like them, it's just—"

"He *hates* them." Angelina's smile is wide and cold. Scoring points. "Says they're cruel." She pulls her phone from her pocket and pokes at the screen. "He's *so* clueless."

"Do you really think cats are cruel?"

"Well . . . I wouldn't want to be a mouse around here."

"Oh, don't worry, our boys and girls wouldn't hurt you. They get special Maine Coon cat food and fresh minced game. Can't make pedigree kittens on a diet of mice and scraps, can you?" She wipes a hand across the tip of her pink nose, catching a drip. "I love them. They're the best thing in the whole wide world."

Angelina squats in front of the cage and holds her phone up, pointing the back of it at the waddling peaches-and-cream cat. Presses a button. An electronic shutter noise. Then she stands, smiling down at her phone. "She's beautiful."

"Ooh, let me see . . ." Ellie scurries over, Wellington boots flapping on the snowy concrete. She peers at the screen, then looks back at Wesley. "Her name's Doctor Bugs. Mummy says I can have the pick of the litter."

Jeanette raises a fleshy hand. "Late birthday present."

"Angelina, you should have been here, it was an *epic* sweet sixteen and we had a barbecue and snowball fight and a great big cake in the shape of a cat!"

Sixteen? She sounds more like a twelve-year-old. Still, it's nice she can still muster up some enthusiasm. Unlike some people.

Angelina fiddles with her phone some more. "Going to text it to Mum. *She* likes cats, even if Wesley doesn't."

Her new best friend puts the mop and bucket down and gives him another flash of those perfect teeth. "Would you like a tour too? We've just finished, but I'd be happy to show—"

"Leave the poor man alone, Ellie." Jeanette points over her daughter's shoulder, back toward the cages. "They've come a long way and they've not had their tea. Now you go finish cleaning out those runs. You can show the gentleman round later."

A sigh. "Yes, Mum."

Yeah . . . that was something to look forward to.

"Now, Wesley." Jeanette takes his arm and steers him into the corridor. "I hope you like venison stew. It's leftovers, but I made plenty. And it's always nicer reheated, don't you think?"

DOZENS OF PICTURES of cats line the kitchen walls. Big, furry, wild-looking cats. Most of them sit next to some sort of rosette or shiny trophy.

Wesley drains the last dregs of tea from his mug. There's a stain on the tablecloth next to his knife and fork, a little drift of crumbs by the salt and pepper, a bottle of tomato ketchup with sticky fingerprints on it. "The stew smells lovely. I hope we're not putting you out."

"Oh, it's no trouble." Jeanette stirs a pot on the range, filling the room with the earthy scent of meat, wine, and garlic. It's warm in here, condensation misting the windows. "We were going to call ourselves a 'boutique hotel,' but that seemed a little conceited. Didn't it, George?"

George plonks a couple of dead pheasants beside the brace of rabbits on the work surface. His hair's a thick shock of white, ending in a swath of pink neck that disappears into the fat collar of his checked shirt. His old man's cardigan is full of baggy pockets with a button missing halfway up, the gray fabric stretched across his impressive stomach. "Don't want to come off as conceited."

"I mean, we're not French, are we?" She shuffles toward the double Belfast sink—deep enough that if she stood in it she'd be up to her knees—and turns on the tap.

"God forbid." George grabs a knife from the rack.

Jeanette rinses out an oversize teapot and jiggles it. "Anyone want another cuppa?"

A petite woman, pushing fifty, bustles in through the kitchen door. Closes it. Stamps her bright white sneakers a couple of times. She's wearing a parka jacket, the fur-trimmed hood thrown back, presumably so it won't interfere with the theatrically bouffant silver quiff that sticks out at a jaunty thirty-degree angle to her head. "It's like a skating rink out there." She peels off her parka, revealing a long red polka-dotted dress. A bit too formal to go with the sneakers. As if she'd gotten dressed up for a special occasion but thought she might need to make a quick getaway.

She cups her hands around her mouth and huffs a breath into them. "Ooh, Jeanette, is that tea? I'm frozen solid."

Jeanette gathers up a couple mugs. "Grace, Mr. Smith and his daughter are staying with us tonight. Wesley, this is Grace Robertson, our midwife. We're *very* proud of her. She's terrific."

The midwife sticks her tongue out at Jeanette. "Don't you believe Jeanette, Wesley; I'm a holy terror when I get going." She steps in close, showing Wesley the wide eyes of a keen listener or budding ax murderer—brown, like caramel, flecked with gold. "I'm in 'Tabby': didn't fancy driving back home in a blizzard. It's been kind of a long day." She sticks out her hand. "Call me Grace."

"Right, Grace." He stands.

Her grip's warm and she holds on tightly, gazing up at him with those big wide eyes. "I love your hair." She turns. "Don't you love his hair, Jeanette?"

Jeanette clunks the mugs down on the table. "Ellie was saying exactly the same thing." She sticks her fists on her hips. "George Constable: you put that filthy thing away, right this minute. We've got guests. And they're about to *eat*."

A pipe sticks out of the side of George's mouth. "Not lit." He demonstrates, puffing on it, lips goldfishing, making sucking noises. "See?" He bunches a handful of gray fur in his fist and pulls, stripping it off the headless rabbit. Then takes a cleaver from the knife block and slams it down on the rabbit's ankles, cutting the feet off. The pelt slaps onto the pile beside him.

"Tsk . . . Have you not finished those yet?" She dries her hands on a dish towel and frowns at the blood-smeared chopping board.

"Had to sort out Boo and Moppet: they keep picking on Ginger. You know what queens are like when they scent blood."

Jeanette sniffs. "Well, he's only got himself to blame."

"Should be ashamed of themselves really. But any excuse for a fight."

"Well, make sure you wash your hands afterward, and don't leave the skins on the work surface this time."

He raises an eyebrow, sucks on the stem of his pipe, then jabs an elbow in Wesley's direction. A hole in the cardigan exposes a snatch of checked shirt. "Anyway, I'm sure Wesley doesn't mind, do you, Wesley? Pipe's a *man*'s habit."

"I don't smoke."

Grace nods. "Filthy habit. But if we don't let George have his little vices, he gets all frisky, doesn't he, Jeanette? Quite the stud in his day."

George roars out a laugh.

Jeanette sucks in her cheeks, pursing her lips. "Why is *everyone* determined to embarrass me in front of guests? Grace Robertson, Mr. Smith doesn't want to hear your smutty talk." She yanks open a drawer and pulls out a handful of cutlery. Slams down a knife and fork on either side of a pair of placemats. A dessert spoon across the top. Then sniffs and turns her back on the midwife. "Wesley, Angelina's a lovely name."

He pulls a chair out from the table and sinks into it. "It's Italian. Means 'messenger' or 'angel.'" Though most days it's hard to believe. "Her mother and I met in Venice." Two lifetimes ago.

Jeanette tilts her head to the side, eyelids closing slightly, like she's waiting to be kissed for the first time. Then smiles. "Ah, right on cue."

The kitchen door swings open and Ellie walks in. She's abandoned the scruffy outdoors look for a pair of orange corduroy trousers and a gray Aran sweater, her long blond hair pulled back from her face in a ponytail. Angelina's right behind her, carrying a huge fluffy gray-and-white cat in her arms, belly up like a well-fed infant—tufty white bib and collar, whiskers an arsenal of miniature knitting needles. She stops on the threshold, frowns at Wesley, then sticks her nose in the air.

Lovely. It's going to be one of those meals.

Jeanette pulls on a set of oven mitts. "Buttons shouldn't really be in here, Ellie."

"Sorry, Mum. Angelina just wanted to hold him, and he likes her: look."

Angelina hauls the mass of fur up in her arms, showing off a swath of belly hair that thrums and vibrates. "He's gorgeous." Buttons is making cooing sounds like a dove.

George pulls the pipe from his mouth—fingers covered in clots of blood and wisps of feathers—and pokes it at Wesley. "EU directive: Pets not allowed in the kitchen while food's being prepared or served. Utter nonsense of course, but try telling *that* to our bureaucratic overlords in Brussels."

"I better put him outside." Ellie picks Buttons out of Angelina's arms and lowers him to the floor. Where he stands, looking indignantly up at her.

Angelina's shoulders droop slightly.

Wesley clears his throat. "The cat can stay in here if you like." He looks at Angelina, gets a smile. "We won't tell anyone."

"Obliged, Wesley. Good man." George puts the pipe back in his mouth.

Jeanette claps her hands together. "Angelina, you sit yourself over there next to your dad, and I'll get the plates out of the warming oven. Hope you're hungry."

Angelina hesitates for a moment, then does what she's told, pulling the woolly hat from her head as she shoogles the chair over a bit. Putting some distance between herself and her father.

George grins. "Well, I never. Look at that." He's pointing at Angelina's hair. It shines like polished copper under the kitchen spotlights. "The apple doesn't fall far from the tree, eh? A redhead, just like your old man."

"And my gran, grandad too. Runs in the family." She gives him a jagged smile, then pulls the hat back on, hauling it down till it covers the tips of her ears.

Jeanette pops salt and pepper shakers on the table. "We call that 'breeding true.' It's so *nice* when that happens, isn't it, George?"

"Wesley, I think you deserve a wee nippie sweetie, don't you?" George digs into a cupboard and comes out with a bottle of Talisker. "Ellie, glasses, please; there's a good girl."

* * *

The venison stew is so dark it's almost black—chunks of sweet carrot and meltingly tender meat in a rich wine gravy. There's something wrong with Wesley's fork though: it keeps shaking in his hand. He grips it tighter. Keeps it still as he stabs up another chunk of deer. A blob of gravy slides down his chin. He grabs a napkin and dabs at it. The napkin trembles too.

Luckily, no one seems to notice. Angelina, Jeanette, Ellie, and Grace are all too busy listening to George banging on about how wonderful it is to live in the middle of nowhere.

"And luckily, the loch's just a stone's throw behind the house." George points at the Welsh dresser in the corner with his pipe. "Good years, when we get a decent freeze, you can skate on it. Even go curling. You ever curled, Wesley?"

"I play squash. The bank I work for has a league."

"Ah. Could never really see the point of squash myself. Too much running about and dropping dead of a heart attack. What about you, Angelina? Fancy skating on Loch Righ tomorrow if the weather clears?"

"Nah. I hate sports." She pushes the carrots to one side of her plate, where they can't contaminate the meat. "I play the clarinet."

As if exercise and musical talent were mutually exclusive.

"Ooh, really?" Ellie sits up straight. "Have you got it with you?"

That too-cool-for-school shrug again. "It's in the car."

Ellie reaches across the table and holds Angelina's hand. "You *have* to play for me! How great would that be?"

Grace cups a large crystal tumbler in her hands, swirling the contents in a slow circle, perfuming the air with its peaty tang. "Do you play anything, Wesley? Other than squash?"

"Bit of piano, guitar."

Jeanette sighs. "You're so lucky. I tried the piano once, but it didn't agree with me. We all sing, though."

"Ha!" George pops his pipe back in his mouth. "Some of us better than others."

"Well, thank you very much, George Constable. That's a lovely thing to say in front of our guests."

"She sounds like one of our cats with its tail caught in the cage door." He drops a hand beneath the table and slaps his wife on the backside, where it overhangs the seat. "I love her dearly, but Jeanette was off shopping when they were handing out the musical genes."

Jeanette's cheeks turn the same color as George's neck. "People are watching . . ."

"You interested in genealogy, Wesley?"

"Can't say I am, particularly."

"Hmm . . . Just because you've got a common surname, it doesn't mean there aren't some pretty special branches on your family tree."

Common surname . . . ? *Smith*—he'd checked them in as Wesley and Angelina Smith. Stupid mistake. People must register here under Smith all the time. Of course it sounds like a fake name. Should have picked something less obvious.

But George seems content to keep any suspicions to himself. "Great thing, genealogy: does a body good to know where he comes from."

"Yes, well, we don't really—"

"I do." Angelina holds up her fork, a glistening lump of venison stuck to the end. "Hugh's a Mormon: they have to trace their families way back to, like, caveman days, so they can get all their ancestors baptized and turn them into Mormons too. We did my side of the family this year, all the way back to 1760."

Wesley scowls down at the contents of his plate. Bastard. Who the hell was Bloody Hugh to change the religion of Angelina's relatives? Posthumously. Without even asking. Her grandmother and grandfather—*Wesley*'s mother and father. Filling her head with all this shit . . .

Grace coughs. "Wesley, are you all right?"

He keeps his mouth firmly shut, holding the knife and fork like daggers. Pressing them into the plate.

George scrapes out the bowl of his pipe with a little metal thing. "Who's Hugh?"

A deep breath through gritted teeth. "He's Angelina's *step*father."

"Ah . . . But you're her . . . biological parent?"

"I'm her *father,* yes." He stares at Angelina.

She stares back. "Yeah, and you're doing such a good job, *Wesley.*" She turns to Ellie. "It must be *so* great living here. Having such lovely parents and all these beautiful cats." She looks back over her shoulder at him again. "I wish *I* was that lucky."

"Really?" Wesley's voice trembles. Keep it calm. No domestics. Calm. "Because I seem to remember paying for music lessons, private schools, phones, computers, clothes, holidays."

"That's all that matters to you, isn't it? Money. You can't bribe your way out of what you did, Wesley."

"It's not bribery, it's because I love—"

"If you loved us, you wouldn't have cheated on Mum. The only thing you ever loved is your bloody bank!"

"That's *enough,* Angelina." He places his trembling cutlery down, getting gravy on the tablecloth. "These nice people don't want to hear you acting like a spoiled child. Just eat your dinner and behave."

"*I'm* spoiled?" She stands up, chair legs scraping the floor. Her face clenches like a toddler's about to have a tantrum. "That's rich coming from you, *Dad*." She marches out of the kitchen, slamming the door behind her.

Silence settles into the room, everyone looking at anything other than Wesley.

"Ahem. Right, better get on." George gets to his feet. Heads over to the worktop, grabs the carcasses, and disappears out through the back door.

Jeanette sighs. "I suppose the washing up isn't going to do itself." She holds out a hand and Ellie passes her Angelina's plate. "Thanks, love. You know, maybe you should go . . . have a word or something?"

Ellie nods, then gets to her feet and hurries out after Angelina.

Wesley picks up his knife and fork and places them in the middle of his plate, then pushes it away. Not really hungry anymore.

"Would you like anything else?" Jeanette looms at his shoulder. "I've got some trifle, or there's syrup sponge and custard?"

"No, thank you. It was a lovely dinner."

She carries the dirty dishes over to the sink and turns on the taps.

"I'm sorry." He takes his napkin and dabs at the splots of gravy left behind. "She's . . ." What? Poisonous? Vicious? Spiteful? Or just an eleven-year-old girl from a broken marriage, lashing out because he's closest? Wesley clasps both hands around his whisky tumbler.

A warmth seeps through his sleeve and into his skin. Grace's hand is on his arm.

He raises his glass. "To happy families."

Grace clinks her tumbler against his. "She'll come round. Teenagers' brains are all over the place, and girls are the worst. I speak from personal experience."

"She hates me."

"At her age, they hate everyone. It's a phase. You'll see."

"She doesn't hate her mother. Or Bloody Hugh. Pair of them have been dripping poison in her ear since day one. I'm not the bad guy, Grace."

She takes a sip of Talisker, rolls it around her mouth, then sits back in her chair, those big brown-and-gold eyes wide, like he's the only thing worth looking at in the world. "Go on then: shock me. What did they tell her?"

It's nice to be special for a change. To be interesting. To be wanted. "That I tried to persuade her mother to have an abortion."

Grace runs a hand through her gray quiff, and when she's finished, it's leaning in the other direction. She places the whisky tumbler down on the tabletop between them. "Wow. That's quite an accusation." Her eyes grow even wider, pinning him to the chair. "Did you?"

Heat rises up the back of his neck and he looks away. "Point is, it's not something you tell an eleven-year-old."

WESLEY PAUSES ON the landing, one hand on the carved wooden railing. The hall light glows pale gold, casting shining reflections on the sea of framed baby pictures. Downstairs, from the kitchen, Grace's and Jeanette's muffled voices are accompanied by the clink and clatter of dishes being washed in the sink.

He takes a breath and marches down the corridor toward Angelina's room.

The door creaks open when he's a dozen paces from it and Ellie slips out. She closes the door behind her, then turns, and her eyes go wide. She jumps. Makes a little squeaking sound. Then clamps a hand over her chest. "Pfffff . . ." A smile makes her face shine. "Sorry, you frightened the *life* out of me."

"Didn't mean to scare you."

Silence.

"Right, well, I'd better . . ." She points along the corridor toward the stairs, a flush blooming across her cheeks.

"Yes."

He flattens himself against the wallpaper as she inches by. And as soon as she's past him, she runs off, thumping down the stairs. Teenagers—completely incomprehensible.

Wesley straightens his shirt, then knocks on Angelina's door. There's no reply, so he does it again. "Angel? Are you okay?"

Her voice is small, barely audible through the wood. "Go away."

"Please?" He tries the handle. It isn't locked. He opens the door a couple of inches.

She's sitting on the bedspread, knees together, feet pointing in toward each other. Buttons is curled next to her, making droning whirring noises as she strokes the long gray fur on his back. She doesn't look up as Wesley slips into the room and clicks the door shut behind him.

"I know you're confused, and you think you hate me, but—"

"Why do you have to ruin everything?"

Wonderful. "It might look like that, but I'm only doing all this because I love you. It really *is* for your own good . . . And I know grown-ups say that all the time, but this time it's true."

She keeps her eyes on Buttons's back, fingers moving through the ash-colored fur. "Hugh says—"

"Hugh's a cock." Shit. Wesley pinches the bridge of his nose with his fingertips. "I'm sorry, I didn't mean that." Yes, he did. And more. "He's not what you think he is, Angel: believe me, I know. Your mother . . ." Deep breath. "Your mother loves you very much, but Bloody Hugh is . . ." He sinks down onto the bed beside her. "Before she started seeing me, they were going out together. She came back from his place this one time all bruised and limping. Told everyone she'd slipped and fallen down the stairs, but it was him."

That gets him a shrug.

"I would never do that." He reaches out and caresses the hair at the nape of her neck. Always liked that when she was little. "I'd never do anything to hurt you, Angel."

A chime sounds in the small room, something electronic, and she pulls out her phone. Buttons stretches his front legs, paws spread wide, yawns, then settles down again as Angelina squints at the screen. "Ellie says I should cut you some slack."

"Well . . . Ellie's obviously a smart cookie."

"She says you don't mean to be a dick."

Lovely. "Look, how would you feel about coming to stay with me for a bit? Not just until your mum and Bloody Hugh get back, but for a couple of weeks, maybe? I miss you, Angel." He licks his lips, then brings out the big guns. "We could get a cat?"

Her head comes up at that, her eyes wide and greedy. "Can we get one of Ellie's kittens when they come? Maine Coon cats are just the best."

Buttons raises his head, that broad white chin trembling as he purrs. Sometimes you have to make sacrifices for the people you love . . .

THE RADIATOR UNDER the window pings and gurgles in time to the rattling pipes. Wesley sweeps his hand through the water pounding into the big enamel bathtub: not quite scalding, but close to it. Good. Nothing like a hot bath after a bad day, and by Christ, today couldn't have been much worse.

Still, look on the bright side—at least now Angelina wants to come stay with him.

He turns off the tap and gives the water another swirl. Perfect.

Okay, so it was going to cost him a pedigree cat—and there was no way something like that was going to come cheap—but it was worth it just to see her smile at him like she used to when she was a kid. Before Bloody Hugh reappeared on the scene . . .

He steps out through the door of his en suite bathroom and back into his bedroom, then gets undressed, laying his clothes neatly on the chair by the wardrobe.

But that's all behind them now. They're going to be friends again. Daddy and his little girl, without anyone screwing it up. Poisoning her against him. Ruining everything . . .

Wesley's reflection frowns at him from the dark window. Pasty naked skin, sagging under the weight of forty-three years of disappointment. Two failed marriages. And today.

A slab of bruises spread midnight-blue and violet stains around his ribs; bite marks carve ragged circles across his forearm.

He pulls on the fuzzy white dressing gown hanging in the wardrobe, wraps it around himself, and ties the cord in a knot at the front. Should really close the curtains, too. Not that there's a risk of anyone seeing him—not unless they're up one of the trees in front of the house with a pair of binoculars. Still. Habits, like so many other things, die hard.

A sharp draft knifes in under the bottom edge of the sash window. Thing isn't shut properly.

He slips a finger through each of the two hooks set into the white-painted wood and stops.

It's not snowing anymore. The night is perfectly still, the landscape blanketed under a smothering of cottony blue as the moon cuts through a break in the clouds. Moonlight shimmers on the surface of Loch Righ, revealing what looks like a boathouse with a small jetty. Must be lovely in summer—take a rowboat out onto the calm water, fish for your dinner.

Have to take Angelina back here next year, when everything's settled down. She'll like that . . .

A familiar voice drifts up from below, muffled by the window, and there she is, skipping through the snow, her breath steaming out behind her. "Come on, then."

Ellie follows her out, stops a dozen feet from the front of the house, and hunches her shoulders. Cups her hands to her face. Then a flickering yellow light illuminates her features. The smoke of a sly cigarette billows out into the night air.

Ellie holds the cigarette out to Angelina. "Want a puff?"

So Jeanette's perfect family isn't so perfect after all. They're normal people, a little screwed up, white lies and secrets, just like everyone else.

Instead of forcing the window shut, Wesley tugs it open and cold air slumps into the room, wrapping itself around him, making the hair on his arms stand up. He fills his lungs, ready to shout down that she better bloody not . . . then closes his mouth. It's going so well—finally, after all this time—why spoil it?

Angelina shakes her head.

"You sure? They're Turkish!"

"Tried one of my stepdad's once. Nicked it from his study while they were throwing this swanky party for his latest book launch. Threw up all over my party frock." She reaches into her coat pocket and pulls out something small and dark. "Besides, smoking and woodwind instruments totally don't go together."

Good girl.

She points the thing in her hand at the BMW and the indicators flash.

No, don't go in there!

She pulls open the back door and reaches inside.

Oh thank God . . . The air rushes out of his lungs, taking all the strength in his knees with it. He rests his arms against the sash window's frame.

"Of course, I'm not very good." She reappears with a rectangular leather case, pops the catches, and opens it. It's the case for her clarinet. She lifts the pieces out and slots the instrument together.

"I'm sure you're brilliant." Ellie takes a long draw on her cigarette, then throws her arms wide. "Play something sad."

"Not today. Today's the best day ever." She raises the clarinet to her lips and the adagio from Mozart's Clarinet Concerto floats out across the moonlight. All that expensive tuition's worth it after all. Her embouchure, tone, and expression are all perfect.

Something swells in his throat. How can a tube made of wood, reed, and metal in a factory in Worthing produce something so beautiful?

Ellie raises her arms, laughter sparkling in counterpoint to the clarinet's soaring notes. She moves her feet through the drifts of white, turning and weaving in slow motion, tracing the melody—trailing ribbons of smoke from the cigarette in her hand—as Angelina sways from side to side. Eyes closed. Lost in Mozart.

It's been so long since he's heard her play. It's the most wonderful . . . And then the music stops.

Angelina pulls the clarinet from her mouth and looks back into the car. "Can you hear that?"

Ellie slithers to a halt. "Don't stop, that was great."

"No, shhh; *listen*!"

The warbling strains of Whitney Houston ruining "I Will Always Love You" leak out from somewhere inside the BMW.

A bitter taste fills his mouth. "Angel? That's enough. Come inside, okay?"

She takes a step toward the car. "Hugh?"

Oh God, it's Bloody Hugh's *phone*. Bastard always did have rotten taste in music. Of all the *stupid* things to miss.

Icy sweat prickles across Wesley's forehead. "It's too cold out there. You'll catch your death."

Angelina looks over her shoulder at him, frowning, mouth slightly open. Then turns back to the BMW.

The ice seeps into his skin, leaches into his veins, spreads into his chest, suffocating him. Make her stop. "ANGELINA, YOU COME INSIDE RIGHT NOW!" Holding on to the window frame, bellowing loud enough to make his throat raw. "DO WHAT I TELL YOU!"

"Hugh?" She's at the back of the car.

Another *plip* from the car keys and the boot hinges up on its own, the courtesy light casting a soft golden glow.

Angelina reaches inside.

No, not now. Not like this. Please . . .

Ellie turns to face him, hiding the cigarette behind her back. "We weren't doing anything wrong. I just wanted to hear her play."

Angelina staggers back from the car, one hand up to her mouth. The clarinet falls, swallowed by the blanket of white. She stares up at him, face pale as the snow. "Oh God, Dad. What did you do?"

His bare feet hit the snow as he stumbles out of the house, the cold drilling up through his soles and into the bones. Angelina looks at him, eyes half closed, mouth slack and open, like she's barely awake. He steps toward her. She turns her head away and her shoulders tremble, then shake, arms wrapped around her stomach—as if she's been punched. He moves toward her . . . but a scream stops him.

Ellie.

She's hunched over by the BMW, hands up at her face, fingers splayed like claws. She screams again. Keeps screaming. The noise pulses in his teeth.

Drag her away from there, close the boot.

Feet numb, he staggers through the snow to the car, breath spuming out in ragged clouds, forehead burning. He grabs her. She tries to pull away, hands pushing against his chest. Convulses with hard sobs that wrench out of her and ping back like stretched elastic.

He doesn't let go.

Over her shoulder, in the boot, a corner of the blanket's folded back. Hugh stares up at them, waxy eyes in his lopsided face, temple bruised and blood caked. Lying on his side. A bare foot pokes out by his chin, the skin like silk, the toenails painted a rich burgundy. A dark line cuts across his cheek, shirt stippled with bloody fingerprints, his pink tie a grotesque tongue.

"What's going on?" George stands in the doorway, shotgun in his hands.

Wesley lets go of Ellie. She steps away; his body grows colder.

Too late . . .

Angelina's mouth moves but nothing comes out. She raises a shaking finger and points at the boot of the BMW.

Snow scrunches under George's slippers as he picks his way over to the boot, the shotgun pointing at Wesley's chest. Then he leans over. . . . His mouth sags open. He takes a handful of the blanket and pulls it out. Lets it fall to the ground. Stands there in silence.

Natalie's curled up in the hollow of Hugh's body. The oversize man's shirt she's wearing rides up on one side, showing a slice of hip and a bare leg. But it's her face that makes Wesley's chest clench. It's swollen and dark, those stunning green eyes bugging and bloodshot. Mouth open slightly, teeth stained with blood. Her neck's a patchwork of purple, blue, and red—pale stripes marking the path of the belt she was strangled with.

Angelina makes a choking sound. Then a sob.

Wesley clears his throat. "Natalie was . . . she was dead when I got there. Bloody Hugh . . . He was dragging her into the boot of his car. Her face was all . . ." Wesley swallows something sharp. "He had a shovel. He went for me. I . . . I didn't have any choice. He *killed* her . . ."

George lowers the blanket again. "Ellie, get in the house."

"But—"

"It wasn't my fault. What if he'd gone after Angelina?"

"Ellie!" Jeanette's voice booms across the driveway. "You heard your father. Inside, *now.* And take Angelina with you."

George raises the gun, points it at Wesley.

Ellie hurries over to Angelina, high-stepping through the snow. "Come on, we've got to go."

Wesley stands there, an ice statue, as Ellie wraps her arms around his daughter, makes little cooing noises, steers her toward the house.

George's gaze doesn't flinch from Wesley. "Jeanette, you see they're safe inside."

A nod. "Come on girls, we'll get you some nice hot sweet tea."

Angelina stops, looks back over her shoulder. "What about . . . *him?*"

Something breaks in Wesley's throat; she can't even bring herself to say his name?

"I'll take care of it." George gives her a smile. "Don't you worry."

Angelina glances at Wesley, then starts moving again, letting Ellie lead her across the drive and into the doorway where Jeanette gives her a hug and a peck on the forehead. She ushers the girls into the house and closes the door, leaving Wesley alone with George, the shotgun, and two dead bodies.

George jerks the barrel of his gun toward the side of the house. "Move."

Wesley has his hands in the air. No idea when he stuck them up. Must look pretty stupid, standing there in nothing but his bathrobe, hands up like it's a bank robbery. But now probably isn't the time to lower them. He swings his left leg out . . . as soon as his foot hits the ground all the bones in his leg are going to snap like breadsticks, sending him sprawling. But no: he stays on his feet. Manages another step without keeling over. "I didn't have any choice."

"Not for me to judge." George pokes him in the back with the shotgun, nods toward a path that leads around the side of the house.

Wesley shuffles his broken-breadstick legs through the snow.

A tall metal gate. George presses a button and a buzzer sounds, then the gate clicks open. "Almost there."

Wesley pushes the gate wide and walks through to a small courtyard with trees and a handful of small stone outbuildings on two sides, and a blank wall of dark gray on the other.

"I was going to find somewhere safe to hide Angelina. Somewhere I could leave her while I . . . while I buried the bodies. She'd never have to know . . ." He wipes his eyes with the sleeve of his dressing gown. Bites his lip. Sniffs. Forces the tears back. "Too late now. She thinks I killed them, doesn't she?"

George is silent for a moment, then he nods. "I don't know if it helps, but I believe you."

"You do?"

"Had a good feeling about you right from the start. And I'm *never* wrong."

"Thanks, George." It's enough to start him crying again. He doesn't deserve anyone's sympathy. But it helps. He wipes his eyes and forces a smile. Mummy's brave little soldier. "You don't need to worry. I won't run away. And I'm not going to hurt anyone."

The gate buzzes again and Jeanette appears, her apron dappled with shadows. She scuffs through the snow toward them. "Angelina's distraught. Poor thing."

Wesley clears his throat. But his voice still cracks. "Can I see her?"

"Actually . . ." Jeanette tilts her head to one side. "Maybe best not. She's fine with Grace and Ellie. Don't expect she'd want to talk to you right now anyway. And you can't really blame her, can you?"

Angelina was right—he's ruined everything. A shudder runs up his body, ice crystals rippling through his core. Feet so cold they're throbbing. He lowers his hands and wraps his arms around himself. "I need my clothes."

"You'll get your clothes. If you behave."

"If I *behave*?" Maybe he deserves to be treated like a teenager. "Seriously: I'm freezing. Let's just go inside and you can call the police." Put an end to it.

"Oh, Wesley." Jeanette pats him on the shoulder. "What makes you think we're going to call the police?" She walks toward the outhouse, triggering a row of security lights—a line of six steel shutters appears from the gloom, running the length of the building. "Come and see."

She flicks a row of switches and the shutters clang and rattle upward.

He limps through the snow, getting closer, the smell of bleach and creosote stronger with every step, George right behind him, gun pointed at his back.

The shutters stop with a clank. Then Jeanette flicks another row of switches and low-energy bulbs flicker on. . . . Wesley stares, mouth hanging open. Instead of cat runs, six barred cages make up this side of the building.

"Hello, sweetie, how's my good little girl today?" Jeanette smiles into the first cage. A wooden nameplate sits in the middle of the upper bars, the name SPOOKS painted in cheery pink letters. She turns to Wesley. "Spooks is a timid wee soul, not very good with people . . ." She points into the cage. "See?"

He hobbles closer. The cage is about the size of a modest bathroom. Toilet in one corner. Shower attachment snaking from the cinder-block wall at the back above a drain set into the concrete floor. A clear plastic corrugated roof, heaped with snow. The back wall is made of cinder blocks, with a cubbyhole-sized hatch at knee height. Wooden kickboards cover the side walls from the floor to a third of the way up.

A skinny young woman in a black sweatshirt and gray jogging bottoms is tucked into the narrow space between the toilet and the kickboards, rocking to and fro, hands clutched around her knees. She looks at him, hunches her shoulders, and looks away.

Jeanette pats a hand against her own stomach. "She's just beginning to show. Can you tell?"

Jesus Christ.

"Next up"—Jeanette sidles along to the next cage—"we have Ginger."

Ginger's a chubby little boy, maybe five or six years old, with curly copper hair, and a bottle-green sweatshirt: I HATE MONDAYS. As soon as they pause in front of his cage, he scrabbles forward, clinging on to the bars, snot glistening on his top lip, eyes pink and swollen, tears streaking the dirt on his cheeks. "I'm sorry! I'm sorry, Mummy, I'll be good, I *promise*." He clasps his hands in front of his chest, as if he's praying. "Please can I come back in the house? Please . . . ?"

Jeanette moves on. "Here's our pride and joy: Boo. Isn't she precious?"

The boy lets out a strangled little wail and hurries along the bars. "Please! I'll be good, I promise! Mummy, I'll be good!"

She stops, raises a hand. "George, flick the switch, there's a dear."

"NO! I'll be good! I'll be—" There's a faint hum, a red LED comes on above Ginger's cage, then he squeals, flinching back from the bars, tucking his hands into his armpits. His face contorts into a scowl, and jagged sobs build into a howl of pain and betrayal.

The LED blinks off, and on, and off, and on, marking time with his wails.

"Anyway . . ." Jeanette beckons Wesley over. "You have to meet Boo."

The girl who waddles toward them, supporting her bloated stomach with both hands, can't be much more than sixteen, her face still round with baby fat, cheeks flushed and shiny. Glowing.

Wesley's mouth goes dry. "What the hell *is* this?"

"Isn't she gorgeous? It's twins. And she's just a year older than Ellie, too!"

Boo looks him up and down with her sapphire-blue eyes, then pokes a hand through the bars. Touches his dressing gown, rubs the fuzzy cloth between her fingers. Her T-shirt has a picture of a laughing cat on it, beneath the words SERIOUSLY, I'M JUST KITTEN.

He reaches down to take Boo's hand, but she snatches it away. Turns her back on him. He stands there, blinking, as she waddles away, kneels, then squeezes herself through the hatch in the back of her cell.

Next door, the little boy's cries have subsided into a gurgling snivel. "I'm sorry, Mummy, I'm sorry . . ."

Wesley backs away from Jeanette.

The next cage contains a woman wearing gray sweatpants and a black sweater emblazoned with the slogan FAT CAT. Her hair's incredibly short, as if she's recently shaved her head. Or had it shaved for her.

Jeanette keeps her distance from the bars. "This is our queen bee. Moppet's produced a litter practically every eleven months for the past ten years. And we've only lost two. Still got a few good years left in her. Very feisty."

Wesley stares at the woman behind the bars. She looks back at him, and something curdles in his gut. Something that makes him step away from the bars too. Out of reach. "Why are they—"

But Jeanette has already moved on to the next cage. "Shame about this one." The nameplate on the next cage has GOLDILOCKS printed on it, but the enclosure is empty. "Just wasn't up to scratch. Had to let her go.

"And here's our resident stud: Max."

Max is a weedy guy with a mane of gray-flecked hair, and eyes that dart from side to side. He's dressed the same as the girls, his T-shirt emblazoned with THE CAT'S BOLLOCKS in big yellow letters. "Got to give me one more shot. I can do it, Mummy, you know I can. I can do it *right now,* if you want?" The smile he pulls on skitters from side to side, as if it's uncomfortable about being dragged into the light. "Let me try?"

"Of course, Max. Why don't we take you inside for a nice warm bath, see if that helps? Get you all nice and clean and ready for Moppet?"

He grins. Performs a little bow.

The word "*Bastard*" comes from a couple of cages along, sounding as if it's being spat out between bared teeth.

"Now, now, Moppet. You know what happens to bad girls." Jeanette takes a clutch of keys from one of the pockets of George's cardigan. Unlocks Max's cage and pushes the door open, then slaps a hand against her thigh. "Come on, Max. Come on, there's a good boy."

He steps forward, moves out into the path, picking his way through the snow, toes turned in toward each other like a crow's, as if he's not used to walking. Elbows in against his ribs, hands curled in front of his chest. He stops in front of Jeanette, shuffling from foot to foot.

George waves the shotgun at Wesley. "Right: dressing gown off."

"*What?* But . . . I'm not wearing anything under—"

"If you don't do what you're told, George will shoot you in the knee. He won't miss." Jeanette takes a bag of Mint Imperials from her apron and digs one out for Max. "There you go, sweetie. Who's a good boy?"

Max snatches the mint from her open palm and jams it into his mouth. Crunching and sucking on it with his eyes closed.

Wesley frowns at George for a second. "I don't—"

"Better do as she says. Shotgun to the knee won't kill you, but by Christ it'll hurt." He lowers the barrel till it's pointing at Wesley's groin. "Five. Four . . ."

"You're all mad. I'm not taking my bloody—"

"Three. Two . . ."

"Be reasonable, this is—"

"One." George brings the stock up to his shoulder and aims.

"I'm doing it! I'm doing it!" Wesley's fingers scrabble at the tie-cord.

He rips open the dressing gown, lets it fall onto the ground. Wraps one arm around himself. Pulls his knees together and hunches over, cups his other hand over his shriveled cock.

Jeanette smiles. "Ooh look, a proper redhead." The smile vanishes. "Now get in the cage."

"Look, I have money. I work for a bank, I can—"

"The lady said get in the cage, Wesley. Don't make her ask you again."

Wesley goes inside, his feet dragging like dead animals. Trembling. Teeth rattling against each other. It's warmer in the cage, and dry—some sort of heater mounted to the wooden roof, its glowing red bars blazing heat down on his naked shoulders.

Jeanette closes the door and locks it. "There we go. All safe and sound." Then she turns and takes out another Mint Imperial for Max. "Come on, sweetie."

Max shuffles over to her and takes the mint. She places her hand on his cheek and he leans into her palm, eyes shut as he savors it. A smile forms on his lips and his chin comes up.

"Who likes his mint? You do, don't you? Yes, you do."

"Ooh, *yes,* Mummy . . ."

"Good boy." She sticks her free hand into her apron pocket, plucks out a stocky lump hammer, and batters it off the side of his head.

He reels sideways, staggers back again, and drops to his knees, eyes rolling up, lids flickering, blood pulsing from the torn scalp. He moans and Jeanette slams the hammer down again, smashing into his right temple. Again. Teeth gritted, scraps of bone and chunks of flesh spattering out onto the snow. Again and again, his body twitching with every blow, until his face is crumpled and flattened, barely recognizable as human.

"Hit him again!" Moppet is on her feet, grabbing the bars of her cage, spittle running down her chin. "DIE, YOU FUCKING BASTARD!"

"Shhhh." Jeanette staggers back a couple of steps, breathing hard, steam rising off her shoulders in the cold air. Looks down at the gore-smeared hammer in her hand. Tufts of hair stick to the metal surface. Blood drips onto the ground, dark scarlet ribbons that turn pink as they hit the snow.

The smell of raw meat reaches the cages and Wesley's stomach lurches, bile burning in his throat.

She steps over Max's body and walks up to Moppet, pudgy face stretched in a wide grin. "Did you say something?"

Moppet bites her bottom lip. Her shoulders tremble, and a sob rips its way out of her.

"Let it out. You'll feel better." Jeanette's forehead glistens. She wipes her sleeve across it, leaving a smear of blood behind. Then she marches over to George. Kisses his cheek. Then on the mouth. And again. Long and slow. Moaning. Tongues writhing. One hand buried in the white hair at the back of his head, pulling him in. She drops the hammer, slides her fingers down the front of his trousers, and squeezes.

She finally pulls away, breathless and beaming. "Let's go upstairs. We can clean this mess up later."

"Ta-da . . ." The security light blooms into life and Jeanette appears again in front of the cage, with her arms out to one side, waving her fingers like she's introducing a magic trick.

Ellie shuffles into view. She's got on a fluffy gray dressing gown clasped around the middle, her blond hair swept back and blow-dried. She's wearing dark eye shadow and pink lipstick, too much blush, dangly scarlet earrings. She plucks at the dressing gown with violent-magenta fingernails. She licks her top lip, then breaks into a grin. "Hi, Wesley." She drags his name out, "Wesssssss-ley," as if she's rolling it around her mouth, tasting it. "How cool is this?"

Cool? Can't she see Max lying there, pinned in the security light's glare? Flat on his back, head smashed in and misshapen, oozing scarlet and gray into the snow. Can't she *smell* him?

Wesley wipes a hand across his eyes. "Ellie, go call the police. This . . . you can't." He pushes himself farther into the corner and draws his knees up against his chest. The cinder-block wall is cold against his back, the concrete floor rough against his buttocks. "Please. They killed him!"

"Now"—Jeanette pats her little girl on the cheek—"I want you to be good. You're a queen now. You're special. You'll make *lovely* babies."

"I know, right!" Ellie bounces up and down on the tips of her black stiletto heels, then unties the cord on her dressing gown and lets the whole thing fall to the ground. She's wearing a red-and-black basque with stockings, garters, and a thong. Her pale skin fluoresces under the spotlights, arms goose-pimpling, all the hair standing up as if she's glowing. Red dots of acne speckle her sunken chest. Dressing her up like a '70s porn star doesn't make her any more mature. She's still just a sixteen-year-old kid. Barbie does Dallas.

It's so absurd it *has* to be a joke.

Ellie wobbles forward on her high heels and twists her fingers through the bars of his cage. "Don't worry, Mum and Dad didn't want to rush things. Said I had to wait till I'm sixteen before they had me covered." She drops her voice to a whisper. "You're my first."

Oh God. He wraps his arms around himself, trembling. "Ellie, listen to me: you have to call the police . . ."

"I'm so glad it's you and not Max. You've got much nicer hair." She looks over her shoulder at her smiling mother. "Do I get to name him?"

"Of course you do, dear. What about . . . oh, I don't know . . . something fiery? Something red?"

Ellie nods. "Scarlet."

"They killed a man!"

"You can't call him 'Scarlet,' darling. Scarlet's a girl's name."

"Oh . . ."

"You have to give him a *boy's* name."

"Listen to me: they killed him. They dragged him out and battered his head in with a hammer!"

"Then I'll call him . . . Weasley! Like Ron. He's got red hair too."

"THEY FUCKING KILLED A MAN!" Wesley jabs a finger at what's left of Max. "He's right there. LOOK AT HIM!"

Jeanette sniffs, bringing her chin up. "I don't think you're in any position to complain about something like that, Weasley, do you?"

"WHAT THE HELL IS WRONG WITH YOU PEOPLE?"

She takes a key from her pocket and unlocks the door to the cage. "I'm not the one with two dead bodies in the boot of my car, now am I?"

Wesley takes a step toward her . . . then stops.

George walks out of the shadows, shaking his head, the shotgun in his hands.

Wesley retreats to the corner of his cage again.

Ellie totters in, giggling. "How many positions do you want to do? I've been looking it up on the Internet: there's *loads*." She claps her hands as her mother locks the cage behind her. Then stands there and stares at him. "Well?"

Maybe he didn't kill Bloody Hugh after all. Maybe Hugh got the better of him, and right now Wesley's lying on the floor of Natalie's house, bleeding out, and this is all a death-rattle hallucination.

The cage blurs, and he scrubs a hand across his eyes. It comes away wet.

Ellie points at the waist-high hatch in the back wall of the cage. "Aren't you going to invite me in?"

"I can't . . ."

She smiles down at him, then adjusts the back strap of her thong. Her voice is soft and soothing. "It's okay, Weasley, it'll be fine. Trust me." She slides the hatch open, then reaches for his hand.

"They killed him . . ."

"Max wasn't a pet, Weasley. He was a breeding stud. If he can't get the queens pregnant anymore, what are they supposed to do?"

Wesley blinks at her. "What?"

"Come on, come inside with me. We don't want anything to happen to you, do we?" Then she bends over and squeezes through the hatch.

Oh, that's just brilliant. That's just spec-fucking-tacular. They battered Max's head in with a hammer because he couldn't get it up anymore. The back of Wesley's skull makes a dull thunking noise as he bangs it against the cinder-block wall. They're going to kill him.

"Weeeeeeeasley . . ." Ellie's hand emerges from the hatchway, index finger beckoning. "I'm waiting for you."

They're going to drag him out into the snow and bash his brains in.

Unless he can get out of here.

He stands. Glances back over his shoulder at the courtyard. But Jeanette's gone. The only one left is Max, lying flat on his back in the snow. *Click*—the security light dies, plunging Max's corpse into darkness. The only sound is the soft patter of snowflakes on the cage's plastic roof.

Wesley takes a deep breath, ducks down, and crawls through the hatchway.

Inside is a crudely finished room just big enough for a double bed, a small wooden cabinet with a lamp on it, and a small stack of Stephen King paperbacks—the spines cracked and broken. Rough wood lines three of the walls, but the fourth is covered in floor-to-ceiling blue velvet curtains. A low-energy bulb swings from the end of a short length of cord. Heat sears out of an electric heater, mounted high above the open hatch.

The air reeks of mildew and stale sex and desperation.

Ellie's kneeling on the bed, her legs tucked under her, smiling. "Oh, Weasley, we're going to make such beautiful babies!" She pats the bedspread. "You want to make out a bit first? I'm a *really* good kisser."

Wesley slides across to her. "You have to help me get out of here."

She runs a fingertip along the top edge of her basque. "I saw this one porno where the man does it with, like, three women at once. Do you think you could do that? I bet you could."

He grabs her wrist. "Will you *listen* to me? Your mother and father are sick. They need help."

She shuffles closer. "I bet you could satisfy a *hundred* women."

"I have to get out of here!"

"I bet you could go all—"

"*Stop it!* They're not well; they're . . . I don't know, psychotic or something."

A little wrinkle appears between Ellie's eyebrows. Her bottom lip pokes out. "It's me, isn't it? You don't think I'm sexy."

"Get me the key. You can do that, can't you? The key in your father's cardigan?"

"I can be sexier! I can! I know stuff off the Internet. Like blow jobs." She grabs for his shrunken penis.

"*No!*" He jerks one leg in front of the other, hiding it, then shoves her away. "Get off me!"

She scrambles back onto her knees again and stares at him, lips pressed tightly together, odd-colored eyes flaring. "They'll *kill* you." She bares her teeth. "They'll cut you open and skin you like a rabbit."

Silence. Then a clunk and the blue velvet curtains judder open.

Instead of wood, or cinder block, the wall's made of thick wire mesh—like the partitions of the cages—with a corridor on the other side. On the far side, rows of cat pens. One big dirty-colored beast with huge brown paws and a matching lion's mane sits on a wooden platform, smirking at him. On the near side, George and Jeanette are seated in a pair of folding chairs. Staring into the room. At the naked man and their daughter.

George tamps the tobacco down in his pipe. "Is there a problem?"

Ellie glowers at Wesley. "He won't cover me. Says I'm not *sexy* enough for him!"

Jeanette wags a finger at him. "Honestly, Weasley, that's not very nice, is it? Say you're sorry."

"You're out of your minds, the lot of you!"

"Nonsense, it's perfectly sensible. Ellie's heterochromia's genetic—that's why we paid so much for her. Your babies will have lovely red hair, with one gorgeous blue eye and a beautiful green one. Oh, they're going to win so many *prizes*."

"There aren't going to be any babies!"

"Now, now . . ." George stands. "It's just first night nerves. I was the same with Jeanette."

He scuffs down the corridor, out of sight, then back again—wheeling a trolley with an old-fashioned portable television on it. The kind with a built-in video recorder. "Sometimes a gentleman just needs a little something to kick-start his motor."

"I demand you call the police. *Right* now."

"This was one of Max's favorites." George unwinds the TV cord and plugs it into the wall opposite the cage. Then he fiddles with the remote control until a crackling picture fills the screen. The colors are washed out, flickering with static from multiple viewings: it's Max, rutting on top of a woman with curly golden-blond hair. He's hammering away, but it's like she's dead. No movement, just rocking back and forward in time to his thrusts. Blank eyes staring at the camera. It's been shot from the corridor—the wire mesh clearly visible in the picture. The only sound track is Max's grunts and the squeak of the bed.

She's not one of the women in the cages outside.

A cold lump settles into Wesley's stomach. Spreads its tendrils down through his bowels and legs. Shriveling everything.

George sits down again, patting through the pockets of his cardigan until a box of matches turns up. He lights his pipe, suckling on it until his head is wreathed in smoke. "In your own time."

"No. This is . . . it's *ridiculous*. I can't. She's too young."

"Nonsense, Wesley my boy, she's perfect. Trust me, they're like rabbits at that age."

Jeanette jabs him with her elbow. "Don't be crude. And his stable name's Weasley."

"Really?" A shrug. "Takes all sorts."

Wesley tears his eyes away from the screen. "This isn't happening . . ." He's at Natalie's house, bleeding out on the garage floor. Or he's crashed the car getting away from the burning house. Or he's having a stroke. A brain tumor. *Anything* other than this. He backs away from the bed. "It's a joke. A wind-up. Right?"

George charges out of his seat and slams a fist against the wire mesh, hard enough to make the whole thing rattle. "*Get on with it!*" His face is flushed, eyes dark.

Wesley flinches. "Don't you get it? I'm not going to sleep with your daughter."

"Daddy . . . ?" Ellie shuffles forward on the bed. "Maybe it'd help if you and Mummy weren't watching? Maybe Weasley gets nervous?"

"You *know* how this works." George's nostrils flare. "If we can't see him, we can't tell if he's doing the business." Then he crashes his palm into the mesh again, glaring at Wesley. "Now get your backside in that bed and *do your bloody duty*!"

Jeanette tugs at his sleeve. "Maybe he's impotent."

"Impotent?" George's face darkens. "Then he's no bloody good to us, is he?"

Ellie clutches her hands together, like she's praying. "You've got to give him a chance! Pleeeeeeeease? I know he can do it. It's just, you know, been a long day and the dead bodies in the boot and Angelina shouting at him and what happened to Max . . . We could try again tomorrow morning! I *know* I can get him all excited if you give him another chance." She pouts. "Pretty please?"

George doesn't move.

His wife walks over and strokes him on the shoulder. "Patience, George. Patience."

He takes a few deep breaths, then steps back from the mesh and nods. "I see. Right. Yes. We'll call it a night then. Try again in the morning." He reaches out and switches off the portable TV. "And if he still can't get it up, we'll just have to get ourselves another stud."

Another stud . . . *Max taking a Mint Imperial from Jeanette's hand. Nuzzling her palm. Lying in the snow with his head bashed in.* Replaced.

Wesley shudders.

"Right, Ellie: out of there. And take the blanket with you. Weasley doesn't deserve bedding." He folds up his chair and tucks it under his arm, then scowls at Wesley. "You'd bloody well better perform next time."

LIGHT FLOODS IN through the open hatch.

Wesley sits up, blinks. . . . Must have fallen asleep, though God knows how.

He crawls toward the hatch, pins and needles jarring through his feet like he's stamping on a hairbrush. He looks out through the pen and into the glare of the security lights, gouging his eyes. He holds up a hand, blotting it out. Squinting till his eyes can adjust.

It's snowing again, flakes floating down like broken gossamer threads under the lights.

Outside the cage, a fox slinks along the path toward him, mouth open, chocolate-brown socks digging into the snow. It stops. Stares at him.

A few seconds . . . then darkness as the security lights click off again.

Wesley waits, looking out into the night. There's not a single sound. Then a little muffled squeak breaks the silence. Then it's quiet again.

The heater mounted to the roof is cold and dark. Either someone's switched it off to punish him, or it's on a timer.

He's about to duck back inside, where it's at least a *little* warmer, when the lights come on again.

The fox stands with two paws on Max's chest, head tilted to one side. It sniffs him. Licks what's left of his face. Then bares its teeth and grabs hold of something. Starts tugging.

A shudder ripples across Wesley's back . . . He swallows and looks away.

He's not the only one woken by the security light—Boo's up too. Jeanette's pride and joy is just visible through the bars, crouched on top of her toilet seat. She lifts something to her lips and bites down. Rips her head from side to side. Chews. Whatever she's eating, it's bigger than her fist—a long, pink tail dangling from her bloodstained hands. Twitching. His stomach lurches.

He looks back at the fox. Its scarlet-flecked snout jerks sideways as it gnaws away at his predecessor.

Oh God . . . Wesley makes it to the toilet just in time, flinging up the lid and heaving venison casserole into the bowl. Each retch is a punch in the stomach, filling his nose with the bitter stench of stomach acid. And then the gagging fades. Stops. One last lurch . . . Then he rests his head against the seat, spittle dripping from his open mouth. He breathes. Spits. Fumbles for the flush and washes it all away. Cups his hand in the stream of water gushing out of the rim, using it to wash his mouth out.

The water's sweet and cold.

The lid goes back down with a clank. Wesley wipes his eyes on his wet palm. Then frowns out at the patch of snow outside his cage.

There's a mound in the snow, a few feet from the fox. Like a deflated body . . . There's writing on it, just visible through the layer of white. He moves forward, one lumbering step at a time, squinting. What does it say? The letters *LOI* stand out in bold black lettering, but the rest of the word's hidden. A few more letters: *OUSE*. And what looks like *8&8*. Shit: *LOINNREACH HOUSE B&B*. It's his dressing gown. Still lying where he dropped it.

He grabs hold of the bars. A ball of needles explode in his fists, in his wrists, slamming straight up his arms and into his shoulders. "Jesus!" He jerks his hands away from the metal, curls his arms against his chest, rounding his back as the ache fades.

A little red LED blinks on and off above his cage; the bars are electrified. Of course they are.

Should have looked first. Bloody idiot.

Wesley gets down on his knees. Eases his hand through the space between two of the bars. Don't touch anything. . . . Don't set it off again. . . . His fingers twitch and claw at the snow. . . . The dressing gown remains stubbornly out of reach. Damn.

The fox looks at him. Bares its teeth like he's going to steal its supper. A high-pitched yowl rips from its throat—outraged, urgent, and insistent, like a roomful of hungry babies.

Wesley's heart kicks against his ribs. His temples buzz. He lies down, the rough concrete freezing his stomach and chest. Stretches his arm out, groping for the dressing gown as the fox screams. His arm bumps against one of the bars. Explosions in his bicep, in his shoulder, snapping his hand up. But he forces it back down and keeps fumbling for the dressing gown. . . . *There!* He snags a pinch of cloth between his fingertips, teases it toward the pen. Inches it closer.

He sits up, hauling his dressing gown toward him. Another jolt tears up through his arms as it comes in contact with the bars, strong enough to shove him backward. But the robe's in the cage now. Success. Suck on *that,* George. Wesley shakes the snow off it. Checks it over to see how wet it is. Only part of the back seems to be soaked through. He bunches it up, squeezes. Forces a thin trickle out. It'll have to do.

The fox's chilling wail trails off into silence and it goes back to its meal.

He stands and slips his arms through the sleeves. The material is cold and wet and clings to his skin. He pulls it tight around him. Ties the cord. Takes one last glance at the fox, then heads back through the hatch.

I once was lost but now am found,
Was blind, but now I see.

Spooks has been singing to herself for a while now, her timid, girlish voice disappearing off into the darkness. It's a pleasant enough sound, but she sings the same song over and over, as if someone's set her on repeat. And it's really beginning to grate. He came out into the pen to tell her to be quiet, but couldn't bring himself to do it. No one else is complaining. It's probably some sort of ritual for Spooks, a coping mechanism, and who is he to make her give it up?

Bloody annoying, though.

No idea what time it is either. The world's disappearing beneath a thick shroud of gray, swirls of fresh snow speckling down from the inky sky. He hugs the dressing gown tighter around his body. Well worth a couple of electric shocks.

Spooks takes a deep breath, ready to start the same damn song all over again, when the security lights slam on, glaring back from the pristine white landscape, making Wesley flinch like he's been punched.

He covers his eyes. Blinks.

The sound of a car engine gets louder. And then the back of the BMW comes into view, reversing toward the cages, running lights glowing baleful red. Turning the falling snow into spatters of blood.

Moppet's head pokes out of her cabin hatch, two cages down. She frowns at him.

The BMW stops just shy of Max's body and George gets out. He doesn't even look at Wesley, just pops the boot, bends down, and wrestles Max's mauled corpse in on top of Hugh and Natalie. A threesome of pale flesh and dried blood. It doesn't seem to bother him that the fox hasn't left much of Max's face behind.

George closes the boot, gets back in the car, and drives away.

The taillights dwindle to two small red points, then they're gone and it's silent. A minute later, the spotlights go *click,* returning the courtyard to darkness. And Spooks begins again:

Amazing Grace, how sweet the sound . . .

Moppet knocks on the bars of her cage. "Was that your car?"

How come she didn't get an electric shock? He scans the roofs of the other cages. His is the only one with a winking red light.

"Bastards . . ." He tightens the cord on his dressing gown.

"Was that your car?"

He raises his voice a notch. "Yes. It's mine."

"There were bodies in the boot."

Beyond the cages, wind sighs in the trees.

Wesley clears his throat. "Have you really been here ten years?"

"Came up on holiday. Our first as a family: me, Beth, and . . . *Doug.*" She pronounces the name as if it's venomous, as if she needs to spit to get rid of the taste. "I went to sleep the first night and woke up in here."

"Doug and Beth. Did they—"

"Doug's dead."

Of course he is.

"I'm sorry." Wesley moves closer to the bars separating his cage from the empty one next door. Raises a tentative finger and taps it against the metal . . . No shock. Must just be the front set that's electrified.

"They said he wasn't breeding material." She lowers her head, twists the gold band on her ring finger. "Our daughter, Beth, was seven at the time. The Constables told her we'd abandoned her, that we'd run off in the middle of the night, and left her here for them to raise. And when she turned sixteen, they locked her up in here too."

She pauses. Then sniffs, shakes her head. "Did you kill them? The people in your trunk?"

"What happened to her after that? What happened to Beth?"

"She's called Boo now."

Boo? The rat-eating heavily pregnant one? Holy *shit.* "So Max . . . ?"

Her smile is colder than the snow. "Got his head caved in so you could have his job."

Jesus. Wesley pulls his chin back into his neck. "So what, he just . . . How could you let him do that? To you, to her?"

"Goldilocks." She looks away. "There was another male stud for a while: Rum Tum. Just a boy, really. But he was moved on three years ago. Leaving good old Max to shoulder the weight all on his own." There's enough acid in her voice to eat through the bars.

Wesley fidgets with the cord on his dressing gown again. "What's your name?"

"Moppet."

"No, your real name."

She pauses. "It doesn't matter anymore."

He presses himself against the bars, lowers his voice to a hard whisper. "How do we get out of here? Ten years: you've got an escape plan, right?"

She just stares back at him. "There's only one way to escape. The way Max did it."

"No. There's got to be a—"

"You've seen what they're like! And you think getting your head bashed in is the worst they can do to you? This cage here, the empty one, that's where Goldilocks was. She got out when they were putting her to Max one night. Made it as far as the loch before they caught her." Moppet turns her back. "George cut off her hands and feet. Jeanette hacked out her tongue. Goldilocks didn't last long after that."

Wesley closes his eyes. He's going to die here. "Oh God . . ."

"Try to sleep, Wesley." Then she ducks down and slips back through her hatch.

He stands there until he starts to shiver, looking through the bars at Goldilocks's empty cage. He's going to die here. And no one's ever going to know.

Inside the cabin, he curls up on his side, wrapped in his damp dressing gown, and cries himself to sleep.

He's wading through knee-high drifts toward Angelina. She places the mouthpiece to her lips. "Abide with Me" pours out in rich, fluid tones, as drops of blood squeeze from the bell of the clarinet onto her bare white toes, the nails lime-green against the snow.

"WAKEY-WAKEY, BOYS AND girls!"

He grinds the heels of his hands into his gritty eyes. Dry-washes his face. Crawls over the mattress and drops onto the floor. Then peeks out of the hatch.

Thick snow coats the ground. The sun sits like a scorch mark in the clear morning sky, but it's still cold enough to make his breath billow out in sour-smelling clouds. Perhaps if he behaves, they'll give him a toothbrush?

Jeanette's outside Spooks's pen, smears of flour and egg on the front of her apron, with a service trolley. "Room service!" She opens a flap, like a letterbox, set into the front bars of Spooks's cage and slides a heaped plate through.

She trundles the trolley along the concrete path to Ginger.

The little boy keeps his eyes on the concrete beneath his feet as she passes his food through to him. "I promise I'll be good, Mummy. I'm sorry I was naughty . . ."

Wesley unfastens his dressing gown, shrugs it off, and tosses it onto the bed. If they don't know he's got it, they can't confiscate it. He climbs out of the hatch and waits by the gate.

When she gets over to him, she's all smiles. "Good morning, Weasley. Did you sleep well?" She reaches up and flicks a switch. The flashing LED above Wesley's cage goes out and stays that way.

A plate of sausage, eggs, beans, black pudding, mushrooms, potato scones, and toast slides through on a tray. Plastic cutlery.

Boo gorging on the rat. The fox tearing chunks off Max's face . . . Wesley swallows. "I'm not hungry."

"Nonsense. Got to keep your strength up." She takes a thermos from the lower shelf of her trolley and fills a polystyrene cup with tea. "We had a lovely funeral service, up by the loch. We sang hymns, and Angelina played her clarinet. She's so *gifted*, isn't she? I was really quite moved by her 'Abide with Me.' And just between you and me, that doesn't happen too often."

"What did you do with the bodies?"

"Left them in the car, of course. George said a few words as it sank." She puts the polystyrene cup on the ground, just within reach of the bars. "Very touching."

Natalie and Bloody Hugh, locked away forever at the bottom of the loch. It's what he wanted, isn't it? Get rid of the evidence? They're gone; he's safe now . . . safe in a cage, with a pair of psychotic B&B cat breeders in charge.

Jeanette clasps her hands together. "I think you'd have enjoyed it."

"You're a fucking nutjob. You know that, don't you?"

Her eyes narrow, wrinkling like crushed paper bags. For a second, it looks as if she's about to drag out that blood-smeared hammer again. But she looks away, toward the house, cocks her head. "Ah . . . They're here."

The purr of a car engine comes from somewhere around the front of the house. Someone's pulling up the driveway.

Jeanette reaches one foot out and knocks over the cup of tea. "When our visitors are gone, I think we might have to work on your attitude, Weasley."

Visitors? Of course: *visitors*. He hauls in a lungful of cold air, cups his hands around his mouth like a megaphone. "HELP! HELLO? HELP! CALL THE POLICE!"

Jeanette shakes her head. "You'll hurt your throat, crying out like that."

"WE'RE ROUND HERE! HELP!"

She sighs, then walks away, wheeling the trolley in front of her.

He's still shouting five minutes later, when a middle-aged man waddles into view: thickset and bearded, dressed for a polar expedition. A woman wearing a matching outfit picks her way through the snow beside him, bleached blond hair held back with a fur-lined headband, knee-high boots slipping on the icy surface.

"OVER HERE! HELP! WE'RE OVER HERE!" Wesley bangs on the bars of the empty cage next to his. Moppet's the only one not in her cabin, eating her breakfast in the relative warmth. "Help me, for Christ's sake!"

She looks at him in silence, then turns and slips through her hatch, taking her tray with her.

"What the hell's wrong with you? They can help us get out of here!"

The couple get closer, and Jeanette appears around the corner of the building, moving fast, panting with the effort, closing the gap.

"WATCH OUT: THERE'S A CRAZY WOMAN BEHIND YOU! CALL THE POLICE, FOR GOD'S SAKE! *PLEASE!*"

Then Jeanette catches up with them . . . and they start talking. Smiling at one another.

Shit. They know each other . . .

Wesley's neck aches, as if someone's just dropped onto his shoulders. He slumps there, breath catching in his throat as they walk toward him. He cups his hands over his groin.

Jeanette leans in toward the woman. "I know you weren't too keen on Max, but I think you'll like this one."

The woman purses her lips, looks Wesley over. Up close she's more cougar than snow bunny. "Well proportioned. Good bone structure. Athletic. Handsome. *Great* hair. Mmm. What do you think, Charles?"

The man rubs his gloved hands together, claps them. "Whatever you think, Petal."

"I'm asking your opinion."

"If you like him, I like him." A cough. "You *do* like him, don't you?"

She turns to Jeanette. "You were right—he was worth tromping up here at this ungodly hour on a Sunday. Ellie's eyes and his coloring . . ." She takes the man's arm. "We'll pay the deposit now."

"Excellent." Jeanette beams. "I knew you'd love him soon as you saw him. That's why I gave you first refusal. Erm . . . will you be planning on breeding from the child?"

She looks at Charles, who shrugs back at her. "To be honest, that's not something we've really thought about. I suppose so. Why?"

"It's quite a bit more expensive." Jeanette moves around behind them, her arms out, taking them under her wings, guiding them back toward the house. "Let's go inside and do the admin where it's nice and warm. I'll give you a leaflet to take away explaining the various prices, payment structures, terms and conditions, the sterilization program . . ."

Wesley drops to his knees.

Tiny gritty snowflakes hiss against the corrugated roof of his cage. There's no sign that Max's body was ever there—even the bloodstains have been buried.

Wesley sits sideways on the toilet lid, beneath the glowing heater. Dressing gown wrapped around him, arms wrapped around it. Feet sideways on the concrete floor—the soles pressing against each other. Breathing fog as the snow falls.

All the other cages are empty. He's the only one daft enough to be out here in the cold. Everyone else is in their cabins, hiding from the weather. He could go inside, but what's the point? Sit on a secondhand mattress with no blanket, waiting for George and Jeanette to haul open the curtains whenever they feel like? No thanks.

Spooks's voice breaks into the stillness. She's singing again.

Amazing Grace, how sweet the sound,
That saved a wretch like me.

He leans his head back against the cinder-block wall. "You do requests?"

I once was lost, but now I'm found,
Was blind, but now I see.

"How about a bit of Rolling Stones? Or Coldplay?"

'Twas Grace that taught my heart to fear,
And Grace, my fears relieved . . .

"Change the bloody record, Spooks."

How precious did that Grace appear,
The hour I first believed . . .

Silence.

"Spooks?" He stands, looking down the row of cages. There's a figure tromping through the snow toward him, her thick padded jacket dusted with white, gray quiff leaning to the right today.

"Grace!" He picks himself off the toilet lid and hobbles toward the cage door. "Over here!"

She hurries over, stops in front of his cage, leaving a trail of footprints behind her that slowly soften. Soon they'll be gone, just like Max. Her face is creased, eyebrows furrowed, those wide brown eyes bathing him in their warming glow. "Are you okay?"

"You've got to get me out of here." He keeps his voice low. "They're all mad. They want me to sleep with their daughter!"

"Oh, Wesley . . ." She bites her bottom lip. "What can I do to help?"

"Thank God . . ." The world blurs and he blinks away the tears, face stretched into a grin. "Call the police. Get George's keys. *Please.*" He grabs her hand through the bars. "Get me out of here!"

Grace's shoulders drop a little and she pulls on a small smile. "But you're replacing Max. You can't have a breeding operation without a stud, can you?"

He lets go of her hand. "What?"

"Isn't this every man's dream? A harem of women, your every whim catered for, somewhere cozy to sleep, three square meals a day? You should be grateful."

"No, no, no, no . . ."

She reaches into her pocket and comes out with a little blister pack of blue pills. "George tells me you've got problems performing. Do you have a history of erectile dysfunction? High blood pressure? Heart disease? Because that's important to know."

"Ellie's sixteen!"

"Exactly." Grace pokes the sheet of pills through the bars. "Take one."

He backs away. "I'm not doing it."

"Seriously, Wesley, you need to take it at least thirty minutes before you have to perform, otherwise—"

"I am not going to fuck Ellie!"

Grace drops the packet and it clacks against the floor. "Just think about it. Okay?" Then she turns and works her way down the cages, running her fingertips across the bars. *Thunk, thunk, thunk . . .* She stops outside the cage at the end of the row, leans forward, and clasps her knees with her hands. "Spooks? Spoooo-oooks? Mummy's got something for you."

Mummy?

"Come on, Spooks, there's a good girl . . ."

Wesley shuffles over to the side of his cage.

Five sets of bars away Spooks is inching toward Grace. Her gray jogging bottoms are stained up one side, her hair all flattened on the left, as if she's been sleeping on it.

Grace holds out a Mars Bar. Spooks shifts from side to side, then edges over to the bars and takes it. Unwrapping it with filthy fingers.

"There's a good girl."

"Is she really your daughter?"

Those big brown eyes swing around. "Isn't she pretty?"

"You let these nutjobs keep her in a cage?"

"Mummy's special girl's a bit . . . fragile. Aren't you, Spooks?"

But Spooks isn't listening, she's nibbling the chocolate from the top of her Mars Bar.

"And I know I probably shouldn't have put her to Max. Let's face it, what with her . . . difficulties, none of the other breeders would touch her. But Jeanette's family. What are big sisters for?" Grace reaches through the bar and strokes Spooks's matted hair. "And I really, *really* want a grandchild."

Wesley just stares at her.

"Anyway, I suppose I'd better get going." She walks back up the row of cages, until she's standing outside his cage again. "Some friendly advice: Take the Viagra. Close your eyes and pretend you're screwing your dead wife. Or your mistress. Or your boyfriend. Do whatever it takes to get Ellie pregnant."

His knees wobble. "I can't . . ."

"Then you'll end up like Max, won't you?"

WESLEY SITS ON the edge of the mattress. It creaks underneath him as Ellie wriggles her way out of bed. He doesn't watch her get dressed; he's too busy trying to haul a breath in between the sobs.

She places a hand on his shoulder, the warmth of her skin like a branding iron. Marking him. She smells of strawberries and apples. "Shhh . . . It's okay."

He hangs his head, wipes a hand across his eyes. "I'm . . . I'm so . . . so sorry . . ."

Ellie settles down on the bed beside him, wraps her arms around him, and gives him a hug. "Don't worry about Angelina. We had a big long talk last night, and I was on your side and everything, and she doesn't think you strangled her mum anymore. I told her you only killed Hugh to protect her. You're a hero, really." A shrug. "She's angry now, but it'll get better."

"I tried . . . I . . . I really did . . ."

"I know you did, Weasley, I know." She strokes the back of his neck. "Shhh . . ."

Something clangs and rattles through in the cage outside, then George's voice rips through the echoes. "ELLIE, GET YOUR BACKSIDE OUT HERE, NOW!"

She sighs, pulls his chin up. Looks at him with those mismatched feline eyes. "Oh dear. Sorry, Weasley; we would have had *such* beautiful babies." She kisses him on the cheek. "I'll miss you." Then she slips her stilettos on and totters out through the hatch.

"NOW YOU, YOU SLACK-COCKED USELESS GINGER WASTE OF SKIN!"

Could just stay in here. Hide . . . Where? Under the bed? The curtain's open—a video recorder on a tripod trained on the bed, the red light blinking. Jeanette sitting sour faced on a folding chair, scowling at him. It wouldn't exactly take them long to figure out where he was, would it?

"DON'T MAKE ME COME IN THERE!"

Die in here, or die out there? At least out there he'd get to see the sky one last time.

Wesley reaches down the side of the bed and pulls out his tatty dressing gown. Slips it on—warm and fuzzy against his skin. Time to go.

He ducks through the hatch.

Snow drifts down from a battleship sky, muffling the landscape. The women and Ginger are out in their runs, watching. Waiting for the new guy to get his brains bashed in.

George stands at the door to the cage, the shotgun in his hands. His face is like an angry bull, the skin flushed and trembling. Spittle flecks the corners of his mouth. "I gave you one simple job to do. That's it, just the one, and you couldn't even do that properly, could you?"

Something cool settles in Wesley's chest. Not cold. Not fear. Not panic. Acceptance. "Go on then, Fat Boy, get it over with."

"Fat . . ." For a moment it looks as if George's head is going to explode. Then he raises a trembling finger. "You, useless, impotent piece of shit. You do *not* speak to me like that!"

"Come on, Lardy, I haven't got all day."

"How *dare* you!"

Yeah, good plan—goad him into a heart attack.
Spooks's thin wobbly voice rises into the air.

Yea, when this flesh and heart shall fail,
And mortal life shall cease . . .

"Out. Here. Now."

I shall possess, within the veil,
A life of joy and peace.

Wesley shrugs. Why not? What difference does it make? His bare feet don't even feel the cold anymore.

George glowers at him. "I had high hopes for you, Weasley. You're a disappointment."

"Daddy!" Ellie holds her hand up, as if she's asking a question in school. "You don't have to put him down: we could go for artificial insemination. We could, couldn't we? All he'd have to do is . . . you know, into a cup and Aunty Grace could squirt it in. He'd be good at that, I'm sure he would!"

The world shall soon dissolve like snow,
The sun refuse to shine . . .

"Your mother would never agree to that. It's not natural."

Wesley sweeps his arms up, like he's about to be crucified: palms front, fingers spread.

But God, who called me here below

George turns on Spooks. "WILL YOU SHUT UP WITH THAT INFERNAL RACKET!"

And everything goes into slow motion. The shotgun isn't pointing at Wesley anymore, it's pointing at the empty cage.

His knees bend then throw him forward, arms swinging, fists balling, toes digging into the snow. Brushing through the falling flakes—paused in midair. Moving like he's running in treacle.

And then BANG—the world's at full speed again. He slams into George's side and the big man topples, the shotgun spinning off to clatter against the empty cage. They both hit the ground in a flurry of snow and ice, arms and legs flailing.

He lands a punch on George's cheek, then another. One more—right on the nose, sending blood spattering across the spotless white.

Then something crashes into Wesley's ribs. Then another. Fire lances up through his groin, radiating out through his stomach like it's full of scorching petrol.

A sharp voice slashes through the grunts and thuds. *"You leave my George alone!"*

His head snaps to the side, making bells ring in the distance, then another blow brings black specks with it, swimming and whirling through his vision. He groans and blinks. And pain bursts across his stomach.

He blinks up at the gray sky, and Jeanette draws back her foot and slams it into his belly again.

Wesley bounces off the snow-covered concrete, slithering to a halt, curled up in a ball, hands over his head.

"Oh, George, what has the horrible man done to you? Shh . . . Shh . . ."

"Get off me, woman. It's only a bloody nose."

A small warm hand rests on Wesley's head. "Weasley, are you okay?" Ellie's face is blurry, flickering in and out. "Come on, let's get you up."

She helps him to his knees. He wobbles. She catches him. Everything aches, a taste of hot copper pennies filling his mouth. He spits out a glob of scarlet.

George is sitting on his backside in the snow, blood streaming down his chin, Jeanette fussing over him.

"Tilt your head . . . no, not like that. Pinch the bridge of your nose. Here, have a hanky . . ."

The shotgun. Get the shotgun.

But it's lying in the snow by the empty cage, and George and Jeanette are between him and it.

"Oh, Weasley, your poor face is all bleeding." Ellie kisses him on the cheek. "You shouldn't fight with Mummy, she's too strong."

There has to be something he can use as a weapon. Something he can turn against the bastards. *Anything.*

Jeanette presses a handkerchief underneath her husband's nose, then turns and glares at Wesley. "You hateful, ungrateful animal."

Weapon. What the hell is he going to use?

Jeanette reaches for the shotgun.

"Mummy, please: Weasley didn't mean it! Please don't hurt him."

Jeanette slips off the safety catch. *Click.* "Get away from him, Ellie. Do what your mother tells you."

Weapon.

Wesley yanks on the end of the cord holding his dressing gown shut. The simple knot unravels and the whole thing slips out of the loops holding it in place.

Weapon.

He jerks backward—so Ellie is slightly in front of him—and wraps the cord around her throat. Pulls it tight. She makes a gagging noise and her hands come up, pulling at the ligature, but he just hauls it tighter.

"Drop the gun!"

Jeanette's mouth sets in a firm line, her eyes like stab wounds in her pale face. "You're in no position—"

"Drop the fucking gun or I'll choke the life out of her!"

"Don't you hurt our—"

"I mean it!" He tugs on the cord, jerking her head back against his chest.

Ellie makes a noise that could almost be his name, one hand slapping at his fists where they're wrapped around the cord.

And then Angelina's voice shrieks out across the courtyard. "Dad? What the hell are you . . . ?"

He looks up and there she is, standing next to Grace, one hand up to her mouth—just like when she found her mother and Bloody Hugh.

"Angel, I need you to—"

"Oh God, what are you *doing*?"

Shit . . . He's half naked, strangling a little girl who's dressed like a prostitute. "It's not what it looks like; they . . ."

Jeanette shifts her grip on the gun.

Wesley pulls tighter on the cord. *"Drop the bloody gun or she's dead!"*

Spittle flecks the back of Ellie's head. She's not struggling as much as she was.

A hiss escapes from Jeanette's thin lips, then she lowers the shotgun to the ground.

"Dad, you're hurting her!"

"Pick up the gun, Angel."

Angelina does what she's told, for once, holding it like a live snake. "Where are your clothes?"

"They tried to make me sleep with her, make her pregnant, it's—"

"Leave her alone! Why do you have to take *everything* away from me?"

"The whole family are insane: ask the women in the cages. Ask the little boy. Go on, ask them!"

Ellie's hands stop scrabbling at the cord and fall into her lap.

Angelina turns to stare at the empty cages. There's no sign of Moppet, Ginger, Boo, or Spooks.

"They must've gone inside, it's—"

"You're sick!" She spins around, mouth hanging open, eyes wide beneath furrowed brows. "You're a sick, filthy, murdering rapist. Hugh was *right* about you, wasn't he?"

"Open the cages and let them out—they'll tell you I'm right. The keys are in George's—"

She brings the shotgun up to point right at him. "Get away from my friend!"

"You don't understand, it's not—"

"Get away from her!"

"Okay, okay . . ." He lets go of the dressing gown cord, and Ellie falls facedown into the snow. She isn't moving.

Oh God, not again . . .

"Angel, it'll be okay. Grace can fix this, she's a nurse. We just need to get Ellie some—"

"All that shit about going to the house and Hugh strangling Mum." The gun shakes in her hands. "I almost believed you. But it was you, wasn't it? You *killed* her. You killed them both!"

Wesley raises his hands. "No, Angel, it was an accident, I didn't—"

"I'm glad this happened. Glad I can finally see you as you really are." Tears glisten on her cheeks. Her face is flushed, her whole body trembling. "Well, do you know what, *Dad*?"

She pulls the trigger.

WESLEY BLINKS. COLD. Numb. Tired.

His arms and legs are made of concrete, his head of broken glass. And when he breathes it sounds wet and crackly, bubbles frothing deep in his lungs. He's lying on his back, staring up at a sea of white.

A melody is blowing on the wind: the adagio from Mozart's Clarinet Concerto, played with a raw beauty that makes his teeth ache.

Wet.

He's lying in an inch of water. He tries to sit up. Grunts. Gasps. Reaches for the plank of wood above his head, hauls himself up to his knees, and the music stops.

Fog rises from the surface of the loch, swirling in thick eddies that curl as the rowboat drifts farther out onto the dark water. Flakes of snow sink through the frigid air, clinging to the wooden hull where they hit.

Something warm drips onto his hand. He looks down and there's a splotch of dark red on porcelain skin. Farther down and there's a gurgling hole in his chest.

The music starts again, picking up where it left off.

For a moment, the fog thins, and there's the edge of the loch—the boathouse with its small jetty. Four figures stand close together: one, small and thin, leaning heavily on the unmistakable rounded silhouette of Jeanette. That must be Ellie. She survived. He didn't kill her.

A smile breaks across his face. That's something.

A fifth figure stands a little way off from the others, swaying in time to the music, playing for her father.

It's beautiful.

The water's getting deeper.

If he sits up, he'll have a better view. He'll hear the music better. Can tell Angelina that he loves her, no matter what. That it isn't her fault.

He pulls at the plank, but he's stuck. There's a chain around his waist, attached to something in the bottom of the boat. He feels his way along the ice-cold links, until he gets to the curling stone padlocked to the end.

Ah . . .

He slumps back against the hull, rests his head against the damp wood, and lets the music wash over him as the boat slowly sinks.

T. RHYMER

Gregory Frost and Jonathan Maberry

1

When the tall, sleek man caught Stacey's eye, she ignored him. He was sitting alone at a table, a glass of whiskey between his palms, watching her.

Stacey turned away. She even made it clear that she was ignoring him. It was too early in the evening to throw anyone too much rope. Let him tread water for a while. If she swam past all the guppies and he turned out not to be a shark, then maybe she'd offer that rope.

Coming to this place wasn't even her idea. The whole Edinburgh club scene was a bore; but tonight it was a necessary evil. The trip to the nightclub was an impromptu minicelebration because her roommate, Carrie, had gotten the promotion she'd been aching for. Carrie celebrated everything of value in her life with tequila, loud music, and a degree of flirtation that would shame Hugh Grant.

And, thank God, it was Friday.

As well as the night before Halloween.

More reasons for Carrie to throw caution, common sense, and—all too frequently—her clothing, to the wind.

Stacey wasn't entirely sure if she was here as a friend sharing a moment, a wingman, a designated driver, or a chaperone. Since moving in with Carrie, Stacey had been all those things. More than once.

She sipped her drink and killed some slow minutes by looking around. Jack-o'-lanterns lit every table; warm drinks came in mugs filled from a bowl that bubbled and smoked like a tub of dry ice on the end of the bar.

A lot of people pranced about in costumes, and some half out of them. At the best of times she would have avoided the lights, crammed crowds, and thumping beats of clubbing. The speakers were loud enough to create little *Jurassic Park*–style vibration rings in her drink. She had a favorite song by The Be Good Tanyas that observed how only crazy people went to a place that was too dark to see and too loud to hear in order to meet anyone. Whatever else she was doing, she was not looking to meet anyone.

No way, José.

Especially after the last time, with the law clerk. She should have fled early from that one. He was twenty-six and had posters thumbtacked to his bedroom walls. Not framed art—posters. Granted, they were classic movies—*Casablanca, Metropolis*—but it was a warning sign she'd chosen to ignore. The law clerk was cute, with a kind of Bradley Cooper vibe that somehow disabled her common sense. The first time he cried during sex Stacey thought it was special, a sharing of something genuinely deep and meaningful. By the fifth or maybe sixth time the word *Flee* was painted on the inside of her head. Even then, she stayed too long, and now she felt wrecked, jaded, and weary of the whole dating thing.

So this field trip was strictly for Carrie. A few drinks and then she'd go home. Otherwise she'd have worn something more stylish than a drab sweater and black jeans over her Nina slingbacks.

And yet . . .

Her attention kept returning to the man. Black jacket over black crewneck shirt. Black hair, too, with a windswept style that looked expensive. Perfect deepwater tan. And eyes the color of hot gold.

Stacey lifted her glass to take a sip and set it down with no conscious awareness of whether she'd had any. She tried not to look at those eyes.

Tried.

He gave her the smallest of smiles. Not a come-on. Not even encouragement. Just a smile. Showing that he knew she was looking at him, just as he was looking at her. It was the first thing he'd done since sitting down. All this time he'd simply sat there, watching the crowd swirl around him, some in work clothes, some in costumes. He was in the middle of it and entirely apart from it.

Stacey thought, *No thanks, buddy. Whatever you're selling, I can't afford it.*

She thought that, but then she realized that she wasn't sitting at her table anymore. In some dreamy and distant way she felt herself moving. Walking across the floor, weaving without thought between clusters of vampires and zombies and a few grinning Guy Fawkeses.

Then she was at his table. Standing so close that the edge of it pressed into the tops of her thighs. And he didn't seem the least surprised when she just came to a rest right before him.

Her mind told her to leave.

To run.

Right now.

But she stood there, leaning into his table, aware on some level that if it weren't there she'd have fallen on him.

Wake up, you stupid bitch!

Her mind kept screaming at her, but it was like the sound track of a film she was watching: happening to someone else.

The man lifted his eyes. They really did look like hot gold. As if they were lit from within. Weird contacts? *No,* came the answer in her mind. *It isn't the contacts that are weird.*

Run. For Christ's sake . . . run.

From across the room the man's eyes were just eyes. From across the room his smile was friendly.

Oh, God . . .

But here . . . within reach, within touching distance, the eyes were alien, and his smile . . .

Oh, Jesus, what's wrong with me?

But she knew—on every level—that what was wrong here was not her.

That smile seemed to somehow touch her. Without lifting a finger or saying a word, this man seemed to touch her. Everywhere. Inside her clothes. Inside her body.

Inside . . .

She could see in the gold of his eyes as he peeled each and every one of her secrets and slipped them like raw fruit between those smiling lips.

Took them.

Consumed them.

Please.

She thought she said it aloud. Maybe she did, but the music crushed it flat.

Please, she begged.

That only made his smile creep wider.

Stacey could feel herself wanting to give in. She knew that she had issues with being too submissive. Five years of therapy hadn't fixed that. She wasn't a total slave, not like the girls she knew who cruised the BDSM waters. But she gave up and gave in too soon.

Too soon.

Too much.

Oh, God, please.

The man's smile seemed to coax her to share her darkest thoughts. It made her unlock the locks and pull open the doors of her mind so that he could see his image there. A dark knight about whom she'd fantasized since before puberty. The shadowy stranger who would come and sweep her off her feet.

A man of shadows. From shadows.

With burning eyes.

And he, without so much as a word, drew from the secrets he'd stolen and pasted before her the images of what he would do . . . and it was everything she wanted. Motionless, staring into his eyes, she grew wet with desire.

The man raised his glass and finished his whiskey, then he pushed his chair back and stood up. Without saying a word, he turned and left the bar.

Stacey followed him.

She felt herself do it and couldn't believe she was doing it.

"Hey, girl!" called Carrie from across the bar, but the thumping beat all but drowned her out. It made it easy for Stacey to pretend she didn't hear.

They left the club.

The man didn't even once glance back to see if Stacey was following but walked on across the parking lot.

"Stacey!"

Hearing Carrie yell her name stalled her in her tracks, and Stacey turned like a sleepwalker.

Here came poor Carrie, looking both angry and concerned. "Wot are you playing at, you daft cow? You're going to abandon me to those carnivores in there? Wot's 'e—"

Carrie's tirade suddenly disintegrated into a meaningless jumble of sounds. Noises.

The man stepped between her and Stacey.

"No," he said.

Immediately Carrie stopped walking, stopped talking, and sat down right there in the middle of the parking lot. Right on the asphalt that was stained with grease and oil. Carrie's rump thumped down, her legs splayed wide, revealing white thighs and blue knickers. Her eyes were as wide as saucers and there was absolutely no trace of anything in them.

"Carrie . . . ?" began Stacey, but the man turned around and focused his eyes on her. Stacey's voice evaporated into a misty nothing.

"Time to go, Stacey."

His voice was like syrup, like the most potent drink imaginable, like heroin.

She forgot about Carrie sitting splay-legged on the ground.

She forgot about her car. Her purse. Her life.

The man took her arm.

She melted into him.

Into his arms.

Into his car.

And into the night.

2

The sleek limousine drove past him, but no one inside—not the brutish driver, the smiling man, or the drowning woman—saw the figure who watched it go. He was in plain sight, but he stood so completely still that the world seemed to move around him. Nothing reacted to him—not drunks on the street, not the dog searching for scraps in the alleys.

He watched the car with eyes that had grown old and fierce and murderous. As its taillights vanished around a corner, he bared his teeth like a night-hunting cat or some darker predatory thing. Those he was hunting were in that limo: the glamoured one, and a skinwalker as a bonus.

When the street was empty, the figure turned, seeming to detach himself from the shadows. He touched his pockets and belt in a reflexive movement as natural to him as breathing. Checking that everything was where it should be.

His knives, the *òrdstone,* his strangle-wire. All of it.

Without haste he turned and crossed the street to where a motorcycle stood, black and gleaming. Waiting for him. The only detail on the bike was a partial handprint burned onto the engine cowling in angry red. It was not put there as a decoration. It had happened during a moment of blood, of screams and slaughter. And now the mark was burned into the metal.

The man swung his leg over the seat, keyed the ignition, and fed gas into the hungry engine.

The roar of his motorcycle split the air like a cleaver as he rode away in the same direction as the limousine.

3

The man's limousine was long and dark and sleek, and there was plenty of room for Stacey to get naked.

She did it slowly, but in a dreamy way, not like a vamp.

Piece by piece. Snaps, hooks, sleeves, straps. The hiss of cloth down her skin.

The air inside the car was stiflingly hot. Furnace hot.

Sweat ran in crooked lines down her arms and legs and back, and despite the heat, her skin pebbled with gooseflesh, her nipples growing hard. Stacey's breath rasped in her throat. It was less like the heaving breath of passion and more like the gasps of drowning.

Her clothes were scattered around her.

She was naked, vulnerable, unable to resist him.

The man sat on the bench seat, legs crossed, hands folded idly in his lap, eyes hooded in thoughtful appraisal.

Stacey felt her arms lift, hands reaching for him. Her mouth opened, and a low moan came from deep inside her chest.

The man did not move. He watched her, still smiled at her. His lips were red, his teeth glistening with spit.

Stacey closed her eyes and waited to be taken. To be used.

To be whatever he wanted.

No, cried a voice deep down in her soul, but it went unheeded.

The limo drove far out of town, leaving Edinburgh behind. Shadow-shrouded trees whisked by on either side.

All the time Stacey knelt there, arms raised, beckoning to him, aching with a need that no part of her mind could understand.

"Please . . . ," she managed to say aloud.

The man looked at her for a moment longer, then he turned his head and stared out at the night-black landscape.

After a long, long time the car slowed to a stop, the tires crunching over gravel and then dried leaves. Stacey sagged back, her arms falling to her sides.

The limo door opened and the man stepped out. He did not tell her to follow, but she followed. Naked, covered in sweat. Cold air licked at her.

They were in the countryside somewhere. It looked like there were huge ruins in the distance, but they were vague shapes against the under-lit clouds.

They walked some distance from the limo. Tiny lights like fireflies began to accumulate around them, dancing, flitting about until they all flew to one spot ahead, coalesced into a vertical line. Then, impossibly, the line split wider, began swelling into a bright green glow. She looked to him, bathed in that light. He was no longer there. Something transforming, inhuman, had manifested in his stead; it still looked upon her with those eyes that held all she desired.

He went ahead of her toward the green light. Around him were shadow-shapes, not the ruins she'd seen in the headlights of the limo but something else. And distance. It wasn't merely light, it was a place. Once inside it, he turned about and held out a hand to her.

"Come," he said.

Stacey looked from his golden eyes to the proffered hand. Her heart lurched in her chest. The fingers were wrong.

So wrong . . .

They were iron-dark, and all along the back of his hand and down his wrist the skin rose and rippled into dozens of tiny mounds, as if something was pushing from underneath. Then it tore as the needle-sharp tips of small spines thrust outward. Each barb curled out from a knot of gristle, like roses rising from malformed stems.

She watched her own arm extend to take that terrible hand.

Please . . . please . . . please . . .

She could hear her inner voice, her inner howls, but she could not act.

No . . . it wasn't that. She had no will to act, no desire. Those howls were an enraged echo of the Stacey who used to claim ownership of this body.

Was that Stacey gone? Was she dead?

Her hand reached for his, and she took a small step forward, toward the creature who, second by second, was changing. The mottling of his skin ran up his ironlike arm, under dissolving clothes, and erupted all over his throat and cheeks and face. His smiling lips thinned, the mouth widened into an ophidian leer.

The scream she needed to scream burned in her chest.

The owner of the golden eyes chuckled, an ugly noise that was painful to hear.

He said, "Now."

He didn't say it to her. It wasn't a demand for her to do anything, but her eyes widened and her mouth fell open as the night *changed*, and the green burned away her world.

The man—if it was ever a man—stood revealed as something entirely inhuman. Huge and bulky, with skin like that of a diseased toad stretched over muscles undulating in strange arrangements.

His eyes remained that compelling molten gold. And despite the utter horror of what he had revealed himself to be, Stacey had but to look into those eyes to know that she was still a slave. Still lost. Still haplessly willing.

The man—the *thing*— turned away as if dismissing her; but that only pulled her harder. He cut her one last glance over his shoulder, and then the green light took him.

He was gone.

Just . . . gone. But the light waited for her.

Finally, the scream that could not find release burst out of her.

Not from fear. Not in horror at his grotesque body or the impossibility of what was happening to her.

No, she screamed because the creature intended to destroy her *and she could not help but follow.*

Arms outstretched, she ran straight at the light.

"No!"

The bellow came from the shadows, and Stacey turned to see a wild figure emerge from the darkness, running at her with the speed and ferocity of a wolf. He was tall, slim as a sword blade, with glossy black hair whipping in the night breeze. One hand was empty, but in the other he held something—was it a gun? A knife?

Still screaming, he leaped at her, wrapped his arms around her, crushed her to his chest as he fell. They landed together with a bone-rattling thud, but the newcomer turned as they hit, taking the brunt of the fall, the spin of their bodies sloughing off the shock of impact. As they rolled away from the light he opened his arms and she spilled out and away from him. Then he was up cat-quick and he flung himself toward the wall of shimmering green light. He raised the thing in his hand and plunged it down as if he meant to reach into the light and smash or stab the man who'd brought her here. But instead, as the object made contact, the green light disappeared.

The stranger ripped his arm back and forth, slashing at the light, destroying more of it with each swipe.

No, she thought as a splinter of clarity jabbed through the strange muzziness in her thoughts. She cried, "Wait, what are you doing? You're closing it!"

He dropped to one knee and with a last vicious swipe sealed the night. The shimmering green light shivered and went out, plunging the clearing into darkness.

4

Stacey sat up slowly.

It was like coming out of a dream. Or a coma. Her body felt new to her, as if it was something she'd never owned before.

The newcomer stood a few yards away, his back to her, his hands loose at his sides, the object still clutched in one fist. The limo lights splashed over him obliquely. He sighed and his shoulders sagged for a moment; then he took the object—which she could now see was a piece of smooth gray rock a bit larger than the palm of his hand—and slid it into a leather pouch on his belt. As it vanished from sight, Stacey saw that its face was covered with complex patterns of strange design.

The man's black hair was shaggy. He wore a light gray jacket over a torn army-khaki T-shirt, old jeans, and lace-up boots. He turned. She took in the thin hair above his forehead, the beard that was maybe a week old. Her mind seemed to be swirling, confused in its attempt to reconcile being here with being at the club, where she knew she must be.

Then he turned and looked past her to the limousine.

"Skinwalker," he said in a terse, eager whisper and broke into a run. Straight at her.

Stacey screamed and flung herself backward, crossing her arms in front of her to try and ward off another of this night's horrors. But he shot past her, heading straight for the limousine. Too late its engine turned over and started. The door she had emerged from still hung open and the man dove through it as the limo lurched forward. The door swung shut and the limousine rolled maybe ten yards before it braked to a stop again and there was a flash of red from inside. The engine kept running.

The door opened again and the man climbed out. He held something in his arms, a bundle that, as he came nearer, she saw was her clothes. Only then did she realize she was naked in the middle of a field. And it was cold. She crossed her hands over her breasts.

The man didn't seem affected by her nudity. He held out her clothing as if holding out a gift. Her slingbacks dangled by their straps from two of his fingers.

"You should probably change in the vehicle," he said. His voice was soft, the accent strange. Irish, but with Scottish overtones. And something else. A strange quality she couldn't quite identify.

"I . . . ," she began and faltered. "I don't . . ."

"You have to hurry." His eyes shifted past her to where the light had been. "They'll open the portal again in a moment, and he won't be alone this time."

He took her by the arm and directed her back to the limo. There was none of the warmth or magnetism of the other man. In fact his grip hurt a little, enough to get her moving. She tried to pull away, but his hand was like a vise.

"You're *hurting* me."

His answer was a short, hard laugh. "What do you think *they'll* do?"

He held the door to let her climb in and slammed it behind her. Her mind was still sorting out a hundred questions, but she remained too rattled to ask any of them.

Then she saw the driver. Still upright at the wheel.

Stacey began to say something to him, to plead for help or an answer, but as she bent forward she froze in absolute horror.

The driver was dead.

More than dead . . . he looked like a corpse that had been rotting for weeks, maybe months. Stacey's mouth worked in a silent attempt to make some kind of rational sound, to *react* in some proper way to this, but that was impossible. She'd expected to see blood everywhere, but there was nothing—nothing to explain that strange explosion of red she'd glimpsed.

The driver's door opened suddenly, and the stranger grabbed hold of the corpse and yanked it out. The neck made a cracking noise and the head dangled loosely. The man got in. He looked back at her. His was not an unpleasant face, but his sharp blue eyes were the saddest she'd ever seen—until they abruptly burned green. It was a moment before she realized they were reflecting a flare of light, and she glanced around.

"Damn it," he whispered tightly.

As he'd predicted, the bright green oval had reappeared. Stacey stared at it with a mind that felt like it was fracturing. Even though she'd seen one like it only a minute ago, seeing this new one form out of nowhere was somehow worse. It promised something, some secret she knew she didn't want to hear.

Through the tinted window of the limo, she made out strange, rough shapes moving within the light.

Moving toward *her*.

"Hold on," growled the stranger as he slammed the door and put the car in gear.

Stacey stared at the green light and saw an impossible shape begin to emerge. All spikes and knobs, with massive shoulders packed with muscle.

"Oh, God! Something's coming through!"

The man stomped down on the gas. The limo pawed at the dirt like a maddened bull, then sprang forward with a roar of tires that left a cloud of dust behind them. He kept accelerating until they reached the main road, and then the vehicle squealed onto the pavement.

The green became a tiny thing seen between trees and then was gone.

5

They drove in silence awhile, and she wasn't prepared when the wave of shock finally slammed into her. Without realizing, she was abruptly gasping, panting, her heart racing. She thought she might be sick, rolled down the window, and stuck her head out into the cold wind. Her eyes watered and she broke into sobs. She reeled her head back in, found him watching her in the rearview mirror. He hadn't closed the driver's compartment panel.

The recognition of her fear exhausted her. She lay back against the seat and stared at nothing. She still hadn't put on her clothes, and how ridiculous was it that they didn't seem to matter? She tried to explain to herself what had happened to her, to Carrie sitting unconscious in a puddle of oil.

Her right shoulder blade itched and she scratched at it. The silence was becoming oppressive.

"Where are we going?" she asked.

He shrugged out of his jacket and thrust it at her. "Cover yourself."

"Where are we going?" she repeated, leaning on each word.

"Somewhere safe."

Stacey covered herself as best she could with the jacket, shivering with cold and the terror that trembled beneath her skin. "Not back to the club then."

"D'ye not know how far from there you are?"

"Um . . . a long way?" she ventured.

He gave a short, bitter laugh. "Not as long as it could have been."

"My roommate's at the club. I left her."

"She'll be fine. They didn't select her. But not the club, no. Nor tae your flat."

His accent really was odd. It wasn't Irish at all, she decided. It sounded somehow old, unevolved, like maybe he lived out on the Orkneys or somewhere else isolated. She couldn't place it.

"Why did you interfere?" She didn't mean for it to sound accusatory that way. The part of her that had acknowledged her lifetime of subjugation seemed to be speaking, but he didn't seem to notice.

"Be happy I did, lass."

"No . . . Why? Tell me."

At least a mile passed before he answered. "It's a very long story. Just know for now that I'm going to keep them from taking you."

"Why?" she asked, leaning forward. "What are you, the Lone Ranger?"

"I don't know who that is."

"Right. Naw, you wouldn't."

Another silent mile, then, "You sound angry that I didn't let him have you."

"I . . ." She couldn't figure out how to answer him, but he interrupted.

"Try to understand; they're good at hearing that in you, that sort of need. It's not your fault, any of it."

"What's not my fault?" She climbed across the center table to the seats behind him, stuck her head through the open barrier. "Who in hell *are* you?"

"Who out of hell, not in," he said bitterly. "The one who escaped but came back like the tide again and again."

"Oh, great. Riddles. I've stepped into the Twilight Zone, and you're feeding me riddles? What are you, Gollum?"

"Hardly."

"Well . . . who *are* you, then?"

He thought about that for a moment. "Rhymer," he replied, though she didn't know if that was his name or some form of behavioral explanation.

"Do you know what's going on?"

"Aye, I do." His voice and face were sad.

"Why is this happening to me?" she asked, and her voice suddenly dwindled to something smaller, more vulnerable. "Why do these people want to hurt me? Did I do something wrong or—?"

"No," he said firmly, "it isn't your fault that the Yvag singled you out."

"*Yvag?* Is that his name?"

"It's what he is."

She huddled behind the jacket, eyes huge. "I saw that, didn't I? I mean . . . all that stuff back there, and him changing. It really happened, didn't it?"

Rhymer nodded.

Tears broke from her eyes. "That man—"

"Wasn't a man," he finished.

"What *was* he?"

He considered the question. "They're what you'd call elves."

Despite her tears, a single bark of laughter escaped her. "Wait, what? I'm sorry, but did you say . . . *elves*?"

"Aye."

"As in the little sods making toys for Father Christmas?"

"Hardly." He glanced sidelong at her, the smile still in place. "Sounds so cute and cuddly, doesn't it? Little wee elves."

"The night before Halloween and I got picked up in a club by an elf?"

"Aye."

"What did he slip into my drink?"

"Nothing."

"Then I'm crazy? Is that it? I've gone barking mad?"

"I know it all *feels* a bit mad," he admitted. "But it's true. Like it or not, this is the real world."

"How?"

"Like I said, there's a long story."

She reached to scratch her shoulder again.

"You might not want to do that," he told her, "or it could start bleeding."

"What could?" she asked, wide-eyed. She pushed her shoulder forward and tried to see her back. Was there something there? She glanced around for her purse, a compact. It wasn't here. Probably back at the club. Great, her ID, credit card. Looking up then, she realized that the ceiling of the rear section of the limo was mirrored. She could guess why. There was probably a highway club that only did it in limos. She looked around till she located the bank of switches, flicked them until she'd ignited lights surrounding the mirror. Now she could see her naked self clearly, curled up on the seat, her dirty soles tucked under her. On her back there was definitely some kind of mark. It looked angry, infected maybe.

"What the hell?" she demanded.

"It's a *sigil.* He marked you. Why you cannae go back tae your flat, nor anywhere close. They're going to track you by that no matter where—"

But by then her hysteria had hit the ceiling. "Track me? What do you mean, *track* me? How did this happen?" Her voice quavered and tears stung her eyes. "Mister, what are you talking about?"

He sighed and gripped the wheel. "Ten centuries and you'd think I'd be better at this," he said to himself. "Look, lass. The short version—which isn't going to make sense tae ye—is that you've become the chosen *teind,* which translates for the Yvag as their tithe to hell."

"Whoa . . . wait. Hell?"

"Aye."

"As in . . . *hell*?"

"Aye."

"Actual hell? Not just hell but *hell* hell?"

"The same."

"I think I need to scream."

"You might at that," he said, either not getting her joke or not considering it one. "The Yvag have chosen you, marked you with their *sigil,* and that means that until they get their hands on you again, they're going to be extremely unhappy, not to mention panicked, because if they don't get you back for their ceremony, then that princeling who snatched you has to take your place in the ritual."

"Good. Fuck him."

"I couldnae agree more."

"Wait . . . princeling?"

"Aye, he is powerful among them. He has great charisma, lass. They all have it, but few wield it with his level of power."

" 'Charisma'?" she echoed.

"Aye. Tae humans that's just a gift of attraction, something to sell cars with, but for the Yvag, it's one of their most powerful weapons. They can make you lay bare your throat for the knife and thank them while they cut."

She thought about all of the absurd things she had done, including stripping naked without a thought, and shivered.

Rhymer sighed. "Had I brought him down tonight it would have crushed them."

"For good?"

"No . . . but it would weaken them for many years to come. Ah well. Meantime, I recommend you switch off those lights before we pass this articulated lorry, else you're going tae give the driver a heart attack. You might want to put your clothes back on, too, as we'll be pulling off the road in a minute. At least your shoes."

"Oh, God."

Everything that was happening was jumbled inside Stacey's head, and she knew, on some level, that she should be reacting better than she was. She also knew with perfect clarity that she was teetering on the edge of some dangerous level of shock. There were too many bizarre and impossible things happening, and despite tears and gooseflesh, she was taking this all too calmly. Her lack of ordinary reaction to it terrified her.

Her nudity, oddly, did not. And it damn well should have. She didn't even like wearing low-cut blouses.

Even so, she punched the switches until the rear of the limo went dark, and they passed the semi. She sorted through the heaped jeans, cami, and sweater until she found her panties.

"Can you answer a question?"

"I can try."

"I . . . just went with that guy. That elf or whatever. I went with him. I let him touch me. I took my fucking clothes off for him. I don't *do* that. A guy tries to grab my ass I kick the piss out of him. I'm not a victim, damn it, and I'm not anyone's casual piece of ass."

"No," Rhymer agreed.

"Well, you seem to understand this madness, so can you tell me why I did this?"

In the rearview mirror she saw him grin again. It changed his face from one of lupine harshness to something else. When he smiled, his face was gentle. Sad . . . but gentle.

"If I tell ye that this is all glamour and magic, will you hit me in the back of the head with your shoe?"

"Why . . . is that the sort of thing you're likely to say?"

"Well . . . elves and all . . ."

"Bollocks," she said, but mostly to herself. An admission that they were no longer driving through a sane landscape.

She pulled on her clothes. "So, what, I have to stay hidden till after Halloween?"

"Well, that's where we get into the long version of things. Normally, they would be hunting you for about a year."

"A *year*?" She did almost whack him with her shoe then.

"It's a question of relational temporalities. A day in *Yvagddu* lasts a year in our world. But they got cocky about things, figured to haul you over and dispose of you just like that, so they waited—"

"Just tell me for fuck's sake!"

"Thirty more hours, more or less."

She fell back against the seat. "I have to call Carrie. I need to know she got back to the flat okay."

"Right. Here." He handed her a cell phone. "It's a burner. You don't want to use your own."

She stared from the phone to him. "Elves can track cell-phone calls?"

For the first time he gave her a genuine and open grin. "Aye, the universe is totally daft like that."

"But . . . why the secrecy? Why not go south? We could go down to London; nobody can find anybody there."

He shrugged. "You're lucky you don't have a family," he said. "If ye had folks, children, it'd be far worse. They could substitute them on account of your blood."

"If I had kids and a family," she fired back, "I wouldn't 'a been clubbing with Carrie in the first place. Pish."

Quite suddenly, Rhymer spoke in a peculiar singsong.

No cause to trust eyes of promise,
Eyes so golden, eyes that burn, down into your darkest soul.
When you fall, and all unbinds
The last of you will scream out for the first.

Despite the words, his singing voice was beautiful. In the strangest way, the sound of his voice comforted her, removing splinters of fear from her mind.

Rhymer fell silent again and drove on as if nothing odd had occurred.

She stared at him, his face bluish like a ghost's in the dawn light. Rhymer—what in hell kind of name was that? Like something out of an old folk song.

6

Stacey had assumed they would be pulling into, at the very least, a lay-by. They weren't all that far from where they'd begun, maybe ten kilometers.

Instead, Rhymer turned the behemoth of a limo onto another dirt track that led into the darkness of another wood. He shut off the engine but left the headlamps glowing onto a clearing among the trees.

When she climbed out after him, she spotted the nose of a blue Fiat Punto backed in on the left. She remained where she was while he headed to the other car. He didn't seem to realize she wasn't following him until he had crossed the clearing.

He met her gaze over the limo. "I don't blame you," he said. "I'd be contemplating scarpering, too, wondering how hard it can be to lose me in the woods. I'll save you the trouble of breaking your ankle on a root—I'll not chase you. You go as you choose. Whatever you do, though, don't wait here. It'll like as not take them the whole morning, but they'll find it."

She took a wobbling step away from the limousine door. "Will they all be like him? Because I didn't have any choice with him . . ." She felt her face burn as she said that. It felt like admitting something bad, something dirty.

"What, you mean his glamour? Oh, they'll be sleekit but none of them's cowrin or timorous beasties."

She said, "What?"

Rhymer took a breath and continued, but Stacey noticed that he dialed down his accent. It seemed to take effort for him to speak in a normal, modern way. So weird, she thought. Rhymer said, "The glamoured ones all gleam like that. They'll have a harder time now on account of you're not wide open, d'ye see? So you stand a chance there; you can get away before they snare you again. It's the skinwalkers you likely won't see coming."

"What are skinwalkers?"

He glanced into the darkness behind the limo. "We should have this conversation while in motion, not waiting for them to catch us up."

"But you took their transportation."

He shook his head. "It's hardly the only way they travel. Even on foot I get from here to there. They won't be on foot." He sighed. "I had to leave a bonny little motorcycle back there, but I couldnae see driving off on that with you starkers on the back."

"Uh . . . no."

He nodded to the Punto. "This piece of junk will do for now. It's faster than it looks, and it's the kind of thing no one pays attention to."

"Nondescript ain't in it," she agreed.

Suddenly something whooshed above the trees. It might have been an owl, she thought, but Rhymer immediately climbed into the Punto and started the engine. Stacey pulled off her shoes again and walked, limped, cursed her way across the clearing toward the compact Fiat. The second she was in, he took off. They swung around the limousine and back up the dark rutted track, then back onto the A68 again.

A stripe of gray dawn painted the eastern horizon. She tossed her shoes into the back, noticing as she did the curving lines of some device laid across the rear seats.

Her inner voice couldn't seem to settle between rage and terror. The urge to yell at him compelled her, but she couldn't identify what for. He had saved her life, and she was reacting as though she resented it. All meaningful questions went unspoken while she asked herself what in hell was wrong with her.

Finally, she prompted, "Skinwalkers . . . ?"

"Mmm." He glanced at her sidelong. "People taken over by the Yvag. Mostly people in positions of power."

"What, like kings?"

Rhymer's features stiffened as if he could see something terrible on the road ahead. She couldn't help looking. But then he sang in the same soft voice as before. It was almost spoken-word but flowed with an elusive interior melody.

Never kings, but always kingdoms.
Never thrones but always ears.
Crucial words, spoke in whispers,
from our hands put power in theirs.

"God*damn* it, what is that? You got like some fucking Tourette's you can't help?"

"What?" He blinked at her, perplexed. "What did I say?"

She repeated the lyrics more or less, then asked, "You don't know when you do that?"

Rhymer took a moment answering that. "I don't, actually, strange as that sounds. I . . . know it's happening, but I'm lost *while* it happens. It's like something is talking through me."

"Oh, fuck me. You're telling me you're possessed?"

"No," he said quickly. "It's not that at all. I don't know how to explain it, though."

"But you do know what it means—what you said?"

"Aye."

When he didn't offer more than that, she said, "Well? How about we both know, since it's my arse they want, not yours."

"It's my *head* they want."

"I thought they wanted me."

"And now I've interfered, you're a pathway to me."

"The fuck I am."

Rhymer shrugged. "It's complicated."

"So's algebra. Try me anyway."

But he didn't.

She ground her teeth. "Okay, then what about the other thing? Tell me about those skinwalker things. Otherwise, you're taking me the hell back to Edinburgh right now, and sod you and your elves."

"Right." Rhymer rubbed his eyes. "So, the Yvag, they're ancient, like more ancient than the earth itself."

"How's that possible?"

"Where they live, it's a space between universes, ours and others. There are lots of others, I gather."

"A multiverse?"

He cut her a sharp look. "Now how do ye know that word?"

"I have every episode of *Doctor Who* DVRed. Keep talking."

Looking vaguely perplexed, Rhymer nodded. "They came from one of the others. It collapsed or something—I'm not entirely clear on the concept and it's not like they feel as if I ought to be included. Their escape, though, tied them to or was dependent upon some other form of life."

"Like what?"

"Like hell," he said. "Not your scriptural one exactly, though I expect our version of hell came from them, too."

"Hold on . . . Judeo-Christian tradition comes from elves?"

"I know how it sounds."

"Not to a history major, you don't."

"All right, history major, just suppose that a lot of people with influence, advisers to the powers that be, were . . ."

"What?"

"Were not really *people,* d'ye see? Suppose the Yvag had colonized them?"

"Skinwalkers, that's what you meant?"

"Yeah. They move in, take control of certain people—the ones who make laws, the ones who decide for everyone else, almost never the central person, almost always the advisers."

"'Never kings but always kingdoms,'" she repeated back at him.

"Exactly. If they were kings, they'd be in view. But manipulating the king? They stay in the shadows."

"Was the driver—?"

"He was one, yeah. I know, he's not someone in a position of power like, but they need others, too, to do simple tasks, move the glamoured ones around."

"Minions?" she said, smiling for the first time.

"Aye," agreed Rhymer, "minions is a good word."

Jesus, she said to herself, *I'm having a conversation in which elves, the multiverse, and minions are serious talking points. And vodka is not involved.* She took a breath. "But why did that skinwalker bloke look so . . . so dead?"

"Because he *was* dead the instant an Yvag took him. When they move in, they rip the human soul out. Whoever that person was is destroyed. Shredded. From that moment forward, the body is dead and only the Yvag is alive. The corpse maintains the appearance of being alive as long as the Yvag is inside, but once it's gone then the magic is broken and the body becomes what it really is—dead and rotting flesh. The longer the Yvag occupies you, the faster you turn to dust when it leaves. Understand, this magic is difficult, it requires a lot of energy and sometimes it slips. Every now and then you see a person who looks more dead than alive, and it's probably an Yvag whose control has slipped. Which is the other reason they choose to keep to the shadows."

"What do you mean?"

"Sunlight is nae good for dead skin. It speeds the corruption."

"Sounds like vampires."

He nodded. "What people call vampires are almost always Yvags."

"*Almost* always?"

Rhymer gave her a crooked grin. "It's a strange, big universe, lass."

"Yeah, yeah, there are more things in heaven and earth . . ." Stacey shook her head, trying to make sense of this. "The driver . . . the Yvag left him?"

"You could look at it that way."

"Which is to say you killed him."

"The Yvag, if I'm lucky. The driver . . . wasn't really there."

"Why?"

Rhymer twitched, ducked his head as if she had finally hit a nerve, a place he couldn't go or explain. In the end all he said was, "It's what I do."

She squinched up her face. There was something he had said—tossed off so casually it had flown right past. She rewound the conversation, listened, came to the moment when she'd freaked, and there it was. "Ten centuries. What was that about you living for ten centuries?"

"Well, give or take a decade . . ."

"Please tell me you're at least cool enough to be a Time Lord."

"A what?"

"Sigh," she said aloud.

"I know it's impossible tae believe—"

"No, see, that's the problem, I *completely* believe it. I just don't want to be a part of it!"

"I'm sorry you are."

She chewed her lip for a moment. "The way you fought? What was that? Kung-fu? Judo?"

"Gutter fighting," he said. "Bit of this and that."

"Nasty."

"It's not supposed to be nice."

"So . . . for a thousand years you've been messing it up with them, right? Interfering with this—this—"

"Tithing."

"Tithing. How often do they have to do that, pay this tithe to hell?"

"Part of a cycle. Here, it's every twenty-eight years."

"And you've been keeping people like me from getting taken."

He had a strangely anxious look on his face now and only nodded.

"No wonder they want your head. So in all that time, you must have saved like, what, five, six hundred people?"

He said nothing, staring hard at the road ahead.

"Rhymer, goddamn it. How many have you saved?"

"Counting you, seven."

"Seven hundred people? Really?"

"No," he said softly. "Just seven."

He met her gaze then, and the misery in his look spoke for him.

Very quietly, she said, "I think I want to go home now."

"Ye can't," he replied. "Not for twenty-nine more hours, or you're just handing yourself to them."

"Oh, really? How's that different from sticking with you?"

"Staying with me means you haven't given up," said Rhymer. "And when they come for you again, we're going tae make them pay dearly."

A moment later he added under his breath, "For a great many things."

7

Stacey awoke with a jolt.

She hadn't even realized that she'd fallen asleep. She sat up, brain muzzy, tongue thick, skin clammy. She had drool on her chin and wiped it away as she glanced at Rhymer. He was watching the road.

"How long was I asleep?" she asked. She rubbed at her eyes.

"About three hours. You've been through a lot. Magic wears a body out every bit as quickly as exertion."

" 'Magic,' " she echoed. "Right. Not a dream. Damn."

Outside, the sky was cloudy, and she didn't recognize anything in the brown-and-green landscape. They had left the A68 at some point.

"Are we there yet?"

"No, we've still got a bit to go," murmured Rhymer. "Sorry, but we couldn't just keep going straight. They would have come at us from ahead, so I've been shifting direction, zigzagging roads to keep them from being able to predict where we're heading."

"Where *are* we heading? Do we have an actual destination, or are we just going to drive around until these Elvis thingies get bored?"

"Yvags," he corrected.

"Whatever. Where are we going?"

"I've a place. But going there will only work once, and I want tae make sure they don't have sight of the car when we turn off."

As if to accentuate his point, a car roared up from behind to pass on the straightaway. As it came abreast it seemed to hold for a moment, and the driver gave them a hard stare before accelerating ahead.

She saw that Rhymer was watching the car, too. She gripped his forearm.

"Oh, God . . . please don't tell me that's one of those bleedin' skin-walker things?"

"Can't tell from here," he said. "You can bet they have every available one out listening for your sigil."

"Listening for it," she repeated, trying to grasp the concept. Her stomach gurgled. "For fuck's sake . . . we're being chased by monsters and here I am starving. I didn't eat last night. What is it, noon?"

"We'll get some food as soon as it's safe and—"

"I'm going to need some real shoes, too. Can we stop somewhere, some town center? Just for, like, half an hour?"

He didn't look happy at the prospect. "What is it about women and shoes?"

"Oh, mock me for being a cliché, that'll help."

"Sorry."

"I need something I can run in. We are fleeing, right?"

"Right. We'll see about getting better shoes, but understand me, lass, we take our lives in our hands every time we stop."

"I get that," she said soberly. "I really do. But if we *are* stopped—by them I mean—I'm no good running through woods and across fields in heels or bare feet."

"Still safer to keep moving," he said.

"Look, you can't seriously expect me to stay in this car for thirty hours! Besides . . . they could run us off the roadway out here and nobody would so much as notice. In a town there are lots of people. Doesn't that make it harder for them?"

He looked at her critically. "You were surrounded by a couple of hundred people at that tavern last night."

"Club," she corrected. "That still doesn't alter the fact that I can't run through the woods barefoot."

Rhymer seemed to weigh that. "All right," he said, and suddenly turned left, heading, so the sign indicated, for the village of Marfield.

"Thank you. Can I try Carrie again?"

He handed her the disposable phone. The signal was lousy, but it rang, dumping her immediately to voice mail. Stacey ended the call as she had done the previous time. Carrie not answering her phone was a bad sign, and Stacey imagined that a car had struck her while she sat stupefied in the parking lot last night. Last night? Christ, it seemed like days ago.

They arrived in Marfield on Creightontown Road, first passing a small hotel and café called the Rowan, and then shortly as they crawled along the main street of the village, a shoe shop. He pulled over and parked across from it. She got out, ran barefoot across the road.

The shop seemed to specialize in Doc Martens, but she found a pair of red sneakers that fit. Rhymer paid, producing a thick wad of bills from his pocket. When he caught her staring at the money, he leaned close and said, "Picking the pocket of a skinwalker isn't actually theft."

"Jeez," she said. Then her stomach grumbled again, much louder this time. "If I don't eat soon, they won't need that effing sigil to find me. They'll just follow the hunger pangs."

He rubbed his eyes and then nodded as if accepting a sentence to be flogged. "Very well," he grousedemphasis. "We'll get some food."

They left the car there and walked back down the road to the Rowan.

They sat by the front window, giving him a view of the street outside. He looked as if he hadn't slept in a year.

"When we're done here," Stacey said, "let me drive."

He started to protest, but his words were interrupted by a jaw-creaking yawn.

"That's settled then," she said.

A waitress came—the only one in the place. Stacey ordered an American-style burger and a Coke. Rhymer had the shepherd's pie and coffee. "I've acquired a taste for it," he explained, though she hadn't asked.

"Do you think we're safe?"

He shook his head. "No way to tell. I don't have an elf detector."

"Hilarious. But they have a tithe detector, don't they?" She meant it to sound light, but it fell over them like a bucket of cold water. "How do they choose? How did they pick me over everyone else in that shite club?"

"You must have made eye contact at the right moment—from his point of view, I mean. It could as easily have been your friend if you'd switched seats."

She chewed her burger, ate some chips, and meanwhile sorted through all that had happened to her, the beautiful monster who had snared her, this strange, slight man who seemed to be some kind of immortal in his own right. Unless, of course, he was barking mad, but then if he was, so was she. "What started you—I mean, ten bloody centuries, you were here for the Davidian Revolution for fuck's sake. I can't wrap my mind around it."

"Me, either," said Rhymer. "Davidian? I think I missed that one."

"What made you pit yourself against them?"

He took a forkful of meat and mashed potato. "The short version is—"

"Does everything have two versions with you?"

"Everything in life does," he said. "Though rarely only two."

She bit her burger.

"Anyway . . . it was the Yvag who set me on this path. Everything that's happened was because of them. *Is* because of them." He ate, and his eyes slid past her, focused upon the street as if something had caught his attention. But it soon became apparent that he was looking deep into the cavern of his own memories. Gray clouds seemed to drift across his face, deepening the sadness in his eyes.

"What's the long version?" she asked gently.

Without looking her way, he answered, "They chose unwisely." His voice was distant, pale, and filled with ice.

She set down her burger. "That's the *long* version?"

He came back to the moment, then his blue eyes closed for a moment. When he opened them, he gave her a hard, grim smile. But he didn't answer. His reluctance was palpable. She found herself reaching across the table to close her hand over his. He twitched at her touch. Human contact was that alien to him?

"It's fine," she said. "You don't have to."

"It's not that. I don't know quite where to start. Tell me, have you ever heard of the ballad of Thomas the Rhymer?"

"Rhymer?" She smiled. "He a relative?"

"Have you ever heard of it?"

"Sure. We read something in school. Let me see . . . 'True Thomas sat on Huntlie bank?' "

He nodded.

It took her almost twenty seconds.

"Jesus H. Christ!" she gasped.

"Shhh," he cautioned.

"You're going to sit there and tell me that *you're* Thomas the fucking Rhymer?"

"What . . . after everything else it's that you can't believe?"

"No, it's just . . . just . . . There are all those legends. And songs. I mean, Steeleye Span did a song. My mum had that album. And that band . . . Alabama 3, they did a song. That's the damn band that did the theme song for *The Sopranos*. You want me to believe you're *that* Thomas the Rhymer?"

He spread his hands.

Stacey tapped the tabletop. "There's a tower in Earlston that's supposed to be connected to him. Well, what's left of a tower. It's a bleedin' tourist site."

He gave her a lopsided grin. "I know. I took the tour once. Just to see. It's called the Ercildun Tower. Actually, I never lived in that tower. They built it on top of my cottage a century after I'd gone."

"And where were you?"

"In Yvagddu." She drew her hand back doubtfully. "I told you I didn't know where to begin."

"You were the *tithe*?"

"Not the first time," he admitted. "The first time, I spied on them carrying off their *teind*."

"And . . . ?"

"And they caught me watching. They don't like being observed."

Suddenly his sharp eyes unfocused, and she knew he'd been pulled into another of his riddles.

The friend who is nae what you see,
The lie not told but in the being.
They close the circle who come tae ye.

His eyes cleared. He drew a sharp breath, set down his fork, and pushed his fingertips against his forehead as if massaging a headache.

"Does it hurt?" she asked.

"Not more than being kicked in the face," he muttered. He blinked a few times and leaned back against the cushions. "All right. Tell me what I said."

She told him. When she was done, Rhymer glanced out the window again, but with such intensity that she turned her head too. Nothing out of the ordinary caught her eye.

"We should go," he said quietly. "If you need to use the loo, this is the time."

She got up and walked quickly across the small hotel lobby. At the restroom door, she glanced back. He was peeling bills from his thick roll of dead people's money.

She didn't take long in the toilet stall, but she lingered at the sink, washing her face over and over again as if the soap and hot water would somehow sponge away the day.

No, that wasn't it, and she had to study her own haunted eyes until she framed it the right way in her head. She wanted to wash away the *reality* of all this.

But she shook her head at that, too.

Not all of it.

Not Rhymer.

She wanted him to be real. He was powerful in ways she didn't understand, and beautiful in a wolfish fashion. Whether he was truly Thomas the Rhymer in reality, or a madman with some kind of psychic powers, or something else, he was real and this was happening. He'd saved her from humiliation and degradation. That alone made him heroic and even . . . sexy, though it was hard to get all hot and bothered while monsters were hunting you down in order to sacrifice you to hell.

Hell . . .

The word smashed into her mind like a fist.

Hell. You couldn't say the word enough times for it to lose meaning. Not today. Not after last night.

Hell.

It was no longer an abstract place in a Sunday service homily. Not a concept from a horror movie. Not a metaphor.

It was actual . . . *hell.*

She started to turn away from the mirror, from the belief she saw in her reflection, but her knees buckled and she crashed into the wall beside the sink. The floor pulled her with unkind gravity, demanding that she collapse into a huddled and quivering ball of tears. Maybe of screams.

"Fuck!" growled Stacey with all the ferocity of a trapped animal. She slammed the wall with her elbows, propelling herself erect. She looked at the face of the woman in the mirror—the face that was filled with fear and wanted to let the enormity of all this crush her.

"*Fuck you,*" she snarled.

She whirled and banged open the bathroom door.

8

She came out of the bathroom and edged past an elderly man who was heading into the men's room. As she crossed to the table she swiveled her head to check every face. To look for . . . what? The elf thing that had nearly taken her had looked completely human at first. So what did she expect to see?

"You ready—?" she began as she slid into the booth. The question died unasked.

Stacey's heart nearly seized in her chest.

Rhymer was gone.

Instead . . . *Carrie* sat in his seat.

Carrie was sitting across from her.

"Oh my Lord, *Carrie.* You're okay? God," she babbled, "did Rhymer tell you to meet us here?"

"Stacey," said Carrie very quietly, "I need you to listen to me."

But Stacey was so happy to see her friend. "I've tried to call you, to make sure you're all right."

"Ah," said Carrie, "that was you. I didn't recognize the number so I didn't try calling back. You left your phone in your bag at the club. Here."

Carrie pulled Stacey's small purse up onto the table and pushed it to her.

Stacey stared at her purse but didn't take it. "The phone's off," she said.

"Is it?" said Carrie. "It doesn't matter."

The elderly man came out of the men's room and made his way across the lobby behind Carrie's shoulder. He paused behind their booth and stared down at the back of Carrie's head as if contemplating speaking to her. Instead, he turned away for the exit.

Where was Rhymer? Was he in the loo? Was he getting the car? What was taking him so long?

"Stacey, I need to tell you something and you have to listen. You *have* to." Carrie leaned closer to take Stacey's hands in hers, holding them firm and giving them small emphatic shakes as she spoke. "Listen to me, the man you're with is a lunatic. He's very dangerous. The police told me about him. He's totally daft. He thinks he's some sort of savior."

"No, you don't understand," said Stacey. "The guy I left with was the loony. Rhymer saved me."

Carrie shook her head. "No, honey, they have warrants out for him. You're not the first girl he's taken. The others . . . well, it'd fair turn your stomach what he's done with them. He's a monster. It's all over the news, the whole country's looking for you. For *him*."

"Did you call the police?"

"Of course I did! When I came to outside the club and you weren't there, I knew something had happened to you. I reported it right away."

"But you don't understand, Carrie," insisted Stacey, "he's not the man who kidnapped me. I got away from the other guy. Rhymer stopped him."

Carrie smiled as if having to indulge a slow child. "You only think you got away, Stace. They're all in it together. See? It's a trick. They're working some kind of mindfuck on you. I think they slipped something into your drink, so who knows what you *think* you saw. The police know the truth."

"No, listen—"

"Stace, you think you've been rescued, which is just how he makes girls think they can trust him. Now he's trying to take you to some secret place. He'll lie and say that it's a safe place, that you have to wait there with him for a while. Has he told you that?"

"I—"

"That's where the other girls will be."

"What other girls?"

Carrie shook her head sadly. "That's what I'm trying to tell you. He's collecting girls. Kidnapping them, rounding them up. He's going to take you to wherever he keeps them. You'll see . . . they'll be there. All of them."

"That doesn't make sense."

"Sure it does. It's a sex trade thing, Stace. That's what they're doing, kidnapping women for the sex market. He tells them it's *him* who's saving them from some evil cult or coven or some such bullshit, but that's just to confuse them. It's all about sex and money for him. Do you know how much money a good-looking white bird like you is worth to some

Arab prince? Or to a brother in Dubai or someplace? All of this . . . all the elaborate steps he's taken are just to make it work. He uses a lot of money and a lot of tricks because the payoff is huge."

"No, Carrie, you're wrong about him. It's not like that at all."

Carrie ignored her; she gave Stacey's hands another squeeze. "Now listen, you need to come with me, okay? The police sent me in to get you away from him."

Stacey felt like the seat was tilting under her. This made no sense at all. She hadn't imagined the man who abducted her, who got her to strip naked, who tried to lure her into a wall of shimmering light.

She could not have imagined it.

Nor could she have imagined that Rhymer came out of the night to save her.

It had happened.

Right?

Now Carrie was telling her that all of those things were false—lies or the product of some kind of drugs, maybe mind manipulation. Did that make sense?

Or . . . which made more sense? A coven of evil elves who wanted to tithe her to hell or a manipulative bastard who wanted to sell her to the sex trade?

Neither seemed to be part of any world Stacey lived in.

Right?

She stared into Carrie's eyes, looking for the lie, looking for something that made sense of what her friend was saying. After all, this was her flatmate, her girlfriend for the past three years, the person she trusted with secrets she would not have shared with anyone else. The boyfriends, the bad dates, the skeevy English professor who'd come on to her last year—that's who this was, holding out a hand with chipped Chancer-red nail lacquer, ready to whisk her away to safety while the police brought down the madman who called himself Rhymer, and the whole network of sex traffickers working with him. Maybe they'd taken him already and that was why he'd vanished.

Or were the police outside waiting for Rhymer to come out of the bathroom? Were the SWAT team, the Lothian and Borders squad cars all poised to pounce?

She looked out the window, but there wasn't anything on the street except a bronze-colored Bentley parked right outside, with two official-looking men in charcoal suits standing beside it, the people on the street glancing as if expecting a celebrity to pop out any moment. Not a policeman in sight. But from here she couldn't see the Fiat either.

"I have to get you out of here," Carrie insisted.

And then like an echo, Rhymer's voice seemed to whisper in her ear. A fragment of his last riddle.

" . . . the friend who is nae what you see . . ."

The blood in Stacey's veins turned to cold slush.

Carrie sat there, eyes intense, mouth . . .

Smiling?

It was so small a thing. Just the tiniest upturn at the corners of Carrie's full lips.

A smile.

Why in the wide blue fuck would Carrie smile?

And where the hell was Rhymer himself?

If this was a trap, how had it been laid? Was the hostess one of their kind? Smiling so nicely at everyone?

Smiling like Carrie.

"Will you come with me, sweetie?" asked Carrie with that smiling mouth.

A word rose to Stacey's lips. It came slowly and reluctantly, and Stacey knew that to speak it would cost her. It would hurt her.

She said, "Skinwalker."

For a tiniest fraction of a second, Carrie's façade slipped, the brown eyes flickered with a degree of intelligence that had never shone in the girl Stacey knew. It was weird.

No, it was *alien*.

In that moment, seeing that different mind look out at her through those familiar brown eyes, Stacey knew—as surely as she knew her own name—that Carrie was dead.

The monsters had come and stolen her friend away. Stolen the light that was Carrie's light. Stolen her laugh, her dreams, her joy of living. Stolen everything. It was worse than murder. Using her body like this was a new, foul kind of rape.

"Oh, God, Carrie . . ." Stacey said as she jerked her hands away. Tears threatened to flood her eyes. And she repeated that dreadful word. "Skinwalker. You're part of that coven."

Carrie's smile blossomed into something overripe, swollen and nasty. She rose and came around the table and clamped a hand on Stacey's biceps. The pain was immediate and intense. "You need to come with us now."

"Why? Why didn't they just take you or somebody else?"

Carrie abandoned all pretense of being herself as she jerked Stacey out of the booth.

"Rules," she hissed, making that word into something hideous. "Your new boyfriend put the sigil on you. Hell has *tasted* you. Nobody else will do."

Tasted. She shivered.

God almighty.

She tried to pull away, but it was hopeless. She twisted around to yell for help, but everyone in the place was already looking at her.

Every single person was smiling.

At her.

Their smiles were wrong. All so wrong.

Like Carrie's.

Stacey sagged against Carrie. "Where's Rhymer?"

Carrie—or the thing that had invaded her body—sneered with contempt. "Your savior ran away like the coward he is."

"No . . ."

"He saw us and he fled."

"He wouldn't do that."

Carrie laughed. "That's exactly what he does, you silly little cow. How do you think he's survived for so many years?"

"No!"

Carrie leaned closer. "Why do you think that so many people have died in his stead? Or hasn't he confessed his failures? His crimes? Thomas the Rhymer is a coward who stole his immortality, and all he does—all he's capable of doing—is bring pain to those he pretends to protect."

"And what are you?" snapped Stacey. "You're nothing but monsters who—"

"Who pay a tithe to hell," finished Carrie. "Yes, we do. And why? Because appeasement is the only thing that prevents the legions of hell from waging war on all the realms of the living. In this pathetic world of yours, and across all the worlds." She leaned close, and Stacey could smell a rotting-meat stink on her breath. "That's the truth that Rhymer won't tell you. He delights in the songs sung about him and the tall tales you humans tell, but his freedom is bought at what cost? He paints us as evil, tries to make us out to be the villains. But it was his own escape that nearly brought down all the infinite worlds. His arrogance is his greatest crime."

"He saved my life!"

"Your life?" spat Carrie. "What is your life compared to a billion billion lives? To a trillion worlds? The tithe to hell is so small a price to pay, you should drop to your knees and thank all of the gods of all the worlds that you were chosen as the true savior of the universe. You—you pathetic bitch. We 'monsters' *killed* your girlfriend, but we chose you to be the sacrifice that would save everyone. She's dead. A waste. Am I supposed to mourn for you? To feel sorry for *you*?"

Dazed and confused beyond speech, Stacey could find no will left to fight as Carrie dragged her outside, leading her to the Bentley. One of the bodyguards opened the rear door. Cold hands reached out, dragged her into the back.

"Here is the tithe," said the skinwalker in Carrie. "Try not to let her tears of self-pity drown you."

There were only two seats in the back, with a paneled elbow rest and divider between them. The other seat was occupied by a heavy older man with salt-and-pepper hair and jowls. His eyes were blue, but watery, almost colorless. She knew she'd seen him before, in the news somewhere. An MP maybe.

Kingdoms, never kings.

The two men in the front seat turned around to look at her. They were both important-looking older men.

"This is the tithe?" asked the driver with an imperious sniff. "How far we have fallen."

"Please," Stacey pleaded. "Just let me go."

Carrie, still lingering in the doorway, said, "I tried to explain the truth to her, but she's too stupid to listen."

"It's always the same with those the Rhymer tries to save," said the other person in the front seat, an iron-haired man with a military bearing. A general, perhaps. "Some whimpering, simpering bitch who thinks that Prince Charming will protect her from the Big Bad Wolf." He made a disgusted sound.

"Please, please . . . this doesn't make sense," pleaded Stacey. "Why would Rhymer do this?"

"Why would he try to save you?" asked the fat statesman in the backseat with her.

They all laughed. Short, bitter laughs that were entirely without humor.

"We have a word for it," said the driver. "Actually there's a word for it in every language throughout all the universes, but they all mean the same thing. It describes people like Rhymer."

"Tell me," she begged. "I have to understand."

"Why . . . he's a terrorist, my dear," said the military man. "I thought that was obvious to anyone. He *wants* to start a war with hell."

"It wouldn't be a war," said Carrie coldly. "Without the tithe . . . it would be fire and slaughter forever."

They all looked at Stacey as she wept.

"That's who Thomas the Rhymer is," said the driver.

Carrie's mouth wore her vicious, secret little smile as she slammed the door.

9

They left Marfield, turned away from the direction she and Rhymer had come, and headed somewhere else. Stacey sat in stunned silence, staring out at the road for signs. The next listed Balnuaran of Clava. She knew that site and where she was if those burial cairns were only twenty kilometers up the road. They passed the Nairn viaduct, and shortly after that they turned onto the narrow paved road past Balnuaran. A dozen or more tourists milled around between the three cairns in the crisp autumn weather, a few of them in medieval or Druid costumes; but the car rolled on past. To the left lay a farmhouse and outbuildings, and a large brown field full of baled wheels of hay or grass. Another farmhouse went by on the right. A sign read MILTON OF CLAVA, directly after which the road banked left at an acute angle. Instead of turning, the Bentley pulled off to the right, effectively blocking a narrow footpath between low wire fences. It seemed to lead straight into the afternoon sun.

The fat statesman remained where he was until her door had been opened and she'd been led out. Then he came around the nose of the Bentley and stepped in behind her to propel her along the path. The two black-suited men remained with the car, no doubt to keep anyone else from coming along after them.

Stacey knew that she could run. That she *should* run.

But her legs wouldn't deviate from the path.

What if it was all true? What if her life was the price that could save so many?

Everyone she ever knew. Everyone in the world.

In . . . all the worlds, if that part was true.

Could she actually run away from that, as Rhymer obviously had? Could she be so selfish? So murderously self-centered?

And yet . . .

Why had Carrie smiled that last little smile?

Who was telling the truth?

What was the truth?

Was there any? Or was this all a two-sided game with no good guys, only bad ones? And her life as the only piece on the board.

Help me, she prayed, mouthing the words but not speaking them. *Help me.*

But she had no idea to whom her plea was directed.

God—if there was a God—seemed to allow this madness. Did that mean that He was complicit in so much misery?

Of course He is, she thought, scolding herself. People died in pain and misery every minute of every day. All she had to do was google the statistics of rape, child abuse, murder, genocide to know that any god of this world did not care about suffering, pain, and death, or it was part of His indescribable plan.

Was there a point to suffering? Or was it some kind of fucking entertainment?

These thoughts slowed her feet, and the fat statesman gave her arm a sharp jerk.

"Come along, you cow," he growled.

People were already gathered ahead to the right, half a dozen in a rectangular space where an open gate led onto a path between an eight-foot-tall standing stone that seemed to mark the site and a smaller clump of boulders. On the gradual downhill slope beyond it lay a bowl-like depression in the ground next to the piled rubble of what might once have been a cairn like those back up the road at Balnuaran. A little farther on, but separated by fences, lay more stones and boulders and artificial depressions in the ground. At the low end of the fenced space stood a line of high shrubs and beyond that a stretch of woodland. She glimpsed the glisten of a stream on its far side.

Because the previous event had occurred late at night, Stacey anticipated that nothing would happen here until after dark. Instead, the six people already there spread out into a circle around the central depression—a runnel surrounding a small mound, like a miniature of a Bronze Age hill fort. No one said a word. The clarity and stillness of the afternoon, the matter-of-fact way they all took their places, made it surreal to her. Entranced, she had escaped from this fate last night. Now, fully aware, she might as well have been entranced again. She couldn't stop it.

"Over here," said the statesman, taking her arm again. He waddled down into the runnel and then up onto the mound. A cold wind blew across the field.

As he spoke, some of the gathered people snickered.

That seemed strange to Stacey. Even now, even with all this.

No . . . *because* of all this.

If she was a necessary sacrifice, then why laugh at her? If her death meant that worlds would be safe, shouldn't these people—these *skin-walkers*—be weeping for her? Honoring her?

It's what she would have done.

But their laughs were like Carrie's secret smile. Wrong and out of place.

The fat statesman pushed her to a spot and then stopped her. "You will take off your clothes and pass naked through the doorway."

"Why?" she demanded.

"Only a *pure* sacrifice will do. Clothes are impure. Plastics, metal . . . no. You will be reborn into the fire as naked as you were born into the blood of this world."

The smiles around her grew brighter. Several of them licked their grinning lips and wrung their hands.

Stacey frowned. "N-no . . ."

"Do it," said the fat man, "or we will do it for you, and we won't be gentle."

She made no move to obey. Instead she looked into his eyes. "Why are you doing this?"

"We told you . . ."

"No. Why this? Why do I need to be naked? I stopped fighting you, so why are you treating me like this? Why are you being so mean?"

His only answer was a lascivious chuckle. Then he reached into the inside breast pocket of his suit coat and drew out a black stone about the size and shape of a large box cutter. It had been polished to a high gloss and sharpened along one side to a wicked razor edge. Like the stone Rhymer had, it was covered with all sorts of markings and symbols. But Rhymer's wasn't knifelike, and Stacey thought of primitive knives or adzes from prehistoric sites. She was sure she'd seen such a tool in a museum display somewhere, but now it was here, not on display, and they were going to kill her with it.

"No," she begged.

"Oh yes," he said. "You are a cow, but you are a comely cow. Let us see the flesh that will burn. Let us delight in the breasts that will suckle monsters and the loins that will spawn the horrors of hell."

He darted out a hand and caught her blouse. Stacey cried out in disgust and pulled away, but the man's grip was strong and buttons flew and cloth tore.

She staggered back, her blouse torn open, her bra and bare midriff exposed to their sight. The eyes of every person in the circle burned with delight at what they saw.

"Tear the rest off," yelled one of the women.

"Let us see the whore," cried a hulking man.

"Cut her!" yelled the others. "Let us see the wine of her heart. Cut her . . . cut her!"

They all began to chant for the fat man to strip her. To use his knife to cut her clothes. To slash her face and breasts and limbs. They hopped up and down, punching the air with their fists, eyes ablaze, passion causing red poppies to bloom in their cheeks.

Laughing with them, the fat man advanced on her, one hand clutching as he reached for her, the other slicing the air with awful promise.

Suddenly, it was as if a cold, clean hand reached out of the darkness of her mind and slapped Stacey across the face.

A coven after all.

Just that.

All around her, hearts beating for the love of darkness.

And everything was lies.

She actually staggered back from him as if struck.

But as her foot came down it landed firmly and she crouched, fists clenched, teeth bared, deep understanding catching fire in her mind.

This was the truth. This carnal madness of the moment tore away the cobwebs in her mind.

"You bastards," she said. "You lied to me."

They heard her words and for a moment they stared blankly at her, and then they erupted into huge, coarse laughter that scared the birds from the trees.

"This is all a game to you, you sick fuckers."

The woman who had yelled gave a few seconds of ironic applause. "And the trained monkey squeezes out a real thought."

Everyone laughed at that.

Stacey spat in her face, but the woman wiped it from her skin and licked her fingers.

"So . . . all of that about Rhymer, that was—what? A joke?"

"Oh, no," insisted the fat man, "it's not a joke."

Stacey hesitated. "But—"

"It's more delicious this way," he explained. "The last turn of the knife, so to speak. The ugly truth, the final betrayal, the realization that you came willingly when you really should have tried to run away and find your fabled savior. So nice. Like whipped cream." He leaned close. "Oh . . . how they scream when they hear that."

The gathered skinwalkers cackled like crows.

Stacey wheeled around, looking for a line of escape, but the people closed ranks around her.

"And how it must turn the knife even harder in Rhymer," said the fat man. "To know that those he fails to save die either hating and damning him or calling for his help, and he is always too late."

"Too late!" chanted the crowd.

"Year after year, century after century, too late." The fat man squeezed his crotch as a wave of erotic joy flushed through him. "His pain is so delicious. So . . . very delicious."

"You *are* monsters," said Stacey softly. "Everything Rhymer said—all of it—was true. You are a coven of monsters."

"Monsters, monsters, monsters," they chanted, laughing and fondling themselves.

The fat man guffawed and held his trembling belly as he laughed. "I wish you had seen it, girl," he said. "When he realized that we were already in that town. When he saw that we were already in the restaurant. He turned as white as a sheet and ran—actually ran—from there. Your hero. Failed once again. The last we saw of him was his back as he ran for his life, leaving you, my dear, to . . . *us*."

And with that he lunged at her with the stone. For all his bulk, the man was terrifyingly fast. Stacey flung herself backward but the edge of the sacred stone drew a red line across the tops of both breasts. Beads of red blood bulged from the cuts and then spilled down, following the curves of her breasts, staining her torn blouse, falling onto the ground.

The crowd cheered wildly.

"Cut her again!" screeched a reed-thin man dressed in a postman's uniform.

The fat man laughed and raised his stone. Stacey tried to back away, but the crowd was a solid ring and they forced her toward him.

"Cut her! Cut her!"

Stacey realized that this was it, that she was going to die. Even with all that had happened since last night she'd never quite accepted the absolute reality of her death. Or its absolute imminence.

The stone knife slashed through the air, inches away, and she saw strands of her hair flutter in the breeze. The fat man was circling her, closing the distance with each pass. Cut after cut whistled through the air and she felt lines of molten heat erupt along her back and arms. Blood ran like rivers.

"Cut her! Cut her!"

The chant filled the air.

The fat man grinned like a ghoul as he closed in. Behind him the air began to shimmer with green fairy lights.

"Cut her! Cut her!"

Stacey braced herself, shifting her weight to the balls of her feet, ready to run, ready to spring. Ready to fight. Ready to do anything but let him butcher her without at least crippling the bastard. She was determined to take his eyes with her. If she had to die, then fuck it. Let them pay for it.

"Cut her! Cut her!"

Stacey timed herself to his next swing, and then she ducked low and snatched up a rock, rose, pivoted, and hurled it with all her strength.

It struck the fat man on the shoulder as he was raising his weapon and then ricocheted off and struck the postman in the mouth. He staggered back, spitting teeth.

The crowd laughed at that, too.

With a sinking heart she realized that they were used to their victims struggling. Worse, they enjoyed it.

The wall of green light intensified, blocking out part of the circle of skinwalkers. Its presence cut down on the amount of maneuvering room she had. She was barely able to stay away from the killer as it was, but as the wall strengthened and grew, Stacey knew that sooner or later she would fall beneath the knife or be forced through that doorway.

The fat statesman slashed at her again, and she dodged, but as she did so she realized that he *could* have cut her. She stumbled away, confused. Surely he wasn't showing her mercy . . .

As he stalked her, the fat man began speaking some words and phrases in a language she didn't know, which sounded like a made-up form of Latin. With each word the shimmering light flared and grew.

He must have seen the look of realization in her eyes. He said, "That's right, we won't kill you here. But we will lap your blood." His tongue waggled obscenely.

She was a tithe to hell. Not a blood sacrifice. She was going into the green light alive, not into the ground dead.

The light bathed the whole clearing, painting the faces of everyone there in shades of sickness and unreality. It was like looking at a pack of madmen through night-vision goggles. All green and black and shades of gray.

The fat man raised the blade high over his head.

He opened his mouth to say something else. Perhaps another phrase in that weird language. Maybe another taunt.

Whatever it was, though, would never be spoken.

Not in this world.

Something whipped past Stacey's ear and for a split second she thought it was a wasp. It hummed, high and sharp.

Then she stared with slack-jawed shock at the thing sticking out from between the fat man's teeth. Long and slender, with brown feathers quivering at the end.

An arrow.

The fat man took a slow, wandering sideways step and turned away from Stacey, revealing the barbed spear point standing out from the back of his skull, slick with blood and strands of gore.

The fat man clutched at Stacey, but his body began to shudder violently. His chest bulged outward—she could hear the wet, muffled sound of his ribs and sternum snapping, then the skin stretched and stretched until it burst open in a spray of blood. Something leaped through the bone-broken doorway, a humped and gnarled figure no larger than a child. It landed on two misshapen legs and stared around with eyes that glowed with real inner heat. Its skin looked like a map of veins and musculature, like some grotesque subject of dissection in a medical school. But it was alive and filled with hate. Intelligence burned in those hot eyes.

Stacey lunged for the fallen stone knife.

So did the creature.

But as they both reached for it—as Stacey curled her fingers around it—a second arrow snapped through the air and struck the creature. This time it hit the chest and transfixed it. If this monster, this *Yvag,* had a pumping heart like a human, then the broad-bladed arrow must surely have torn it in half.

The creature looked at Stacey, its burning eyes seeming to lock on her, and its inhuman mouth opened, screeching to the sky in furious terror. Then it abruptly ruptured into a gray-green mist that spattered Stacey and every shocked and now silent person in the circle. Bones and raw meat flopped to the ground.

The statesman's body—the fat empty shell—still stood impossibly upright; but it was rotting before her eyes in swift, freakish decomposition. Skin bruised, sagged, the wide eyeballs liquefied and fell back into the skull, and the whole corpse deliquesced inside the suit, collapsing with a wet squelch to the ground. He had been in the press for years, decades she thought. Dead far longer than the driver of the limousine.

The wall of light suddenly changed from green to red. Furnace heat roared out across the clearing.

"Push her in!" screamed the woman who had applauded with such vicious irony. Her words broke the others out of their shock. The postman was closest; he made a grab at Stacey.

A third arrow came out of nowhere and punched through his chest. It stood there, the shaft thrumming from the force of impact.

The postman juddered to a stop, and he managed to croak a single last word, raised his arm and pointed.

"No . . ."

Everyone turned.

A figure stepped out from behind the border of tall shrubs below them.

Lean as a wolf, with eyes that were bottomless and dark with incalculable rage. He was dressed in jeans and a vest made of rough doeskin. Belts crossed his hips and from them hung knives of every description. In his hands, though, he held a great yew bow, and a quiver heavy with arrows hung from a strap behind his shoulder.

Stacey watched as he quickly, deftly drew another arrow, fitting it to the string without effort, as if he'd done this a hundred times. Or a thousand.

Or ten thousand.

"Rhymer," she breathed.

10

As Thomas the Rhymer raised the bow, the crowd of skinwalkers howled at him.

They howled with seething hatred for their ancient enemy.

They howled in burning rage for this disruption of their ritual.

They howled in fear of this man.

And they howled in terror for the consequences of his attack.

Stacey heard those roars and yells and she understood them. A scream ripped its way out of her own throat.

Beside her, the postman's stomach exploded as the red monster within tore free. It dropped into a crouch like a bloody ape, head swiveling back and forth as if seeing with new and more cunning eyes than it had used a moment ago. Those eyes came to rest on Stacey, and the thing's lip curled back from rows of gore-streaked fangs that were bracketed by wicked tusks. Its muscles tensed for the spring.

Stacey gave it no time.

She swung the sharpened stone knife with all her strength, and the razor edge slashed through the Yvag's throat so deeply that the stone grated on its knobbed spine. Green blood sprayed outward as the creature dropped.

The postman's body shriveled to dusty rags in a heartbeat.

As if the collapse of the empty clothing was a signal, the elves attacked, and though the real hell waited beyond the shimmering veil of light, there was enough of it to be had in that clearing.

As one they surged forward—a dozen monsters in stolen bodies. The nearest lunged at Stacey; the rest barreled downhill toward Rhymer.

For his part, Rhymer stood his ground, firing arrow after arrow, filling the air with death—first to kill the hijacked bodies and then to slaughter the Yvag who dwelled within. His jaw was tight, his mouth curled into a sneer of disgust, but Stacey saw that his eyes blazed. With madness? Or was he enjoying this? After all these centuries, was this the only time he was truly alive?

Then she had no more time to think. A woman dressed in expensive furs and jewels tried to stab her with a diamond-crusted dagger, but Stacey bashed her arm aside and drove the tip of the sharpened stone into her chest. Over and over again, tearing through ermine and powdered flesh and tough bone. As the woman's chest collapsed, the Yvag inside tried to burst free, thrusting its clawed hands outward to try and snatch the sacred stone from Stacey's hand. But Stacey bellowed and hammered at the scrabbling fingers, smashing them, shattering bones, battering the emerging Yvag even as it fought through blood and ragged tissue to escape its dying frame. Sagging halfway out, the Yvag and its host collapsed onto the ground.

The man with the military bearing leaped over the fallen body and drove a savage punch at Stacey that would surely have broken her neck, but an arrow crunched through the balled fist and pinned it to his chest. Before he could react, Stacey finished him with a slash to the throat. His blood sprayed everywhere.

Bodies fell and clogged the clearing, and Rhymer used those obstacles to advance over the fence. He fired and fired. One bolt struck a skinwalker in the stomach and it fell forward. Its body heaved, then lay still, and Stacey realized that the arrow had found and killed the Yvag within as well.

Then there was a loud *CRACK* and Rhymer spun backward, his bow falling from his hand as red blossomed from high on his left shoulder. A figure—the driver of the Bentley—stood with braced legs, aiming a Glock nine millimeter at Rhymer. Only the wild panic of the crowd prevented him from ending it there.

"Get out of the way, damn you!" cried the driver, and when one of the skinwalkers didn't move fast enough, he shot it in the head. Rhymer leaped the fence and dodged behind the shrubs again. The driver fired into them, but Rhymer had already bolted for the woods. Furiously, the Yvag plunged after him, bounding over the fence and into the trees.

A second man bent and rummaged inside the folds of the military man's empty clothes and straightened with a mad grin on his face and a big .45 Navy Colt in his hand. When he turned toward her, Stacey saw that there was something strange about his eyes. They weren't like the rest of the skinwalkers.

They were more like the eyes of the man who had abducted her from the club. They generated a strange and overwhelming attraction. She knew that this could not be the same man, the one Rhymer said was a princeling among them—he had shed his skin and gone into the green light—but the power was similar. It was so normal and natural and warm that it nearly stopped her in her tracks.

What had Rhymer said about the charisma of these elves?

To humans that's just a gift of attraction . . . but for the Yvag it's one of their most powerful weapons. They can make you lay bare your throat for the knife and thank them while they cut.

She could feel her hand begin to open. The sacred stone began to slip away from her even as the creature raised his pistol and pointed it at her face.

She closed her eyes, waiting for the bullet.

Almost . . . wanting it.

The shot never came. She opened her eyes to see him lower the pistol.

The creature sighed. "Alas for everyone that the tithe must be alive and able to scream."

"I . . ." she began, but there was nowhere to go with words.

"Take her," said the Yvag. He turned away and ran after the others into the woods to hunt for Rhymer. A few moments later there came a burst of shots and a solitary scream of agony.

Only two skinwalkers remained in the clearing, and they closed in on Stacey. They were as splattered with blood as she was.

"You will scream for a thousand years," whispered one of them, a woman with masses of blond curls. "That's the truth of hell, bitch."

"You will become the whore of a hundred thousand demons," said the other.

Stacey closed her fist around the sacred stone. The spell of the princeling had snapped as soon as he turned away.

She bared her teeth at them.

"Fuck you," she said, and sprang from the mound. She cut them to pieces with their own stone knife.

11

There was another scream and Stacey ran downhill. As she reached the wire fence, the skinwalker with the Glock came stumbling backward through the shrubs. He hit the fence and fell on his back at Stacey's feet. His face and throat and chest had been slashed to ribbons. The Yvag—mortally wounded—struggled to tear free from the shriveling body, but Stacey kicked it over and stomped on its head.

Within the forest, Stacey could see Rhymer moving among the skinwalkers. He held a knife in each hand and stray shafts of sunlight struck sparks from the steel as he wheeled and cut and slashed and stabbed. If the bullet had done him any damage, it was not evident. Two skinwalkers, both of them trailing blood and streamers of torn flesh, crawled out of the forest and into the clearing, making for the wall of light and, perhaps, a chance of escape.

There was a sudden howl of rage, and heat struck her back like a wave. It sent her reeling, and the stone flew from her hand. She whirled to see that the wall of light had grown brighter and bigger, filling more than half of the clearing now. It was as if the sky were being sliced apart in pursuit of her. The light seemed to expand toward her like the chest of some great dragon.

A grotesque face peered through, spotted her—a baleful eye that she remembered from last night.

The *princeling,* Rhymer had called it.

It strained to reach for her through the glowing opening, barbed and knobbed fingers gleaming with the sheen of cast iron. Stacey staggered back and wrenched her head away before the princeling's charisma could conquer her.

One of the remaining skinwalkers had crawled out from the trees; they stared at each other for a second. Then he jumped for the cutting stone. Stacey kicked him in the face. The stone flew out of his grasp and blood spurted from his nose. She took a step to kick him again, but with both hands cupped over his face he skittered away from her.

Then someone called her name.

It spoke in a voice like thunder. The force of it shook the clearing and shivered the trunks of the trees. Birds fell dead from the air, as the rocky ground beneath her cracked.

Stacey screamed.

It wasn't just her name that was called. It was her whole being in two syllables, shouted by the prince of the elves from the mouth of hell.

The power of it enfolded her again, the charismatic force as clinging as tentacles, dragging her toward the blazing light.

With everything she had, she fought to pull free, but her captured body betrayed her. As had happened at the club, her mind became compartmentalized, boxed in, trapped.

"The ritual," she heard him broadcast to the surviving Yvag. "Bring the other two. Complete it from your side."

Another of the skinwalkers ran out of the woods—a solid woman with red hair and dressed in a lemon-yellow tracksuit that was smeared with a bloody handprint. She scrambled over and retrieved the blood-smeared cutting stone, cringing back immediately as if expecting to be kicked, too, but Stacey could no longer work her legs. Although she was screaming inside, not a sound came out. Her eyes flooded with tears at her helplessness. They had her. She understood now how Rhymer had only managed to save a few, how tenacious, unstoppable these monsters were.

The woman clambered up beside her to push Stacey up the mound and through the opening.

And then Thomas the Rhymer stepped out from behind the tall standing stone above them.

He was covered with blood, his shirt torn halfway off his body. His limbs were crisscrossed with cuts and the vicious welts from bites and tearing fingers. But he had recovered his bow and he held it in his red, gleaming fist above which the shaft of an arrow rested.

"Rhymer . . ." whispered Stacey. With sudden horror she realized that he was pointing the arrow at her. Was that how this would end? If he couldn't save her from hell, then he would deny the demons the living sacrifice they demanded?

His eyes were hard and merciless as he stared along the shaft at her.

Stacey wanted to curse him. To hate him for this. He had used her to find this coven, hadn't he? To bring the princeling back into this world. Now here he was ready to sacrifice her life. She should hate him with her last breath and thought.

She said, "Do it."

He took careful aim and let his arrow fly.

Stacey closed her eyes.

The arrow whipped by so closely that she felt it pass, viscerally shared the thud of it into the breastbone of the tracksuited woman beside her. Stacey's eyes snapped open to see the woman spin around and stumble backward—straight into the wall of light, her arm extended as if to hand the cutting stone to Stacey. At the last, her shaking, dissolving hand flung it to the ground.

Stacey's arms were free, but she stood there for a moment, too stunned to know what to do.

"The stone!" cried Rhymer. "Now, before it's too late!"

That was like a bucket of water in the face. Stacey snapped out of her shock and dove for the sacred stone.

"You dare not!" bellowed the Yvag prince, and Stacey spun around in horror as the monster dragged the tracksuited body aside and stepped halfway from the light, reaching for her, swiping at the air with its claws.

An arrow thudded into the princeling, but instantly glowed and caught fire, the ashes blowing away in the superheated wind.

"The stone," Rhymer cried again.

But Stacey had it seated in her palm now, her fingers wrapped tightly around it, her body turning—not away from the Yvag prince but toward him. She slashed at him with his sacred stone. The razor-sharp edge of it drew a glowing green line from shoulder to elbow.

The Yvag's shriek of pain came like the screech of grinding metal, like a train wreck inches from her face. It picked her up and slammed her back against the shrubs. Even where he stood, Rhymer fell, too, his arrows spilling from their quiver.

The Yvag prince thrashed in place, like a wasp caught in a spider's web. As Stacey watched, the green lines of glowing blood spread like a vine into the red of the shimmering wall and somehow seemed to bind him there.

Or did it?

The creature threw its twisted body against these new lines of force and step by step the resistance yielded, one line then another snapped, and he emerged. He was almost all the way out now.

Stacey pushed herself up. Thunder seemed to pound through her head. She pressed a palm against one ear, found that she was bleeding from it. And from her nose. Rhymer, sprawled in the dirt, was coughing, and with each cough a bloody foam rimed his chin.

Somehow Stacey still had the stone in her hand, but the monster in the fiery gateway was reaching for it. She raised it for one last stab. Maybe she could cut a tendon or . . .

"Hell and eternal suffering await you," whispered the prince in a voice that was so inhuman that Stacey did not know how to describe it. Words forced out of a throat that was never meant for human speech.

She jabbed at the thing's knobbed fingers and it twitched back, careful to avoid her. They both knew who would win, but the elf did not want to suffer more damage in the midst of its victory.

"The . . . wall . . ."

Stacey heard those words distantly, from a million miles away.

"What—?"

The elf grabbed her ankle in its steely hand and began to pull her across the ground.

"Not the . . . Yvag," croaked Rhymer as he fought to climb shakily to hands and knees. "The wall . . . close it."

Stacey twisted back to the Yvag prince. His goblin face leered at her.

"Too late," he mocked. "Give in to the suffering that is your destiny."

Stacey raised the sacred stone.

"Fuck you!" she screamed, and stabbed.

Not at the monstrous hand that held her.

Not at the grinning impossibility of the black, golden-eyed skull that laughed at her pain.

She stabbed the shimmering wall of light.

There was a dazzling explosion that erupted without sound. A ring of bright green light punched out from the glowing red wall.

"Again!" cried Rhymer. He was crawling toward her, his body broken and bleeding.

"No!" howled the prince of the elves. He yanked at her foot, tearing her sneaker off.

Stacey stabbed again, then raked the stone blade from top to bottom.

Across the line she made, the fiery light vanished.

She stabbed and stabbed.

Wherever the blade touched, the red wall disappeared.

The elf prince was still half in this world. One leg, one arm and shoulder, and his misshapen head. He roared at her and slashed her leg with his claws. Her blood seeded the air.

Then an arrow struck the clawing hand, pinning it to the ground for an instant before dissolving. But a second struck. And a third. Rhymer was on his knees, scooping up fallen arrows, tearing them from rotted corpses, and firing them as fast as he could nock and pull and release. They held him off for seconds, long enough for her to pull her leg out of the prince's reach.

The wall collapsed bit by bit. Line by glowing line, shrinking in on the struggling Yvag.

Rhymer fired a final arrow, and it struck the elf in the left eye and knocked him backward through the fiery wall, out of this world and back into his own or into hell. Which it was, Stacey did not know and did not care. She swept her arm up into the remaining angry hole, and that other place vanished.

The sneaker torn from her lay on the mound like some failed sacrifice.

Overhead, clouds scudded across the sky, and birdsong echoed from the woods below. Had the fenced site not looked like an overturned cemetery, it might have been a lovely afternoon.

She heard Rhymer's bow thud to the dirt, and as she collapsed onto the rocky ground the sacred stone slipped from her fingers, struck on its edge, and rolled away into the grass. It lay there, looking like any other polished black stone.

12

Thomas Rhymer did not call an ambulance or any other aid.

As darkness closed over Stacey, she was half aware that he was dragging her up the slope toward the parked Bentley.

When she opened her eyes for a moment, the light outside had changed. Rough bandages were wrapped around her wounds. She wasn't bleeding, but she didn't know if she had any blood left to lose. She lay in the plush backseat of the Bentley watching treetops flicker past the windows. She had only one red sneaker on, but her other foot was bathed in enough blood that it almost looked like a match.

She said, "Where are we?" Managed to turn her head enough to see him.

Rhymer was hunched over the wheel, his face gray, his fists white-knuckle tight on the wheel. He did not have the strength to answer.

"Oh, well, that's fine then." Darkness came for Stacey and took her down again.

13

The café was quiet. The waiter came and poured fresh coffee into their cups, murmured something in French, and walked away. Traffic whisked back and forth, but no one seemed to be in a hurry.

The bandages beneath her long sleeves chafed, the stitches itched. They would have to come out soon.

Stacey sipped her coffee, wincing at the pain in her lip. It had been split and was taking its own sweet time to heal. Rhymer wore sunglasses even at night. A broken nose had given him black eyes.

People walked by, some of them laughing, a few hand in hand.

"Is he gone?" she asked. It was not the first time she'd asked the question since that day. For a lot of that time Rhymer had remained silent, morose, lost in his own inner darkness.

This time he answered her. "We hurt him," he said softly. "That's the most you can say for certain. He's not like most of the Yvag. He's royalty. I'm not sure if he *can* die." He paused a moment. "But either he steps into the well of the damned or someone else of his bloodline has tae. 'You'll scream for a thousand years' was nae hyperbole."

"God . . ."

"At the very least a princeling of the elves has been wounded by a mortal, a woman, and that's only happened once before in the whole history of the world, to my knowledge." He added sugar to his coffee, stirred as if everything depended on it.

"Will it stop them?" she asked.

He shook his head. "It'll complicate things for them. Opening the gateway takes a lot of power. I . . . don't know if he can accomplish it with what we did to him. Others will, though, next time. And next time they'll come early to the party. You came dear."

She nodded and they sat together for a quarter hour without talking. Then she said, "Rhymer . . . I *was* the tithe."

"Aye."

"Now we spoiled that."

"Aye."

She looked around at the square. Paris glowed with life. "The Yvag said that my life would buy the safety of the whole world. Of all the worlds. Is that remotely true? Has saving me opened everyone up to something bad?"

"They sold you a lie tae make you cooperate in your own sacrifice. Their idea of fun."

"So . . . hell *won't* take revenge?"

Rhymer smiled. "Not on us, lass," he said. "Their bargain."

She opened her mouth to reply, but all she said was, "God . . ."

"Some believe that the Yvag were angels once," said Rhymer. "When certain angels revolted, God ordered that the gates of heaven and hell be shut. Any angels left in heaven became the true and sanctified angels. Those who were shut into hell became demons. But there were many who were trapped in the worlds between."

"And they became the Yvag?"

"According to that version of things." He nodded. "Not pure enough for heaven but not evil enough for hell." He laughed. "More like us than they want to believe."

"Or . . . maybe they *do* believe," she suggested. "Maybe that's why they mess with our world so much."

He considered it, sipped his coffee awhile before speaking again. "As I said, that's one version of it. The tithe paid is to stay free from hell. As fallen angels they belong to hell, and the tithe buys their freedom."

"So . . . why would hell take it out on us if the tithe isn't paid?"

"It wouldn't. And that's your version of them filtered through Christian theology. I know a deal more. They're older than our religions. Older than our race, maybe our world."

She thought about that. "Hell will go after the Yvag, then?"

"Aye. It's a war they cannae hope tae win. But hell . . ." He looked grimly at some memory. "Hell is like nothing Christianity ever dreamed up, and vaster than worlds."

"The well of the damned?"

His mouth twitched at her repeating his own phrase back at him. "The universe balances on a knife edge."

"So saving me you forced an immortal creature to sacrifice itself to buy the Yvag time?"

"Which runs differently in their world between worlds. But, aye. The span until the next *teind* comes due."

A cold wind seemed to blow among the tables. "Twenty-eight years, you said."

"Your being their tithe is done now. The mark on you is no good to them anymore. Like the one on me."

"Then I'm safe, am I?" She knew the answer but needed to hear it laid out.

Rhymer's mouth pulled tight with sadness and weariness. "They won't come after you as their tithe, no," he said quietly. "But the Yvag are a bitter race. You injured their prince. Maybe slew him. They'll ne'er forgive you. Never stop hunting you."

Stacey felt like she wanted to cry, but she didn't. She'd known it already.

Instead she asked, "You said only one woman has ever injured a prince of the Yvag before."

"I did."

"Who was it?"

He finished his coffee, then looked into the cup, head bowed. When she thought he wasn't going to say anything, he replied, "Someone that mattered. A long, long time ago."

"And you've been running from them and fighting them, what, ever since?"

"Ever since."

"Alone?"

"It's not a journey ye . . . Of course, alone."

She reached across the table and took his hand. "Well, not anymore."

He smiled at her, but there was so much sorrow in that smile that Stacey knew that behind the sunglasses his eyes weren't participating. She turned and looked away, looked out at the passing traffic on the rue de Rivoli. Every once in a while one of the people in the passing cars would catch her eye. The looks were brief, except sometimes they went on just a second too long.

Rhymer squeezed her hand, and they sat in silence as the world turned around them.

SHE, DOOMED GIRL

Sarah MacLean and Carrie Ryan

I stood alone in the gray, surrounded by cloud.

My throat burned and my eyes watered as the frigid wind snapped at my face. I'd never felt emptier in my life. It was like that sensation you have after waking up from a dream, when your emotions are still trapped somewhere else and all you're left with is a feeling that you don't understand.

Sure, I'd left everything behind when I'd stepped onto the ferry, but I hadn't expected it to hurt like this. There'd been nothing keeping me in my old life—nothing I couldn't bring with me.

Nothing that wouldn't be forgotten.

Silently I cursed the airline for losing my luggage, leaving me to finish the trip with only my purse and a handful of change.

And a deed. And a key.

And no idea what I was getting myself into.

"You're headed for the castle."

The voice startled me, coming from the fog like in some old gothic movie, where the terrifying Vincent Price character growls the words, all skeletal angles and crooked fingers. But I wasn't in a gothic movie. I was on a boat. In Scotland. And despite the rolling fog that had come down off the hills and pooled in dark cinematic swirls along the banks of the North Sea, hiding both the land I'd left and the place to which I was headed, there was nothing gothic about the bearded Scotsman in front of me.

There was nothing skeletal about him, either.

I swiped at my eyes to clear them, but the bitter wind drew fresh tears. It was obvious looking at the Scotsman that he'd spent his lifetime out on these waters. His cheeks were weathered red from the sting of cold salt air whipping across the deck of the ferry and his words disappeared into a laugh that betrayed a lifetime of whiskey and cigarettes.

I wrapped my arms around myself, bracing against the wind and wishing I had the winter coat I'd packed when I left Los Angeles. The Scotsman was wearing one of those beautiful, warm fisherman's sweaters—the ones that are probably knitted using wool spun from the sheep outside the house. The ones you don't need in Southern California—but that you absolutely need here. I'd have to buy one tomorrow.

Now, I just wanted to get to where I needed to go. I was tired. And I wanted a bed. I'd always been a terrible traveler, and I couldn't remember the last time I'd slept.

The man stared at me, expecting an answer. His eyes gleamed nearly silver in the strange light of dusk and the bleak, gray sea, and I realized that I'd forgotten what he said. "I'm sorry," I said, shaking my head, "I didn't—"

"I said, you're headed for the castle."

I nodded, feeling numb. At least there was good news in that he'd confirmed there would be a castle at the end of this trip.

At least that hadn't been a lie.

"I'm Charlie." He extended one hand, the size of a Christmas ham, and added, "Charlie MacLaron. And you're Emily."

My hand stilled inside his massive grip.

"How did you know that?" I mean, this might be quiet Scotland, and this guy might be wearing a sweater no doubt knitted by his loving wife, but it didn't mean a girl shouldn't be careful.

He grinned then, revealing a gold-capped tooth. "Few make it all this way on their own," he said, as though it explained everything. "I've been keeping an eye out for you."

I suppose it made sense. The key and the deed to the castle had been left for me a few days earlier, and while I didn't know much about castles or land, I did know that it wasn't every day a waitress living paycheck to paycheck was given a castle on an island halfway around the world. Add to it the fact that this place didn't seem to be a booming, bustling metropolis, and I should expect a fair amount of curiosity and gossip.

The wind blew again, harder than before, bitterly cold, knocking me off balance, toward him. Charlie laughed, reaching out to steady me, and said, "Don't have legs for the boat yet? You'll get them. There's plenty of time."

I shoved my purse high on my shoulder. "How long is the ride?"

His eyes lit up. "As long as it takes, lassie."

I faked a smile and looked away. Now was not the time to tell my new neighbor he was more frustrating than funny. I wrapped my arms around myself once more, trying to rub feeling back into them. "In that case, I really wish I had a coat." When he didn't reply, I added, "They lost my luggage."

"You've lost more than that," he said.

I snapped my attention back to him. "What did you say?"

He was looking out over the prow of the ferry, toward the bank of fog that marked our destination. A wide, blank future. Untouched. Pure.

Paradise.

"I said you've lost more than your luggage. You've lost your way."

I have.

"What makes you say that?"

"You're on a boat in the North Sea with nothing but the clothes on your back and a key to a castle. It's not exactly ordinary."

He was right, of course. I opened my mouth. Closed it. Opened it again. "It was a gift."

He looked back to the shore. "Was it, now?"

He wasn't talking about the key or the deed to Castle Anaon, and neither was I. The trip had been a gift. The change. The offer to walk away from everything I was. Everything I had.

Which wasn't much.

Which was nothing.

And the day it all came to a head and I realized that I had nothing—that I was in danger of becoming nothing—everything had changed.

My grandmother used to have a silly saying about doors and windows. I always thought it was the kind of thing that poor women said to keep hope alive. But in that moment, as I'd stared down at the old, weathered piece of paper and the large brass key on the linoleum countertop at Sal's Truck Stop Café—which was neither a truck stop nor a café nor owned by someone named Sal—I'd heard that stupid saying whispering in my ear.

A castle.

Escape.

"What are you running from?" Charlie said. "If you don't mind my asking."

The question made it seem like I was on the lam—like I'd done something terrible. Maybe I had. Maybe I had wanted too much. Loved too hard. Let myself believe that happily ever after was real.

After I'd been punished for it, a stranger had marched right into Sal's Truck Stop Café and opened a window. One that looked out onto the mist-covered banks of the North Sea.

So here I was—to start over. To try again. To be reborn.

Somehow, Charlie's question still hung in the air. *What are you running from?*

Trust. Love.

I finally settled on, "Truth."

"Sounds like something that you run toward."

I smiled. "Maybe I'm doing that, too."

"Well, if you're to find it, then here's where it'll be."

The Scots loved their Scotland, that much was true. I reached into my pocket, fingering the heavy brass key that now seemed like the only thing that hadn't been left or lost on this long, unyielding journey. "I hope so."

The ship lurched at the words, giving a great, heaving groan and sending me to one knee as Charlie cursed. "It always shocks the hell out of me, that," he said, helping me up.

When I was on my feet again, I asked, "What happened?"

"We've run aground. The tides are never where they should be on this side."

It occurred to me that tides are regular as . . . well, tides . . . and that ferries have schedules, but it seemed not the appropriate time to question the ferryman's knowledge of his trade.

"We're here?" I looked past him to the shoreline, where the fog was thick enough to shield everything but the dock.

"Aye, you're here."

I started forward, getting only a few steps before I turned back to Charlie. "I didn't pay you."

He looked at me for a long moment with his strange silver eyes and said, "No, you didn't."

"What do I owe you?" I asked, reaching into my pocket and extracting a handful of change, holding it out to him in that way that tourists do when they don't entirely understand how a new currency works.

I'm not really a tourist now, I had to remind myself. *This is my new home.*

Home.

There was something in the word. Something that felt at once good and right and strange and desperate.

There was no time to dissect the feelings before Charlie leaned forward and picked through the coins in my hand, extracting two heavy golden pieces. "That'll do." He then nodded toward shore. "Up the path to the castle."

I followed his directions and was halfway down the dock when he called out to me. "Emily!"

I turned back, fog swirling around me, cold and wet and fresh on my skin, to find him peering at me intently. "Yes?"

"Sometimes it's best for everyone if you don't look back."

And then he turned away to tend to his boat and I stood in confused silence trying to understand what he meant. The moment was broken when a large man jostled past me on his way down the dock. I pressed myself against the railing to let him pass, but not before my legs were tangled in the leashes of the trio of Labradors following him toward the ferry.

"Wait!" I called out, not wanting to pitch face-first onto the dock, and not wanting to crush the smallest dog—a sweet-faced black puppy who sat the moment I spoke, staring up at me with the most loyal of faces. "I'm caught in your dogs," I added, carefully trying to extract myself from the leashes.

The middle dog, full grown and eager, leaped up at me, his massive black paws catching the strap of my purse and pulling it off my shoulder. It fell to the ground, the contents spilling everywhere. The grayed muzzle of the third dog extended to the bag, sniffing at the honeyed almonds I'd packed for the journey. I snatched them away before he could claim his prize and shoved everything back into the bag.

The dogs' owner didn't say anything, instead waiting patiently until I was clear of the leashes before turning without a word to board the boat, dogs following along behind him.

"Charming," I said under my breath, turning back to the dock, which led to a dirt road and, not too far away, a narrow path that disappeared into a thicket of willow trees. It didn't look inviting.

Few things dark and foreboding ever do.

A sharp shiver of unease sent goose bumps crawling along my spine. Perhaps this entire trip wasn't a good idea after all. I turned back toward the ferry, intending to ask Charlie to take me back across, but the shore was empty. Only a soft sweep of fog curled against the dock in the boat's wake—the tide must have risen fast.

The yipping of his passenger's dogs faded as they began the return journey to the other side of the North Sea.

And, like that, alone on the bank, something felt off. Terribly so. Like I'd forgotten something important.

My sanity, perhaps?

Whatever it was, it was too late now. Charlie had left, which meant I was stuck. Unless I wanted to swim. I took a step toward where the dark water lapped against the shore and was just about to dip my fingers in to test the temperature when I laughed.

I was in Scotland—the very *north* of Scotland, where it may as well have been the Arctic. There was no way I could swim back to the mainland. If I didn't die of hypothermia, I'd disappear into the fog never to be seen again.

And if that happened, who would even know I was missing? Charlie? The stranger who'd left me the key?

There was no one else. *How could that be?*

I had only one option, and it was forward. As Charlie had said, sometimes it's better to not look back.

Ahead, the path loomed, waiting for me. Tendrils of fog spilled from the sea and seeped into the forest, leading the way like a campy horror set. What did I have to lose?

Nothing.

Everything important, I'd lost a long time ago.

With a sigh I shifted my heavy purse from one shoulder to the other and began walking. The ground underfoot was soggy, and within a few steps my shoes were wet, my toes almost frozen.

I silently added wool socks to the list of supplies I'd need to buy whenever I figured out where the nearest town was. In the distance I heard what sounded like sheep bleating, and I shook my head, fervently hoping I wouldn't be expected to rely on them for my new attire. I didn't know how to knit.

The trek through the forest seemed endless, and more than once I feared I was walking in circles. Maybe this was some sort of elaborate prank. Of course I'd already wondered this before—more than once. The moment I'd seen the deed, the first thing I'd asked was, "Is this a joke?"

But then I'd picked up the brass key lying on the countertop, and it had just felt . . . right. Something in my head had whispered, *home,* and I'd known this was where I needed to go.

And, just like that, the path ended and I found myself on the edge of a mist-shrouded field. Something dark loomed ahead, a shadow through the fog. A sharp wind blew from the forest behind me, carrying with it the moaning sound of poplar trees bending until they ached.

"That's ominous," I murmured to myself. And then I had no words because the clouds cleared and I caught my first glimpse of the castle.

I burst out laughing. I'd assumed *castle* had just been a fancy word for "impressive house." I'd been expecting something modest—perhaps nothing more than a quaint Scottish cottage.

I'd been wrong.

This thing was one hell of a castle.

A wall of weathered dark stone rose several stories from the ground, all climbing vines and heavy oak doors and thick windows that hid as much as they revealed. The place was immense and looked like it came straight out of a fairy tale, complete with towers and turrets and crenellations.

There was no way this was mine. Things like this didn't happen in real life—not to people like me.

What else could I do but head for it? I'd come all this way . . . taken all this risk. As I approached the immense wooden door, dotted with heavy iron nails from top to bottom, I pulled the brass key out of my pocket. It had seemed so large in the diner—bigger even than my hand—but now, in comparison to the door and the castle looming above, it was downright tiny.

Holding my breath, I slipped it into the lock and turned. "No. Way," I muttered when the door swung open. The gray light from outside spilled into the dim interior, revealing a threadbare rug and a tarnished suit of armor propped against the wall.

The castle. Had a suit of armor.

Of course it did.

Suddenly, I felt giddy. Ridiculously so. It was like that first moment you open the door to a hotel room on vacation and you have no idea what lies ahead but you know it's going to be awesome.

And this castle was so much more than awesome. My jaw dropped when I stepped inside. The ceiling in the front hall was so high it was lost in darkness. The walls were covered in ancient-looking tapestries and dusty paintings of scowling men wearing kilts and brandishing intimidating weapons. On the far side of the room a curved staircase with an elaborately carved banister swept toward the second floor.

I clapped my hands, no longer frozen, no longer wet, no longer hungry, no longer interested in anything but deciding where to explore first, when a dark, booming voice stopped me cold.

"What are you doing in my house?"

My heart exploded, fear making me light-headed. I jumped back, stumbling into an antique side table. The table tipped and crashed to the ground, one of the legs splintering.

I winced as the sound echoed through the house.

A curse came harsh and wicked from the darkness, and out of the corner of my eye I caught sight of a shadow moving at the top of the stairs. Coming closer.

A complete stranger.

A male stranger, judging by the voice.

He took his time, moving purposefully, step by step, until I thought my heart would beat from my chest in equal parts panic, terror, and something less ominous—something like desperation.

I glanced around the room, looking for anything I could use to defend myself. My eyes fell on the suit of armor, its hands clutched around an ax. Without thinking, I leaped for it, wrenching it free. It was heavier than I expected, and it took all my strength to face him, brandishing the weapon.

"Don't come any closer."

He reached the bottom of the stairs and stopped, just beyond the reach of light from the open door. His shadow spoke. "That ax is four centuries old and designed for someone much stronger than you."

"I think I can handle it," I replied with bravado I didn't feel, even as my muscles protested the heavy weight. He stayed in the darkness. *Good.* "Now why don't you tell me what you're doing in *my* house?"

He didn't say anything, but his shadow moved, crouching over a nearby table. *Looking for a weapon, probably.* I was going to have to duel with this man. Using an ax. And he would no doubt have something more useful. Something portable. And mechanized.

The stink of sulfur rose in the air as he lit a candelabrum there—I watched as flame burst over five tapered candles, all with a single match. I would have singed myself more than once, but his long, graceful fingers didn't waver in their task. I was transfixed by the play of candlelight over those fingers, and the hands to which they were attached—the rise and hollow of muscle and vein, the strong knuckles and long bones.

And that was all before I got to his face.

Good Lord. He was stunning—all dark hair that looked like thick sable, skin bright and bronzed in the candlelight, and cheeks and jaw and brow strong and powerful like some kind of statue—a Greek god. A Roman athlete.

Except there were things about him that weren't so perfect: a scar above one eye, long and wicked; a mouth set in a cruel line, like he'd never in his life smiled; and cold, gray eyes filled with weariness. With tragedy.

Why?

No. I wasn't transfixed. I wouldn't be transfixed.

He was an intruder. In my house, lighting my candles.

And he must be stopped.

I hefted the ax with renewed vigor. "Are you a squatter?"

One side of his mouth twitched, just barely. "I appear to be standing."

This wasn't a joke to me. "I have a key."

"Where did you get it?"

"I—" Wait. I didn't have to answer him. "It doesn't matter, as I also have a deed."

"I assure you, not to this castle."

I raised a brow. "No, you're right of course. To a different castle. Scotland is, I'm sure, overrun with castles just waiting to be inhabited."

"It is, rather," he said.

I ignored him. "Look, whoever you are, this is *my* castle. You're trespassing."

"Where is this deed?" He sighed, as though it was he who was put out and not I—exhausted, without my luggage, my only worldly possessions a half-eaten package of almonds, a pocketful of change, and an ax.

"I'd get it for you, but as you can see, my hands are occupied."

A very heavy ax.

"You can put it down, you know. I don't plan on attacking you."

"Would you tell me if you were?"

"Probably not."

Oddly, his honesty was a comfort. I let the ax fall to my side with a heavy thud. "How long have you been living here?"

"Long enough to know that you shouldn't be here." With that, he turned away. Taking the light with him into the dark bowels of the castle, leaving me no choice but to follow, ax trailing behind me, through the massive entryway and down a long, unlit corridor to an enormous library, spanning two huge floors with a balcony of bookshelves that stretched high above us. I caught my breath inside the door.

He turned to face me at the noise. I shrugged my shoulders and said, "What every little girl dreams of."

He placed the candelabrum on a desk littered with papers and sat in a large wing chair. "You like books."

In hindsight, I should have been surprised that the words weren't a question, but there was a fire roaring in the fireplace, and he had already stretched his long legs toward the heat, the wool of his trousers pulling tight over muscled thighs and knees, shielding the tops of his shoes. He wore a fine white linen shirt, sleeves rolled to the elbow, collar open to reveal a perfect triangle of skin.

The man was dressed for business and draped in wealth. He was no squatter. "Your deed," he said, extending one long arm toward me as though saying the words could produce the document.

And they could, apparently, as I was already reaching for my purse. Extracting the paper, I passed it to him. He looked at it, turning it over, inspecting every inch of it before setting it down on his great mahogany desk. *My desk*. "Where did you get this?"

I inched toward him, dragging the ax along the floor. "I was left the deed and the key."

He looked bored. "An inheritance?"

"Not exactly." *Not at all.*

"How, exactly?"

"As a tip."

His eyes widened, and if I wasn't mistaken, there was a hint of laughter buried in their depths. "As in, a gratuity? For services rendered?"

It hadn't seemed so insane until he said it aloud. My cheeks suddenly felt warm. "Yes."

"For what kind of services?" The question was filled with lascivious curiosity, and warm quickly became hot.

"Not what you're thinking, I assure you!" I crossed my arms at his disbelieving expression. No wonder this man lived alone in a castle. He was insufferable. "Someone should shave that eyebrow right off your head."

"That happened to me once," he said, the smile edging toward fondness. "All right . . . you are not a lady of the evening."

"I am not."

"The gratuity, then?"

"I'm a waitress."

He stilled. "A waitress."

I nodded.

"And someone gave you a castle."

"Yes."

"In exchange for soup."

I scowled at him. "And a sandwich."

He let out a big, booming laugh. "Let me guess, a woman wearing red gave it to you."

"How did you know that?"

"The same way I know she gave you the key."

Nerves made it easy for me to steel my voice and repeat myself. "How did you know that?"

Instead of answering, he turned away and poured himself a glass of amber liquid from a large crystal decanter on a nearby sideboard. A brief smile played across his lips as he lifted the glass into the air and murmured, "Giving a castle to a waitress as a tip—fairly inventive."

He downed the scotch and poured himself another, without offering me one. After a sip, he leaned back against the sideboard, swirling the glass lazily in his hand. In the candlelight the scar slashing through his eyebrow appeared stark and severe.

"How did you know that the woman who gave me the key was wearing red?" I said, clenching my hands by my side.

The stranger grinned, but it was not a grin of mirth. His eyes bored into me. "Lucky guess?"

Before I could argue, he cut me off. It was like a switch had been thrown, and whereas before he'd begun to soften, he'd once again turned cold and immovable.

"You should leave here. Now."

Maybe he was right. But I wasn't going anywhere. "No."

He turned on me, gray eyes flashing. "You can't imagine where you are. What has brought you here. You don't belong here."

"You don't know that," I said.

"I know you're lost," he spat out. "I know you have traveled an immense distance—farther than you've ever gone in your life because you're afraid of where you've been and even more afraid of where you are going. And I know it never occurred to you that where you were going might be worse. That *here* might be worse."

His words startled me, and I hated him then, this dark, handsome stranger in his stupid gothic castle.

My stupid gothic castle.

He didn't seem to care, turning away. "You took the last ferry to the coldest, dreariest place in Scotland, Emily—to an isle at the end of the earth—and you thought that you'd find rainbows and faeries on the banks of the North Sea, all because some red-dressed bitch whispered a promise that offered you escape from the life you lived." He drank, finishing the scotch and setting the glass down next to the castle deed before he added, "Following whispered promises isn't brave adventure. It's sheer idiocy."

For a moment the room was silent. In the distance came the far-off sound of something howling—a dog baying for its master. The sound brought the stranger's attention back to me, the mask dropped from his face. His eyes glistened with something familiar.

Pain.

"You should leave this place and never come back."

Cold raced up my spine. "How do you know my name?"

In two steps he was in front of me, his hand held out as though to cup my cheek but his fingers never quite reaching me. "Oh, Emily . . ." he whispered.

Did he think it was a game? That I was a pawn, willing to be maneuvered?

No. I was through being maneuvered. And this man was obviously everything that was wrong in my life. But I had a key and a deed, and if he wanted some fight, he'd get it. I'd get a lawyer. I'd fight for this.

Like I'd never fought before.

" . . . You fall for it every time."

The words stung. I wanted to throw something at him. Wanted to clear the desk in a single dramatic gesture, sending his ordered papers and pens to the floor. Wanted to plant the ax that was still in my hand into the center of the heavy mahogany, through deed and blotter and centuries-old wood.

But I didn't. Instead I lifted my deed from the desk, folded it carefully, placed it into my back pocket, and said, "I'll take idiocy over isolation any day."

I stormed from the room, leaving the ax and the man.

I'd just made it to the front door when he caught up with me. "Stop," he said, as though he'd never had to make a request in his life.

I yanked open the heavy oak and stepped into the rain that had blossomed in the minutes since I'd entered the castle. His hand closed around my arm. "Where are you going?"

Without bothering to answer, I wrenched free and stormed down the path marked by poplars and willows toward the boat landing.

"The ferry won't be back tonight."

I kept walking.

"The castle is the only thing on the island!" he called out.

The rain intensified. I turned back. "What?"

He emerged from the fog, inches from me. "The island is all deeded to the castle."

I blinked. "So you're the only one here?"

"Yes."

"Nowhere else to stay?"

"No."

A gust of icy wind whipped around us, my hair coming loose from its moorings and whipping my face like a harsh, stinging lash. "Where am I supposed to sleep?"

He looked as furious as I felt. "I think the better question is where are you *going* to sleep."

"Not with you."

"I do not recall inviting you."

I narrowed my gaze. "A good thing, too. I wouldn't if we were the last two people on earth."

He leaned in close enough that I could feel the warmth of his breath against my lips. "If I could do so, I would leave you out here to spend the night with the wolves and the rain. Maybe that way, you'd resolve to leave here forever."

Something lodged in my throat—fear perhaps. Because I didn't think he was joking. A shiver passed through me at how callous this man could be, if he wanted to.

And I was alone with him. Great.

He turned away and headed back through the fog, which seemed to have thickened in the mere minutes that we'd been outside. The rain began in earnest now, and that's what pushed me over the edge; I'd trade my pride to be warm and dry. I had to follow the godforsaken man or get lost on this godforsaken island in this godforsaken weather.

What an idiot I was.

Once we were back inside the castle, the door tightly closed, he lifted the candlestick from a nearby table and started up the large winding staircase toward the upper levels.

I didn't follow, watching him go, taking light and warmth with him, until he spoke again, the heavy, dark words falling down toward me. "Do you want a bed? Or not?"

Like that, I was bone tired, as though the word *bed* were all it took to make me ache for sleep. It filled me with a desperate desire for rest. For peace. And like a stray animal, I followed him, desperate for the promise in the words, even as I hated myself for giving in to him.

Even as I hated him for having power over me.

For making me need.

I stared at the ceiling, my eyes burning from lack of sleep. Wind pummeled against the castle, howling almost as though it were otherworldly. Of course it was storming. As if this night and this place weren't foreboding enough already. I snuggled deeper under the covers of my bed, but that did nothing to block out the flashes of lightning.

My jaw ached from clenching my teeth, maybe from the storm, maybe from the man . . . but every muscle tense, waiting for the next clap of thunder. For another wave of fury thinking of his words—of his insults. Whispered promises. Silly dreams.

He was keeping me from sleep. He, who claimed the castle belonged to him, and who looked so much like he belonged to it.

He, who'd laughed when I'd told him about the deed and the diner.

He, who hadn't bothered to tell me his name. Who was rude, inhospitable, brooding. Who'd all but promised he'd rather leave me to the wolves.

He, who had shown me to the room and closed the door, saying nothing. Offering no comfort, no apology.

But those weren't the things that kept me from sleep. Instead, it was the gray eyes, the square jaw, the wicked scar across his brow. The cords and sinew of his hands and forearms. All things I shouldn't have noticed.

The sound of my name on his lips.

All things that shouldn't be keeping me from sleep.

In despair, I crawled from the bed, pulling a warm tartan around my shoulders and heading for the window to look out on Scotland. On this place that had held so much promise. Closed doors. Opened windows. But tomorrow I'd no doubt find myself without a home, without my luggage, and without a way back to L.A.

Not that there was anything waiting there for me anyway.

Why did that suddenly feel like such a betrayal? It wasn't the stranger's fault I'd made this choice and walked into what was increasingly seeming like at best a prank and at worst a trap. He owed me nothing.

He owes me everything.

The thought stilled me, my breath catching. I felt my pulse thrumming through my fingers.

It was a ridiculous thought.

Thunder crashed, loud and close, like hell itself was just beyond the castle battlements. Needing to distract myself, I moved to the window and pushed aside the curtain. Rain washed against the mottled glass, wind howling through unseen holes in the walls. The room felt colder, and I pulled the tartan closer, willing the wool to keep me warm. Failing.

Just as I was turning back to the bed, lightning streaked across the sky, and everything outside shone as though lit by the sun. Wild, wide fields rolled toward the forest beyond, the willows there a twisted tangle.

Darkness fell again, the landscape burned against my eyes, and it was only then—in the ghost of the image—that I realized I'd seen something moving outside.

More than something.

A sick feeling crawled up the back up my throat.

You're imagining things, I told myself. I was exhausted from lack of sleep and the feeling that I'd been traveling forever.

I tried to force myself back to bed, but I couldn't move. Thunder rolled, hitting the castle with a physical force that vibrated through my body like an earthquake. But there was another noise too. Something creaking. I'd heard it before in the forest, the wind bending the trees, but now the sound was too close.

My hands shook as I reached to check the latch on the window. As soon as my fingers fumbled on the lock, lightning struck again. The world turned bright. I immediately wished for darkness.

Dogs everywhere. Not just dogs. Massive black beasts, their coats darker than midnight of a new moon and their eyes a glowing red that sought me out. As the storm gathered strength and the ground shook, the demented-looking dogs spilled from the forest and slunk toward the castle.

And then a woman appeared, stepping from the fold of trees. For the barest moment I wanted to shout a warning, but as she passed through the hounds she traced her fingers over their backs and none moved to attack her.

She stopped in the middle of the field and looked up toward my window. As one, the hounds threw back their heads and let loose their tormented howls. I could hear them through the walls.

And in the sound I heard my name.

I recoiled and the window blew open. Lightning continued to streak across the sky, illuminating the world like a strobe light that echoed the wild pattern of my heart. I recognized the woman and the red of her cloak.

She was leading the creatures closer. They were coming for me. There were no barriers between us anymore.

Only an open window.

I let the scream come, a single word—the only one I knew. "Owen!"

I WOKE SOAKING wet and cradled in his arms. He whispered into my hair, over and over, the words soft and nonsensical, and rocked me, wrapped strong and solid and safe around me, one hand stroking the hair from my face, and for a moment, I allowed myself to sink into the solid comfort of him. The warmth of him. The way he smelled of rain and ruin and truth.

Owen.

At the memory of the name, I scrambled from his lap, hating the way I went cold at the loss of his touch. I wrapped my arms across my chest. "What are you doing here?"

A hint of hesitation crossed his face. "You had a nightmare."

I glanced toward the window, now closed, the only sign of the storm the still-damp floor. Tentatively, I crossed the room and peered outside. Though the moon was new and the sky mostly black, the rain had eased enough that I could see the grounds below. Nothing.

Normal.

No woman. No hounds.

But it had all felt so desperately real. I shivered. There had been more to the dream—something that had come before, but the harder I tried to remember, the more it slipped from my grasp.

I stared back at Owen. Shook my head. Not his name. He hadn't told me his name.

Even though he knew mine.

The dream—it had something to do with him. Something wonderful and sad at once. I recalled feeling betrayed, but had that been in the dream? Or had it come when I was still awake?

"What are you looking for?" He gestured toward the window.

"I thought I saw . . ." I began, but stopped. Why should he care about my dreams?

He never had before.

"What did you see?" he pressed.

He would laugh, but I couldn't stop myself. The words were a whisper. Like they had come from the trees. "There were these horrible beasts—some kind of dog. They were led by a woman wearing red." I paused, swallowing. "The one who gave me the key."

He didn't laugh.

He stood then. Came toward me. I stiffened before he could reach me and give us both what we wanted. He stopped inches away, warmth pouring from him, a promise. Something had happened in the night. Something had brought us to this moment.

Somehow, I knew him.

I shook my head. "How did I know your name?"

He stepped closer, nearly touching. Not touching.

Owen.

"Because you're remembering, Emily." He said my name like he'd said it a hundred times before. A thousand.

We stared at each other, he the only anchor in a spinning world.

"Have we met before?" I asked, hoping there would be an easy explanation. "In L.A.? Somewhere else?"

Silence.

"You should change out of your wet clothes," he murmured. "I'll make tea."

And then he left.

I found a thick cashmere robe in the closet along with a pair of shearling slippers and headed for the kitchen with my heart pounding in my chest. I knew the way through the castle, the turns through the twisting corridors familiar, natural, like I'd been navigating the halls for a lifetime. For longer.

When I stepped into the warm glow of the kitchen to find Owen at the stove, it was all so . . . simple. Safe.

And then he turned to me, his gray eyes serious as they scanned my body, lighting with something at once familiar and foreign, and I didn't feel safe anymore. I felt naked. I tugged the sash tighter, ran a hand through my tangled hair, nervous.

His.

Where had that come from? We'd only just met . . . we'd never . . .

But somehow, *we had.*

He was staring at me, knowledge in the hint of a smile curling the corners of his mouth. His feet were bare, and the waist of his gray wool trousers hung low on his hips. I imagined slipping a finger into his pocket and dragging him closer, pressing my face to the warm hollow of his neck. Breathing him in. Turning my face up to his.

I knew how he would taste.

My stomach flooded with warmth.

But my spinning mind was still uneasy.

On the stove a teakettle screamed, breaking the moment. I didn't know what question to ask—each one I formulated seemed too preposterous to force past my lips. He didn't seem to be quite ready to volunteer any information, and for a while we went about the kitchen in silence, wary. I pulled down the mugs and set out a plate of cookies. He snatched the empty cookie bag from me and tipped it over my tea, tapping in a handful of crumbs.

I gasped at the gesture, and his gaze snapped to meet mine. A flush colored his cheeks. "I'm sorry," he said, reaching to clear the mug. I stopped him, my hand on his arm.

"How did you know?" I whispered.

"You crumble cookies in your tea."

Without my realizing it, we'd spent the past few minutes in a sort of dance, moving around each other in the kitchen as though we'd lived out this pattern a thousand times before. Kettles and stoves and cream and biscuits.

He'd told me I was remembering, but remembering what?

I met his eyes. "How do we know each other?" Images raced through my head, and I began to pace. "How do I know that you love blackberry tarts? That you shave with a straight razor? That you like Shelley?" Poetry came to me like lightning. "*He does no longer sit upon his throne of rock upon a desert herbless plain.*" He closed his eyes at the words. "You've recited it." I put my hand to the scarred oak worktable in the center of the kitchen. "Here."

With me.

My heart ached with the memory. With the words, full of promise, full of hope, full of happiness. With the loss of them. I looked to him. "But how?"

He was close enough to touch now, big and broad, blocking out the world as he lifted his hand and touched my face, running the tips of those strong, remarkable fingers over my cheek and down my jaw, taking me in hand. Tilting me toward him.

I was gone, lost in his gray gaze, filled with time and truth and heat and something more . . . something I didn't dare identify.

I felt it too.

When he kissed me, I was home.

There was nothing tentative about the kiss; it was filled with knowledge of where we'd been, of what we liked, of how we fit. It was touch and breath and heat, his arms around me, my hands in his hair, and I was robbed of all thoughts save one—

This was truth.

This moment was all I'd ever wanted. All I'd lived for. This was the promise for which I'd come. This man. This place.

He broke the kiss, trailing his lips across my cheek to my ear, his breath warm and harsh there, my name coming in dark, liquid syllables, a benediction. A curse.

"Emily," he whispered, his strong, warm, remarkable hand stroking down my neck, beneath the collar of my robe, setting me on fire with sound and scent and touch until I couldn't bear it anymore.

I gasped and pulled back. "How do I know you? Know this? I don't understand." But I did understand that I had never in my life wanted anything the way I wanted this man.

He knew it, one side of his lips lifting in a wicked smile before he took my mouth again, claiming me with softness and strength before he lifted his head, leaving us both breathing heavily.

He pressed his forehead to mine and spoke, the words low and desperate. "All you need to know—all you ever need to remember—is that I love you."

I DIDN'T KNOW how to respond.

I love you, too.

But that couldn't be. He was a stranger. I needed distance, and so I retreated, putting the table between us. I tried to stay calm, but my emotions ran too hot, everything in my head too bright. My question came out rushed. "Who are you?"

He took a deep breath, grasping the back of his neck with his hand.

And then a murky memory invaded my thoughts, turning the blood heavy in my veins. I ran from the room, Owen chasing after me, calling for me to wait as I tore through the castle, finding my way through the maze of corridors with ease.

I stopped in his office, panting, and heard Owen's steps slow as he approached me. His breath caught as he slipped his fingers into mine, giving comfort. Taking it.

"It's you," I whispered. The painting was ancient and larger than the rest, the color dulled with dust and age—two hundred years old—but the image was still clear. A man in hunting plaid, surrounded by poplar trees, Anaon in the background. He carried a rifle in one hand and a gray-muzzled black Lab sat by his side, a pheasant at his feet. Gray eyes. Strong jaw. One side of his mouth twisted in a tiny, almost imperceptible smile. One I loved.

I faced him and touched my finger to where a scar slashed through his eyebrow. It was the same as in the painting. Every detail exact.

He's a ghost.

The thought entered my mind like a whisper and then turned into a shout.

I shook my head.

Normal people don't think this way, I reminded myself. My life wasn't a gothic novel, no matter how many times I'd read *Wuthering Heights* and dreamed my way into Heathcliff's arms.

"What's happening?" I asked him, dreading the answer.

"How much do you remember?"

I shook my head, ready to say "nothing," but then I realized that wasn't true.

"Do you remember that each time you come to me with a different story? An art student wanting to catalog the castle's paintings. A hotelier hoping to find the perfect spot for a bed-and-breakfast . . . you've inherited from a long-lost cousin . . . *you were given the key as a tip.*" He laughed, the sound harsh and unamused. "Once you came to me as a horticulture specialist looking into a new species of poplar."

My brow furrowed.

"She has a terrible sense of humor. They all do. Sometimes you remember who you really are late into the night and sometimes you never do." His voice deepened. "And sometimes you remember early in the evening, like now."

I glanced around the study, gasping when my eyes landed on his massive desk. I walked over to it, spread my hands across the surface. "You've made love to me here." My cheeks burned red before the words left my mouth. "A dozen times."

"A hundred." He came up behind me, pulling my back against his chest. "I've made love to you everywhere in this castle, Emily," he whispered in my ear. If his arms hadn't been crossed around me, I'd have fallen. Not just from the words, but from the memories.

I nodded, the ache in my chest almost unbearable.

He spun me then, lifting me onto the desk and stepping between my legs. His lips took mine in a frustrated, furious kiss—one I gave in to without question.

After a long moment, he pulled me tight to him, as though he could hold me fast enough to keep the world at bay. The world—or whatever else was out there. "This castle is darkness," he spoke to the top of my head, with barely there sound. "You are light."

I clung to him, hating the words. The pain. The weariness. "This castle is a curse, Emily." His breath was hot against my neck, sweet in my ear. "And you are my savior."

My heart pounded, blood roared, and as he spoke, the memories tumbled through me.

He took my hand and placed it to his chest, at his heart. His gaze was hot, fierce. "We've been here before. Done all of this before." His fingertips curled into my hair, desperate. "Every evening you come to me, and every morning you leave."

No. Impossible.

He was everywhere: the smell of him, the feel of him, the taste of him, and I shook my head, desperate to clear my thoughts. To find reason. Logic.

None would be found, but I knew one thing. "I could never leave you. Not here." Not to this. Memories surged around me: Owen leading me up the staircase, Owen lowering me to his bed, Owen leaning over me, deliciously playful, then deliciously serious.

Night after night.

Again and again.

First pleasure beyond my wildest dreams, then anguish, so powerful that it took the breath from me. "Why?" The word was so simple, and yet I feared the answer wouldn't be easy. For a hush of a heartbeat, I thought I heard howling in the distance. I shuddered.

Owen pulled away from me, the answer on his face. He knelt in front of the fireplace, stoking the fire until it roared. "I'm not a good man, Emily," he said, "and every day . . . you realize it. And you leave."

His eyes were fixed on the flames. "You leave the way you did when I was alive."

I didn't want to believe it. But how else could I explain why I knew his name? How I knew the corridors of this place as though I'd lived here before? How else could I explain the way I felt in his arms? That I would give up everything to be near him?

"How?"

He wrapped his arms around me and buried his head in the crook of my neck. "All I know is that it is always dark and gray and cold. And when you arrive, you bring a taste of the sun with you."

All those years of loneliness . . . a lifetime of emptiness, and here, now, with him . . .

Home.

His eyes shone when he looked back up at me, his lips against mine in fevered, frenzied kisses, as though we were running out of time.

"Please, Emily . . ." His words broke and my tears spilled over, and I was filled with the fear and desperation pouring from him. "Don't leave me. Not again. Not this time."

Or maybe it was me talking. Maybe it was me, my lips against his, and the words, "I love you. Please, don't let me go."

Or maybe it was both of us.

I COULD HEAR his heartbeat as we lay together, and it occurred to me that he shouldn't have a heartbeat. Nor should his skin feel warm on sturdy bone and threaded muscle. Nor should he bring the kind of deep, undeniable comfort that he brought.

We were wrapped in a hunting plaid I remembered from other places—stunning green and black in his portrait, and on the bed in which I started the night, and draped across a chair in the library. It was warm enough beneath the tightly woven wool for us to spread out across the mammoth bed, but we remained tangled together, a mass of breath and limb, of stroking fingers and teasing hands.

He was reciting Shelley again, the words tumbling in rhythmic beats beneath my ear. *I have drunken deep of joy, and I will taste no other wine tonight.*

I laughed as he rolled me to my back with a nip at my jaw and another at my ear, "The man was mad; I fully intend to have another taste," and sighed at the pleasure that pooled deep in me at the words, as though the joy of which Shelley wrote and that Owen felt could not help but find egress through me, like a raven into the dark sky.

I froze, hating the thought. Not a raven. Not anything so ominous.

With a shiver I remembered the earlier storm, the monstrous hounds crawling across the fields for us. The woman in red leading them, her mouth a gleaming slash in her face.

Owen had promised me it was a nightmare. But for a moment I thought I could hear them again in the wind outside. The sound of them howling. Coming for us.

For me.

Owen sensed the change in me, lifting his head, worry furrowing his brow. "Emily?"

I swallowed around a heavy weight in my throat. "How did we get here?"

He smiled, the expression lopsided, making him look younger. More dear. "Well, first, I removed that robe . . ."

I laughed, but not for long before the tears came, quick and painful. "Stop. How did this happen?" I paused, one tear welling over, falling back into my hair before he could stop it, and then I whispered, "What did we do to deserve this?"

He kissed me then, as the answer came. As though he could make the truth disappear along with fear and disappointment and devastation . . . and betrayal.

I gasped against his lips. *Betrayal.*

"You lied to me."

He looked away.

I kept talking. "Every night. We do this."

"We love."

Love. Love and distance. Love and fear. Love and sadness. Love and betrayal. "And every day, I leave."

I could see the pain in his beautiful eyes—those eyes the color of the sea I cross every day. "Every day."

"Every day I remember." And I did remember. I remembered all of it, suddenly, and he knew it. He saw the memories come and he rushed to stop them. To explain them. Like he had a thousand times before.

"I neglected you." His voice cracked. "I ignored your pain, your sadness, in part because I did not know how to chase it away and in part because I was terrified of what it would do to me."

The words hurt. They hurt as much as the memories that came with him. The nights alone, aching for him. The days of wanting him. The way I had to stand by and watch him become less and less of the man I'd loved . . . more and more of the man I married.

The way he'd changed.

The way I had.

And then, the night I'd left, tired and angry and filled with sorrow and unwilling to go another moment here, in this house with this shadow of a man who resisted love and passion. Unwilling to live without it.

Unwilling to ask him for it.

I'd left. And he'd died.

And I had vowed to forget him.

Since then . . . years . . . centuries . . . we've danced this dance. Given what we thought we wanted. Every night: me, alone in a changing world without memory; him, alone in an unchanging one, remembering everything. Filled with regret.

How we were both filled with regret.

And then, after we've finally found each other and seen the mistakes we made—

"I leave. And I forget you. I forget the truth."

That I hate him. That I love him.

"But I never forget you," he said, and pain seeped through me like dye cast in the ocean, infecting every drop. "I never forget what I've done. I never stop regretting that I did not cherish you. I never forget what I feel."

"What do you feel?"

He leaned back against the massive pillows on the bed, the tartan baring him to the waist, revealing a wicked scar crossing his chest from shoulder to hip. The wound that killed him. The wound that took him from me.

The wound that brought him back.

I reached out to touch it, and he caught my fingers, bringing them to his lips. Kissing their tips. "I feel the moments we have missed. The eternity we have been apart. I feel the way I long for you when you aren't here."

He punctuated the sentences with soft, lush kisses. And, finally, he said, "I feel the way you ache for me when you leave."

The words were the worst possible blow. We had lost everything but the memory of what might have been and lived in a place where everything was gray and we were so alone.

Each lost in the mist without the other.

And yet . . . "I would live this night again and again—forever—if it was all I had of you," I told him.

"No," he said. "No more," he whispered at my temple, holding me in strong, steel arms that seemed able to keep everything at bay. "Not again."

"Of course again," I said, refusing his words. "This is how we have each other."

"But, Emily, you can have so much more . . . the other side . . . away from this dark place and its hounds and its wickedness . . . you can have it."

He lifted my lips to his, kissing me again, as though the caress could force me to understand. To choose. To leave him.

As if it didn't make me want to stay forever.

I pulled away. "I don't want it. Whatever it is. I want you."

He cursed, soft and sweet in the waning candlelight. "This is *my* hell, not yours. They were *my* sins, never yours. You deserve paradise."

I shook my head. "You always thought I was the perfect one."

He pulled me to him, holding me as tightly as he ever had, strong arms, harsh breath, fierce love. "You *are* perfect."

But I wasn't. I was as imperfect as he was. Blessedly so.

And because of that I did not have paradise.

I had him.

"I WON'T LEAVE you," I said, eager to start again. To throw open the sash and toss ourselves through. "Not again."

Outside the sky was turning a dishwater gray as the sun struggled to rise. Inside, Owen and I lay tangled in the sheets of his massive bed. He traced a finger down my neck, along my collarbone, over my ribs. His lips followed in the wake of his caress, stilling at the hollow above my hip, his words like a prayer there. "Please, Emily, I beg you. Please leave."

The words stung. Lacerated. Demolished. "You *want* me to leave?"

"Don't you understand? This is agony. Every minute with you is unmatched pleasure and unbearable pain because I know that you shall leave, and I shall be alone again, weeping for your loss, aching for you. Desperate for more than a handful of hours. For a lifetime. For an eternity where we don't have to worry about time or torture or hell."

He looked to me, eyes full of anger. "And every day I know it will happen again. You will come and I will love you and I will lose you. And perhaps I could face it, if it weren't for you. If I did not know that you, too, ache. If every bright memory were not clouded over with the memory of your tears day after day. Tears I have caused." His voice wavered, more breath than sound. "It's been this way for centuries, Emily. And I am so tired."

A tear trailed down my cheek, and he pressed his lips to it.

"I don't want you to suffer."

At my words he left the bed, paced across the room before coming to kneel by me, my legs now dangling over the edge. He gripped my knees with his hands, dropping a kiss onto each of my thighs before saying, "That's the torture of it. Not my own pain—but the pain I cause you. Every morning I break your heart and I can't . . ."

His voice cracked and he squeezed his eyes shut and pressed his lips together. His entire body was quivering. When he finally looked up at me, his eyes were bright, anguished. "I can't keep hurting you like that. Please. Please, you have to end it."

I slid from the bed until I, too, was on my knees.

"Why can't I just stay here, like this?" I asked him. "Never leave, never go to the dock, never get on the ferry?"

He shook his head. "We've tried that before. Hundreds of times. The woman in red always comes for you with her hounds and drags you away screaming." His thumb traced circles at the base of my throat. "We've tried resisting, we've tried tricking and outsmarting. We've tried it all so many times that I've lost count. And the end is always the same."

A sad smile played across his lips. "Every morning I beg you to leave me and never look back, but you always do. But please, Emily, *please,* this once . . . step onto that boat and stare only into the fog. Don't look back. This island is a curse—a hell that imprisons both of us. Across the water is paradise—it's love and light and everything you deserve."

"Except for you," I whispered.

He dropped his gaze. "I bring you nothing but misery. That's all I've ever brought you."

I cupped my hand under his chin and raised his head until he met my eyes. "Not now. Now, you are paradise."

His lips found mine, desperate and yearning. He trailed kisses across my jaw, down my neck, across my collarbone. His hands dug into my back, pulling me closer as if he could somehow make us one being.

Around us, the morning light grew stronger, and I heard the trace of a dog's howl in the distance. Owen stilled, his muscles going tense. "I love you," I said, wishing I'd said it in life. When it might have changed this.

There were tears in his eyes when he pulled away, stood, and helped me to my feet. He thrust my clothes from last night into my hands. "If you truly love me, Emily, please, board the boat and don't look back; it's the only way for you to be happy."

"And what of your happiness?"

"My happiness means nothing if it comes at the cost of yours." He paused, the words catching in his throat. In mine. "I should have seen that in life."

Sadness coursed through me. Regret. Anger.

Fear.

Outside, the hounds gathered.

Owen waited for me just outside the front door. Fog lay heavy on the ground, but it wasn't thick enough to block out the glow of the eyes of the hounds standing near the edge of the forest. Their breath turned to cloud in the chill morning air, and I could almost smell their rancid stench from where I stood.

I latched onto Owen's arm, and he slipped his fingers through mine. "They won't bother us. They're here to make sure we go."

True to his word, we followed the path into the tangle of trees without incident. The hounds kept their distance, shadowing us through the damp forest.

I'd remembered the hike to the castle as being long and arduous, but on our return we found the shore too quickly. Already the boat was there, bobbing at the end of the dock. The man I'd seen before—the one with the three Labs—stood to the side and he tipped his hat when I glanced at him. Next to him stood the woman in red. Hounds paced behind her, anxious and ready.

I hesitated, and one of the dogs bristled, taking a step toward us. The woman in red stopped him with a hand on his head, a smile in her cold, black gaze. She was enjoying our torture—the prolonged pain of our endless good-bye. I wanted nothing more than to run at her and gouge her eyes out.

But I knew Owen was right. That would solve nothing. It would merely rob me of these last moments with the man I loved.

Owen faced me, his hand cupping my cheek. In his eyes I could easily see the question: Would I leave him? Would I stop this agonizing cycle?

I couldn't answer. I didn't know.

The pain in him was overwhelming, and my heart ached with it. His anguish was more devastating than anything I had ever experienced—this moment worse than I could endure. But when I stepped onto that boat, it would vanish. I'd forget. I'd heal.

But he wouldn't.

And if I looked back, I was dooming him to another morning of torture. A day of agony. So I could see him again. So I could touch and taste him and feel his hands on my body.

"Leave me." Owen's mouth pressed against my own; his tears salted our lips. "Save yourself from this nightmare. Please . . ."

It was his last request . . . that I leave him here, to this hell. To the fog and the gray and the hounds.

I stepped back and took my last look at him, my chest tight, tears stinging my eyes and closing my throat. How could I leave this man? Our love? How could I accept an eternity without him?

What was heaven without him?

I turned and began the long walk down the dock. Charlie waited for me at the other end, his hand held out to bring me aboard.

And this pain was nothing compared to what Owen suffered each day, compounded. His hell grew worse every time I arrived.

I was the instrument of his torture.

I had to leave him.

The tears came as I slipped my hand into Charlie's, feeling his strength in opposition to my weak knees, my trembling body. I lifted a foot and placed it onto the boat and I took a deep breath.

Behind me I could feel Owen waiting. Wanting.

He wanted to save me. But he didn't understand that the only time I was saved was in his arms. That he could never save me by pushing me away.

My heart screamed against my ribs, wind off the sea stinging my face.

I knew I was being selfish. I was dooming him again, as I had every day before.

But I couldn't let him go.

When I turned back, Owen was on his knees. Behind him, the man with the dogs stood next to the woman in red: his face streaked with tears, hers awash in triumph.

But it was Owen I cared about, Owen I needed to see, and in his eyes I saw it all: the agony and the elation. Devastated that I would not leave him, even as he rejoiced that tonight, I would return.

That he would have another chance to beg me to leave. That I would have another night wrapped in his arms.

In our twisted paradise.

Owen's lips moved and even though I couldn't hear him, I knew it was the word he said each morning. Every time. "Farewell."

And then he was drowned by the fog.

I stood alone in the gray, surrounded by cloud. My throat burned and eyes watered as the frigid wind snapped at my face. I'd never felt emptier in my life.

Behind me a voice sounded, all smoke and whiskey. "You're headed for the castle."

I turned, startled. I'd been lost in my thoughts, though what they were I couldn't remember. I shook my head, trying to clear it.

"I'm Charlie." He extended one hand, the size of a tree trunk, and added, "And you're Emily."

HAND JOB

Chelsea Cain and Lidia Yuknavitch

One day, her hand began to speak.

It was not the thumb, old opposable standby. One would think perhaps the thumb would have the resolution and guts, being the evolutionary head of things and all, but it was not the thumb. To her astonishment, it was her pinkie finger. That seemingly useless dangler, good for next to nothing but hooking into a grip with the others or carving out an especially stubborn bit of ear wax or applying lip balm.

"Well, this is it," her pinkie said, out of the blue.

She stared at it. Though it made her feel foolish, she spoke, sitting back down on the couch to steady herself. "Excuse me, but this is what?" was all she could think to say.

She placed her nonspeaking hand over the speaking one gently like a woman crossing her hands in her lap.

"Do you mind?" her pinkie said. "I'm trying to talk to you." And so she quickly gave her louder hand air and space. "That's better," her pinkie said.

They sat for a moment in silence. She didn't want to be rude so she did not stare at her pinkie. Instead, she looked out of her bedroom window at the tall camellia tree with its happy little rosen faces and waxen leaves. She looked at the Restoration bird feeder—so squirrel proof, with its brushed metal and black iron. She looked at the wind chimes—the larger pewter ones with minor-keyed song, and the smaller golden-rodded ones with a major-keyed hymn.

"Oh, for Christ's sake . . . can you stop daydreaming for a second? You call this a life?" her pinkie said, raising up a little with indignation. "This is a slack-minded grotesque cartoon version of a life. An air-freshened glossy magazine prison. Look at all this domesticity shit. What are you, Martha fucking Stewart? At least Martha had some chutzpah and went to jail. Knitted ponchos with black women. What've you done lately? Run the dishwasher?"

Taken aback, she looked over toward the kitchen, where the dishwasher hummed dully: it was exceedingly efficient.

"Yep, best keep those motherfucking dishes clean!" her pinkie continued. "I mean, Jesus, woman, what the hell has happened to you? Did you honestly think we wouldn't . . . you know, notice?" Silence sat between them the length of her arm.

She coughed up a response: "When you say 'we,' who do you mean, specifically?"

Her pinkie shot out straight away from the other fingers on her hand. "Oh my God. Have you gone brain dead? Hello?" And now her entire hand was in front of her face, her phalanges all waving vigorously like fat flesh-colored worms. "This we, you stupid meat sack!" her pinkie screamed.

She glanced a bit too hopefully at her other hand. It just sat there, passive and limp. *Typical,* she thought. What was all this about? A pinkie rebellion? What did she even use her pinkie for that mattered? Briefly she got an image of herself in her mind's eye, doing that thing she did every morning on her monotonous commute to work, letting the freeway sort of take control, hooking her pinkies only around the base of the steering wheel. Almost not driving. Just gliding along a path already laid out for her—her whole life . . . Right about the time she gathered the courage to make a fist out of her speaking hand—I mean, really, this was nonsense, she could simply make a fist and curl that little mouthy bitch up and under if she wanted to, or even better, run to the closet where the winter clothes sat neatly in a box and slip on a mitten—her pinkie launched itself at her face. She panicked and slapped at it with her free hand, like she was fending off an attacking bat. Then there was a sound, a blade slicing through ham, the pop of the skin and then the soft give of the meat. Her nose felt like it was full of cold water, and pain seared between her eyes. Then she heard something hit the floor, a little thud, just before she managed to grab her offending hand by the wrist and wrestle it to her thigh.

She tasted blood, all acrid tin warmth. It filled her mouth and snaked around her lips.

A triangle of bloody flesh was on the floor, there on the Persian rug, under the coffee table. It looked like something a cat might vomit up, a chunk of a hairless baby bird scarfed down and then violently regurgitated. She let go of her wrist and reached her good hand toward her nose, only to find a slippery bony hole where her nose had been.

She would not have thought it possible. She looked at her pinkie in horror. It had blood on its knuckle.

"It wasn't me," her pinkie protested. "I'm innocent."

She rushed to the bathroom while blood spurted from the center of her face. She instinctively grabbed the white of the toilet paper and pulled it into great swirls and crammed the three-ply paper into her naked nasal aperture. She frantically searched with her free hand for the first aid kit. Her eyes so filled with tears it was like searching for something underwater. Her head throbbed. She felt dizzy and fevered—was she having a stroke? She managed to locate gauze patches in the first aid kit and added to the drenched toilet paper with gauze pads—she shoved them in, wincing, and thought about how boneless noses were . . . how vulnerable and defenseless. She sat on the toilet with a thunk, her middle-aged ass bigger than the seat. With her good hand, her gentle, compassionate hand, she held the gauze and paper in her nose hole. She eyed what was left of the toilet paper roll. She closed her eyes. Tried to regulate her breathing. Was she going into shock? Would she keel over off the toilet and hit her skull on the bathtub rim and crack it open and die? But wait, was the bathtub clean?

After a time, her pinkie spoke. "OK. Fine. I'll admit it. This looks bad. But I've been set up, hoodwinked, framed. I don't even have a weapon."

"Your fingerprints are all over that nose," she said.

"I've held my tongue for fifty years. I've watched you do this mind-bogglingly stupid thing with your life little by little, year after year, and I kept to myself. Minded my own hand business. But there comes a time in the life of every finger when enough is enough. Do you realize how many times I've had to do things against my morals? Do you have any idea what my life is like connected to your body? I could have belonged to a concert pianist. A cellist. A star quarterback. A surgeon. A painter! But with you? Noooooooo. For Christ's sake, I can't even hold a decent martini."

She thought she heard her pinkie weeping. It drooped a bit and shook, almost as if it had shoulders that were heaving. Briefly she considered petting it with her calm hand. Like a mother would. Or a wife.

But then she snapped out of it: "You sliced off my fucking nose!" she said, in a fit of rage, spitting the words down at her hand. Didn't we all have an edge, a place in our bodies where we could go hard like steel?

"Well, all right!" her finger shot back. "Yes! OK? I did it! I confess. I can't undo it! But losing your nose is nothing compared to what you've done with your life! It's a wake-up call, I'm telling you, like a message from God! Well, except for the fact that I'm an atheist . . . but those other ludicrous fingers, they believe in God! I hear their incipient whispering at night. Losers. So you can think of me as . . . I'm like a . . . like a commandment! Got it? I'm the motherfucking Moses finger of this bunch!"

"What do you want from me?" she sobbed. "What on earth have I done? What are you talking about?" she screeched. The mirror shuddered. The shower curtain wavered. She caught a glimpse of mold. *There should be more bleach,* she thought. *Why is there never enough bleach?* She pictured her nose, alone, cold, probably blue out there on the rug. Dust bunnies gathering around it. Could it still smell?

"Look," her pinkie said, "it's actually quite difficult for me to control myself just now. I mean, I've really had it. I can't take it anymore. I'm a finger on the edge, I tell you, and I could use a drink. Do you think you could get us a stiff scotch before we continue this conversation? Just dunk me in it."

"I'm not getting you a scotch to dunk in!" she screamed, and then turned to the mirror and caught a glimpse of herself, bloodied and frantic, yelling at her own hand. What if the neighbors could hear her? Shouldn't she call 911? Was her blood loss nearing a dangerous place? What the hell would she say when they got there? Should she put her nose in a Tupperware container and bring with? Her thoughts tumbled in her skull like drunk dice.

"Oh no? NO? No scotch? FINE." And then her hand swept up like a terrorist pledge of allegiance and lopped off one of her breasts right through her blouse. It splatted on the ceramic tile floor and jiggled like a jellyfish for a second—blood and corpuscle and vein guts and fatty tissue glistening in the halogen light. Her chest poured blood. There wasn't enough toilet paper in the world for the wound where a breast should be. With the one hand she could trust she grabbed at a towel before falling to the floor, breathing "My God, my God . . ." Her breathing became like feathers. Her sight went all television snow. She had trouble forming word thoughts. The ceramic tiles were cool. Her chest exploded. Pain locked her jaw and dismantled her spine. This must be what soldiers feel when a grenade explodes, she was almost able to think. But really it was just a retinal flash from a scene in *Apocalypse Now*. Blood pooled before her there on the bathroom floor.

"Yeah, well, God's not here. I am," her hand said quietly. "So here it is, straight no chaser." Her speaking hand inched up near her face. She did not open her eyes, but she thought she could feel its breath on her face.

"I've been offered a job," her pinkie said. "By the government."

"A job?"

"They want me overseas immediately. I can't be lugging around your sorry ass. It's nothing personal."

She opened her eyes. Her finger was mad, deranged, half cracked. "You'll die without me," she mumbled. It would, wouldn't it? It couldn't drive certainly, not without a thumb. How far could it get?

"Ha!" cackled her finger. "That's just like you, always the center of the universe, always making decisions for the rest of us. Newsflash, sister. I don't need you, I never did."

How had she not seen this coming? The nail on that finger was always breaking. It had always had a mind of its own.

Her life played out in front of her as blood spread on the floor. When had this phalangeal resentment started? Was it when she slammed that finger in the car door when she was ten? Was it when it got rolled over by another skater at the roller rink? Had she used it too often to feel around for hemorrhoids? Had her rings been too tight? It was true. She had been hard on that finger. This was her fault. She had to stop it.

"Like, I don't know what you are thinking. Would you just stop for a second and really think? Remember in college at the job fair when the government folks came and you interviewed with them? Remember how that one guy said to you, 'You know, you have covert ops potential. Here's how to access applications to the CIA'? Remember how excited you were?"

Clutching her bleeding chest with her nontalking hand, she pushed herself up into a sitting position. It hurt to breathe. But she forced herself up onto her knees and started to crawl. Her leg nudged the raw meat of her dismembered breast and it skidded in the blood on the floor and came to a rest against the toilet.

Her pinkie tried to slow her down. It clawed at the wall, at the pedestal of the sink, but she pressed on, across the hall, through her open bedroom door. The bedside table was painted purple, the color of a bruise. The drawer was already open an inch.

Undaunted, her pinkie ranted, "Remember when you met that James Dean–looking dude your senior year and he said 'Let's go to Joshua Tree' and you jumped on his motorcycle and hugged his ass with your thighs and held on for dear life, laughing your ass off like a banshee?"

But then, with a shudder, her finger seemed to grok what was happening. How many times had that hand been in that drawer, rooting around for sleeping pills, a hair band, her mouth guard? It had seen the gun.

The finger struck her on the side of the face, and she heard the sound of skin ripping and felt a flash of cold air and pain.

"This is your last chance! This is it, woman!"

"Fuck!" she cried. Her ear hung by a bit of skin at the lobe. Her skull was wet with blood. The ear flapped against her neck as she lunged toward the drawer and plunged her good hand inside. This was really the last straw. Her fingers found the grip of the Glock and she pulled it from the bedside table and leveled it at her pinkie.

The pinkie made a run for it, and her arm went straight as a board as the little digit strained and fluttered at the end of her hand, an arm's length away.

"Stop or I'll shoot," she cried.

Her pinkie turned back, defiant. It wagged itself at her, the cocky motherfucker. "You can't shoot me," her pinkie said. "You don't have the hand-eye coordination. You can't even find the B on a keyboard."

She could feel the pulse in her palm, rapid and thready, her flesh a bloody sponge. She was on the cusp of losing consciousness. She steadied her trigger hand and fired.

The bullet hit her pinkie square in the middle phalanx, severing the interphalangeal joint and blowing off tendon, skin, and nerve, leaving a jam-filled hole in a stubby one-inch sausage casing of flesh. A mound of shredded muscle sat on top of the hole, like a scoop of sorbet on a cone. It didn't hurt. She brought her hand to her face and looked down at the bloody stump, ringed with a thin layer of skin.

Thin-skinned. Figured.

Dizzy from loss of blood, she crawled forward, looking for the phalangeal corpse. She found her pinkie on the bed. It was still alive and making quite a scene. She could hear a faint, pitiful rasping coming from it as it twitched on the chenille bedspread. Her finger seemed helpless without a hand to anchor it, unmoored.

She curled next to it on the bed.

"I'm pressing charges," her finger coughed. "You won't get away with this."

"Oh, shut up," she said.

SHE WOKE TO the sound of her own heart—or the awful bleeping of a heart monitor anyway. Everything around her looked beige and blurry. She could only be in a hospital. No place else smelled like someone shit air freshener. She tried to focus. Her face and head felt heavy, almost like lead. With her good hand she reached up and felt around; bandages covered her nose and ear. Something was under the bandages. Firm body parts, it felt like, splints. They had sewn her back together. Reattached her veins, arteries, bone, muscle, nerve bundles, and skin—sutured, cauterized, and clipped. She jutted her chin down toward her chest—yep, judging by the pain, they'd reattached her poor boob, too. She shuddered to think what it might look like—a bruised deflated balloon? There was only one place left to look.

She brought her hand of violence and terror up toward her face. The finger was there. As if it had never left. She tried to speak, but a cough came out. Finally she said "*Hey*" to her betraying appendage.

The pinkie swayed back and forth a little.

Was it still . . . alive?

Nothing.

Two nice-looking policemen came in later to take her statement. Her neighbor had heard the gunshot, they said, and called for help. She was lucky to be in one piece, they said. The policemen opened their notebooks and gave her grave stares. "What happened?" they asked her. "Who did this to you?"

She glanced at her bandaged finger. It throbbed slightly.

"I don't remember," she said.

Nurses came and went, checking on her vitals, speaking in hushed tones about the tragic, brutal attack she'd survived, shaking their heads back and forth with sympathy. Noses, ears, fingers—they had slow metabolisms, the nurses said. They were quite durable, really. You could misplace an ear for a few hours, and as long as it was a clean cut, the surgeon could pop it back on, no problem. Penises did especially well when they got lopped off. They could last fourteen hours in a bucket of ice.

She drifted in and out of sleep. There were two more surgeries on her breast. The doctors cut into her lower belly, loosened skin, fat, and muscle, and then tunneled the tissue up to replace the flesh that had died. She had long talks with surgical residents about nipple sensitivity.

The police came back twice. She pled the Fifth. No one asked to talk to the finger.

SHE WAS RELIEVED when her chest drain came out and they finally let her go home to her beautiful Restoration sofa set and her carefully crafted floor-to-ceiling bookshelves and her array of Pottery Barn knickknacks, candles, bowls of rocks and thistles. But instead of feeling at home, she felt like she'd stepped into the scene of a terrible crime. Her kitchen suddenly looked too shiny and unwelcoming, like things cooked in there would be toxic. Her bathroom held dark, unseemly, naked secrets like in a horror movie. It scared her a little to sit and pee. She eyed the toilet paper with strange trepidation. And her bedroom, her beloved, safe, gigantic bed with its 600-thread-count sheets, the velvet sage-colored curtains, the corresponding soothing sage walls, somehow seemed menacing now, like it had all turned against her—the bedroom, the house, her very life. All these beautiful things. Were they laughing at her?

She looked at her pinkie—the stitches rather Frankensteinian-looking, even if they were the self-dissolving kind. Her pinkie remained silent, black and blue, swollen.

The next morning she prepared for work like she always had in the past, coffee in the coffeepot, but she couldn't help a strange feeling coming over her. Why hadn't anything in her stupid house lifted a finger to help her in her time of need? She stared at the knife rack. Shiny useless inanimates. She leered at the pots and pans dangling swankily from the ceiling. Typical hangers-on. She ignored the dirty dishes in the sink. They would have to wait. Fuck them. What had they ever done for her? Her kitchen suddenly seemed like everyone else's in the universe. A cartoon kitchen.

She showered, washing all her fingers as though they were fingers. One ached and hung slightly askew compared to the others, but she tried to ignore it. She avoided the mirror—her nose and ear had not quite settled into their old positions—and she dressed for the weather, red boots, a rain jacket, and red leather gloves she bought to make herself feel special in the brick cubicle that was her office and destination.

On her way to the door she took a quick detour back upstairs to her bedside drawer. There, she dug out the Glock and tucked it among the day's paperwork and to-do lists. It comforted her, the Glock.

On the freeway, her car merged with all the others, traveling at a constant speed not faster than traffic and definitely not any slower. For the first time she saw the road as four lanes wide of nothing but asphalt leading to a million dead and middle-aged ends. Her commute was forty minutes, and midway there she dialed down the heater and removed her gloves. A text buzzed in her purse. It started to rain again. Her exit loomed ahead of her . . . Exit 17. Why did it suddenly seem ominous? She could almost hear the minor notes of scary theme music. A voice-over booming out "Exit 17 . . ."

Then quite suddenly her pinkie hooked around the steering wheel. She stared at it. It was difficult to know whether the actions that followed were intentional or due to some force outside her—some metaphysical power steering the car crazy fast across all four lanes of traffic, almost clipping Suburus and Priuses and mom vans en route. Her pinkie had the lightest touch, and yet her car drifted toward a completely wrong, completely unknown exit ramp that swung back over the freeway in a giant sky loop. When her exit was executed, she faced a strange and previously unknown long narrow road. Soon, signs presented themselves. Her pinkie acted like a finger at the end of her hand. It said nothing. Though she thought she might have heard a sigh, a long outtake of breath that sounded as if it had taken a lifetime to build . . . with her good ear.

She looked ahead of her. This was not going to work. She looked in the rearview—all she saw was her own eyes, and the receding image of the job she was supposed to get to. Who was she and where was she going? She was a woman with a nose job. A boob job. Plus an ear job. A hand job. But so not like advertised on TV. Her breast burned, her nose ached, she still had two black eyes from surgeries, her ear felt hot and fevered, and what she used to regard as her pinkie, well, who the hell knew what it was thinking? And why did she suddenly want to know?

"Hello?" she said in the glass cave-world of her car, and then almost in a whisper, aimed at her pinkie, again, "Hello?"

To the north, the narrow road led to a giant air traffic control tower in the distance. Planes leaped into the air all around her. People flying away from their lives—maybe to clandestine government jobs where they got to play spy or carry weapons. To the east, the desert . . . roadkill and scrub brush and red dirt and heat, where a woman could even lose herself, or find herself, or where murder-suicides were, in fact, common.

HOLLOW CHOICES

Robert Jackson Bennett and David Liss

What struck me was that I didn't feel happy in any way at all when they walked me down the hall. I'd seen other prisoners whoop and cheer as they were paraded through the doors and gates and checkpoints, nodding to friends or enemies—especially enemies—as they made their big exit. I'd seen smirks and shit-eating grins and knowing smiles. I didn't feel like celebrating. I couldn't. I couldn't even imagine how.

Maybe it was *who* was walking me out. The guard on my right I knew pretty well. I knew his baton for sure, which I'd felt on my shoulder or cheek occasionally when I didn't look at him the right way, or when he just needed to show off. The guard on my left had never hurt me, or at least never struck me or wounded me: but he had been the one to look away and slink off on the afternoon when Hutchins and his friends, who I'd apparently slighted, crowded into the shower with me, slowly penning me in the corner . . .

I wondered, as this guard walked beside me, if he had listened. He must've known what they were going to do to me. And I wondered if he'd known then, as I had not, that it wouldn't be the last time.

They showed me the papers. Recited the appropriate texts. Notified me of all the strictures that'd be placed upon me when I walked out those doors. They were telling me, in a way, that though I was free of this place, though I'd served my time and paid my debt to society, I was not truly free, for they still had some part of me, some part still locked up in here. I nodded, and nodded, and nodded.

The squeak of cheap shoes on linoleum. The flutter of fluorescent lights. Then doors fell open before me, one after the other, and there was a blast of chill and the gray, flat light of an overcast sky.

I walked out. Snowflakes danced down to my shoulders and hands. The guards pointed the way toward the bus I'd be taking to a halfway house. I thanked them, bag in my hand, and started walking.

I smelled exhaust and seawater and winter wind and snow. I smelled the tang of a Swisher Sweet and the rot from a Dumpster. I did not smell freedom. None of it smelled free to me. Maybe I'd forgotten what that smelled like.

WHEN YOU GET out of prison, it's like visiting a foreign country: you watch, amazed, as people go about their inscrutable tasks that feel loaded with threat, meaning, subtext. What would have been impossible for you to do a mere week ago—getting a soda, opening a window—is white noise to them. You realize that these people are not yours, nor are you part of them. You can walk through a city where you once belonged, but now you're an alien.

This was the world I now lived in. I slept at the halfway house ("ST. MART N'S MEN'S TRAN ITION L HOUS NG" read the sign), awoke every day at 6:30 A.M. (expecting each time to hear the blare of the morning alarm), and applied for jobs, with no response. That was no surprise: I wasn't in the front of the line for work by a long shot.

I wandered the city. It felt so strange to move freely. I was so used to tight rooms and winding corridors, to the musty aroma of underoxygenated air. . . . To have the sky spilling in on me from all directions was terrifying and thrilling.

One day, while waiting on one corner for the signal to walk, I looked up and saw a woman standing beside me. There wasn't anything especially notable about her. Her heavy winter coat was wrapped around medical scrubs, like she'd ducked out of her workplace to run an errand. She was neither beautiful nor ugly. She wasn't even plain. There was nothing about her appearance to make an ordinary person take note, but when I looked in her eyes, I saw it.

Nothing.

Well, not *nothing*. Her eyes were *there,* like actually in her skull, but there was nothing *in* them. There's a spark to eyes, an aliveness when there's an intelligence behind them, looking out, watching, learning. You forget it's there, and only realize what's missing when you see the eyes of the dead, or those in drugged stupor, or—a third option—those like her.

She looked at me and said, with a note of some irritation, "Can I help you with something?"

I was so surprised to see her move and speak, I had no idea what to say. It was as though a mannequin had suddenly come to life. She scoffed, assuming, I guess, that I was a perv, and when the walk sign came she hurried away.

I DIDN'T KNOW what she was, but I *suspected,* and it was a pretty good suspicion. Better than a guess. I'd seen men with empty looks in prison, but that was the norm. The men inside were beaten down, defeated, dispirited. They had surrendered to a life without possibilities or choice, but there was more in those men than there had been in that woman.

I began following her without intending to. I was half a block behind her for five minutes before I even realized what I was doing, and let's be honest, what I was doing was dangerous—for so many reasons.

Maybe trouble was exactly what I needed. I had a ticking clock and a lot of grudges, and I was either going to spend my days watching the sand dribble out of the glass or I was going to settle some old scores. I knew which one I wanted to do, but the path of least resistance is sometimes hard to resist.

I felt the need growing inside me, all the time. I had to do something. I couldn't let it all go. I wanted justice, or at least something that felt like justice to me. I was going to rebalance the scales of my little corner of the universe, and I'd do it with a hammer.

That was the plan, anyhow, until I saw the woman. Because she was so like *them,* the ones who had put me in prison in the first place. She reminded me of decisions I'd made, questions I'd never gotten answered. More than anything, I had to know if she had . . . well, if she had *done it.*

If she *had,* then I had to know why, because if she'd had to make the same choice I did, she would have been asked the same question I'd been asked once. Only her answer had been different.

She turned the corner at a coffee shop. I rushed to catch up, but when I came around, she was waiting. She leaned against the building and looked at me, those dead eyes revealing nothing, her lips twisted in maybe amusement, maybe pity.

"Jesus," she breathed through pursed lips, sending a lock of blond fluttering against her forehead. "You again. What do you want?"

I realized I was panting, blowing out puffs of wintry breath like a chimney. "You did it, didn't you?" I said. "You got the offer and you took it."

She looked frightened or caught or guilty. And then she didn't. She steeled herself and met my gaze. "How do you know? Who told you?"

"I don't know *how* I know. I just . . ."

"Just what?"

"I just . . . looked at you. And I knew."

She watched me a second longer, maybe gauging if I was a threat. Finally she said, "I took it. Yeah, I took it. I'd have been an idiot not to."

There were so many things I wanted to ask her, to make her explain, but I knew I could not have that conversation. It would take hours. So I asked the most important question I thought she might be willing to answer: "Do you feel any . . . different?"

She thought about it. Shrugged. "I guess I feel different because my life doesn't suck anymore. My kid's kidneys aren't failing. I'm not about to lose my house. That feels different."

"That's it?"

"Yes. That's it."

I was silent. She couldn't have known it, but her simple answer had reached inside me, broken me up, crumbled me to dust. I felt faint, but I didn't fall. I stumbled backward, nodding to her, and managed a weak, "Thanks."

"You said *no*?" she asked.

I nodded.

"Why?" It was the incredulous voice of a parent speaking to a child who had done something utterly stupid and inexplicable.

"It seemed like the right call at the time." I turned away.

"Hey," she said. "How did you know? What gave it away?"

I almost said it was her eyes, but then I stopped myself. Obviously she did not know, and I didn't think it was right to tell her. Even though this woman had done something unspeakable, it wasn't my place to judge her. She was already, in a very real sense, damned. There was no need to make her feel like crap about her appearance.

THERE ARE A lot of ways to go to prison. Most of them are stupid. Criminals, after all, do criminal acts because they can't make a straight living, either because circumstances prevent it, or because they can't figure out how to get their shit together.

I was a little of both. Me and my friends Marco and Teddy had been busboys at this restaurant for what felt like years. In truth, it'd only been a handful of months, but when you're young, time is different: the days move slowly when you're miserable, and in that steamy restaurant, elbow deep in gray water scummed over with old cheese, they moved even slower.

So when Marco heard that we could make more money as movers, Teddy and I jumped at the opportunity. He didn't mention that we'd be moving gambling machines. And he didn't mention until after we'd already worked a few jobs that what we were doing was highly illegal. By then we'd been paid, many times over, and it's hard to say no or think straight when you've got a wad of money burning a hole in your pocket. So we kept going back to the well.

At the time, it seemed like things could never go wrong. That's the problem with being young: it seemed like it would be beer and dancing and money and pussy forever. But when I look back on it now, all that was over in an instant.

I remember everything about how it ended. When you're in prison, that's all you ever think about. So much more than getting out.

I remember the call in the night. Marco's girlfriend, telling me Marco was hurt. Then I remember rushing into his apartment, the tile of his bathroom a raw, brilliant red, lakes of blood stymied in their crawl across his floor, and the gray-white hand twisted in the shower curtain.

When I pulled the curtain aside, it was not Marco: it was an old man, white, midfifties. He was dressed like a security guard, and his throat had been slashed so wide I could see inches into his neck.

Then I heard the sirens. I remembered how Marco and Teddy had been so secretive the last few days, always pulled aside to talk to the bosses, presumably arranging a big score.

What I remember most, out of all of it, was the way their eyes had looked the night before I was arrested. Empty. Dead. Something had been in those eyes once, but it was gone. They had smiled at me, and it had tasted false and wrong, like someone had drawn a smile on a mannequin.

When the cops brought me in, booked me, and questioned me, I learned piece by piece that a huge amount of electrical equipment had been stolen at the docks. The guard had gone missing along with it: to be found, of course, in Marco's bathtub, beaten about the face and bathing in several gallons of his own blood.

They never found the thieves, but they'd found me, and they were intent on keeping me. Among all the riffraff in Marco's apartment, they'd found a Glock with my prints on the barrel hood, a Glock whose handle just happened to have traces of the guard's blood on its grip. The bruising on the guard's face matched the pattern of the grip. And while you can explain away some fingerprints on a handle, a fingerprint on the inner workings of a gun is a tall order.

I told them I didn't know anything—even how my fingerprints got on the gun. That went down about as well as you'd think. They asked me who else was involved. They told me it would go easier if I gave up the guys who had left me flapping in the breeze. They used words like *deal* and *probation* and *first-time offender,* but even a fuckup like me knew what that meant. They wanted me to flip.

In some distant part of my mind, I'd always known things could go south. I hadn't believed it would, but I'd known it *might*, and I understood there was a way you accepted these things. You took your lumps. You did your time. You didn't sell out your friends. A man who turns on his friends is vermin—that's why they call it *ratting*. And he deserves to be dealt with like vermin. I wasn't going to go that route.

I stayed silent, and they seemed to accept that pretty easily. They didn't beat me. They didn't press me too hard on accomplices. They didn't need to. They had a crime, and they had a suspect. Somewhere some suit who worked in the D.A.'s office was saying they had enough to convict. Why sweat the small stuff?

So that was that. They were done with me.

I spent my first night in jail that night. The first night of what would be fifteen years.

I didn't spend it alone.

I'm still not sure when he arrived. He was just *there,* like he'd always been there, slouched in the cell across from me.

"You look," he said, "like someone in a world of hurt."

I looked up at him. He was a thoroughly unremarkable man: skinny but not too skinny, with salt-and-pepper hair but not that old, his eyes a plain, dull shade of brown. His clothes were nice but nothing particularly special: he could belong anywhere and nowhere.

"What?" I said.

"I said, you look like someone in a world of hurt."

I looked away, said nothing. I was terrified. I was angry. And I was aware that there was a very good chance I'd be spending a lot of time in a place like this.

"I've seen a lot of people in your state," he said. "Tons. God, I can't even *count* 'em. I've seen so many folks at the end of their ropes, I guess there must be rope ends all over the fucking place. I really do."

"Shut the fuck up," I moaned.

But he didn't. He sat up and leaned against the wall at the far end of the cell, all nonthreatening-like. "Now, the thing is, I don't usually see them in such a sorry state for long. You know why?"

"I sure as shit hope you're not going to tell me they find Jesus."

He was quiet. Then he burst out laughing. He laughed long and loud, a rough, throaty laugh that sounded like it hurt. "Oh, *man*! That's good.

That's some good stuff, it really is. Shit, no! That Jesus stuff, it only works on folks who are buried deep in."

"Deep in what?"

He flicked the bars of his cell. "Deep in bars. Folks behind bars behind bars behind bars. And that's the only place it lasts, too. Once they get out, *poof,* it's gone. They forget all about it. Back to their old tricks, y'see." He smiled. "No, these people . . . the ones whose fortunes *really* turn for the better . . . they find something different."

I glared at him. I wished he was dead. Him, and Marco, and Teddy, and the detectives who'd asked me, seriously, a total of six questions, because they'd known they had me dead to rights. "What is it?" I asked angrily.

"Oh, now hold on there," said the man. "Let's not blow our wad just yet. You don't want to jump into this, now do you?"

"I didn't even know there was a 'this.' "

"Well, there *is,* and you're trying to jump into it. To get what I'm offering, you have to give something up. You have to give *me* something. It's an exchange. Get it?"

"If you want my ass, man, you can fucking forget about it."

He smiled. But I noticed his eyes didn't smile. Most people when they smile, even if they don't mean it, some part of their eyes move. It's just what a human face does. But his . . . didn't. "No," he said. "I want something a little bit more valuable than your anal virginity, my boy."

"What?"

He leaned forward, the top of his forehead poking through the bars. "Son . . . do you believe in the soul?"

I stared at him. Then I burst out laughing, just as he had done. "You've got be fucking kidding me! Oh, *man.* You seriously had me for a moment!"

He didn't laugh: he just kept smiling through the bars.

I asked, "Are you, like, some drunk that's in here every night, and this is how you get your kicks?"

Still, he did not laugh. But then he said, "You know, I'm not surprised to hear you laugh. Marco laughed too, when he heard my offer."

I stopped. The world went dead. "What?" I asked. "What did you say?"

He kept smiling.

"What the fuck was that?" I shouted. "What the fuck did you just say to me?"

"You'll want to keep your voice down," he said. "Otherwise the guards will come, and you'll never hear the rest."

The man leaned against the wall and folded his arms. He half closed his eyes like he was remembering something sweet. "Here's the deal," he said. "Marco took it. And Teddy took it. That's why they're out there and you're in here. But the good news—the *real* good news, my friend—is that when you take it, you'll be out there, too. It's as simple as it sounds: you give me your soul, and I give you an easy life."

"So, what," I said with a snort, "you're like the devil or something? Like in the stories?"

"Stories are stories," said the man, "because reality is so much more complex. Here's how it works: I'm not going to offer to make you rich, a movie star, or any of that. I won't make you immortal or irresistible to women. All that is crap. What I *can* offer you is an uncomplicated, pleasant life. You won't get sick before your time, you won't end up living on the street. You'll be luckier than most people. The things you shoot for will have a better chance of working out. Hopefully some high flying, but absolutely a lot of smooth sailing."

"Uh-huh," I said. "Okay, that's swell. That's a pretty good pitch. Now, I'm going to get some sleep."

"You want to get some sleep?" he asked. "You'd rather get some sleep than, say, be set up for life? You'd rather get some sleep than get out of jail free?"

"Tell you what," I said. "Get me out of jail free, and I'll listen. Transport me to the VIP room of some club and stick a supermodel on my lap, and we'll talk terms."

"Doesn't work that way. I can get you out of here, but the clubs and the models are up to you. And I can't give you the goods without getting the payment. That would be bad business on my part. I will promise to get you out of jail in exchange for what I'm asking. All you have to do is agree. Even if you don't believe me, then what do you have to lose? And if I'm right, then you've got your proof, plus so much more."

I was awake now, and I was paying attention. The thing was, somewhere along the way, I started to believe this guy. This wasn't just an annoying cell mate, this was a business negotiation. I told myself I was being ridiculous—it was fear and fantasy thinking—but I believed him, not myself. On some level, I understood that his offer was for real.

It wasn't just the sincerity in his voice, the confident ease with which he delivered a sales pitch I knew he'd delivered countless times before. There were other things. The cell was colder than it had been before, and the air felt charged, like just before a storm, and there were pockets of heat. The man was not attractive—he kind of looked like Andrew Jackson on the twenty-dollar bill, with his long face and high forehead and dour expression, but that was not it. He looked perfectly normal, yet he was also *off*—his eyes and nose and mouth sat on his face slightly wrong, like their proportions were mixed up, but just so slightly you couldn't quite say how. The color of his skin seemed strange too. I had never seen a shade precisely like that—no, I decided, not the shade but the color saturation. It made him look like a man out of an old photograph.

"Can you prove all this?" I was interested now for sure. Not interested in the deal precisely, but in the situation. "Can you show me what you're talking about is real?"

He grinned. "You mean like *magic*?" He waved his hands around, like a magician performing a trick with invisible props. "There's no such thing. There's the reality you know and the reality you don't, but everything follows the same laws of physics. I just might know a few more of those laws than you do. But I can't turn you into a donkey or make vines grow out of the toilet. That sort of thing doesn't happen."

"But the soul is an actual thing?"

"Absolutely. Just like an appendix is an actual thing. That wart on your left big toe is real too, but if I were to remove it, you wouldn't miss having it, and it doesn't do you any good."

"And there's no way to prove you're telling the truth?"

He looked at me, and his eyes glistened strangely. "You know I am."

The thing is, I did. Or at least I thought I did, because when I thought about them, his words had the weight and texture and sound of truth. "Let's say you are telling the truth. Then that means there is such a thing as a soul. If that's true, then all the fucking bullshit we've learned about religion and heaven and hell and all that is also true, or *could* be. Right?"

He didn't nod or shake his head. He just watched me.

I asked, "Wouldn't I be a moron to sell my soul for a shot at a decent life on Earth and then trash my chance for eternal happiness? Who would take such a dumb-ass bargain? If anything, the idea that you're telling the truth would give a person the strength to endure all the shit life throws at them because it means that they're safe from hell and destined for heaven."

The man thought about this for a second. It looked like no one had ever confronted him with these ideas before, but they seemed obvious to me.

"You're basing your assumptions on medieval ideas about the soul," he said. "That's very much like basing your flight plan to India on medieval maps. The soul is real, but that doesn't mean it's what priests and philosophers tell you it is. To be blunt, it is a commodity, one I can use and profit from. This isn't about heaven and hell. It's about supply and demand. This is the economics of the marketplace, so don't go thinking that just because you have a soul you can use Dante's *Inferno* as a travel guide."

"But it's a soul," I said. "Isn't it, like, the essence of who I am?"

He waved his hand in the air in a dismissive gesture. "Who says? Listen, if you needed a heart transplant, and I offered to sell you a compatible organ, you wouldn't worry about the love and goodness and hopes contained in the donor's heart, would you? It's a piece of flesh, and it serves a function. The soul is the same thing. It's a part of you, and one you can live without. Giving it up doesn't necessarily mean you are giving up anything else."

"But it doesn't *necessarily* mean that I'm not."

He shrugged. "You want to do business, I'm your man. You want to talk metaphysics, there are some deep-thinking hard timers in maximum security. They'll be happy to discuss this once they've knocked out all your teeth so they can rape your mouth."

I'd had a chance to ease my way by selling out Marco and Teddy, but I hadn't done it. I'd taken the hard way because the hard way felt like the honorable course. So I sure as hell wasn't about to take the easy way now. I knew—and you have to understand this—I *knew* what he was offering me was the real deal. I knew all I had to do was say yes, and I also believed him when he said I wouldn't miss having it. It would be like that wart, useless and there, and then useless and gone.

But fuck it. I didn't like his attitude. I didn't like the idea of some stranger buying and selling pieces of people, pieces of *me*. I didn't like that he danced around the details rather than answering my questions. No matter what I got in this bargain, he would always have power over me.

"Not interested," I said.

His smile made me want to punch him in the teeth. So smug and satisfied. "Marco said you might not. He said you were too much of a pussy."

"Oh, then I'll show him and prove he's wrong," I said in a lilting voice. "Did you actually think that was going to work?"

"The thing about Marco and Teddy," he said, "is that by getting out of jail, they created kind of a vacuum in the legal system. They'd been arrested for the crime, and then they were let out. Someone else had to look guilty, and that's where you came in. You're sitting right here because those guys took the deal. And now you're going to do time for them."

He wasn't going to force me into making a decision I didn't want to make, but I needed to know if this was for real. "When they made the bargain, did they know this would happen?"

He shrugged. "They knew it might. But they also thought you would get out of it, just like they did. Teddy was sure you'd say yes. Everyone says yes. Just about."

"Not me."

"I won't come back," he said. "There are perfect moments for trading, and this is yours. If you say no, you're saying no forever."

"Fine by me," I said.

He coughed out a mocking laugh. "When you're shitting on that public toilet tomorrow morning, and you're struck by the realization of what your life is going to be for a very long time, you'll be sorry. And then it'll be too late."

I looked over at the toilet, and it did seem a pretty good metaphor for what was coming, but I wasn't about to let him talk me into it.

I turned back to say that, but he was gone. Vanished. Just bars and darkness across the hall. Any doubts I had about the truth of what he'd been saying were gone. I'd been offered a deal, and I'd said no. And now I had a long time to think about whether or not it had been the right call. And I knew something else. Whatever the world was, and however it worked, it wasn't like I'd always thought. It wasn't like how any of us had always thought. But the real deal—that was a big fucking question mark.

Now that I knew there were others, I started walking the city, more and more. I watched the crowds in the street, watched how they looked at the world, how they interacted with it: stabbing at the buttons of cell phones, dancing around little dogs on leashes, haltingly raising their arms for a cab.

And the way *they* watched things. The way they looked at one another, and the way they looked inward. Lots of people look inward when they walk, but maybe sometimes they looked inward at what wasn't there.

I saw it more. Flashes of it. People with dead, painted-on eyes, people who I knew without a doubt were hollow and empty and drifting, like something had just fallen out of them as they walked down the sidewalk.

So many of them were . . . well, not *rich,* but healthy, whole: they looked like Gap models, like bit players in a commercial, not the image of howling rock star success, but the image of comfort, of contentment, of having bought something and found genuine fulfillment in it.

I hated them. I hated them and the cold and the snow, and I hated how it made me feel colder on the inside. They'd said yes, and I hadn't, and I hated myself for it.

It took weeks for me to notice the next big thing, though, weeks of roving and walking in circles. And when I first saw it, it took me a while to realize what I was seeing was true.

There was one block where I saw more of them than anywhere else. Not just the random outliers, drifting down the pavement. Flocks of them. *Gangs* of them. Dozens and dozens of them.

This was where they lived. This was where they congregated, all the ones who said yes.

I felt like I'd penetrated some foreign territory, like a spy on the other side of the Berlin Wall. Were they watching me? Would they suddenly turn hostile, now that I'd found their big secret?

As I huddled in a doorway, I realized they wouldn't. In fact, they didn't give a shit. It took me a minute to realize that to them, to these gleaming, effervescent, happy people with empty eyes, I was probably just some homeless guy. I looked the part, at least. I was scruffy, beat-up. I was someone who'd seen a lot of things and been changed by it. I was not like them, but neither was I anything to care about.

I kept coming back to that block, not sure what I was looking for. Somewhere behind the cold stone walls of that city block was the truth, the thing that had been hiding from me all along, and I had to find it.

Or *him,* actually.

It was sheer random chance that I saw him. The door of a very upscale apartment building opened, and I expected to see, well, anyone walk out. At first, I couldn't even really tell it was him, since it was so dark at the door's threshold.

When he took a few steps out, I realized I knew that walk. That swinging-dick swagger . . . It was unmistakable.

"Marco," I said softly.

He was dressed in a cream-white jacket and corduroy pants, and he wore his beard trimmed so neat and clean it might have been cut by a surgeon. As he walked out, he flipped out a pair of sleek little sunglasses, and he slipped them on with the air of a man confident that he's the protagonist in the movie of his life.

Marco turned back to the door and said something. I saw a shadow at the threshold, and a gorgeous woman in a faux-fur jacket and stripper stiletto heels came clip-clopping out. Usually these ornamentations would make any woman look ridiculous, but she was the sort who used and worked them effortlessly, so that you didn't even notice how impractical they were.

The girl put her arm in his, and they walked off into the city, she with the pristine, pneumatic efficiency of practiced beauty, he with the relaxed contentment of a man freshly scrubbed and refreshed after a long bout of athletic sex.

I stood there in silence for a long time. It started snowing again. When the snow covered the toes of my shoes, I left.

THE NEXT TIME I came back I brought a knife.

I wasn't sure what I was going to do with it. I mean, I vaguely knew. I knew that I wanted to see Marco die, and if that meant I had to do it myself then, well . . . that would need to happen.

Everything had a faint unreality to it as I huddled in an alley outside of his building. I was aware how all this should go—I follow him, wait until he's alone, then confront him, cut his throat—but it felt like I was trying to live someone else's story. I had never killed anyone, even in prison. I'd been in fights in prison, but I hadn't much enjoyed them. I'd seen men die, and I hated seeing that.

I wanted Marco to die. I never ratted him out. I took his years, gave him my own. But I'd never realized how different my life could have been.

He was so happy. Even though his eyes were as empty as all the other hollow people's, he just . . . he just looked like someone everyone wanted to be.

I stood and watched as his apartment door opened. Two young girls came out, trotted down the street. I relaxed. I realized that I'd actually been dreading it: if it was Marco, then I'd have to do what I set out to do.

Then the door opened again, and out he came.

My whole body went rigid. Again, he composed himself on the sidewalk, before setting off with his confident swagger.

I knew that if I took one step after him, I'd have to follow him the whole way, and the more I looked at him, the more I'd want to do it.

My body quivered, frozen. I watched impotently as Marco blithely strolled down the street, turned the corner, and was gone.

Coward, coward. Always such a coward.

I WANDERED THEN. I think I wept. I wasn't sure.

The buzz of yellow sodium lights. The endless tumble of snow. Hallways of towering granite cliffs, riddled with dead little windows. Not unlike the hallways I'd left mere weeks ago. Was this place not unlike a prison? Faceless, miserable people bundled in bright clothing, shuffling along empty stretches, returning to their cells.

I walked down, down into the subway, found some miserable little line hidden in the exposed guts of the city, and sat there listening to the trains, thinking, alone except for a homeless man slouched in the corner.

I looked at my face in the reflection of the knife's blade. The bright, happy young man who'd dabbled in crime had long been erased by sunless years and unspeakable abuse.

How I wished I'd said yes. The hell with all the spiritual navel-gazing. There could be no worse punishment than this, to be alive, and powerless, and empty, and forced to see people living lives that could never be yours.

There was a voice in the subway station. "You look," it said, "like someone in a world of hurt."

I turned my head. The homeless man in the corner raised a hand and pulled his hood back. A familiar face, as familiar as the twenty-dollar bill, smiled out at me as it emerged from shadow.

"Hello again," he said.

"You've seen Marco," he said. He had the same odd, off-color skin, the same weirdly placed features, but he was older and certainly more haggard, even more like an old photograph than before. "Don't tell me you haven't. That could be you, my friend. The deal's a better bargain if you make it before you waste your youth in prison, but that doesn't mean there isn't value to be had. You've got many fine years before you—or, shall we say, they *could* be fine. That's option number one. Number two is that hepatitis C drags you down any day, any minute, poisoned blood washing into your body . . ."

He knew about the hep C. I hated his advantage over me, but whoever this guy was, he wasn't Satan. At least I didn't think so. There was something about him this time that smacked of desperation, like a salesman down on his luck. He had the same jolly, confident tone, but I'd picked up a few skills in prison, and one of them was learning to tell when a guy was talking out of his ass. This guy wasn't just making me an offer, he was trying to save his own bacon. Maybe he had a quota to make. Maybe it had cost him something when he'd let me slide the first time. Who the hell knows how it works in the soul-selling business? Whatever it was, I wanted to find some way to work it.

"I thought it was a one-time offer," I said.

"It was," he said with an easy grin. "And now it is again."

I thought about what he was offering, and what it might mean. I thought about Marco and that woman and all those people in that neighborhood who didn't seem to know or care that they'd lost something. If you don't know or care, how important could losing it be?

"Let's talk," I said.

* * *

We sat in a local coffee shop that fortunately wasn't very crowded. Maybe it had been before we came in, but if so, it soon thinned out. The few other patrons shot menacing stares at us, but I ignored them. None of those people had anything on me, and I sure as hell wasn't going to be intimidated by the evil gaze of a bleach-blond mother who had been ignoring her toddlers while typing into her phone. So I sat with Andrew Jackson while retro cool jazz played over the sound system and strange coffee machines belched out steam like ancient factory equipment.

"The hepatitis goes away?" I asked him.

He raised a saucer full of latte and savored the scent. "Mmmm. Caramel. Yes, my friend. Health is yours for the asking. And more than that—good fortune, friends, women. People will want to help you, give you what you desire, open the doors that now block your every move. No one will want to cheat you or kill you or rob you or rape you—a little protection that might have come in handy over the past few years, I suspect."

Was that why I had been too cowardly to kill Marco? Was I feeling the effects of Marco's deal, and he'd been protected against me?

"Health is good," I said. "So's people being nice."

"*Women* being nice," he said with a wiggle of his eyebrows. "Girls gone *wild*, my friend. Wild."

I said nothing for a long time. He drank his latte and appeared content to wait.

"In the stories," I ventured, "you make a deal, and then something you didn't think of comes back to bite you on the ass. People will be nice to me and luck goes my way, so how do I know a brick won't fall on my head or I won't be paralyzed in a car accident?"

"The brick won't fall," he said, "and you won't get in that car. It's a matter of chance, a matter of choice. The world operates in patterns. I can put you in a place where the patterns always work in your favor."

"What guarantee do I have?"

He appeared curious now. "What kind would you like?"

"I don't know. I just don't want to be ripped off."

"I assure you, no one's out to trick you. It's all aboveboard. If we don't keep our part of the bargain . . . if you fall victim to the wrong sort of pattern, I suppose, and experience devastating bad luck . . . then we are obligated to void the contact. You will, of course, be dead or paralyzed or otherwise unfortunate, but you'd be out of the contract. We can't keep what we take if you don't get what we promise."

"Would that be bad for you?" I asked.

He cocked his head, like an animal hearing something not quite disturbing. "It wouldn't be *good,* no. But we're not here to discuss me. I see you're interested. There's no time like the present to commit."

I nodded. There was, in fact, no time like the present.

His expression brightened. "Then shall we proceed?"

"Give me twenty-four hours to think about it."

"I'm afraid I can't do that," he said sadly.

"You seem to want this deal," I told him, "so I think you can. I'll be back here, in this coffee shop, in twenty-four hours. If you don't show, we'll just say I lost out again, forever. Until the next time."

"You drive a hard bargain, my friend. A very hard bargain."

I went back to the neighborhood, the one full of people with dead eyes. I bought another cup of coffee and stood leaning against the wide of a building, breathing into the cup, letting the steam blast my face.

Those people walked past me, happy and smiling and full of life, hardly seeming to notice that they appeared dead. At least they did to me. Maybe they didn't look that way to each other. Maybe, I thought, they didn't look that way to anyone else. What if you had to say no to the deal in order to spot all the people who'd made deals of their own? The more I thought about it, the more sense that made. A beautiful woman walked past me, her face so lovely it almost hurt to see it, but she had the eyes of a corpse. How could it be that no one else was repelled? The only answer was that they didn't see it.

I did not choose her. A woman like that would be used to turning away strangers. Instead I waited for an older guy, perhaps in his fifties, out walking his little dog in its blue sweater. He seemed like the sort who enjoyed talking, so I walked up to him, my posture relaxed and unthreatening.

"Hey," I said. "Can I ask you something?"

This question appeared to be the highlight of his day. "Sure!" he boomed, his voice low and deep and cheerful.

"When you made the deal, what did the guy look like?"

He lost some of his friendliness now, and he stared at me with fear or shame or regret, I couldn't quite tell.

I raised my free hand. "Just curious. Not looking for trouble. I just kind of need to know."

"Okay," he said, nodding vigorously, like maybe he really wanted to talk about it. "He was kind of strange looking, with a big forehead."

"Like Andrew Jackson?" I asked. "The guy from the twenty-dollar bill?"

"I *know* who Andrew Jackson is," he said peevishly. "I teach American history. But yes, that's exactly it. I could never quite put my finger on it, but that's what he looked like. Except not."

"Except not," I agreed.

I found three more people willing to answer my question, and I got the same response. Andrew Jackson, every time. Either everyone making these deals looked like my guy, or this entire neighborhood was all serviced by a single merchant.

So much the better.

That night I went out. I wanted to enjoy myself before everything changed. I drank a lot of whiskey and paid for a woman, but I didn't particularly enjoy either. The next morning I told myself it was better to have made the effort.

It was just after eight in the morning when I rang the doorbell. I rang it three times and then knocked. Then I pounded. Finally I heard feet on hardwood, and then an awkward hand fiddling with locks. He didn't ask who it was. Why should he have to? No one ever meant him any harm.

He answered the door in his bathrobe open to his waist. He was in great shape, but his face looked like shit—red eyes, unshaven, puffy.

"Rough night, Marco?" I asked.

His face contorted in confusion and then he got it. He remembered. He opened his arms and drew me into a hug.

We sat in his beautiful kitchen, at the table in the nook, away from his own hissing and puffing espresso machine on the marble island. Natural light poured in from the windows. Marco ran a hand through his mussed hair and sipped from his mug, leaving a momentary foam mustache. I passed on the coffee. I didn't need any more caffeine.

We spent half an hour on bullshit. He told me about his life, his job as a consultant, whatever the fuck that was—even he didn't really seem to know. It was just some kind of high-paying boondoggle that had fallen into his lap. He told me about his fiancée, who was not the woman I'd seen the other day. That was someone else, a little thing on the side that didn't mean a whole lot, but sure was fun. And then, after all this wonderful conversation, the topic turned to me.

"I can't tell you how sorry I am about how things went down. Teddy and I never forgot how much we owe you for keeping quiet."

"It's what any one of us would have done," I said. "I just had bad luck."

He opened his mouth, and I was sure he was going to say—*In this world, you make your own luck*—but he thought better of it. Bright boy.

Instead, he said, "Still, I totally owe you."

Maybe he forgot that I received the same offer he did. Maybe he never knew, and the business about him calling me a pussy had been pure bullshit. Whatever the reason, he didn't tell me about the deal, and I didn't bring it up.

After hearing more about how much he owed me, I finally decided to put it to the test.

"I hate to ask," I said, "but the truth is, I'm kind of in trouble. Some guys I knew from inside are trying to shake me down. I could use something to get them off my case."

"Something?" he asked. His face went dark. He loved telling me how much he owed me, but maybe he didn't like so much actually following up on it.

"I need a gun, Marco, and it's kind of hard for an ex-con to get one. You always had a few pieces stashed away. I can't believe you've changed *that* much."

"I don't know," he said, his eyes drifting toward the window. He gazed at his watchless wrist and considered the busy morning ahead. "It's getting kind of late and—"

"I'm not going to shoot anyone," I said, rushing to get the words out, earnest and nervous. "I just want to let them know they can't push me around."

He sipped his drink, thinking. Now he looked at the wall clock.

"You know what, forget it," I said, my voice easy and apologetic, my palms flying up. "I had no right to ask. You dodged a bullet all those years ago, and I shouldn't have asked for you to tempt fate now that you're clean." I pushed back my chair.

If I had tried to lay a guilt trip on him, he'd have left me high and dry, but this worked like a charm.

"Hold on," he said, and he got up, pressing a hand on my shoulder to set me back down. He went upstairs and came down a few minutes later with a Glock. Nice piece. Nine millimeter, seventeen-round magazine. It felt good in my hand.

"Sweet," I said, as I weighed it in my palm. I then held it and pointed it toward an imaginary target.

Marco smiled nervously. "Just be sure you don't kill anyone with it," he said.

"Not a living soul," I assured him.

Something shifted in his face, and he knew. He understood everything.

That instant, less than a full second, hung between us, and the years and experiences and fortunes that separated us collapsed. It was just me and just Marco, old friends. Marco, a good guy, the kind of guy who always attracted good fortune and favors—even before he made his deal. Marco, who walked when I went to jail.

I fired the gun into his forehead. Blood sprayed out the back of his head against the window, a brilliant blossom around the spiderweb of cracked glass.

I hadn't wanted to hurt him. Andrew Jackson had been right about that. I hadn't wanted to do anything that might have done him harm. But I knew that what I was doing was helping him.

"You're welcome," I said to Marco's corpse.

Sixteen rounds left. I headed outside to make the most of them.

I wish I could say it made me feel different. I wish I could say that when I sat in the coffee shop, staring at the cream dancing slowly with the coffee in my cup, I felt like a man on the run, fraught with paranoia, expecting danger from every corner, to hear the air fill with silence and have SWAT officers descend in a coordinated onrush.

But no. I watched the happy couples and young parents stand in line, fussing and chatting, and I felt exactly the same as I had the day I left prison.

I lifted my coffee cup to my lips, but my hand expected the grip of a Glock, and the kick of a firing pin, and when I drank, my nose expected not coffee but the perfume of cordite.

I shut my eyes, and drank. It was like it was all still happening.

. . . A housewife stands in the doorway of her apartment, shouting to her husband that they're six minutes late already. When she sees me, she frowns, curious, and that curious frown never leaves her face as I lift the Glock and point it at her cheek . . .

. . . The teen boy and his girlfriend leap to their feet when I kick in the door, the black sheet of her hair withdrawing from his crotch to reveal a half-flaccid penis dangling from the front of his boxers, and the boy raises his hands to me and screams but the gun is already going off . . .

. . . The old history teacher grumbles as he tries to fix a plastic bag around his hand while his dog yaps mindlessly at me, standing mere feet away. I don't wait for him to look up. The left collarbone of his thick vest spews stuffing, followed shortly by blood. He shouts, slightly outraged, and falls to the ground on his side. His dog shrieks, rears up, tries to bound at me, but the old man's hand holds fast. When he sees me, he blinks and says, "Oh, my goodness. Oh, my goodness," and I take aim again . . .

I swallowed. I put the coffee cup back down and opened my eyes, expecting to see police converging on the coffee shop.

But there were no police. Only him, the curious vagrant with a striking likeness to Andrew Jackson. He was staring at me through the window with a look of slight betrayal. He opened the door and walked in to sit before me.

He stared at me as I sipped my coffee. I did not meet his eyes.

"So," he said. "It was you?"

I didn't answer.

"Of course it was you," he said. "Who else?"

"Who else," I echoed.

"*Why?*" He sounded genuinely shocked. "Why would you do this? Why?"

I looked around the coffee shop, sullen, and did not answer.

"Ten people," he said. "Ten of *my* people. I . . . I told them they would live happy lives."

"I guess maybe I wanted to see if the bullets would bounce off them. To see how charmed their lives really were. Or maybe I thought they'd be better off this way."

"You . . . you don't understand what you've done!" he hissed. "You don't understand how you've hurt things!"

"Did I fuck your sales quota? Is that it?"

"You've *ruined* me," he whispered. He looked like he was on the verge of tears. "You've *destroyed* me."

"I guess your firm must be pretty pissed at you. I can't say you get a lot of my sympathy. After all, I just voided a lot of contracts. Set a lot of souls free." I smiled. "You know, there was a guy I met in prison who'd spent almost his whole life in solitary."

"They'll . . . They'll eat me *alive* for this . . ."

"I only saw him once," I continued, "for about a week, before he wound up going back—back to that empty cell, all by himself. He'd spent *years* in there, they told me. And it was all his fault, you know? Because this guy, whenever they let him out, he always went *wild* on everybody. A huge guy, and he'd just pummel anyone he could get his hands on, beat them to shit. Maybe a week or two would go by before he did it again—the calm before the storm—but then he'd be raging like an elephant, hurling chairs and desks over stairways, breaking glass with his fists . . ."

He buried his face in his hands.

"And I asked him, while I had the chance—why do you do it? What's the point? I was terrified to ask, you see, because I thought he'd kill me—but he didn't. He thought about it, and he just laughed. It was a nasty kind of laugh. And he said, 'We only got a handful of choices. Figure I'll use mine to spit in their goddamn eyes.' And it didn't make a lot of sense to me then, but yesterday, it did."

The vagrant slowly looked up at me. His face drained of expression, then turned to rage. "You did this all . . . for *spite*?"

"Spite's all you've allowed me. It's all I have left. You and the world, you take away my choices, bit by bit, until the only ones I've got left are the ones that destroy me. But I guess you never thought I could take you with me."

"I'll . . . I'll *ruin* you," said the man. He snapped his fingers. "The police will come and they'll take you away, back to your rotten little cell! And you'll *die* there, you'll die coughing and fouling yourself as your body eats itself alive!"

I shrugged. "Out here, I'd be in a cell, too. A little block of life you'd have arranged for me. I don't much see the difference. Except with *your* cell, I'd never have made a choice."

"You would have chosen to be *happy*!"

"I would have chosen to allow you to *make* me happy. Which isn't the same. But here's the thing—having done what I did, and having made the choice I made . . ." I took another sip of coffee, knowing it'd almost certainly be the last I'd be getting for a while. " . . . I am happy as *shit*." And I grinned at him.

The man fumed for a second. Then he spat in my face, a thick, warm blob, turned around, and stormed out, cursing.

I laughed. I laughed long and hard as I wiped his spit away. I was still laughing when I heard the sirens.

AMUSE-BOUCHE

Amber Benson and Jeffrey J. Mariotte

The first thing is my head. It's *pounding.* I wish briefly that my heart would stop, because with every pulse of blood (I can hear it in my ears, like cars passing on a nearby highway) the pain blooms, then starts to fade, but comes back again before it goes away altogether.

Then I realize that I'm thinking about the pounding, that realization dawning so slowly that at that first moment, when I wanted my heart to simply cease pumping blood, I wasn't yet awake. Because now I am, and the pain is so much worse that I'm certain, for a few instants, I'm going to puke. I'm lying on my back, and that's going to be bad, so I roll over onto my side.

Or try to.

That's when I discover the collar ringing my neck and the straps around my wrists. When I try to turn, the leather of the collar catches my throat. I choke a little, which cranks up the volume on the headache, so I roll back to where I was. Test my hands. A few inches of give, but not much.

Now I'm awake enough to think, *What the fuck?*

Wherever I am, it's dark. I'm on a table or a platform of some kind, a theory based mostly on the distance to the ceiling—not as far as if I was on the floor. Plus, when I try to look around, I see things, objects I can't quite make out, lower than me.

I have awakened in some strange places—usually the wrong guy's bed—but never in quite this sort of situation.

I am not, I must add, fond of it.

It's hot in here too. I stink of sweat and maybe pee. So rank, anyway, that I can't smell anything else around me. Not fond of that, either, but there you go.

"Hello?" Someone had to have put me here. I didn't do this to myself. If that someone is still around—although I can't see or hear anyone—then he or she (no, *he,* without question) can undo it. And right now, that's the most important thing. "Hey, where are you? What is up with this shit? Hello, whoever you are!"

Nobody answers, and panic bubbles up inside me like coffee in my grandmother's old percolator. She always made terrible coffee, weak and a little sour. But when I was a kid, I liked to watch it dance into the little clear well in the lid, and I'm trying to think about things I like because it lets me, for almost a second at a time, not think about the reality of what I'm doing here and how I got here and who did this and for fuck's sake why, *why,* and what's next?

And then it doesn't work anymore.

The panic hits and I'm sobbing and my nose is running, my eyes overflowing with hot tears, and I'm saying something, or trying to, but it's not coming out right. It's sort of *hey untie me let me out of here what's the fucking idea if this is supposed to be all fun and games or something you have failed miserably,* but it comes out in a blubbering burst of word stew that even I'm a little embarrassed by. Which, given my situation, is, I know. Stupid.

Not my first encounter with stupid, though.

Was it stupid to walk into that bar last night? A place I've never been, a block off Sunset. Should have been safe enough, right? It was crowded, and loud, and I'd had this argument with Jen and just needed to be away from everything for a while, have a drink, chill. Was it stupid to drink on an empty stomach?

I can't remember anything after that. In the bar, I recall a guy hitting on me and me shooting him down, and then that other one, more persistent. Pushy. A little familiar, maybe, like I'd seen him around the neighborhood. He had dark hair, kind of curly but oily, so it clung to his scalp, and a prominent beak of a nose, and this gap between his front teeth big enough that I could sometimes see his tongue through it, like a fat, pink worm trying to escape a cage. He had a sort of spoiled-meat odor about him. I remember telling him, no thanks, and then getting up and going to the bathroom. When I came out, he wasn't sitting there anymore. And after . . .

After that, nothing. Blank.

Then here. The head, the darkness, the straps holding me in place. The panic.

Which is starting to come back when I hear a voice—his voice, as distinct as that spoiled-meat stink he wore—coming out of the dark. I freeze but miss the words, lost under my own sobbing. A moment later, he speaks again. "I was just wondering, do you know what human myoglobin is?"

I press the button on the remote control and, through the monitor, the iris of the camera becomes my eye. I can already tell that the actress I chose for the part is working out splendidly. She is a real method actor, her fear palpable even from the control room.

There are seven cameras set up around the studio, the angles chosen to capture every nuance of her performance. As I watch her work, I find I cannot tear my gaze away.

Technologically speaking, I am a fan of the Canon 7D—I find it to be a very filmic digital camera with the right lenses, and a lot more forgiving than the more expensive 5D model. For a long time, I chose to shoot on film, but dealing with Super 16 became so cumbersome (I've never been willing to let anyone else process my dailies—I'm a bit of a perfectionist) that I finally gave it up in favor of the more streamlined digital video format. Besides, I am in exalted company. All the modern greats are working in this new medium: Soderbergh, Cameron, Rodriguez. Who am I to be a film snob when the directors I most admire are leading the charge in this bold new world?

I always edit my own material. *Always.* Over the years, I've found I have a real knack for the subtlety of the subject matter. I believe in anyone else's hands my films would seem exploitative. Tarantino is always being maligned for this, and, thankfully, with my skill and the forgiving nature of my audience, I have so far escaped this negative label.

For me, the pleasure of the filmmaking process is twofold: the actual filming is by far the highlight of the adventure, but the splicing together of raw footage, the crafting of an Oscar-worthy performance, is an almost orgasmic feeling that words cannot express.

I have cast talented actresses—and I enjoy working with them immensely—but, in truth, it's the hacks who have supplied me with the most joy. My ability to take their subpar work and make something magical from it, well, that, too, is an orgasmic feeling.

I've ignored my actress for too long, and now the tears have started. I think unmotivated emotion is déclassé. It must be something they all learn in acting class, because they all do it. I have yet to work with one who does not, at some point, trot out the waterworks, expecting to get my directorial approval but finding themselves the object of my derision instead.

Actors are a funny lot. Always looking for the director's praise and willing to subjugate themselves to all kinds of humiliation to obtain that approval. I once called the trade my own, but quickly realized how much better suited I was to directing and producing. I am an *auteur,* not an actor. I crave capturing my singular vision on-screen. I was not born to be a pawn in someone else's game, to breathe life into another man's creation.

I press the intercom and speak into the microphone again.

"I'd like to try that once more. But without the tears."

The actress stiffens, her long-lashed eyes wide as she tries to figure out where my words are coming from.

She was the prettiest girl at the audition. Not the best actress, but from her reading I intuited that she would be easy to mold. That she would take to my directing style without the need to fight me—as some of the more talented ones did in the beginning, before I'd refined my casting criteria. I press the button on the intercom and speak slowly into the microphone, my lips almost, but not quite, touching its thatched head. "Do you know what human myoglobin is?"

She shakes her head, nostrils flaring as she fights the urge to cry. It seems once an actor slips inside the world of a sense memory, it's hard for them to escape its orbit. But my actress contends admirably with the task.

As I stare into the monitor for camera A, I can see her internal struggle. I call the view from this camera the "money shot" angle because of its proximity to my actress's face. I am so tight on her eyes that I can see the jagged red capillaries, like molten tributaries feeding the sclera. They remind me of the bright red streaks of blood I found inside one of my eggs this morning.

It was a pleasure to watch the blood absorb into the gelatinous whites as I scrambled them for breakfast, my gourmand's tongue enjoying the barest hint of blood as I slid the first bite into my mouth.

Delicious.

"NO," I SAY, shaking my head. "I don't—what is—?"

I can't even form the question in my head. There are too many and they all bash against each other and I can't figure out which one to ask first so I go silent, tugging at my bonds, trying to swallow back terror. For the first time, I realize my nausea is not just from fear, but hunger. I rack my brain, trying to remember what I ate last: a bagel. From the twenty-four-hour coffee place near my house. Maybe an hour before I went to the bar. Before the bagel, I'd only eaten breakfast. Greasy eggs and bacon. The memory only adds to my nausea and I push it away.

"Never mind," he says, snapping my attention back to the present. His voice has a strange quality to it. I think it's electronic, like he's not in the room but somehow broadcasting to me. Which would explain why I didn't hear anything until he spoke, and still can't smell him. "Let's try a little exercise. Show me love. Not lust, not romantic love, but motherly love."

"What?"

"Look, I understand you're not a mother. But you've been a daughter. You've seen mothers. Maybe you had a pet, or a doll, something you cared about. Reach inside and give me motherly love."

"I don't know what you're talking about!" I try not to scream, to keep the edge of fear and fury from my voice, because a few things are becoming clear.

I don't do a very good job of it. "Just let me go!"

"That's good," he says. "I love that complex mix of emotions. Confusion, concern, rage, all telegraphed by those remarkable blue eyes, the tension in your muscles, the almost strangled timbre of your voice. It's nicely played. However"—and here his voice changes, not as calm as it had been, his words becoming clipped, his tone like that of a schoolteacher disciplining a problem student—"it is not what I asked for!"

"I don't know what you want! I don't know what I'm doing here!" I wrench at the straps around my wrists but can't tear free. I fight for some semblance of control. "I'm not trying to, I don't know, disappoint you. But, you know, you brought me here, abducted me or whatever, and it seems like the least you could do is explain what's going on."

A long stretch of silence. Then his voice comes back, still with that disapproving tone. "Just a minute."

And it's quiet again. I try to peer through the darkness. Now that my vision has acclimated, I can see things that don't make any sense. I'm in a big room. No windows are visible from my admittedly limited vantage point. There are floor-to-ceiling posts, random furniture. None of that is especially surprising. But then there are what look like lights on stands, and others on racks suspended from the ceiling. Way off to my right is a clothing rack, on wheels, with what appears to be a variety of women's clothes, mostly long dresses, hanging on it.

So I've been abducted by a women's clothing salesman? I think about the boutique Jen and I had ventured into, on Beverly, where everything looked like it had been made for size zeros and smaller, and blind at that, with no concept that some people wear clothes for comfort and protection from the elements instead of to make a statement on the red carpet and the gossip pages. We were kind of stunned at first, then amused, and finally we laughed out loud.

The salesgirl was not entertained.

The image of her—blue haired and impossibly skinny, with black plastic cat's-eye glasses, using some sort of voice-changing device that makes her sound like a man—flashes through my mind, and I can't help myself. I crack up. Giggling at first, then guffaws, genuinely hysterical laughter. My body tries to fold, my neck scrapes against the leather band, my hands flail to the extent allowed.

Through my laughter I hear the scrape of a door, the scuff of feet approaching. I try to look in that direction, but it's off my left shoulder and I can't turn that far. I'm straining, and I know he can see that. He stops, just out of view. I can actually see a little of one of his arms, I think: a black shirt, the arm slightly crooked.

I give up and slump back to my table.

"We have to get some things straight," he says. Now I can smell him. Definitely the guy from that bar I wish I had never walked into.

"We can start with you letting me go," I say. "I won't tell anybody about this, believe me. We'll just forget it ever happened."

"You must know that's not possible," he says. "Besides, we're just getting started."

"Started with what?"

"You have to remember that I'm directing this piece. As an actress it's important that you be flexible. You have to be able to move from one emotion to another, on cue. I realize we haven't had a lot of rehearsal time, but I'm counting on you to overcome that tiny obstacle."

"I'm not an actress!" I cry. "You've got the wrong woman! I work in the financial aid office at UCLA. My name is Mad—"

"Aaaap!" he says, cutting me off. "*Louise!* You're Louise. And you're wrong. I recognized you at the audition. I knew right away that you were the one."

"What audition? I haven't *been* to any audition."

He moves closer, and now I can see him, all greasy hair, nose, and gapped teeth. He puts a hand on my shoulder. I try to shake it off but he holds tighter, his fingers biting into my flesh like he wants to tear off a chunk. "Let's just try it my way," he says. "Later on, if you want to try something different, you can. But for now, Louise, do it my way."

THEY ALWAYS GIVE themselves stage names.

My parents were no different. Once under the influence of the glittering Southern California sun, a nobody Jewess from the Bronx named Esther Smirsky became the much-beloved actress Eleanor Smart. The same went for the orphaned kid from Atlanta they called Henry Cohen. Yet my father loved his given first name—given by whom, he never knew, since he grew up with no knowledge of his true parentage. Not that he ever went looking for his birth parents once he had the money to do it. He chose only to excise the Jewish-sounding "h" from his name and call it a day.

OSCAR-WINNING ACTRESS ELEANOR SMART SECRETLY MARRIES BOX OFFICE SMASH HENRY COEN!

This was an actual headline from a *Los Angeles Times* article that ran right after they eloped to Maui without having told a single soul of their intention—not even Eleanor's only living relative, her mother in the Bronx, who, if Eleanor's nicotine- and alcohol-fueled tales could be trusted, had cried herself to death over the slight.

Speaking of slights . . . I'm not an idiot. Of course, while I was filling out her paperwork last night, I had to look at her Ohio driver's license. The name on it is not Louise, as I'd been led to believe, but Madeleine Newhall. I don't care one whit she changed her name for her career or that she still hasn't gotten around to getting her license in California—even though it's illegal not to apply for a California license within ten days of becoming a resident. Not that I am going to be the one to turn Madeleine Newhall in to the police for her obvious violation.

An obvious violation, especially if she is, indeed, collecting a paycheck from UCLA for part-time employment.

I know how it goes. Every struggling artist, be they actor, painter, or musician, must have a day job to support themselves in their endeavor. You'd think the privileged son of two famous actors wouldn't have an inkling what that's like.

But you would be wrong.

Dead wrong.

Eleanor and Henry had suffered terribly as children. It made them humble, made them work hard for any success they got. They did not believe in sparing the rod and spoiling the child. They treated me as they had been treated.

Even when I was a baby none of the creature comforts my parents enjoyed belonged to me. I was relegated to a small back room ostensibly called "the Nursery"—and it is there I still reside. Once they were both dead, I tried to move into the master suite of the old Outpost Estates mansion, but there's something about the rooms, a moldy-rotten smell, really, that puts me off. Makes it impossible for me to sleep there. So I stay where I feel safest. In the nursery room where I have always lived, alone, like a leper in a paradise I will never be allowed to fully enjoy.

My actress is struggling against her bindings again. I'm afraid she's going to hurt herself, so I take the already-prepared hypodermic needle from my pocket, uncap it, and slide her underwear down, gently pressing the tip of the needle into the firm, round flesh of her naked left buttock. Having done this several times already, I have the dosage down. Instantly, her eyes begin to flutter, the bright lapis irises rolling back into her head. I begin to release the restraints, finding her arms and legs flaccid in my hands. I unhook the shock collar from its moorings, leaving it in place around her neck.

I've found the shock collar, on its highest setting, is a wonderful way to control my actors. It helps them quickly learn that I must be obeyed. I don't know why more directors don't use the technique.

With very little exertion, I manage to flip my actress over and worm my hands underneath her limp body, picking her up easily. I wonder if she's awake, because it feels as though she's nuzzling my neck, but then I realize it's just her steady breath wheezing against my skin and the way her head lolls as I carry her across the room. She is heavier than she looks. Though she's slim, she's muscular and long-limbed. But I'm up to the task. I lift weights every morning out on the veranda with my trainer, Mike.

I may not be able to fully enjoy the gated compound my parents left to me when they died, but I've discovered a consolation prize. It gives me great, almost physical pleasure to know my parents are silent partners in my filmic endeavors. I think if they knew just how much I've grown as an artist, they might finally be proud of me.

I keep one hard-backed chair in the center of the second basement room. It is the room's sole occupant—that is, until I bring one of my actresses inside and seat her on it. I have sat in the chair myself and I can assure you that it's very uncomfortable: perfect for the work we will be doing.

I step away and immediately, as though she is mocking me, the actress slumps forward in her chair. I sit her back up, draping her arms over the chair back so she won't slide again, but this position makes her large breasts jut forward under the thin cotton of her chemise. Most men would find the pose erotic. They would spread her legs and touch themselves as they looked at her.

I am not most men.

I am an artist.

I reposition her into a less wanton, more supine, pose and then I inject her with adrenaline.

My actress wakes with a start.

MY HEART HAMMERS so fast in my chest that I wonder if I'm having a heart attack or a stroke or something. A panic attack at the very least. I haven't had one of those in almost seven years, since I got away from Cuyahoga and my lush of a mother and her useless husband, old Wandering Hands McGee. I can't say I've missed them. The 'rents *or* the panic attacks.

So it takes me a little while to realize I've been moved. I'm sitting in a rigid, straight-backed chair. It's the only stick of furniture in the room. He, the guy—let's call it what it is, my abductor, my captor, the man I'm convinced means to be my murderer—stands a few feet away, watching me. He wears a half smile: Mona Lisa in drag. His eyes are wide, expectant. His right hand is buried in his pocket.

"Good," he says, in reference to I don't know what. "Let's get to work, shall we?"

"You know I haven't the slightest idea what you're talking about."

The hand in his pocket moves, and at the same instant I'm jolted by sudden, darting pain. My back arches, my feet come off the floor and slam down again, and I almost fall out of the chair. It's gone in a moment, just a remnant tingling sensation left behind, and my heart feels like it's been kick-started again.

"We're wasting daylight, Louise. A little cooperation would make this all so much easier."

"Why all the drama?" I ask. I know I'm risking another jolt—my neck is burning and I realize that it's probably the collar around it, some sort of shock device, and he's holding the remote in his pocket—but I'm scared and I'm pissed and I've really just had it with this guy. "If you're going to kill me, get to it."

His hand twitches again and I wince, knowing what's coming, but it doesn't. For an instant, I'm grateful. I think about offering him head. That might make him angry, though, and I figure if that's what he's after, he'll tell me. Besides, the idea of him filling up my empty stomach with sperm makes me want to gag.

"Here's the scene," he says. "You've been hurtfully, unceremoniously dumped by the guy you thought was the One. The wound is still raw. He told you that he only wanted you for your body, for what you could offer him sexually. That stings, because deep down inside, you always suspected that. So you're going to make sure that never happens again. With me so far?"

Not in the slightest, I think. But I'm not looking for another shock. "Sure. I guess."

"So how will you accomplish that?"

"I don't know. Wear baggy clothes. Hide my figure. Maybe gain some weight."

"Temporary fixes!" he snaps. "Sooner or later you'll be out there again, with your breasts on display like some common streetwalker. You've got to take real action. You've got to show your commitment to change. This is the emotional meat of the scene, Louise. He's coming back to see you, and you've got to show him your determination to become someone else, someone who's not ruled by your sexuality. Someone who can break free from the bonds of the flesh."

Just when I think I've got this guy figured out, I don't. I'm confused all over again. I thought my flesh was why he snatched me in the first place, and I've been waiting for him to make his move. But now it sounds like I repulse him.

Pretty much the same effect he has on me, so I guess we're even. Except he's the one with the remote control and I'm the one in the chair.

"You've lost me," I tell him. "I don't know how I'm supposed to convey that, or even what you mean by it. What do you mean, 'break free'? How do I transform myself?"

He allows himself a smile, showing me the gap between his teeth. "See? Isn't this better, Louise? Give and take. We figure out who your character is, what makes her tick, and then you inhabit her. As for your transformation . . ."

His pocket moves, just the slightest bit, and once again I'm spasming, this time lurching from the chair onto the floor. When it passes I climb back up, and I know I'm giving him *What the Fuck* eyes but I can't help myself.

He reads me like a newspaper. "A gentle reminder," he says. He shoves his left hand into his other hip pocket and pulls something out. Holds it up for me to see.

A folded razor.

He bends forward, sets it gently on the floor, then straightens and gives it a kick.

It skids toward me, spinning, hits a leg of the chair and stops.

"I WANT YOU to cut your face," I say, the words like tiny electrical shocks as they dance across my tongue. I'm so excited about this actress, about all the possibility that lies before us, I can hardly contain myself.

My actress stares at the straight razor, blinking rapidly. I can see the thoughts flickering like ticker tape through her mind. She has such expressive eyes—windows to the soul, they say—that I can almost guess what is going on in her mind.

She takes a ragged breath, trying to decide what might be the best way to approach the situation. I am amused by her. She is trying to figure me out. I want to tell her that after five years even my psychiatrist still hasn't been able to get a bead on me, so I find it highly doubtful the actress who mans the reception desk at the UCLA financial aid office is going to be able to put Humpty Dumpty back together again after five minutes in my company.

She lifts her chin, having decided that a good offense is the best defense.

"No."

Her voice is low and husky. Reminds me of Sophia Loren, but without the accent.

I lovingly caress the button on the remote control in my pocket, my thumb sliding over its polished plastic surface. My eyes lock on hers as I remove the device from its hiding place, holding it up so she can see how small, slim, and discreet it is. I want her to see it. I want her to watch me press the button. This way she has no doubts about who is in control.

The shock sends her sliding off the chair. I've ratcheted it up all the way now—I'd only had it on the medium setting the first time—and her whole body thrums with the electricity I'm shooting through her. I release the button and the pain stops, her body going slack on the floor. She shudders once, a string of drool oozing out of her mouth. A puddle of urine pools around her hips, but it doesn't bother me. I just go to the supply closet behind me, unlock the door with one of the keys hanging around my neck, and retrieve a roll of paper towels, a brown paper grocery bag, and a bottle of Nature's Miracle, placing it at her feet.

"Clean yourself up," I say.

I take care not to let her see the interior of the supply closet: the plastic sheeting, the extra-large roll of garbage bags, the bottles of Clorox, the boxes of disposable cotton gloves, paper jumpsuits, and paper booties. I like to leave things to the imagination, and a look inside my supply closet would give away part of the ending.

Dazed, she collects herself, takes the paper towels and mops up her waste, deposits it in the brown bag—which, unbeknownst to her, I will burn in my fire pit later. She looks up at me through fringed lashes, her long, brown hair falling over her face. There is defiance there. But there is delicious fear, too.

I slide the remote control back into my pocket but do not remove my hand again. Now she will be in the dark, will not know when the next shock is coming.

"Cut yourself," I whisper, encouraging her with my words.

"Where?" she says.

Where? I wonder for a moment, until inspiration strikes. "Take off the tip of your nose."

She stares at me, uncomprehending. I distinctly hear her stomach growl. I know she has been on set for twenty-five hours without a meal, but hunger makes the senses sharper, gives a better performance.

"I said, take off the tip of your nose."

Almost against her will, she reaches out and takes the blade. Her arm rises—my excitement mounts—then she stops, the blade an inch from her nose.

"I don't want to," she says, her tone perilously close to whining. "Do I have to?"

I nod.

She swallows, her chapped lips compressing into one thin line. She places the blade against the tip of her nose and closes her eyes. The blade—razor sharp, I've made sure—slices through the dermis and then the cartilage. It happens so quickly, the thrust of her hand so decisive, that, at first, it doesn't bleed. But as her pale flesh falls to the ground, exposing the raw inner parts, the blood begins to flow in earnest. She screams at what she's just done, the pain registering, finally. She looks down at the floor where the tip of her nose lays, the flat, bloody part pressed onto the concrete. She looks at the blade in her hand, then she lifts her eyes to me. Whatever she sees there, whatever the open window to my soul reveals, makes her scream and scream and scream.

And then the ground begins to shake.

WHATEVER HELL I'VE fallen into must be of my own making. I don't know what I've done to deserve it—no, that's a lie, and if I can't be honest with myself at a time like this, then I'm a hopeless case. I've done plenty; I've been petty and vindictive, dishonest, I've made an art form out of situational ethics, and if I have any personal principles, they're subject to change without notice. Mom rarely emerged from her alcoholic miasma long enough to teach anything about morality, and her husband was no saint, unless there's a patron saint of diddling stepdaughters. But I understand that a person has to set her own standards and live up to them, and in that pursuit, I have failed miserably.

But this, now . . . I must have brought it upon myself, because a neutral universe wouldn't allow it.

Or else the universe isn't neutral, but insane. Yes, that must be a possibility, too. The universe is insane and the "director" is insane and me—with a razor's edge held against my nose, the cute, petite button of a nose I've been unreasonably prideful of for so long, upturned at the very end—well, I'm either insane or simply a victim, unmoored, haplessly floating in a river of crazy.

He stares at me. That fat pink tongue emerges from his mouth, laps across his lips once. He looks famished.

Hapless. Hopeless.

I make the cut.

Nothing. Did I miss? But then it hits, a shock of pain almost electric in its suddenness. At the same instant, a pale dollop of flesh hits the floor in front of me and I realize what it is and I look up at the man who made me do it and my mouth falls open and the screaming begins. I fall off the chair, certain I've pissed myself again, not giving a damn.

But the chair keeps moving behind me, and the floor's moving too. I think it's me, but then I see him throw his legs apart for balance, arms outstretched, and he eyes the ceiling. Dust cascades from above. The motion continues, harder, jolt after jolt.

I find myself embracing sanity again. Because this is an earthquake, and I've felt a couple of those before. Frightening as they can be—and this feels like a serious one—at least they're somewhat familiar. The quake tethers me to reality, and I realize I truly have cut off the tip of my nose. Blood spatters the floor and my stomach heaves, and I spew my guts onto the floorboards, noticing as I do that they're buckling. All around me are the sounds of the structure cracking and snapping and heaving and groaning.

He—the director—tries to run. He bolts for the door, but the ground bucks and hurls him down. At the same time a crashing noise sounds from above. He cranes his neck, looks up, and screams, his hands and feet skittering, unable to find purchase.

And a ceiling beam—in a brief instant of clarity I recognize it as a six-by-six and suspect it's redwood—snaps and plummets, jagged end first.

It hits him dead on. It spears his lower back, I can actually see an immense shard of bloody wood erupt from his abdomen. As he slumps to the floor, plaster and debris tear loose from overhead and fall across his legs.

More crashing sounds from outside this room, as if the whole—whatever; I think, because of the lack of windows, that we're in a basement, but that's only a guess at this point—as if the whole rest of the house is collapsing on us. I brace for more falling beams, ready to die in the crush. Almost eager for the end.

Almost, but not quite.

The shaking ceases and after one more thunderous roar, all is still. Dust has filled the room. It settles slowly, softer than snowfall. I gag on it, spit blood and puke and phlegm.

I force myself to my knees, to my feet.

I've lived in L.A. long enough to know that there will likely be aftershocks. For the moment, though, the earth is quiet, its wad shot. Awareness dawns slowly, but dawn it does, and I know these things:

- I have mutilated myself.
- Even so, I'm not as injured as he is. He's alive, but maybe not for long. He's moaning and writhing under the weight of the beam that pierced his midsection and maybe broke his legs.
- The house is a wreck, but the power, remarkably, remains on.
- Maybe the universe contains mercy as well as madness, because it has given me a chance.

On unsteady legs, I walk around him, giving him a wide berth. He's awake, looking at me, his eyes pleading. Blood runs from his mouth in a steady trickle, and although his jaw moves, the only sound he makes is a wordless gurgle.

Beyond him is the door. I'm almost afraid to test it, but the knob turns easily in my hand. Opening it is a challenge, but that's because of debris behind it. I give a shove and I'm through.

On the other side is the room I was in earlier. I recognize the lights, the rack of clothing, a big slab of butcher block that's probably where I was lying. As woozy as I am, I know I've got to get out of here before I faint. I go to a wall, moving with my fingers always in contact with it for support, and explore the perimeter, beyond what I could see before. Somewhere, there's a way out.

I almost trip over the staircase before I recognize it. Light barely penetrates this corner of the space, and at first it just looks like a pile of lumber. Then my eye distinguishes the regular perpendiculars of stairs, and I feel a surge of hope. But these steps are lying on their sides, and when I look up, where the staircase should be, there's a massive clot of wood and plaster and stone. I could dig through it, perhaps.

If I had a month or two. And a shovel. Or maybe a backhoe.

If this is the only exit, then not only is the universe insane, but it's got one hell of a cruel streak.

As I stand there, looking at it, tears welling in my eyes, I hear his voice call out weakly. "Louise?"

It's all I can do not to pass out from hunger, exhaustion, and hopelessness.

THE PAIN IS exquisite, deep and heady. Like the smell of gasoline just before you light the match that sends whatever you've drenched in it off to hell.

I wonder if this is how my actors felt. Or were they merely shocked . . . reeling, unprepared? Did any of them understand that by making them stars, I was breathing life into them? I like to think they did, that they accepted my gift graciously and were, in the end, pleased with what I had given them.

As I watch Louise scurry through the doorway leading to the next room, yanking at her collar as she goes, I start worrying that I may have let her down. I want Louise to have the gift, to be purified and released from her burden, but fate has intervened and I don't think it's going to happen. At least, not by my hands.

I begin to wonder how long it will take to die. I twist my head, looking behind me to the closet where I keep all my materials. If only I could get closer, just a few feet really, I could open the door, knock the gasoline can over, light the flowing liquid with my Zippo. It wouldn't be a complete success, but I would release us both and that would be something. I find that I do not want to die. Correction: I don't mind dying, just not this way. Just not if my body is left to rot like a common animal. If there are no flames, then there is no point.

That's when I notice the forgotten piece of Louise's nose where it lies on the floor, just beyond my grasp. The savory red-and-peach color catches my eye, enticing me. I reach out my right hand—the left is pinned under me, useless—and stretch my fingers, inching toward it. My index finger grazes the edge of the tip, but no matter how I strain, I cannot reach it, and the pain I engender in my attempts fills my eyes with tears, sends searing fire through my abdomen.

I hear Louise struggling with something in the other room. After a few moments, she returns—she has put on a long brown sweater from the wardrobe rack in the other room, and the sacklike clothing has walled her away from me. There is nothing she can do about the collar, though. It still hangs from her throat like an untried noose—so there is that. Too bad the controller is in my pants pocket on the left side of my body, totally inaccessible.

She walks over and squats down in front of my face. I can see disgust in her eyes, and I realize the damage to my body must be massive. I wish I could stand outside of myself and view it objectively.

"Is there another way out of here?" she asks, her voice controlled, even.

"Why?" I reply, genuinely curious.

She sits back on her haunches, sighs. I can see that she is conflicted—or maybe my severe injury has upset her. Maybe she is just queasy about blood and viscera. Some people are, I've found.

Finally, she responds. "Because the earthquake caved in the ceiling above the stairs. We can't get out that way."

I nod, pretending to think, but really waiting to see what else she is going to say.

"I can't get you to a doctor," she adds. "Unless you tell me how to get out of here."

She is a sly one. I doubt she will call a doctor if she gets out. She will leave me here to rot. That's what she'll do—and it's the one thing I cannot abide.

"There's no way out, then," I say. "That was the only exit. I had it built that way on purpose."

The calm façade leaves her and she stands up, starts pacing. To my delight, she unwittingly kicks the tip of her nose, scooting it much closer to me than it was. Before she can stop me, I reach out my hand—the pain from my guts sliding up my vertebrae and into my throat—and grab the thing.

"Stop it!" she shrieks, squatting down again, snatching at it.

She's too late. I slide the delicious piece of skin into my mouth and begin to chew. Her eyes pop almost out of her head, and she grabs me by the jaw and tries to pry my lips apart. *Not smart,* I think as she forces her fingers into my mouth. I have very sharp teeth and I like to use them. She screams when I chomp down on the index and middle fingers of her right hand. I feel flesh and sinew start to give way, but she manages to extract her fingers before I can sever them.

She falls back on her ass and scuttles away from me, glassy eyed with fear. I settle back and finish eating the tip of her nose, savoring its chewy texture and the saltiness of the coagulating blood. All in all, it's a rather scrumptious treat.

"You're insane," she whispers, more to herself than to me. She shakes her head, as if she can't believe what she's seeing, what's happened to her.

"I have a phone," I say once I've swallowed the last morsel of skin, having had to flick it out from between my teeth where it had gotten wedged.

She sits up, fire burning in her eyes again. *Hope.* "Give it to me," she says, starting to crawl back toward me.

I shake my head.

"There's a condition."

This stops her cold. She sits down, stares at me.

"You must watch one of my movies first."

I give him time. It seems like hours, but the analog clock in the control room tells me it's only been forty-five minutes. Waiting is the hardest thing I have ever done, but I have the advantage over him. He's dying, bleeding out on the floor of that wretched basement room. He knows it. Sooner or later, he'll break, will give me the phone or tell me where it's hidden. Or he'll die and I'll be able to search his ruined corpse for it. I can outlast him. My nose is hardly bleeding anymore, and I've wrapped the fingers he bit in rags torn from his "costume" rack. I could use some first aid, but I'll live.

While waiting, I'm not idle. I tear the place apart, looking for it. I find his studio or whatever, full of high-tech equipment I don't know the uses of, monitors and microphones and switches and dials, dozens of soft blue and red lights glowing. I should be able to land a 767 with what's in here, but I can't find anything that will allow me to communicate with the world outside.

I do find shelves of DVDs in plain plastic cases. These must be the movies he's talking about. *Has* been talking about, since I first woke up here. One of the movies he wants me to star in.

If I watch one, he'll let me have the phone. That's the deal, right? I'm not sure how he'll know if I've actually watched it, since there's no monitor in the room he's in, and he's sure as hell not coming in here to watch me watching. But I suppose he could ask questions about it, to verify that I paid attention.

Another idea strikes me, and I go back into the empty room. The stench of his dying is thicker now, flavoring the air. "Where are we?" I ask. "I mean, where's your house located?"

His face is pale and drawn, his voice weaker than it was before. "I asked you a question before. Human myoglobin. You admitted your ignorance."

"What the fuck does that have to do with anything?"

"It's a protein found in muscle tissue. It's what makes meat red. It's only found in the bloodstream if there's severe muscle damage. When anthropologists find it in the fecal matter of ancient peoples, it's a certain sign of cannibalism."

I stare at him, knowing the horror must be evident on my face.

"We're in a side canyon, off Coldwater," he tells me. "Well off the main roads. If that was a major quake, it'll be quite a while before anybody gets here to help."

"If?" I look at the wooden beam piercing his middle. "I'd say it was pretty damn major."

"Then we're here for the duration," he says. "Hungry yet?"

I storm from the room, unwilling to give him the satisfaction of a response. My head aches from the drugs he's given me and the lack of something to eat in my belly. Ever since I was a little kid, my moods have always been dictated by mealtimes. If I don't eat, something hormonal or blood sugar related gets set off inside me and I turn into a real bitch. I channel that feeling now, hoping the hungrier I get, the better able I'll be to do whatever horrible things need doing.

I hate to admit it, even to myself, but in that room with the raw, bloody meat smell of him, my mouth filled with saliva. It's not to the point yet that I'm bent over, crippled with hunger. But it will reach that point if I'm not rescued. Even if I can call, it could take hours or days to be freed from this basement.

"Okay!" I cry, so furious that I think about going back in there and finishing him off. "Okay, you bastard, I'll watch one of your mother-fucking movies! If that's what you want, I'll do it!"

My hands shake so much it takes me a few tries to get the DVD in the player. Once it's in, I punch Play and sit back in his studio chair to watch.

The screen starts out black, but then a light comes on and shines on a girl in a chair. At first I think it's me. She's got my round face, my brown hair, a little shaggy, parted in the middle. My blue eyes. My figure, a little on the thick side, heavy boobs. And she's got that collar around her neck, as I do. But the white top she wears is different from the one he dressed me in. As the camera moves closer, I see that she's not me, after all. He's got a type, like most guys, and we both fit that mold. She might be prettier than I am.

She's every bit as scared.

The camera pushes in more and I see that she has also been cut, or cut herself. What I first took for a deep dimple on her right cheek is a slash, with blood still dripping from it, down to her jawline and running to her chin. A drop hangs there until she speaks, when it plummets toward her lap.

"M'lord," she says, her voice quaking. She can barely get the word out. I release a sob along with her, knowing her terror. "I have been awaiting your return with . . . with profound . . . desire." She's reciting a script, I can tell. The script is awful, and she's awful in the role. I could have done better. As if remembering a stage direction—or maybe he reminds her, off camera—she licks her lips. It's an awkward, artificial moment. Maybe it looked good to him when he was shooting this travesty, but not to me.

"I have been lusting for your touch," she says. "Longing for it." She couldn't be less convincing.

"Show me what you've been waiting for," his voice says from off-screen. The whole scene is ridiculously artificial.

In a move as smooth and sensual as a fourteen-year-old boy at his first makeout party, the woman grabs her own right breast.

I have to look away. It's so bad it embarrasses me to watch. And I understand, I get it. She's not an actress, she's a woman just like me, snatched from someplace and forced to humiliate herself. Like he would have had me do.

I know he'll ask about what I've seen, but I can't bear to view it. I look around the room, letting the DVD play, hoping he can hear the absurd dialogue he wrote for her. So he thinks I'm still watching.

I don't look back until I hear her screaming.

I watch the rest through a screen of my own tears, my own horror. She has the razor in her trembling hand, and when she hesitates he activates the collar. She is thrown from the chair, slowly gets up, listens to unheard instructions, and takes the razor to herself. Slices her forehead, her other cheek, her breasts. Blood everywhere. The razor slips from her hand. She refuses to pick it up, so he shocks her again.

This time, she doesn't get up.

After a few minutes, he moves into the frame. Takes up the dropped razor. Draws it across some part of her I can't see, his back to the camera blocking my view. Pulls off something that can only be flesh.

When he turns around again, he's tucking it into his mouth. He chews, swallows, smiles at the camera.

And I am, I realize, so, so hungry that even what the monster just ate looks absolutely delicious.

She's watching one of the DVDs. I can hear the screaming from the other room, still as real and frantic as it was on the day I recorded it. I think she might be watching Lisa or Dolores, but I'm too far away to really say for sure—and, frankly, it's getting hard to focus on the things around me. I have stopped being able to feel my feet and legs; my arms are nearly useless. I can turn my neck, but all that allows me to do is see the closed utility closet door. This just makes me feel terribly sad, so I've stopped looking that way.

Louise comes into the room, eyelashes wet from crying. She storms over to where I'm lying and squats down beside me.

"Why do you do this?" she asks, grabbing me by the hair and lifting my chin off the floor. "It's disgusting. You're murdering people for what . . . ? So you can eat them?"

She has no idea what she's talking about. She doesn't understand that there is a method to what she considers madness. That there always has been. I want to explain to her, but I'm not sure she will get it. Still, I am dying—I know this now, an absolute truth—and I want to tell someone about my work. I turn my head to look at her, to catch her eye, because eye contact is imperative for understanding.

"I am your God," I say to Louise, holding her gaze with the last of the energy I possess. "Your creator."

I can see that I am losing her. My words are not penetrating. I try another tack.

"You want to know why I eat them?"

This is what she wants to hear about. I have finally penetrated her, it seems.

"Yes, I want to know why."

Her stomach growls, aggressive and insistent. Of course she is starving. It's been more than a day since she last ate. I wonder if she had dinner before going out the night before. These actresses are always so worried about their weight, she'd probably only nibbled at something, a kale salad or a piece of baked fish.

"Why?" she presses, slamming my chin down, hard, on the concrete, recapturing my attention.

I feel the skin tighten, then burst apart like the seams on a child's stuffed toy. Blood flows from the wound, mixing with the blood that's already all over the floor. I am losing blood with every breath. Dying one exhalation at a time.

"They are my creations, my actresses," I say. "Through them I give birth to my films, and my films give life to them. When they have concluded their part, I complete the circle. They belong to me, and no one else."

She stares at me, eyeballs darting back and forth in their sockets as she tries to process what I've said.

"You're sick," she says finally. "A fucking monster."

She releases her grip on my hair, and I use the last of my energy to lay my cheek against the concrete floor. The blood that coats the ground—my blood—is wet and sticky, but even through its viscosity I can still feel the coolness of the earth coming up through the concrete, reaching for me, making me shudder.

I am not a monster, I want to say to her, but I have nothing left inside to defend myself with. It would just expend too much energy.

"You're just hungry," I whisper. I say it so quietly, she doesn't hear.

"What?" she says, leaning closer to my face.

"You're just hungry," I repeat.

"Yes, I am," she says. Then: "You promised me that cell phone if I watched your movies."

I nod as best I can.

"Cut a little of my cheek for yourself," I say. "Eat a little of me. So you don't starve."

She rolls her eyes.

"Not a fucking chance."

We are at a stalemate. She did as I asked. I owe her the phone, I concede.

"Phone is on my ankle."

She doesn't believe me, shakes her head.

"Holster on my ankle," I say.

She is suspicious. Slowly, she picks her way over the rubble that traps me, lifts my pants leg. I can feel her shaking with relief. She can't believe I held to my promise. Though I may be many things, a liar I am not—but she doesn't know this. She knows nothing about me, really.

"Thank you," she says, crawling back over to me so I can see her face. "Thank you for this."

She is crying. Tears are leaking from her eyes, falling onto her cheeks and then the floor, melding with my blood. Bringing us even closer together. I think part of her wants to kiss me in gratitude, but she doesn't. Instead, she powers on the phone, her excitement growing . . . and then it is dashed before my eyes.

"It's password protected," she says in shock.

"Eat a little of my cheek and I'll tell you the password," I say.

She glares at me. "No."

I try to shrug, but my body is a lifeless thing.

"Eat a little of me and save yourself," I say. "It's the only way."

She doesn't want to do it, but I have her in an untenable position. She holds my gaze for too long and I think she is not going to do what I want her to—but then she gets up and walks over to the corner of the room. The blade she used to cut off her nose lays there, still red with her blood. She picks it up and comes back to me, kneels down. She places the blade against my cheek and quickly slices off a piece of flesh, lets it drop into her palm.

The pain makes my blood sing.

Her body thrums with rage as she cradles the piece of me in her hand. With a shudder, she lifts the raw flesh to her mouth. I close my eyes, savoring the knowledge that my body will become one with hers, but when I open my eyes again, I see that she has not done as I asked. My flesh still rests in her hand.

"Do it," I say, encouraging her. "And the password is yours."

Her body trembles as she raises the flesh to her lips. She grimaces, then shoves my cheek into her mouth. She can't even chew, just swallows hard, forcing me down inside of her. She starts to gag, then she vomits, the unchewed skin splatting on the floor in a puddle of bile and stomach acid.

I grin up at her.

"There's another way out," I say—and there is. I don't lie. "I'll tell you how to get to it, but first you need to promise me one thing. My movies—"

"Fuck you," she says. "Tell me the password. You promised."

I sigh. She may have spewed me back up, but technically she did do what I asked. There is also the fact that I am dying, and I need her to live so that she can bring the world my masterpieces, my films.

"The password is 3337," I concede.

She presses in the code and the phone comes to life.

"Now listen. It's important that you—"

At first, I don't realize what she's doing, but then, as the life ebbs from my body, I understand: she is stabbing me repeatedly with the blade. I try to open my mouth, to tell her the way out before it's too late . . . but then the moment is gone. I am out of my body, floating away. I look down at my lifeless corpse, devastated that all my glorious work will be forever lost to the ages.

Because unless she gets over her distaste for flesh, she's doomed. Rescue will come eventually, but no time soon.

And my phone has never had a signal down here in my secret studio.

BRANCHES, CURVING

Tim Lebbon and Michael Marshall Smith

So what did she do now? Did she get up out of bed or try to go back to sleep? Did she continue to doze or try to wake up?

SHE LAY THERE, arm still held rigidly down by her side, and could not make the choice.

Jenni hated choices. Always had. She took forever to order in restaurants because she wanted every meal to be perfect and couldn't bear the cost of selecting one thing over another. She spent so long browsing Netflix that by the time she'd chosen her evening's entertainment she wound up nodding off halfway through the movie. Even a simple trip to Starbucks could strand her blinking up at the menu board, becalmed and indecisive, while people muttered in line behind her. Sometimes there was just too much information. Too many choices, and no telling what to choose.

It was a peculiar trait, this inability to decide, because in other ways she was notably impulsive; two ex-husbands and a string of failed affairs before and after each barren marriage (and also during, regrettably) stood testament to that. Fleeting closeness is not about choice, however. It's living in the moment, however ill-advisedly. It wasn't as if she was ever faced with a room full of men to select from. Perhaps that would have been better. At least that way she might still be choosing, still dithering . . . and would not have spent so very, very long looking for whatever was missing from her life. That elusive something, hidden from view, and yet the one solid anchor in the storm of her mind. The thing that would close the circle and make her complete.

She didn't want yes/no. She wanted a continuum, a permanence, something that would hold her steady forever and put a stop to the endless circle of selection. She was still searching. Still dreaming her life away.

Still waiting to be awake.

AND IN THE meantime she sat at the fork in the road, unreasonably furious at whoever was responsible for the absence of direction. The road to the left angled up a steep slope and soon disappeared around a high-hedged bend. To the right it continued across the hillside, disappearing eventually into a dip in the valley a quarter of a mile away. Both routes were the same width, both imbued with the promise of roads untraveled, and there wasn't even a road sign to help make a decision. She knew they'd taken down a lot of signs across the countryside during the war—to confuse the Germans if they ever invaded—but that was a hell of a long time ago now, surely. Maybe there was simply nowhere interesting to go from here, and so they'd never bothered putting them back up.

"Nowhere," she said, the dull word swallowed by the car's upholstery. "Or somewhere."

Which was which? If she'd had to bet, she would have put money on the road to the right being the way to go. But there was no way of knowing for sure.

Just follow the road, the kid in the village had said. Attractive little place, church, old pub. The kid had pointed without looking, wearing a hoodie and high-tops and with a phone grafted onto his left palm, eyes welded to the screen. He'd had strange eyes, and Jenni had thought he looked like one of those kids from that movie she'd seen a month or two ago. She couldn't remember its name. That had been on a bad movie night, one of the few when she'd wished she'd taken longer to choose.

The car coughed before settling back into a tired grumble. Even her Mazda wanted her to stop prevaricating and decide.

Fuck it.

She nudged into gear and pulled forward, and it was only at the last moment that she changed her mind and swung the wheel to the left, scraping the bumper and wing through a bramble hedge as she aimed uphill at the curve in the road.

But she'd committed herself, at least.

A hundred yards along the road an ancient stone mile marker was half buried in the hedge. It felt like she'd seen it before, but with its skewed carved cross and a McDonald's cola cup pressed onto the top, it was nothing she could have dreamed. It was too specific. It troubled her that she couldn't *remember* seeing it, but there was a comfort in that, too. Oftentimes in life, as with ordering a meal or a movie, she needed to be shown the way.

Driving the country lanes, she expected déjà vu to close around her at any moment, bringing dislocation but also joy. The many times she'd experienced the feeling before, she'd felt as if she was in her own movie, a loop separated from the world and part of something else. The smallest of things—the path of a raindrop down a windowpane, the flight of a bird, the way a stranger in a coffee shop cocked his head and raised an eyebrow before turning the page of a book—made her ache for such moments to last, perhaps forever.

But they never did. She was sucked back into the circle like a fly that had almost escaped a patient spider's trap. Almost, but not quite. She was not convinced that this quest was aiding her escape either. She feared instead that it was tugging her closer, as if she was forever circling a web, pulled inexorably toward the center.

She passed several country houses with no people in their gardens. A tractor headed back the way she'd come, its driver not making eye contact. A smear of roadkill steamed and twitched, and she paused until she had decided what it was.

Rabbit. Yeah, a rabbit. One leg still kicking. That tractor . . .

At last, just as Jenni began to believe she'd taken the wrong turn after all, she rolled to a halt in a gateway and saw, at the field's center and close by a small pond, exactly what she'd been looking for.

The tree.

It was an old oak. Dead a long time, its trunk had split heavily down the middle, enclosing a large shadowy space that had doubtless proved a hiding place for countless kids, and even a few illicit lovers. There was plenty of room for two inside, and wasn't there some legend about making love within the shadow of an oak tree's canopy? She couldn't recall. But if there wasn't, there should have been.

It was beautiful, and haunting, and her gaze was drawn up and to the left, to one stretching branch upon which a few errant leaves still fluttered. Not quite dead, then.

She parked the car and got out.

SHE COULDN'T REMEMBER how long she'd been having the dream. There'd been no particular night when she'd woken breathless, sitting bolt upright in that way they do in movies. It wasn't even a nightmare, really. Just unsettling.

And, eventually, repetitive.

Slowly she simply became aware that, when she found herself dreaming of a cold and isolated country lane with an old oak at the end of it, she'd been there before.

And now here she was again, but for the first time.

She turned back, looking toward the bend beyond which the road-killed bunny lay. For a moment she had the feeling she'd seen the rabbit before, too—that perhaps in one of the dreams she'd even run over it. Couldn't be, of course. Roadkill is everywhere. All she was doing was retrofitting it to the uncanny sensation of being here.

Which wasn't even, after all, especially strange. In the small hours of a recent night, waking from the dream for the sixth or seventh time, she'd tried to lead herself back toward sleep by idly wandering the Internet on her laptop, her hand held by Google search. She sometimes found this soothing, half an hour spent meandering the unexpected roads revealed by typing random words into the search box; the way it presented you with pages of choices, none of which really mattered. Half led to porn, of course, or would by the time you'd clicked a couple of times: trying to navigate the back roads of the Internet *without* joining the highway of people's obsession with nakedness became a kind of game within the game.

On this particular night, still haunted by the dream, she'd typed in the words *old oak* to see where that led her, tired but cozy in her bed, face lit by the screen's glow.

At first it led mainly to links to bars and country clubs and small towns in America. After a while, to the myths and legends that surrounded this most eldritch-feeling of English trees. And then . . .

She'd frozen, her fingers hovering over the keyboard.

The last link she clicked led to a report in some never-heard-of local newspaper for a town way out in the west country. At the top of the story was a photograph. It was of an old, misshapen oak tree.

More than that, it was *her* oak tree. The one that stood in her dreams.

She read the scant report and quickly realized (or decided) that this probably wasn't coincidence or weirdness after all. She must have simply seen the report somewhere before. People were forever posting up this kind of thing on Facebook and Twitter. You flitted across hundreds during an average week, occasionally grunting with mild interest before getting back to e-mail or work or whatever you were supposed to be doing. Her conscious mind had forgotten it. Some other part, evidently, had not.

She got out of bed and took the laptop to the kitchen, where she could make a cup of tea and print the story out.

AND NOW, TEN days later, she was here. The tree looked exactly as it had in the online photograph. Oddly so, in fact, as if the photographer had stood *exactly* where she now stood. But several months had passed since the piece, too, so you'd also expect at least *something* to have changed.

The tree looked identical, however. As if it had been her who'd stood here taking the picture, and she'd subsequently seen it on the Internet.

She pulled out her iPhone to take a photograph of her own. The twisted branches, bare but for those few stray leaves, stood out starkly against the leaden sky, like cracks across a windshield or roads mapped spreading out into unknown territory. Her phone felt awkward, the fingers of both hands painful, as if strained by some great effort. Gripping a steering wheel for hours in the freezing cold, she assumed.

The moment she pressed the shutter, it started to rain. "Christ," she muttered. Had she brought a coat with her? Of course not. That would have been a *sensible* choice.

She hesitated, knowing she should run back to the car but that if she did she'd just drive away, and the journey would feel incomplete. Instead she stuffed the phone into her jeans pocket and withstood the cold, bitey raindrops, walking across the field closer to the tree.

The hole in the split lower portion of the trunk was very dark. There was no sign of disturbance around it, which was no surprise, because the discovery had been several months ago. A pair of local children—maybe even related to the hoodie kid who'd given her directions—had been playing inside the big hollow trunk and found a button amid the dirt. Old, tarnished.

Thinking they might be on the trail of buried treasure, they'd grabbed a couple of tough sticks and started to rootle around in the soil. Jenni considered it a testament to how bored you could be as a kid living in the country that they'd kept digging for an hour, until finally they'd found . . . something else.

She looked into the hollow, her hair soaked and hanging in freezing lines down her cheeks. The earth in there was now flat, and undisturbed. It was too cold, too wet.

Too sad.

She abruptly realized she didn't want to be here anymore and turned and walked quickly back to her car.

The rain had become a deluge that soaked her to the skin and made her shiver, her teeth chattering autumn's song. Stupid to come this far without a coat, and without a clue about why she had even come. As she sat in the car, heater on full blast and the steamed-up windshield slowly clearing, a gust of wind rocked the vehicle on its suspension.

She rubbed her hand across the side window. Through the downpour she could still see the tree. It appeared untouched by the storm, immovable.

Now I know where it is, at least, she thought.

The idea didn't comfort her, and as she drove away, concentrating on a winding road that was already awash with too much surface water, the tree suddenly felt lost once more.

I won't be able to find it again. The roads will lead elsewhere.

She arrived back at the junction where she'd waited earlier, debating which way to go. This should have been another of those endless decisions she was so bad at making, but this time it seemed to have been made for her. Night was drawing in. Her wipers barely held their own against the rain, even on full speed. Wind roared across the landscape, sweeping darkness before it.

She would stay in the local village that night. Jenni tried to convince herself she decided this because of the storm, the risk of getting lost in a network of signless country lanes, the threat of falling trees.

She had a perfectly good sat nav on her iPhone, however, and it was probably only ten or fifteen miles back to the nearest main road.

Maybe she just wasn't yet ready to leave.

The Horseshoe turned out to be a pleasant, cozy pub, larger than it looked from the outside, with a friendly atmosphere and no hint of the tumbleweed moment she'd feared as she entered. Yes, they had a room available. Yes, they were still serving food. Jenni took a corner table, close to the roaring open fire—something she wasn't used to, a city girl through and through—and with a view across the rest of the pub. A group of locals sat at the bar chatting and laughing, and several other tables were taken with families or couples eating. If she caught anyone's eye, they traded smiles.

There was no discernible reason for her anxiety. But then . . . there rarely was. Anxiety is never about cause. Presumably it must therefore be about effect. Or perhaps something hidden in the circle between the two.

It took two glasses of merlot for her to settle, and halfway through the third drink her meal arrived. The food was extremely good, but she only ate half of it. Both of her ex-husbands used to comment on her childlike appetite.

"My dad caught that," a voice said.

Startled, Jenni looked up to see the hoodie-wearing boy from earlier in the day, the one who'd given her directions. His sweatshirt was unzipped now, hood down, and though the phone was still in his hand, he seemed to be back in the land of the living. He even offered a tentative smile.

"The duck," he said, nodding at her plate. "Dad caught it."

"It did taste very fresh," Jenni said. The boy did not reply, so she tried again. "Very tasty."

"You didn't finish it, though."

"I ate a big lunch." She wasn't sure why she lied, but she *was* sure that he saw the lie.

"He shot it at the pond by the Dying Tree."

Jenni pursed her lips, nodded, looked into her wine again. She'd been staring there when the boy had startled her, but she could no longer recall what she'd been thinking about. Debating whether or not she should have another, perhaps.

"You find the tree?"

"I did, thank you."

"You a copper? Or a reporter?"

"Have you had a lot of reporters around here?" It felt strange, talking to someone else about the tree. It made her feel naked, as if she was sharing her dream.

"Couple," the boy said. "Not for a while though." He knelt by the fire and poked at it, throwing on two more logs. Sparks flew. A knot popped. One of the locals—a woman, perhaps the boy's young mother, or older sister—glanced across at Jenni and the boy. She looked away again just as quickly, laughing at something said by the barman, unconcerned. "Talked to the coppers, too, for a few days after I found it."

After I found it.

Jenni picked up her wine and took a big swig to still the thudding of her heart. She closed her eyes as she drank, seeing the tree. Its branches offered so many possibilities. Enough to trap someone forever.

"Oh, so it was you," she said casually.

"Me and Billy." He became more animated. "Found the buttons first, when we were exploring the big hole in the trunk. Been in there before, loads of times, but it's always different when we go back. Found a dead squirrel in there once, and a used condom, and a wine bottle filled with piss. So we got digging, and Billy found the first bone."

His eyes clouded, just slightly. Jenni wondered how haunted he was by their discovery.

"Ran away when we saw the bones were inside a sweater. Told Mum." He nodded back over his shoulder, and Jenni caught the woman's eye once again. This time the woman looked mildly troubled.

"Buttons?" she asked the boy. "I thought you only found one. That's what the papers said, and the local news site."

The boy's smile changed. He was just a little boy, for all that he wore a teenager's clothes and carried a phone, and he'd been caught out.

"Kept one each," he admitted, looking into the fire. When Jenni did not reprimand him, he asked, "Wanna see?"

Jenni smiled and held out her hand. Her other hand tightened around the wineglass.

"Tom?" a woman's voice called.

Jenni nodded at the boy, biting back a comment. *Come on, quick! Before someone stops us.*

He dug around in one pocket and then dropped the button into her palm.

"Tom, leave the lady alone."

She looked at it for a moment, then rolled it around her palm, working it up between her fingers. The sight of it, old, metallic, tarnished by its time in the ground. The feel of it. And when she rolled it between thumb and forefinger, it felt so familiar.

Her mouth dried. "The Dying Tree."

"Yeah. That's what they call it around here."

"Why?"

He shrugged. "Because it's dying?"

She nodded, though it seemed unlikely the tree had been ailing for long enough for the name to become embedded local custom. "I thought you'd found a body in there?"

"Tom, here, now!"

The young boy stood to leave, but he looked at her almost in fear. At her, down to the button, up again. He wanted it back. He knew it was important to him, even if he didn't understand why.

"Oh, he's no bother," Jenni heard herself say. She dropped the button back in the boy's hand and watched him walk away, wondering how he—or his mother—could not have noticed what she had about the left sleeve of his hoodie, about what was missing there. She reached for her phone to look at the photo of the tree one more time.

As she had rolled the button between her fingers, time had rolled as well. When she looked at the image of the tree, she was not surprised. The fuller branches, the healthier hue, the narrower maw in the tree's wounded trunk . . . perhaps she had projected her dream onto the tree earlier and it wasn't actually as old, as gnarled as she'd believed.

Perhaps.

There was one way to know for certain.

Looking at the rain-speckled window, Jenni finished her wine.

The short walk across the pub car park had her half drenched once more, but by the time she'd been driving for ten minutes, the storm had started to abate. It didn't fall to nothing but reduced at least to a persistent, thoughtful kind of rain.

The first thing she noticed were the road signs. It wasn't like there were so many, but they were at least there, revealed by the sweep of her headlights. At several points where she'd decried the lack of them that afternoon—or thought she had—stood sturdy little poles with small signs pointing in opposing directions. This was so inexplicable that at first she grew concerned she'd somehow taken a wrong turn out of the village, gotten herself on some entirely different and yet eerily similar set of roads, roads whose signs had always been there.

Then, however, she found the junction where she'd sat becalmed, and she saw a sign there, too. An old sign on a weathered post right in the base of the Y, as if its presence had been what caused the roads to separate and go their own ways.

She jammed on the brakes and skidded to a halt, stopping a few feet short of the sign. She stared up at it through the windshield. Two arrows, one either side. Both pointing up one of the available roads.

Both blank.

She opened the door and got out. Looked back to check that no one was heading toward the junction. No sign of lights, and it was hard to imagine why anyone would be out driving these roads at this time of night.

Anyone apart from her.

She approached the sign. Two little metal panels, both battered and old-looking. Still blank. She stretched closer, expecting or hoping to see the remnants of previous village names or destinations on them, scrubbed or chipped off at some point, for some unknown reason.

But there was nothing. Either someone had done an immaculate job of erasing any names, or there had never been anything there.

Never, or not yet.

She got back into her car and shut the door. Reversed a few feet. Now she was here it seemed impossible not to go ahead and do the obvious thing. She indicated left and drove along the road that led to the old oak.

SHE WAS SOMEHOW not surprised to see that it looked different now. Different even from her own photo from earlier in the day. She pinched herself, feeling absurd, but all this achieved was raising a pinky-blue weal on the back of her freezing wrist. She wasn't asleep, or if she was, she was sealed within an experience impervious to simple solutions.

It didn't look like an old oak now. It just looked like an oak. A huge, robust tree, in the prime of life. The tree itself was not dying, if that's what the name had ever been about. The gap in its side, the wound, remained, but the opening was narrower.

Still wide enough for a boy to crawl into, however. A boy hiding from the rain, or from a playmate. A boy who for some reason never made it out again, and whose flesh slowly rotted until the only thing left to find were three tarnished buttons from the left sleeve of the sweater he'd been wearing. The hoodie he still wore, and which still had the ornamental buttons on the other sleeve.

Jenni bent closer and looked into the hollow. The space inside remained the same. Easily large enough for two to play. She knew what she'd seen in the eyes of the boy when she'd first happened upon him, earlier in the day—when he'd given her directions to the tree. He'd looked away, keeping his eyes on the screen of his phone, because he knew there was no escaping what had already happened.

Jenni wondered how many times he had dreamed of it. More than her? Perhaps. Impossible for her to know. She did know, however, that people would later say that they had seen the boy talking to an unknown woman in a pub, the night he disappeared.

She knew this because she'd read it online.

Awkwardly at first, and after quite a lot of effort, Jenni managed to squeeze herself through the gap and into the hollow in the oak. Once inside it was more roomy. If she curled up, it would be a comfortable enough place to spend the night, and the next morning or day, or however long it took.

She retreated back into the darkness to wait.

To wait for the boy to come again.

SHE WOKE RELIEVED, as always, to realize that she was at home in London, safe in her own bed. She'd slept like a log, curled tightly on her right side. Her back protested and her knees clicked as she straightened, as though they'd been locked up in the same position from the moment she'd closed her eyes.

She rolled onto her sweat-dampened back and pushed the covers down, yawning massively and releasing the arm that had been trapped beneath her. It was a little numb, but not too bad.

As she opened her fingers to waggle them back into life, she heard a soft plopping sound.

She looked down and saw a tarnished button, lying on the sheet beside her hip.

RENASCENCE

Rhodi Hawk and F. Paul Wilson

New York City
1878

1. UNDER A HARVEST MOON

Rasheeda Basemore hid her impatience as one last relative lingered over Graziana Babilani's coffin. Finally she approached the old woman.

"You were close to the deceased?"

The woman turned. She had a lined face and wore widow's black.

"Graziana and me," she said in a thick Sicilian accent, "we was family. She's a-my baby cousin from Palermo."

"I'm sorry for your loss." *Now please leave.*

"She just a-come over here to America and now she die." She dabbed her eyes with a yellowed lace handkerchief. "Such a shame."

Rasheeda took the woman's arm and gently tugged her toward the door. "We have to close the coffin now. Will you be at tomorrow's ceremony?"

"Oh, yes. I'm a-come. And you? You be there?"

"Of course."

The woman patted her hand. "You nice. You pretty. But you got no ring. No married?"

Rasheeda shrugged and put on a smile. How many times had she heard this? She looked a decade younger than her forty years, but to these people you were an old maid if you weren't married with a clutch of bambini by the time you exited your teens.

"My fiancé was killed in a dirigible crash." She worked a tremor into her voice, a quiver into her lips. "There will never be anyone else for me."

She'd repeated the lie so many times she could almost believe it.

The woman squeezed her hand. "I'm a-so sorry."

"Besides . . ." Rasheeda gestured around at the funeral parlor. "This keeps me too busy for anything else."

The woman leaned close. "You do a-beautiful work, but this a-no job for a woman."

"My darling dearest left it to me. I continue it in his honor."

Finally Rasheeda ushered her out into the Harlem evening. She locked the door behind her and leaned against it just long enough to take a deep breath, then she was on the move again.

"Toby!" she called as she headed back to the viewing room.

She approached the coffin again and looked down at its occupant. Graziana Babilani was thirty-eight years old but looked fifty. She'd been healthy until last week when she'd come down with pneumonia and died, leaving behind a husband and two teenage sons. While preparing her for the viewing, Rasheeda had noted her sturdy peasant body with approval. She'd succumbed quickly to the infection with only minimal wasting of her musculature. She was perfect.

Rasheeda leaned over the coffin and sniffed. Not quite to the peak of ripeness. But by tomorrow she'd be perfect.

"Yes, Miss Basemore?" Toby's voice.

"Is the grave dug for Mrs. Babilani?" she said without looking around.

"Yes, ma'am."

"Time to fetch us a warm one then."

"Can I do the ritual this time?"

She turned to face him. Toby Hecker stood a brawny six foot plus two with fair skin and blond hair and spoke with a barely perceptible German accent.

"Not till you've perfected your technique on animals."

"But I have!"

"Do you really believe that? The result of your last trial was rather pathetic, don't you think?"

He dropped his gaze to the Persian rug under the coffin. "I never get to do the important stuff."

"What could be more important than procuring a warm one? I hope you don't expect me to—"

"No, of course not, Miss Basemore. I'll go now."

He turned and hurried out. Rasheeda shook her head as she watched him go. If only his mind were as strong as his back.

Returning her attention to the coffin, she patted Mrs. Babilani on the cheek.

"Not to worry, dear. By this time tomorrow we'll have you up and about again."

Toby picked up the elevated Third Avenue pneumatic line at the 125th Street station and took it downtown. His car was crowded with Negroes, Jews, and Italians. The latter two groups were chattering in their native tongues, and he found himself, as always, resenting that. His own parents had fled the midcentury revolutions in Germany, but he had been born here and had grown up speaking English. He was an American. These were foreigners.

The Negroes spoke a form of English that Toby found hard to understand. Slave-speak, he called it. That's what they'd all been until twenty or so years ago. The invention of the steam-powered spindle picker in the mid-1850s had dropped the bottom out of the slavery market—one machine could do the work of a hundred slaves—so most of them had been set free. And where did they come? New York, of course, making an already tight job market much worse.

He spotted a tattered copy of the morning *Tribune* under his seat and shuffled through it to the shipping news. He nodded as he found a notice that the German freighter *Von Roon* out of Bremen had docked yesterday with a cargo of fine fabrics and precision machinery. That meant clumps of German sailors staggering through the streets in search of wine and women. Perfect. All he had to do was find one who had strayed from his fellows.

That settled, he turned to the major news. As usual, all the bigwigs were decrying. President Greely had issued a statement from the White House decrying Germany's superiority in the dirigible field and urging America to develop a superior alternative. Governor Westinghouse had already electrified Albany and was making progress in Manhattan; he wanted to run electric power through the entire state but was decrying the shortcomings of direct current.

Toby dropped it and kicked it across the floor. Why did he even bother reading the news? Nothing ever changed.

Just like his life. Sure, Miss Basemore paid him well—very well, in fact—but he wanted more. He wanted her respect. Truth be told, he wanted even more than that—he wanted *her*. Yes, she was an older woman, probably fifteen years older, but she didn't look it. Her olive skin and her dark, dark eyes, and her voice . . . oh, Lord, she spoke perfect English with a British accent and an Indian lilt that sent shivers down his spine. Even her name: Rasheeda . . .

He knew she'd had an English father, but she'd spent the first half of her life in India. What had she learned there? He'd heard it said that Hindu women knew fabulous secrets about sex, and that a single one of them could please a man in more and better ways than a brothel full of whores.

But she didn't seem interested in men. At least not the living kind. She seemed to prefer the dead. Toby could count on getting admiring looks from women almost everywhere he went, but never the slightest sign of interest from Miss Rasheeda Basemore.

He sighed. Perhaps his own interests would be best served if he could stop thinking of her as a beautiful woman and see her simply as his boss. Becoming personally involved could only lead to trouble for him. Not that it would ever happen. She was above and beyond him . . . unobtainable.

Still, he wished he could find a way to impress her. Just the slightest expression of admiration from her would complete his life and allow him to go on admiring her from afar. But all she assigned him were menial tasks like preparing the dead for burial and hunting down a "warm one" when needed.

When his train hissed to a stop at the Bowery station, he exited the tube and hurried down the stairs to street level. The Bowery area was full of brothels, faro parlors, and German beer gardens, just the sort of neighborhood visiting sailors from the *Von Roon* would seek out. If Toby came up empty here, he could always head a few blocks west to Five Points. That journey had proved unnecessary in recent years since a group called the Young Men's Christian Association had opened a combination gymnasium–boarding house for, well, young men.

He had just crossed Delancey Street when he saw a lone sailor weaving along the sidewalk in his direction. He recognized the German merchant marine uniform.

"*Guten Abend!*" he called.

The bearded sailor grinned. "*Sind Sie die Deutschen?*"

Toby told him his parents had moved here from the old country. He and the sailor made small talk in German and he learned that the man's name was Gustav and he was indeed on shore leave from the *Von Roon*. It didn't take long for the inevitable question to surface.

"Where can I find women? Where's the best place?"

Toby made a face. "Not in this neighborhood, that's for sure. I mean, if all you're looking for is a bend-over-and-lift-the-skirt type, fine. But if you're interested in quality, you'll have to travel some."

"Where then?"

"Uptown."

He frowned. "How far?"

"Harlem. The tube will take you there in minutes. Fine, clean women, good brandy and cigars for after."

The sailor's eyes widened. "Can you show me? Can you take me?"

Toby backed up a step and shook his head. "I don't know. I'd feel like a procurer."

"Don't be silly. You're helping a new friend from the old country who's a stranger in your city."

Toby pretended to think about it, then shrugged. "Very well. I'll do it for a countryman. But let's buy some wine for the trip."

"Excellent! I'll buy!"

"No, I won't hear of it. You are my guest."

Buying the bottle would put Toby in control of it, allowing him to add the envelope of opium waiting in his pocket.

Rasheeda sat at the steel mixing table in the top level of the tower and stirred the latest batch of sustaining oil. She'd brought it up from the safe in the cellar for addition of the final spice. It had been curing for one lunar cycle now and had one more to go before it would be ready for use. Tomorrow she would have to start a brand-new batch.

She sighed. The process never ended.

The limited wall space of the tiny room had been put to full use—the exotic ingredients needed for the sustaining oil lined the narrow shelves. She'd been mixing a new batch on a monthly basis for over a decade now—she had no choice in the schedule since the oil didn't keep—and knew the proportions by heart.

She heard the house creak below her. Although not that old, it always creaked. Initially she hadn't cared for the blocky Second Empire building with its mansard roofs and central tower and feared the wrought-iron cresting would require extra maintenance. But it had come with the graveyard, and so she hadn't had much choice. As the years passed she'd changed her mind, however. The first floor had proved perfect for the viewing rooms, and she'd put the basement to excellent use. Plus, the roomy backyard offered more than enough space for her gas-fired crematorium.

But the central tower was the best. The four eye windows in its fourth-floor room, one facing each point of the compass, let in the moonlight, which was crucial to this step in the process.

She rose and gazed up at the high moon through the north window. Tomorrow would mark the last night of its full cycle; she'd have to get an early start in the morning to finish the third and last round of monthly anointings for her clients. If only Toby's fingers were a little more dexterous, she could send him on the monthly rounds. He'd like that—he'd think he was doing "important stuff." But although he could repeat the chant phonetically, he couldn't seem to master the necessary Sanskrit—*Vedic* Sanskrit, to be precise—and the sacred words had to be transcribed accurately or else they were useless.

A flash in the moonlit cemetery below caught her eye. Was someone out there—in *her* cemetery? Grave robbers perhaps? She couldn't help a tiny smile. Slim pickings out there, fellows.

She picked up the telescope from a nearby shelf and extended it to its full length. Usually she used it to watch the stars, but now it could help her spot intruders.

She scanned the entire grounds but saw no one, and the flash never repeated. Probably just a trick of the light. She—

The outside door to the cellar slammed four stories below. She hadn't imagined that. Toby most likely, but she wasn't going to take a chance. She pulled her Remington derringer from the compact work desk against the wall and checked the over-under double barrel to make sure each chamber was fitted with a cartridge. Yes. Good. She placed the tiny pistol in a pocket of her lab coat. With the flask of sustaining oil in one hand, she slipped through the trapdoor and descended the ladder to the tower's third floor.

She hurried down to the ground level. As she unlocked the door that led to the basement, she heard the metal clang of the cell door and knew it had to be Toby. Only she and Toby were allowed down there. Descending the steps, she found him hanging the cell key on its hook on the far wall.

The walls were heavy granite block, broken by the stairs to the first floor, the steps to the backyard entrance, and the heavy wooden door to the earth below the cemetery. The furnishings were minimal and functional: an extra embalming table, the iron-barred cell, and the steam-powered burrower, resting under a tarpaulin. The only items that might pass as decorative were the map of all the plots in her cemetery and the pair of silver collars linked by a ten-foot silver chain, all .999 fine. These hung on the wall next to the cell key.

"Well," she said, eyeing the limp form of a bearded seaman on the floor of the cell, "that was quick."

Toby smiled. "Yes, ma'am. He's German. And since I speak the language, he was ready to follow me anywhere."

"And a sailor. Excellent."

Not uncommon for one or two to jump ship in a larger port. No one would be looking for him once his ship set sail again.

She spun the dial on the safe embedded in the wall near the cell and placed the sustaining oil within, next to the remainder of the ripened batch. If those flasks ever broke or spilled, there would quite literally be hell to pay.

Toby said, "He drank enough of the spiked wine to keep him out well into the morning. I left him the rest of the bottle just in case he wakes up."

Adding the derringer to the safe's contents, she relocked it and turned to smile at him. "What would I do without you, Toby?"

He blushed. She could always make him blush.

"I'm sure you'd survive, ma'am."

"Yes, but you make it so much easier. See you in the morning then?"

"Yes, ma'am."

"After we get Mrs. Babilani up and about tomorrow, we'll try another Sanskrit lesson, yes?"

His eyes lit. "I've been practicing." He made a squiggle in the air with his index finger. "I know I'll be able to get it right this time."

"I'm sure you will. Good night, Toby. See you tomorrow."

She hoped he did get it right. And soon. Her business—Renascence Staffing, Ltd.—was expanding steadily, and she needed someone to share the monthly burden of anointings. If he couldn't get it right, he'd wind up in the cell like the sailor.

Just like his predecessor.

The next morning Rasheeda escorted the last of the Babilani mourners through the cemetery gate—the same cousin who'd lingered at the wake last night had lingered again at the graveside—and then locked it. When she returned to the open grave, she found Toby waiting.

"Let's get this over with."

He nodded and jumped into the grave. Straddling the coffin, he lifted the lid and reached down past Mrs. Babilani's corpse where he unfastened a set of latches. He climbed out and closed the lid. Anyone watching from a distance would assume he'd simply adjusted the position of the coffin.

As Toby slipped on his goggles and fired up the gravedigger/filler, Rasheeda walked back to the house and descended to the cellar. The German sailor was still out cold. Good. She didn't want to have to listen to pleas for release—in German, no less.

She pulled the tarp off the burrower, revealing its fusiform shape and screwlike nose. On the wall above it she consulted the grid map listing the coordinates of every plot in the cemetery. According to the map,

Graziana Babilani was buried in plot G-12. Rasheeda lifted the hinged cover over the navigation board and placed a peg in the G-12 hole. The Babbage analytical engine nestled beneath it would do the rest, guiding the burrower to plot G-12.

She closed the lid and patted the machine. It had made her life so much easier. Before its arrival, she and her assistant would have to go out in the dead of night and dig up the recently buried, then cart the remains back to the basement. It was not only difficult physical labor—they couldn't risk the noisy gravedigger—but dangerous as well. They might be discovered in flagrante delicto, or a family member might notice alterations in the surface of the grave and raise an alarm. Or worse, demand an exhumation. The burrower obviated all those concerns.

All thanks to Purvis. He had been her second assistant and a bit on the lazy side. But laziness is often the mother of invention, and Purvis had found a way to modify a diamond-mining probe into an efficient grave-robbing device.

Purvis was long gone now. As valuable as he had been, his growing avarice and ambition—not to mention his pathetic attempt at blackmail—had outstripped his usefulness and so he'd wound up in the cell, just like this sailor. But his legacy of innovation remained.

Toby, goggles pushed back atop his sandy hair, arrived then.

"Time to start the burrower," she said.

He nodded, lowered his goggles, and ignited the steam engine. While that was warming up, she opened the wall safe and removed the carafe of ripe sustaining oil. This older batch had perhaps twenty-four hours of usefulness left before it spoiled.

"I wish I could help you with that," Toby said over the hiss of the burrower.

Rasheeda forced a smile. "I wish that too, Toby. Later we'll try another lesson."

Toby returned her smile, then pulled open the thick wooden door to reveal the entry tunnel to Rasheeda's own private underground. Over the years the burrower had riddled the earth beneath her cemetery with wandering passages. It no doubt resembled a giant anthill in there.

Toby rolled the burrower to the entrance until its drilling head was just beyond the threshold, then put it in gear. The machine hissed as it trundled into the opening and disappeared from sight. It would follow existing tunnels and dig new ones until it reached plot G-12. Once there it would expose the bottom of Graziana Babilani's coffin. Her body would fall through the trapdoor cut into its floor, and the burrower would return her here for the ritual.

Rasheeda waved. "See you in a few hours."

"Can I perform the ritual when you come back?"

"We'll see." She gave him a hard stare. "I'm sure I don't have to warn you against trying your undeveloped skills on Mrs. Babilani while I am out, do I?"

He blanched and raised his hands. "I wouldn't even consider it! She's too valuable."

"Remember that."

"'WE'LL SEE,'" Toby muttered after she was gone, mimicking her accent. "'We'll see.'"

He knew that phrase too well. Her way of saying no without using the word itself. Why didn't she have more confidence in him? He was sure he was ready to graduate from being a laborer to participating in the really important stuff. He just needed a chance to prove himself and convince her.

For a moment—a fleeting instant, no more—he considered defying her and performing the ritual on Mrs. Babilani himself. That would show her.

But then he remembered the lady's cold rage when a certain client had stepped way out of line. That particular client had sickened and died in agony within a week. His doctors never determined the cause of his pain, but even the strongest opiates could not touch it.

Just as Toby would not touch Mrs. Babilani.

He busied himself around the basement while awaiting the burrower's return. He checked on the unconscious sailor to make sure he was still among the living. He'd seen people stop breathing from too much opium, but no, this one's chest was moving with regular respirations.

Finally he heard a whirring noise in the tunnel, growing louder: the burrower returning. He stood aside as it lurched out of the tunnel and hissed to a stop. He closed the door behind it—no telling what vermin might wander in if left open—and turned to the burrower.

He froze when he saw what lay in the receptacle atop the machine. A body, yes, but not Mrs. Babilani. Instead of a clean, middle-aged woman, this was a dirt-encrusted man. But equally dead.

Toby lifted him out of the burrower and placed him on the embalming table. Not that they ever did any embalming down here—they had a back room upstairs for that.

He looked him over. Dark hair, even features. Forty years, perhaps. Even though the clothing was caked with loose dirt, Toby could see it was of good quality. His shoes were shined beneath the grime. Something glinted in the corpse's right hand. A gold ring? Toby looked closer and was shocked to see all four fingers fitted into a set of brass knuckles.

"Who were you, my friend?" Toby muttered.

Certainly not a savory fellow, despite his quality clothing—not if he was wearing brass knuckles. How did he die? Where was he buried? And by whom? He—

Toby noticed dried blood on the left breast area of the coat. The soil had mixed with it some, so it must have been still fresh when he'd been consigned to the earth. The blood surrounded a horizontal slit in the fabric. Gingerly he lifted the coat and suppressed a gasp at the grand expanse of red-brown stain on the embroidered vest and linen shirt beneath. The vest showed a slit similar to the one in the coat.

No doubt about the cause of death: a knife blade—a large one, from the size of the cut—driven deep into the heart. Death must have followed almost immediately.

"At least you didn't suffer. But the question is: Are you an innocent victim or did you get what was coming to you?"

But a more immediate question: Why had the burrower delivered him instead of Mrs. Babilani?

He went over to the machine and checked the programming board. Not at all like Miss Basemore to make an error of this magnitude, and no, she hadn't: the destination peg was firmly set in the G-12 hole.

What was going on? None of it made sense. Toby saw everyone who went into the ground here and he'd never laid eyes on this man. From the looks of him, he hadn't been in a coffin, just thrown into a hole in the ground and covered up.

And then Toby Hecker had an epiphany.

This corpse, this unaccounted-for body from who knew where was like a gift from God—or perhaps Shiva. This stranger would allow him to prove himself to Rasheeda Basemore and demonstrate beyond all doubt that he was ready to handle the important stuff.

He ran to the wall and removed the chained silver collars from their hooks. He clamped one around the corpse's throat, then threaded the other through the bars of the cage and fastened it around the neck of the unconscious sailor. He opened the safe—he knew the combination—and there among the fermenting batch of new oil and Miss Basemore's derringer lay the book that contained the ritual.

He positioned himself between the two men and began reading . . .

"KATRINA!" MADAME LOUISA said. "Put that down and let Miss Basemore anoint you."

The young woman, dressed in an extremely brief French maid's uniform, lowered the heavy armoire she'd been carrying across the room and did as she was told. Rasheeda used the oil to draw the Sanskrit words on her forehead, cheeks, and the backs of her hands while muttering the chant. She worked to make sure the oil penetrated the thick rouge someone had troweled onto her cheeks.

"Fit as a fiddle till the next full moon, I assume?" Madame Louisa said with a broad Southern drawl.

She stood on a short stool in the center of the room while a tailor pinned and chalked a dress of golden velvet he was fitting to her curvy form. Her eyes were close-set and her jawline wide, a look that had probably made her appear vulnerable when she was younger. She was about Rasheeda's age and pretty, but her gaze was cold and calculating. Rasheeda supposed those qualities were necessary in the madam of one of the city's premier seraglios.

"Rest assured," Rasheeda said, slipping the carafe of oil back into her satchel. "Renascence Staffing guarantees it."

"I remain amazed that this oil of yours imparts such wondrous strength to those skinny little arms."

It didn't, of course—that was just one of the many fictions Rasheeda had concocted about her revenants.

"Yes. It's miraculous, in a way."

"And it's really true that my dear Katrina would become torpid and useless without your monthly upkeep?"

Rasheeda nodded. "Yes, the ministrations are necessary. You know that."

"No, I don't know that. I have only your say-so."

"Why would I make up a story?"

"Perhaps it's just some excuse you've concocted so you can come by every month to collect your rent. I've half a mind to lock you out next month and see what happens."

Oh, you don't want to do that, Rasheeda thought as the muscles at the back of her neck tightened.

"That would be . . . regretful."

Louisa gestured to one of her minions. A beefy fellow with long blond hair—one of her bouncers, most likely—stepped forward to hand Rasheeda a cash envelope to cover the monthly lease. That too went into the satchel along with the other payments collected today. This was the part about these rounds that Rasheeda didn't mind at all.

"Tell me," Louisa said. "Where do you find such perfect servants? They're strong as oxen, don't speak, and do whatever they're told. Whatever is in that oil of yours?"

They're dead, Rasheeda thought, but smiled and said, "Trade secret."

Louisa's affable expression wobbled. Obviously she wasn't used to being refused and didn't like it.

"I understand. However, I have a business proposition I wish to discuss with you."

"I look forward to it," Rasheeda said, backing away, "but I have my monthly round of anointings to complete."

"Some other time, then." Her gaze became pointed. "We will talk soon."

"Of course." Rasheeda turned to leave, then turned back. "Mister Traugott is a client of yours, I believe?"

Louisa's eyebrows lifted. "I do not discuss my clients with anyone. They are assured of discretion here."

"I appreciate that, so let me rephrase: Are you acquainted with Mister Traugott?"

Louisa smiled. "Come to think of it, I do believe I am. Why?"

"The Traugotts don't seem to be answering their door. I tried yesterday and the day prior."

"That's because they are on holiday."

Holiday? A wave of cold passed through Rasheeda. She'd had no idea.

"But if they aren't back today, their maid Eunice will miss her anointing."

Madame Louisa laughed. "Well, I guess that anointing'll have to wait, because they don't get back till tonight."

Rasheeda noticed that she'd slipped her façade to reveal a more working-class manner of speech. Madame Louisa seemed to catch herself, and when she spoke again, she did so more slowly.

"Anyhow, what's the worst that could happen? As you say, she'll go all sleepy and someone else'll have to bring Fritz his brandy and cigar after dinner. I'm sure Fritz'll survive."

Don't count on that, Rasheeda thought.

Despite what Madame Louisa had told her, Rasheeda went directly to the Traugott house. Mr. Traugott was a member of the Rhinelander family, which had made a fortune in sugar and shipping. He and his wife and children lived in a Yorkville mansion on East Eighty-Fourth Street, so Rasheeda took the pneumatic tube uptown from the brothel.

Despite repeated poundings of the heavy brass knocker, no one answered their front door.

This could be bad, she thought as she hurried back toward the Eighty-Sixth Street pneumatic station. *Very bad.*

RASHEEDA RETURNED HOME to find an unaccountably exultant Toby.

"I've got a surprise for you, Miss Basemore!"

Oh, no.

"What is it, Toby?" she said, not wanting to hear the answer. "Not Mrs. Babi—"

"No no no! I wouldn't touch her!"

She let out a breath. Well, that was a relief.

"Good. Excellent. What's all the ado then?"

"It will be easier to show you." He was vibrating with excitement. "Down in the basement. Come!"

He dashed ahead and she followed, hefting the satchel of lease payments that was bound for the safe. She entered the basement, where the burrower rested near the tunnel entrance like a faithful mastiff, pressurized air still burping from its tubes.

Toby spread his hands to the cage. "You see? I told you I could do it!"

The cage door was closed. Stretched across the stones beyond it lay a sailor, Toby's donor, dead, still tethered to the silver chain. And on the opposite end of the silver sat—

Not Mrs. Babilani.

No, the fellow next to the dead sailor was dirty and scarred, drool sagging from lip to lapel.

Toby rattled the bars. "On your feet, now. Say hello to your new mistress."

The man did not blink. The stream of drool neither slowed nor coursed afresh. He was beyond stupor.

Rasheeda felt her fingernails tighten around the satchel. "Toby, what have you done?"

"Give me a minute. I'm sure I did it right."

Toby slipped the key into the lock and threw wide the cage door. He shook the man, though *man* was a generous word for this creature. No more animated than a bull thistle. And so covered in dirt he looked like he'd been buried without a box and crawled up through the soil on his own. Facial scars indicated that during his life some of the bones had broken and healed over a few times; and yet, were it not for his pallor and ghastly stupor, he might be otherwise handsome.

Toby shook him, but the man's head lolled back without resistance. Only when Toby released him did the head slowly right itself to its normal posture.

This revenant was useless.

An inch at a time, Toby raised his gaze to Rasheeda.

"It was the burrower. It should have picked up the Babilani lady, but it brought *him* back instead."

Rasheeda swung the satchel of coins and bills, catching Toby on the side of the head. He howled and stumbled backward, then jabbered about how he'd only been trying to salvage the situation. Wasn't there something they could do? After all, this was Toby's first revenant.

Rasheeda looked at the thing. "Certainly. We could sit him in Central Park as a means of attracting pigeon shite to spare the statues. I'm sure the Borough of Manhattan would pay . . . oh, let me see . . . *nothing?!*"

Toby sank to his knees and retrieved a gold eagle coin that had escaped Rasheeda's satchel.

She snatched it from him. "You can't revive just any old corpse. This one's clearly been dead too long."

"But he seemed so fresh. He was still leaking from the stab wound in his chest."

Rasheeda pinched her brow. "Well, then, he probably wasn't dead long enough. The timing is sensitive. There's a reason I'm the only one who can do this. A good revenant is lively but dumb, docile, and compliant, and very plain to the eye."

"But I never—"

"And you never will. We'll have to get rid of this rubbish as it is. And the donor, too, which you've wasted. Now we have two bodies to dispose of, with no usable revenant to show for it. I should take the money I'd be getting for the Babilani woman out of your wages."

"I'm sorry. I'm sorry, Miss Basemore."

"You're lucky he came to as a houseplant. These things can be dangerous."

"I don't know why the burrower didn't bring her back. That part's not my fault."

Rasheeda scowled. But the burrower *had* made an error that she could not explain. She'd set it herself. She glared at Toby, then at the drooling heap he'd created.

"Oh, just . . . take me to the Babilani grave."

EVEN IF TOBY hadn't utterly failed, the man who sat liquefying back in the basement would have made a terrible revenant. Who would want *that* lurking around their pantry? Revenants sold best when uninteresting and unintimidating. And sexless. Wealthy ladies resented pretty maids; gentlemen hated chisel-jawed butlers. No one wanted a servant who was too feral. Or too exciting. Unless they were perverts.

Once the gravedigger excavated the soil, Toby clambered out from behind the controls and hopped into the hole, then opened the coffin. Rasheeda hated to risk exposure like this, but she needed a look inside.

Mrs. Babilani lay as they'd left her. Rasheeda stepped back from the grave.

Now that the gravedigger had gone quiet, the frogs' calls filled the night. *Ah-ah-ah*. It sounded like they were jeering.

"Get the casket out," she said.

Toby nodded and closed the cap over the corpse. He pulled the chains from the gravedigger, affixing them to the casket. Under his guidance, the gravedigger farted, reared, and plucked Mrs. Babilani's casket from its not-so-final resting place. Dirt rained from its contours and sent dust billowing out in a ring.

Rasheeda lifted her lantern over the empty grave site.

Beneath the clean, chiseled, machine-cut grave: a crude hole. One just large enough for a man. A loose clod of dirt tumbled from its rim to the tunnel left by the burrower.

Despite herself, Rasheeda smiled. "Clever."

"What's that?" Toby asked as he jumped down to the grass, panting and slapping at a mosquito.

"*That* explains the light I saw in the graveyard last night. *That* is where your drooler got ditched."

"I don't get it."

"Which fails to surprise me." She drew a breath. "Someone or some *people* killed your man and dumped him beneath Mrs. Babilani's gravesite. They must have spread dirt over his body, knowing that the Babilani casket would cover him forever. That's why our burrower brought *him* back. *He* was under *her*."

Toby gaped.

"Oh come on, you have to admit it's clever!"

Toby said, "I still don't get it."

Rasheeda sagged. "Just . . . put Mrs. Babilani back, Toby."

Rubbing her jaw, she turned away and headed for the house. Clever or not, she wouldn't tolerate marauders in her graveyard.

This city knew all sorts of criminals. She couldn't care less about any of them or what they did. But any criminals who trespassed on her property and cost her time and money—well, they'd soon wish they'd been caught by the police.

She'd take a better look at Toby's drooler. Maybe she could find out who he was, where he came from. Maybe something on him could lead her to the trespassers who felt so entitled to her graveyard.

From somewhere behind her, the gravedigger resumed its coughing and groaning. The moon, close to the end of its full cycle, cast the lawn in tones of brown and gray. Rasheeda realized she was panting. She'd been striding faster than she'd intended, and her cheeks burned with blood. It occurred to her that she'd never felt so alive.

IN THE BASEMENT, the cage door still lay open. The sailor still lay dead. But Toby's revenant was no longer drooling on the floor next to him. He wasn't drooling anywhere. He was gone.

So were the keys—last she'd seen them, Toby had left them dangling in the cage lock.

Oh, no!

Rasheeda panned the room. The safe stood open. And empty.

Oh, no no no!

The implications were appalling, but not so appalling or *urgent* as a slavering revenant run amok.

There. A trail of dirt. Leading up the back staircase. The *in*side staircase.

She hitched her skirts and dashed halfway up before pausing and running back to the basement to retrieve . . . her derringer was gone. All she could find was a long embalming needle. It would have to do.

Back up the stairs, and when the clumps of dirt continued, up another flight to her own quarters.

He was in the lavatory. Probably rooting around, clumsy and mindless. She raised the needle and kneed the door open.

Toby's revenant was seated in Rasheeda's own bathtub. A pistol in one hand, a bar of soap in the other, the bathwater milky gray.

"Ah. I guess you'll be the fine hostess, then."

A thick Irish accent. And no drool.

This revenant was perfectly coherent. Perhaps a little too coherent. He eyed her embalming needle and lifted a brow, his fingers going snug on the pistol.

"You wouldn't be having any men's clothing around here now, would you?"

SHE DID. IN fact she had quite a stock of spare clothing, male and female.

"What's your name?" she said as he dressed behind her screen.

She'd turned away just long enough to give him a pretense at modesty, but then watched him from the corner of her eye. He cleaned up well enough for a man who'd been killed and buried raw. The scars couldn't be helped.

"Liath."

"Lee?"

"Close enough. Liath O'Shea. Now I'll be having a few questions for you, Miss Basemore."

He knew her name! "How—?"

"I was listening to every word."

She ground her teeth in frustration. Toby had a lot to answer for.

"Playing possum, as it were?"

"So to speak. Apparently I was dead and buried and you brought me back to life." He stepped out from behind the screen, shirtless, dressed in ill-fitting gray trousers. "What sort of blasphemy is that?"

She sniffed. She didn't believe in blasphemy or sacrilege or any of that nonsense.

"The kind that allows you to ask that question."

He smiled. "Touché, as the French say."

Not a bad smile. He reminded her of Alastair back in England. They'd been lovers. Poor boy had thought he was her one and only. When he found out about Rupert, he challenged him to a duel. It hadn't ended well for Alastair—a bullet through the heart. She'd used the ritual—and Rupert—to bring him back but that hadn't ended well either. That and complications from other impetuous acts had precipitated her flight to the New World.

"Well?" she said. "Out with it. What happened?"

Liath's eyes clouded. "I don't remember. All I know is that some guttersnipe stabbed me in the back."

"Toby—the man who resurrected you—said you were stabbed through the heart from the front." She pointed to the sealed wound in his chest.

"Was I?" He touched the spot. "Well, this is a new one. See, I don't even remember that. I do remember walking past the docks on Pearl Street and then . . ." He shook his head. "I never saw him."

"Come now. You can tell me. What happened that night?"

"Well . . . I remember I was on me way to me sister's. She's quite a cook, that one. Always stuffs me with brown bread and coddle—"

As he pulled the tunic over his head she saw her chance. She grabbed the parlor pistol from her bedside drawer—

"Hate to be disappointing you, dearie," he said as his head popped through the collar, "but that toy is just a Flobert, and I removed the flint."

She pulled the trigger anyway only to be rewarded by an impotent click. Silently cursing him, she tossed it on the settee.

He added, "And before you draw out that ghoulish-looking needle again, ask yourself a wee question: What's become of them lovely liniments you were keeping in your safe, mm? And might you be wanting them back?"

Rasheeda fixed her teeth. "You . . ." She moved toward him, extending her neck. " . . . impudent . . ." And drew in so close she had to tilt her face up to meet his gaze. " . . . reckless philistine. How *dare* you steal my oil? Without me it's no use to you or anyone else!"

"Seems of use to *you,* luv."

"Oh, is *that* what this is? Imagine, a simple revenant, looking to make a penny!"

He shrugged, fastening his trousers.

She said, "The only reason I indulged your drivel was to learn who stuffed you in my graveyard so I could find them and grind them into sausage. Not because I give a fig about *you*. It's my *graveyard* that's been violated. And if you think you can blackmail me—"

"Ah, now look how you've got yourself in such a lather. You'll get your liniments back. And not for money. Just give a helping hand in this."

"In what?"

"Finding me killer, of course. It's good for both of us. You said yourself you wanted to know who stuffed me in your garden."

"Not that badly. And not likely I'd trust you. You've already fooled me with your drooling act."

"Seemed the only way to get out of your basement on me own two feet. You'd've either thrown me in your oven or sold me off to rich folk."

"How would you even know what I do?"

"Because I'll be living in a part of the city that watches how the rest live. I've heard rumors about the strange house staff you rent out." He eyed her. "And now I know where you recruit them: from graves."

She straightened. "I prefer to refer to them as domiciliary revenants."

"I don't care if you call them coddled eggs, do we have a deal?"

She shook her head. "I don't have time for this. I have a revenant who needs anointing before the moon changes. Tonight."

She still had enough of the properly fermented oil for Eunice, the Traugott revenant, but what about the next lunar cycle? The mixture took two cycles to properly ferment. If he didn't return that flask, she would lose everything by the end of the next cycle.

"I'll be tagging along, and we can start looking for me killer along the way."

"What? You've already been murdered once. I do not intend to be at your side should someone try again."

His expression grew fierce. "Well, I'll not be locking meself away, I can tell you that. I'll find me killer and make him pay."

LIATH STRODE ACROSS the dark New York City cobblestones in a long dress, a veiled hat, and pinchy heeled boots. The only visible emblem of his masculinity was the brass knuckles he wore on his right hand. What a fine state.

But the lady—whose name he'd learned was Rasheeda—was right: it wouldn't do at all to be recognized by the one who murdered him. Better to let him think he'd succeeded. He'd be off his guard then.

But Liath felt he had to go out tonight because he didn't want to let Rasheeda out of his sight.

She was striding next to him, all cat eyes and gilded scarlet in the streetlamps' glow, and not the least bit sympathetic to his boots. Quite a specimen, she was. Her skin was flawless. Obviously from India but not as dark as others he'd seen from that mysterious subcontinent.

Liath's attire had once belonged to a grand if horsey lady who'd outlived two husbands and then been trampled by a spooked gelding. No doubt the lady's family believed that Rasheeda had disposed of the dress. But no. It went into one of many basement trunks. Fortunate for Liath that Rasheeda hoarded death clothes the way a spinster collected cats. She said she never sent a revenant out in clothes they died in, but they most certainly went out in clothes that someone *else* died in.

"How do you make your living, Mister O'Shea?"

"I guess you could be calling me an importer."

"Importer of what?"

He grinned. "Anything with a high tariff—the higher the better, I always say."

She laughed—a musical sound. "You're a smuggler!"

"You prefer 'domiciliary revenants,' I prefer 'tariff-free importer.' Me trade is made possible by the wonderful Republicans down in Washington, bless their souls. They love tariffs so much they place them on *all* imports—averaging thirty-six percent, would you believe? Without them I'd be out of business."

"Do you think one of your fellow smugglers did you in?"

He shrugged. "Could be, but I doubt it. There's plenty to go round." But he wasn't interested in his trade. He was thinking about all the revenants that had come before him. "So, considering me new circumstances, have you got any advice for a man like me?"

"Yes. Stop thinking of yourself as a man."

Considering the dress, her advice rang obvious. "You know what I mean. As a pet monster, or . . ."

"Domiciliary revenant."

"Fine. What's me upkeep? A dab of that oil now and again?"

She eyed him. "Not that simple. The anointing has very sensitive timing. *If* the revenant is salvageable. And there's a recitation involved."

"What, a spell?"

She shook her head. "The entire process is a delicate balance. Your existence is completely . . . anomalistic." She shrugged.

He turned his gaze back to the stones down the alley. So. Maybe he would not continue to exist as the coherent, functioning lad from Meath. Maybe he would degenerate into . . . what?

No use giving over to dread. He'd long since been doomed.

Vengeance was all he had left. Vengeance and wrath, rich as whiskey in the blood. He'd have a taste before his final bow.

The streets were dark and quiet. They'd left Toby behind to handle disposing of the donor sailor in the crematorium. Later Rasheeda would use the ashes as substitutes for corpses she *should* cremate but would resurrect instead. All so very ghastly, but Liath could respect her business sense.

He himself had dabbled in racketeering, bribery, or whatever was required, but he'd found he had a knack for the smuggling trade. He considered it more of a gentleman's racket, although every once in a very long while he might have to doff some bloke and shove his body off the pier. But those were rare and unfortunate circumstances, and then only if the bloke were a true maggot.

Rasheeda gave Liath an annoyed glance.

He realized he was whistling, same as he'd done on the night he'd died. Whistling along, thinking of his sister's brown bread and coddle . . .

He snapped to. A shadow moved at the far end of the alley.

Liath cleared his head and squinted. The shadow swayed. Just some drunk. But something familiar about him just the same.

Ah. Liath knew him but couldn't place the fellow. He was singing some made-up lyrics to an old opus, something about "promenading in the park, goosing statues after dark . . ."

. . . and Liath nearly groaned. Ricky the Rake. An alcoholic thief who was known for laying hands on the ladies. Usually without consent. And he often combined his lechery with pickpocketing. More the worse, he was stinky. To graze past him was to be saturated by him. Yes, Liath knew Ricky all too well.

And Ricky knew Liath.

Liath moved to Rasheeda's other side so that he was now striding—actually, scrabbling in his pinchy boots—between Rasheeda and the Rake.

If that lout didn't accost the two "ladies" in the alley, it would be a first. And if he laid one hand on Liath's bum, he'd figure out that Liath was a he.

The Rake seemed at first to take no notice, but then: "Oh, ladies. Hullo and good—"

Liath swung the brass knuckles in a roundhouse punch to the left side of the Rake's chest. Ricky crumpled to the stones.

Liath and Rasheeda kept walking. Behind them, a low, long squeak escaped from Ricky's throat.

At the end of the alley Rasheeda finally asked, "Are you going to explain what just happened or are you counting on my frisky imagination?"

"Just someone I knew. Didn't want to risk being recognized."

She glanced back over her shoulder. "Did you stab him?"

"No, luv. Just a little trick I learned from Five Points. They call it the Dead Rabbit punch."

"He's dead, I think."

"Naw. That punch can stop a heart but our man there will see tomorrow, though he'll remember that blow for weeks—every time he draws a breath."

AS LIATH WORKED on the bit lock with an iron pick and a crooked finish nail, he heard Rasheeda grousing behind him.

"We're too late, I think."

He turned and saw her staring up at the moon. "Too late for what?"

"The moon . . . it's past its full cycle. Damnation!"

The cylinder turned and he pushed the door open. The house was quiet, of course. Rasheeda had said the Traugotts were on holiday. Or supposed to be.

Then beyond the foyer, from the drawing room, came the sound of breathing. Loud, steady; a restless sleep sound.

And a wicked odor.

Rasheeda squeezed Liath's elbow. "I was afraid of this! Turn on the light, I'll cover the windows."

She rushed to the far wall, pulling the sash and letting the drapes fall together. Liath switched on a Tiffany floor lamp.

There on the silk rug sat a gaunt and pasty waif, forearms resting on her knees and her skirts hitched so that her bloomers spilled apparent. A revenant dressed in a maid's uniform. Her mouth was covered in gore. It formed a muzzle and stained her neckerchief and skirts.

The maid took no measure to conceal her disarray. She merely sat, staring, unresponsive to Rasheeda or Liath or the light that now bathed the room.

"What has she been . . . ?" Liath started and looked toward the hall.

"Oh, dear," Rasheeda said softly. "Eunice, Eunice, Eunice."

Kneeling next to the maid, she removed a carafe from her pocket and began streaking oil onto the revenant's face.

"Go find the family," she told him.

"And where might they be?"

"They will be dead and . . . not pretty."

"Dead?"

She waved him on. "Go, go! See if anyone survived."

Liath ventured deeper into the house. And one by one he found them: the husband, the wife, the children, a butler. Rasheeda had been right: not pretty. Each had been savaged as though by a rabid boar. Some were barely recognizable; others merely had their throats torn.

Of all the degenerates Liath had known, from Five Points to the Bowery, from the Dead Rabbits and Bowery Boys to the Municipals and the Metropolitans; not from any rank of thuggery had he witnessed such wanton disregard for human life as what that revenant had done in the Traugott home.

Worst of all: Why didn't he feel shock or revulsion? Was it because he was . . . oh, well, might as well be saying it: dead?

He stood in the kitchen and gazed at what was left of the butler. The poor man lay eviscerated atop tiny little black-and-white tiles, a cloth still draped neatly over his arm. Shattered bits of china and a tea tray lay at various points around the baseboard.

What disturbed Liath more was that his own stomach was not turning flip-flops as it ought to. Instead it felt . . . peckish.

"Well, you can't say I didn't warn them," Rasheeda said behind him.

Liath jumped in his boots. "Godsake woman. Don't be sidling up on me like that."

"Wasn't sidling. I was just saying that I'd warned them."

"You mean to tell me, all these people *knew* they risked slaughter and still they dallied in their return?"

"Well, not *slaughter* exactly."

"No? Well, then, what *were* you after telling them—*exactly*?"

"I told them what I tell all my clients: without the lunar anointing, their servant will become inactive—as you can see by that wretch in the drawing room."

Liath looked in the direction of the revenant maid. "But if I might be hazarding a guess, it appears she went into some sort of berserker rage first."

"Yes. They do tend to do that when the anointing is delayed past the full moon."

"Well, if these folks knew she'd do that—"

"They didn't know *that*, exactly."

"What? You don't tell your clients their lives could be at risk?"

"Of course not. Why would I do that?"

"Don't you feel some sort of responsibility to give fair warning?"

"Don't be silly! Who would lease from me then?"

"No one!"

"Exactly!"

She was cold, this one. Colder than his own dead arse.

"That's . . ." He found himself at a loss for words. "That's unconscionable!"

She raised her chin. "I'm not sure I care for an air of moral superiority in a career criminal—and a dead one, at that."

"An air? Me? I'm not one for airs of any sort. I may be having a few failings now and again but—"

"A *few*? You've told me you're a smuggler. That means your modus operandi is bribery, thievery, and probably extortion as well. I wouldn't be surprised if you didn't have a murder or two on your hands to boot."

"Oh, listen to herself talking about murder. As if there's not a drop of blood on her lily-white hands."

"I have *no* blood on my hands, and what you imply as murder on my part is anything but. It is a simple transfer of life force."

"The poor bloke's just as dead as a man with a bullet in his noggin."

"Besides, it's not as if they were doing anything useful with their lives in the first place. We're careful in choosing the types who tend to go missing anyway. No one is looking for them, I assure you. But you—how many have you killed?"

"Only two, and never with glee, and never a one who didn't deserve it."

"And what criteria, in your estimation, are required for one to find a place on your 'deserve it' list?"

He hesitated, scratching his cheek even though it didn't itch. This wasn't a comfortable topic.

"All right: both times was because of a double cross."

"A betrayal?"

"Yes. Someone who says he'll be doing one thing and then he does another."

She rocked her head back and forth. "Oh, and I suppose you, as a career criminal, never break your word?"

"Never. And I don't think of meself as a criminal."

"Smuggling is a crime."

"It is, but I'm after thinking of meself as a businessman whose trade simply happens to be against the law."

"One who's never gone back on his word?"

"Well, sometimes I may not be delivering on a promise—"

She jabbed at finger at him. "Aha!"

"—but only because of circumstances beyond me control. Never because I had a better offer elsewhere, or something heinous like that."

"You mean . . . let me understand this: you mean to tell me that you hold to your word no matter what?"

"If I say I'll be doing something, I do it. People have to know that when Liath O'Shea says he'll be delivering, he delivers. How else will business get done?"

"Even when it turns unprofitable?" She shook her head. "That's like some silliness out of a penny dreadful."

"It's a matter of me personal pride."

"So you fancy yourself a character from a penny dreadful then?"

"I do no such thing! You sound as though you think keeping one's word is silly."

"Of course it isn't!" She looked mildly offended, then shrugged. "Unless of course it becomes inconvenient to do so."

"How can you say that? Your word is your bond!"

"I always reserve the right to change my mind if things don't go my way."

Liath could only stare. Was it because she was from India? Was this how heathens over there conducted business?

Rasheeda stared back with a puzzled expression. "What?"

"Well, then, you can't be expecting other people to hold up *their* end of a bargain, can you?"

"Of course I can—they gave their word!"

"B-but—"

She waved her hands in the air. "I'm tired of this discussion."

"*You're* tired! I'm exhausted!"

Rasheeda left with Eunice to take her back to the house and secrete her in the basement. After all, the maid had suffered no damage and, as Rasheeda said, no point in wasting a good revenant. She'd be cleaned up and rented out again in no time.

She left Liath to ransack the Traugott household and make it look like a robbery. Liath set to it, but only to get it over with. A week before and he would have been gleeful for the opportunity. But tonight the only thing that interested him were the Traugotts themselves. And their butler. He tried to ignore his growling stomach, but . . .

Mrs. Traugott lay on her fainting couch, her macerated liver exposed—Eunice had apparently dined on that. Liath stared at the bloody tissue. It looked so tempting. He'd always loved liver and onions—he did a lot of cooking and that was one of his favorites—but never raw . . . and never human.

God help him, his hand took on a life of its own and tore off a piece. He hesitated, then shoved it into his mouth. He closed his eyes and let his head fall back as he chewed. Ambrosia.

He swallowed, then, remembering it was supposed to look like a robbery, slipped the pearls from the lady's neck. He glanced again at her liver. He wanted more, but a wave of self-loathing prevented it.

He fled to the second floor to remove himself from temptation. He might have sobbed had he still the capacity.

Not only was he dead, but a cannibal as well.

2. UNDER A HALF MOON

A whole week wasted.

Worse than merely wasted—wasted wearing a dress and a veil.

Liath had crisscrossed the Five Points area and the Bowery time and again. He'd even dared the East River docks, which weren't suitable for a lady, fending off more than one proposition. With the towers of the half-constructed Brooklyn Bridge looming in the background, he'd spied many a fellow smuggler wandering the streets there. He'd paid particular attention to the boyos he'd worked with, but not a one of them was giving anything away.

He'd spent his nights as a shadow in the city. Difficult work when you've got no coin. And yet he'd learned nothing of his murderer.

He'd had enough.

Wearing his own comfortable boots and a dark suit from Rasheeda's collection, he headed for the rooms he rented on Fletcher Alley near the docks. The key had been missing from his suit pockets, but he went there anyway, figuring he could break in—and not by bashing down the door. Rasheeda had been quick to peg him as a common back-alley beef. Rasheeda and her opinions! No, he'd never met a lock he couldn't pick. Even the new Yale tumblers.

As it turned out, no need for picking: the door sat ajar. He pushed it open and stood on the threshold surveying the premises. He could afford better but had never liked to advertise his affluence. The important thing was it had a gas stove where he could cook to his heart's content. Otherwise he spent little time here, so a bit of shabbiness was tolerable. But now . . .

His room had been ransacked.

His pipe lay on the floorboards with the tobacco trampled into the cracks.

The ginger jar his sister had given him: smashed. His teakettle lay overturned. Every hinge bent on his gas stove; the basin upended. Clothes plucked from the line, the drawers pulled from the dresser, the mattress cut up. Even his calendar was torn—well, that might have been torn before.

Liath gritted his teeth. Not enough that some goat dogger should stab him through the heart. But his home? They had to vandalize his home? Looking for . . .

What?

If only that last night alive were a bit clearer.

He righted a stool and sat on it. He leaned back, rested his boot across his knee, and closed his eyes, trying to remember. He'd been on his way to his sister's for supper. That much was firm in his mind—but not a reason to have got him killed.

No . . . nothing came to him but bits of his past. He'd been ten on his arrival here in New York with his parents and his older sister, Moira. That had been 1846, during the great Irish diaspora at the height of the potato blight. Two years later folks discovered gold in California, so his father took off to make his fortune in the rush and was never heard from again.

As a teen Liath worked in a chophouse where he learned to cook, but he supplemented his income—he was pretty much sole support of his mother and sister—by running with the Dead Rabbits gang in the Five Points area, stealing, rum-running, and helping them put the squeeze on illegal gambling dens and faro games.

Eventually he developed his own smuggling enterprise. Liath chose the items with the highest duty and smuggled them in quantity. His policy was to split the difference with the merchant so they'd both make out. His business had been thriving because he gave everyone a fair shake. Why not? Plenty to go round.

Of course he, like everybody else, had to pay a tribute to the Whyos, the current rulers of the city streets, but that was just the cost of doing business. And he always paid, so he couldn't see them doing him in.

Ah, well, nothing was coming. He opened his eyes and was about to stand up when he noticed that his right boot heel was just a tad off center. He pushed on it and it swiveled, revealing a hollow.

The diamonds!

He rechecked the hollow to be sure it was empty, then swung it back into place before leaping to his feet.

Yes! He remembered. On the night he died, he'd received his cut of a shipment of velvet, plus half a dozen uncut diamonds. He'd hidden the gems in his heel and sold off a goodly portion of the fabric. He'd been paid in gold coins.

The coins . . .

He raised his gaze to the ceiling. The rusted tin squares were still in place. Flaking and sagging, but in place. Even the loose one.

He dragged the stool over and positioned it under the loose tin. It folded back on concealed hinges he himself had crafted. The loose square revealed the small hole in the lathe and beyond that, the gap between his ceiling and his neighbor's floorboards.

They were still there, round and sweet, stacked in the little cubby between all that board and lathe. At least he had some spending money.

But the diamonds . . . now he knew the motive for his murder. Who had known about the diamonds?

As he stuffed some of his clothes into a duffel bag, Liath came to a decision: no more slinking around. Time to come out in the open and rattle some cages.

RASHEEDA STOOD BETWEEN a recently disinterred middle-aged man and a scrofulous drunk Toby had acquired from downtown—both connected by the silver chain—and chanted the ancient Vedic verses. This fellow would make someone an excellent butler.

The book was not the original Vedic manuscript, but a transcription hand copied by her father. She missed him. A little. Well, not really.

He'd been an archaeologist who'd married a descendant of Siraj ud-Daulah, the last Nawab of Bengal. Rasheeda had been born in Bengal and grew up in a bilingual household. In 1857, at age nineteen, she and her parents had fled India because of the Sepoy rebellion. A year after their arrival in London, her father had been killed during a robbery. Oddly enough, the only thing taken was an ancient Sanskrit Vedic manuscript that had been in her mother's family for many generations.

Stolen, but not completely lost: her father had transcribed a copy before his demise. Rasheeda had never been interested in the book before, but now she delved into it. She found a ritual for supposedly raising the dead. As a lark, with no hope of success but little else to occupy her time, she tried it out on animals and, to her shock, found that it worked.

Alastair was the first human she resurrected—sacrificing her other lover, Rupert, to bring him back. She'd kept the revenant around for a while, but he proved such a dullard that she rekilled him.

The experience had kindled a fire in her, however. To gain access to more of the recently dead, she learned the undertaking trade—even though a woman undertaker was unheard of—and perfected the resurrection process. In 1865, under a cloud of suspicion and ugly rumors connecting her to disappearances of wastrels from the Limehouse district, she took her share of the money her father had left—not a great amount by any stretch—and emigrated to the States.

Shortly after opening her mortuary in Harlem, she innovated the first crematorium in the United States. Although she offered the service to her clients, few opted for it. No matter. She had her own uses for it.

She wished Toby were around to assist today, but she had sent him off to help that shanty Irishman find his killer. Anything to speed the return of her sustaining oil.

LIATH AND TOBY stood in a doorway on Bleecker Street, just east of Lafayette. The sun had dropped below the rooftops and traffic was light. Across the street, on the corner of Bleecker and Shinbone Alley, stood the Stone Ox pub.

"All right," he said, pointing, "that's where me boyos gather of an evening. I'll be going in and buying a few rounds for the house. None of that crew will be leaving while there's free drink to be had unless—"

"Unless they know you should be dead."

"Exactly." He clapped Toby on the back. "You're a smart lad, that's why I asked your help."

"I don't work for you," Toby said stiffly. "Miss Basemore told me to help."

"Only because I *asked* for you. I don't think she appreciates your abilities, Toby. I know you can handle this."

Toby visibly swelled with pride. Liath had noted his frustration and reluctantly decided to play on it. Reluctant because he did owe the young man his renewed life, such as it was. And as for Rasheeda, she had threatened Liath if anything happened to him. Toby had plenty of faults, she'd said, but she had no time to train a new assistant.

"I'm sure I can," Toby said. "But what exactly do you have in mind?"

Liath pointed again at the Stone Ox. "Only two ways in or out. Obviously the front entrance, but there's also a delivery door in the alley there. This vantage offers a view of both. If you see anyone come out, follow them."

"That's all? Just follow?"

"Yes. He knows me, but he'll not be knowing you. I'm sure you could easily apprehend him, but I have a feeling that more than one miscreant was involved in me untimely demise, and I want them all."

"We could catch him and make him talk."

"Shaky business, that. You're never knowing whether you're hearing the truth or just what the fellow thinks you want to hear. Better if I see it with me own eyes."

"Right, then," Toby said with a confident nod. "Simple enough."

"He'll probably be slipping out into the alley. If he comes this way, just get behind him and follow. If he heads deeper into the alley, don't follow him there—you'll give yourself away. Shinbone turns left and opens onto Lafayette, so head over to the corner and watch for him there."

Toby nodded his understanding.

Liath squared his shoulders. "Here I go."

He crossed the street, dodging a mix of horse-drawn carriages and steamers. When he stepped through the Ox's swinging doors, he wanted to have maximum impact on the guilty party. To that end he'd made a point of wearing the suit he'd died in—cleaning away the dirt and bloodstains first, of course.

He burst into the room and raised his hands.

"Who'll be wanting a drink on me?"

Pipes and cigars were puffing, drinks were sitting on the bar and the tables, spilled beer wet the sawdust on the floor. Every eye in that smoke-filled space turned toward him, and every face, the familiar and the not-so, broke into a smile.

No, not every face. Jesse Timbers, a smuggler he'd worked with on occasion, went white as a virgin's wedding dress.

Liath's vision blurred for an instant as he remembered Timbers's face looming out of the dark that night, just as his life faded. But Timbers hadn't attacked him. His assailant had been extremely powerful, and skinny Jesse Timbers was anything but.

Liath staggered a step, then someone grabbed his elbow.

"Whoa there, mate. Looks like you're a bit buckled already," said Sean Healy, one of Liath's oldest friends in the city.

"I've had a few."

"And you're so pale," Sean said.

"Been off me feed, but I'm okay now."

Pretending not to notice Timbers, Liath bellied up to the bar and slapped a gold piece down. "Give these beggars one of whatever they want!"

As a cheer went up and all the mild porter drinkers suddenly switched to whiskey, Liath kept watch on Timbers from the corner of his eye. His pallor was shading toward green now. And instead of shouting out a drink order like the others, he was edging toward the side door.

What was driving him away? Fear? Guilt? The need to get word to someone about how the man they'd shivved and robbed and buried was alive and well and in the Stone Ox buying for the house?

All three, he hoped.

As his mates yelled "Sláinte!" and slapped him on the back and asked him where he'd been hiding the past week, Liath watched Timbers slip out into Shinbone Alley.

All right, then. He had to trust Toby to take it from here.

He sipped his whiskey and almost gagged. It tasted like shite. He looked around. His mates were downing theirs with gusto. What had happened to him? He had no appetite for food and never slept. Was he to be denied strong drink as well?

All he had an appetite for was human offal, and he wasn't giving in to that again. He'd bought slices of calf's liver and tried it both raw and cooked, but neither did the least to assuage his hunger. What sort of a thing had he become? He couldn't see spending year after year with this foul craving.

He shook his head. Once he found his killer and evened the score, he'd find a way to die again—permanently.

He waited around, resisting the urge to be out on the street following Toby. Instead he increased his popularity by buying a second round. Too soon, Toby appeared at the swinging doors, his expression grim.

"The news isn't good, I take it," Liath said as he joined him on the sidewalk.

Toby shook his head. "I'm afraid not. I followed him up Lafayette but lost him in the street by Cooper Institute."

"Aw, no."

"Well, it was dark, and he simply disappeared into the crowd around there."

Liath wanted to scream that no one simply disappears but resisted the outburst along with the urge to throttle the boy.

"Don't worry," he forced himself to say. "All is not lost. After seeing him, I'm surer than ever that more than one snake was involved. He's run off to tell someone. Five'll get you ten there'll be a viper slithering back here to confirm the dead man sighting."

So they retreated to another doorway farther east on Bleecker but on the same side as the Ox, where they couldn't be seen from the tavern.

"You're sure he's involved?" Toby said.

Liath nodded. "It fits. Jesse Timbers is a fellow smuggler, mostly gin."

"We have plenty of gin here. Why smuggle it?"

"He specializes in Old Tom gin, which you can get here but only after paying a forty percent duty. But here's the thing: Timbers knows I smuggle gems among other things and knows about me boot heel. He didn't stab me, of that I'm sure, but that expression on his face when he saw me says he knows who did—maybe even put them up to it for a share."

They waited, and, sure enough, less than a quarter hour later who appeared but Jesse Timbers himself, accompanied by a hulking, thuggish fellow, a hardchaw if Liath had ever seen one. The streetlamp revealed a long scar down his right cheek. He might have been the one who wielded the knife, though Liath was not convinced.

"Keep watch," he told Toby, pressing himself deeper into the doorway. "I don't want them to see me."

"They're entering the Stone Ox," Toby said. Half a minute later he added, "Now they're back on the sidewalk, looking around." After a few seconds his voice rose in pitch: "They're coming this way!"

"Good," Liath said, fitting his fingers into his brass knuckles. "The time for watching is over. Tell me when they're almost here."

Toby stared into space, looking like he might be drunk or just banjaxed. Liath heard footsteps and voices approaching.

"—swear I saw him, big as day," Timbers was saying.

"You been down Chinktown, suckin' on a pipe? He's dead! We buried him."

"Wasn't just me. You heard the others. They saw him—"

Liath jumped out in front of them. Timbers was the closest so he swung at his face. "Here's your proof, you traitorous guttersnipe!"

The git tried to turn away, but Liath caught the side of his head with a brass-bolstered fist and he went down like a dead man.

The scarred man was quick. An automatic knife appeared in his hand as if by magic. He was already slashing at Toby as the blade snicked open. Toby cried out as it gashed his flank and blood splashed from the wound. Scar whirled toward Liath, aiming a backhanded slash for his throat. Liath raised his arm to fend it off, saving his throat, but the blade pierced his arm through and through.

The man's mouth dropped open as he recognized Liath.

"You!" he cried, releasing the knife handle and stumbling back. "It's really you!"

He turned and ran and Liath would have given chase but for Toby, who was down on his knees, groaning with pain and clutching his bloody flank.

And then the matter of Liath's pierced forearm. Why didn't it hurt more?

Never mind that now. He turned to Toby. "We need to be getting you to a hospital."

"No! Miss Basemore can fix me."

"Well, then, what about Timbers? How do you think we'll get both you and him all the way to Harlem?"

Toby was staring at Timbers. "I don't think he'll be much use to you in Harlem or anywhere else."

Liath turned and saw the weasel's blank staring eyes.

"But I hit him only once!"

"That was all it took, I guess."

"Do I not know me own strength then?" Liath looked at his pierced arm. "And why aren't I bleeding?"

Toby struggled to rise and Liath helped him to his feet.

"Revenants are terribly strong. And they don't bleed."

Liath grabbed the knife handle and pulled the blade free. He felt only mild discomfort, and not a drop of his blood had spilled.

"YOU PROMISED TO keep him safe!" Rasheeda said through her teeth as she stitched up Toby's flank.

The young man lay on his side on the resurrection table while she worked on him. Scar's knife had pierced the skin and underlying fatty layer—lots of bleeding but not deep enough to damage any organs.

"Well, he's safe enough now, isn't he?" Liath said.

"I'm fine," said Toby. He winced as Rasheeda jabbed a curved sewing needle through the skin at the edge of his wound, but otherwise seemed to be enjoying his boss's hands on him.

"You've lost a lot of blood."

"He's young," Liath said. "Feed him a steak and he'll be good as new in two shakes." Liath raised his arm. "Meself, on the other hand . . ."

He'd rolled his shirtsleeve up to the elbow and was inspecting his own knife wound, such as it was. The edges had sealed over, leaving two opposing seams on the upper and lower surfaces of his forearm.

"I told you," Toby said. "Revenants don't bleed."

"How can you bleed?" Rasheeda said. "You have no blood."

"No blood . . ." Liath stared at his arm. "How is that possible?"

He'd refolded Scar's automatic knife down on Bleecker Street. Now he removed it from his pocket, found the button on the fancy ivory handle, and pressed it. The blade snapped out, bright and fine-edged. He pressed the point against the belly of his forearm. It felt dull rather than sharp. He pressed harder until it pierced the skin, causing only mild discomfort. He dragged the point toward his elbow, opening a four-inch gash that revealed the layers of the skin and the yellow fat beneath, but not a drop of blood.

"Like cutting open a dead man."

He looked up to find Toby and Rasheeda staring at him.

"Well?" she said.

"But I'm *not* dead. I walk, I talk. I may not be knowing a lot about science, but I know that blood powers the muscles and the brain. Cut a man's throat and he bleeds to death. If I've no blood, what's powering me muscles?"

Rasheeda frowned. "That has long puzzled me. The ancient *Veda* never explained it. It calls revenants *khokhala* and—"

"What's that mean?"

She concentrated on knotting the thread of her latest stitch. "Hollow."

Liath looked at his bloodless wound, already healing. "Well, I guess I'm that. Hollow of blood anyways. What else am I hollow of now? A soul, perhaps?"

She looked up at him. "Some philosophers say there's no such thing as a soul."

"They'll be heathens, then."

"Irrelevant. Lots of 'heathens,' as you say, believe in souls. I was raised a Hindu, and Hindus believe in souls."

"You say that like you no longer believe."

She shrugged. "When you've resurrected as many of the dead as I have, it gives you cause to wonder. Consider: If your soul truly traveled on after your murder, then how can you be alive again and still be you?"

"Who else would I be?"

"I don't know. That German sailor's life force went into you—why aren't you speaking German and yearning for the sea?"

"That so-called life force doesn't pump blood through me veins."

"That's because your heart's not beating."

"What?"

He pressed his hand against his chest and felt nothing. He pressed harder—still nothing. He'd not noticed.

"Dear God!"

"You don't need to breathe, either."

"But I do." He drew in a breath and let it out. "See?"

"I didn't say you couldn't. I said you don't need to—except to talk, that is."

Liath felt as if the world were pulling away from him.

Her earlier words came back.

. . . *if your soul truly traveled on after your murder* . . .

"I've been robbed of me soul!"

Toby grimaced as Rasheeda again jabbed the needle through his skin.

"Don't be ridiculous!" she said. "Even if you had a soul, I didn't send it on. Your murderer did."

Hollow . . . no blood, no heartbeat, no breath, no soul, and a hunger for human offal . . . he'd become an unholy thing.

"You've robbed me of an afterlife then! I'll never get to heaven!"

She made a clucking noise. "Assuming there's such a thing as a soul, and assuming there's such a place as heaven, did you really believe yours would be welcomed there?"

Liath opened his mouth, then closed it. Good point, but that still didn't lessen the feeling that he'd lost something of infinite value.

"What in God's name *am* I then?"

"A *khokhala*."

"Just a word! What allows me to move, to think?"

"The *Veda* says a *khokhala* is animated by *Ajñata*."

"Another heathen word! And what, pray tell, would that mean?"

She shrugged. "It translates to English as 'Nameless,' which I suppose is a way of saying they don't know."

"Well, *something* is powering me muscles and me brain—such as it is."

"My theory is that it comes from the aether—Aristotle's fifth element."

"Well, if you're calling it 'aether' it's not exactly nameless now, is it."

"Well, no . . ."

For the first time since he'd met her she looked unsure. Liath found he preferred her usual supreme confidence.

He waved the knife at her. "See, aether or not, something is fueling all your cocoa-holidays—"

"*Khokhalas*," she said.

"Whatever the name, something is powering us all, and that means you're running up a terrible bill."

She laughed. "It's not like electricity!"

"How do you know?" he said, feeling uneasy. "We're tapped into something. Call it aether or fifth element or 'nameless'—"

"Ajñata."

"—or whatever you like, but someday the bill is going to come due. What then? What will the price be? And who will be paying? You? Me?"

She shook her head. "You're being silly."

"Nothing is free, luv. There's always a balance to be struck. It's a rule of the world—of the whole universe. Sure as the sun rises tomorrow, that bill's gonna come due someday, and I'm fearing there'll be hell to pay when it does."

3. UNDER A NEW MOON

Rasheeda had been under the impression she'd be meeting with a bereaved widow wishing to arrange a funeral for her husband. With a shock, she recognized the woman as soon as she entered the room, and knew she wasn't married.

"Madame Louisa?" she said, rising behind her desk. "I don't understand."

Louisa's smile had a smug twist. "Don't fuss at your assistant. I played the grieving new widow for him." She faked a sob as she dabbed at her eyes with a lace handkerchief. "And rather convincingly, if I do say so myself."

Rasheeda hadn't grown up in the States, so she wasn't familiar enough with American dialects to know if Louisa's drawl was real or affected. The lady was dressed fashionably in a long-sleeved, form-fitting dress with a square neckline and a cuirass bodice. One never would have guessed that she ran a high-end bordello.

"And now I understand even less."

Louisa laughed. "Y'all have some wine perhaps?"

"I keep a bottle of brandy in my desk for some of my more fainthearted clients."

"That'll do, I suppose. Pour us both a taste. You may very well need it before I'm through."

Rasheeda did not like the sound of that.

"Whatever do you mean?" she said as she withdrew two snifters and a bottle of Armagnac from her bottom right drawer.

Louisa lowered herself into one of the chairs on the far side of the desk. "The subject is the servant I hired from you."

"Katrina?"

"Well, yes and no."

Rasheeda poured two fingers into Louisa's glass and only a dollop into her own. "Again, I do not understand."

"Of course you do, Miss Basemore. You're just being coy. Yes, I mean the servant I'm hiring from you, and no, her name ain't Katrina. It's Leni Schmidt. She's the daughter of Otto and Margaretha Schmidt who emigrated from Germany in 1847. Or perhaps I should say, the *deceased* daughter of Otto and Margaretha Schmidt."

Rasheeda hid her shock. She'd feared this day might come. She added another two fingers of brandy to her own glass.

"Wherever did you acquire such an outlandish idea?" she said, pushing a snifter across the desk.

Louisa reprised her smug smile as she swirled the brandy under her nose. "Smells like the good stuff." She tossed it back in one gulp.

Rasheeda sipped. She didn't enjoy brandy—didn't like the burn—but she felt she needed the alcohol right now.

"VSOP. But you were about to explain . . . ?"

"Oh, yes. Well, just last week I was researching one of the newer, more affluent patrons of my establishment—I like to make sure they are who they say they are. I keep a file of *Leslie's* because that seems to be the best source."

Frank Leslie's Illustrated Newspaper . . . more like a magazine, a new copy appeared every Tuesday, and Rasheeda read it herself. It more than lived up to the *Illustrated* part of its name.

Vetting her patron? Rasheeda wondered. Or setting him up for blackmail?

"While I was perusing a back issue, I lay that you'd never guess what I found."

"I'm simply dying to know." Quite the contrary, she was dreading to know.

"A tragic story about the poor daughter of German immigrants, born soon after their arrival, who was caught in a cross fire between the police and some robbers outside a Harlem bank. A stray bullet pierced the heart of Leni Schmidt, killing her on the spot. *Leslie's* printed a picture of the poor girl. Imagine my shock when I recognized my dear Katrina. And then my further shock when I read that the wake was to be held at the Basemore Funeral Home."

Rasheeda tossed back her own brandy and, coughing from the burn, began to pour a second.

Louisa laughed softly. "I knew you'd need that." She held out her glass. "Don't forget the guest."

When they each had another two fingers' worth, Rasheeda leaned back.

"They say every person has a double. You must have seen Katrina's."

"My thought exactly at the moment. Then I remembered the remark of a patron who bedded her."

Rasheeda wasn't surprised, but reacted as if she were. "*Bedded?* That is not part of her duties."

She shrugged. "I dress her in that frilly little French maid outfit for show, but one of my wealthier regulars took a shine to her and offered a pretty penny for an hour alone. I ordered her to do whatever he told her. He returned shortly and was good and angry. He said he could probably expect more response from a corpse. I gave it no further thought. I did try to school her in the French style—you know what that means?"

Rasheeda nodded. "I'm familiar with the term."

"Well, that failed too. She had no, shall we say, head for it. Some women are simply not cut out for the life. But I remembered that patron's 'corpse' remark as I gazed at Leni's photo, and I began to wonder."

"You can't be serious."

Louisa stared at her. "Must we continue this charade, Miss Basemore? Katrina, as you call her, doesn't talk, never sleeps, doesn't drink, and doesn't eat—if she's served a meal she simply pushes the food around on her plate. And now that I've been watching her, she doesn't even *breathe*. Plus, she has a small round indentation on her left tit, just the size a bullet might make as it pierced through to her heart."

Rasheeda quaffed half of her second brandy, then stared straight back. "What is your point?"

"My point is: when you brought her to me you said she was mute and mentally defective but could follow instructions. You didn't tell me she was dead."

What to say? What to *say*?

"She is obviously not dead if she—"

"She was killed, she was buried in your cemetery, and shortly thereafter you hired her out." Louisa fixed her with a narrowed gaze. "Somehow, some way, Miss Basemore, you brought her back to life."

"Madame Louisa, really—"

Louisa waved a hand. "Rest easy. I ain't here to report you to the authorities or blackmail you. We're both women in business, and as such we must stick together. I've come with a proposition: I could use young, attractive women who are like Katrina in all ways except, well . . . they should be able to put Nebuchadnezzar out to grass."

Rasheeda gaped at her, perfectly confused.

Louisa rolled her eyes. "Come on, now, sugar. You know what I mean. They should be sexually responsive—or at least be able to fake it."

Rasheeda drummed her fingers on the desk. She could see no way to win this showdown. Louisa had deduced all the important aspects of her resurrections except the *how*. The *how* was beyond ratiocination. But the more important *how* right now was how to play this shrewd woman . . .

She leaned back and steepled her fingers.

"Let us, for the sake of argument, assume that your accusations—"

"I don't feel I've been the least bit accusatory. I prefer to think of them as deductions."

"Very well. Let us assume that your deductions are accurate. You must then appreciate that I simply could not supply hirelings to order. I do not choose my clients. The dead must be brought to me, and I must work with what comes through my back door."

"I've thought of that. But nubile women who have, shall we say, suffered sudden death without disfigurement could be brought to you."

Rasheeda nodded. On the surface the plan had its merits, but Louisa was lacking some critical facts.

"Again, just for the sake of argument, let us stipulate that the timing of these supposed resurrections is critical. Too late and they are barely animate. Too early and they retain a mind of their own and can be quite willful." As Rasheeda knew all too well these days. "But if reanimated somewhere in the middle, they are docile and obedient without any original thoughts in their heads—like Katrina."

Louisa sighed. "The wonderful thing about Katrina is indeed her lack of will. I don't have to worry about her running off or pilfering the silver or stealing the receipts."

"Renascence Staffing personnel are all like that. But I fear one capable of the faux enthusiasm you desire would be lacking in the traits you find so attractive in Katrina."

"Still . . . I would not be adverse to a trial."

Rasheeda saw disaster looming but did not want to antagonize this woman. She knew too much.

"Continuing in the realm of supposition, perhaps there is a way the process can be modified to meet your needs."

Louisa's smile was genuine this time. "That'd be wonderful. My current crop of girls're so unreliable, so unprofessional. They tend to drink too much, and some are opium eaters. A few have tried to rob my patrons." She shook her head sadly. "Good help is so hard to find." She brightened after finishing her brandy. "But I'm trusting you will solve that for me."

Rasheeda showed her to the door and wished her well, while secretly hoping she'd fall out of the pneumatic on her way back downtown.

But after closing the door, she realized that none of this would matter if that Irish scoundrel didn't return her sustaining oil in time. Madame Louisa would then see another side of Katrina. One she never dreamed existed.

Two weeks . . . two weeks from now and it would be too late.

4. UNDER A GIBBOUS MOON

The only way to recall was to relive that night and retrace his steps—at least the steps he remembered.

So Liath stood outside the door to his rooming house on Fletcher Alley and started walking toward his sister Moira's place just as he had done that night some three weeks ago. She lived on the far side of the ramp to the half-finished Brooklyn Bridge, an easy trip.

He wore the same suit, he wore the same boots—although the hollow heel was empty this time—and across his shoulder, instead of fine velvet, he carried a bolt of cheap burlap. The velvet had been for her, as well as the tin of Canadian nutmeg in his pocket.

The main difference was the moon—it had been high and bright and full that night, shedding its pale light on the docked ships and reflecting off the bridge towers jutting from the East River. Tonight it gave only half the light.

He walked down the slope to Pearl Street and turned left, just as he'd done then. He continued north toward the ramp. The bridge builders had left space for Pearl Street to run beneath, but it was a dark place. Governor Westinghouse's grand electrification project hadn't reached the waterfront yet, and the underpass was a popular spot for low-end harlots to ply their trade. He remembered whistling, thinking of his sister's kitchen and how she'd fill his bowl when she saw what he'd brought her. No public house in the city could measure up to the simple foods of Meath.

As he approached the dark rectangle, he stopped and re-created that night.

He remembered switching the bolt of velvet from his right shoulder to his left, and slipping his fingers through the four loops of his brass knuckles—just in case.

When he'd entered the shadows, he remembered noticing that the underpass was strangely deserted. No calls from the harlots to dally in the dark for a quick bit of the old in-and-out. He'd picked up his pace and had just reached the midpoint where he could see the glow of the gaslit street on the far side when he sensed movement in the darkness behind him. A shadow had separated from the wall and was approaching. He pivoted to his left, swung a hard right, and landed a solid brass-encased Dead Rabbit punch to his would-be assailant.

A heart punch! He'd forgotten. And he'd struck a solid blow.

He remembered an instant of astonishment that the blow had no effect. Not even a grunt of surprise. And then astonishment turned to horror as the knife point drove through his suit and between his ribs and into his chest. He remembered the excruciating pain of it piercing his heart, and even worse agony as it was yanked out. And then a ghastly sense of drowning as he dropped to his knees. He remembered falling over backward and landing hard against the cobblestones. As his vision faded he saw a wash of light and heard the hiss of a steamer pulling up. A quick glimpse of Jesse Timber's face and then all went black.

Liath stood now and stared into the darkness. The heart punch . . . who could withstand a blow like that? Not as if his attacker had been wearing armor. He'd heard no clank of metal on metal. His fist had landed on flesh . . . soft flesh . . .

"Oh, dear God," he shouted to the night. "Oh, dear God!"

RASHEEDA NEARLY DROPPED her flask as Liath clambered up the ladder into the top floor of the tower. She'd been adding the half-moon ingredients to her next batch of anointing oil—a batch that wouldn't be ready for another five weeks.

" 'Twas a woman done me in!"

She stared at him from behind her mixing table. His eyes were wide as he stood in the doorway, panting.

"What? How do you know?"

"I remember!"

"What did she look like?"

"I don't know!"

"Then how—?"

He held up a brass-knuckled fist. "When I struck with me heart punch, I remember me fist hitting something soft and just realized I'd struck a bap."

"A what?"

"A bap! A diddy! A knob!"

"What?"

"Goddamn it, woman! A *breast*!"

"Well, why didn't you say so?" she said, gently placing the glass flask on the table.

"I just did—numerous times."

Rasheeda recalled the man who had accosted them on their first outing together and remembered how he had dropped after Liath struck him that single blow.

"She must have been a very heavy woman, then, with quite ample padding."

"That's just it. She wasn't. I could feel me fist hit her ribs through her bap. But she didn't even flinch!"

As he paced the tiny room, which allowed no more than two steps this way and two steps that, an idea niggled the back of Rasheeda's brain.

"What else do you remember?"

"I remember that as I lay on me back, gasping for air, a vehicle pulled up. Great puffs of steam and doors slamming, and I had a brief glimpse of that blackguard Jesse Timbers's face before I passed on."

"This Timbers is the one you killed down on Bleecker Street?"

"The same."

"When was the last time you'd seen him before that?"

"At the Stone Ox." Liath's eyes narrowed. "I told the weasel-faced maggot I was going to visit me sister and take her some fine velvet. The sleeveen gave me a seed of nutmeg from a shipment he'd smuggled in from Canada as a gift to her. I was thinking what a fine fellow he was, never having met Moira and all."

"Did he ask where she lived?"

Liath frowned. "Come to think of it now, he did. I wasn't after giving him her exact address, but I said she was on the north side of the ramp they'd built for the bridge."

"The Brooklyn Bridge?"

"Well, what other bridge would I be talking about?"

Rasheeda drummed her fingers on the mixing table as the pieces fell into place.

"I'll assume he knew where you lived and knew you had gems in your boot heel."

Liath's expression grew sheepish. "It's possible I may have been in me cups one night and mentioned something to that effect."

"Well then, he would know the path you would take from your place to your sister's and have his confederates waiting."

"But that means he would have sent a woman to accost me—a strong woman who feels . . . no . . . pain . . ."

She nodded as the light grew in his eyes. "You were attacked by a revenant. Which means that one of my customers is behind your murder."

He slammed his fist on her mixing table and would have upset her flask if she hadn't grabbed it in time. "Who?"

"I have a list right here." She leaned to her left and plucked her black ledger from a shelf. "Names and addresses."

She allowed Liath to snatch it from her fingers and leaf through it. After a few pages, he glanced up at her.

"You're making a nice living from this, aren't you."

"I manage. I don't plan to be in it forever."

He resumed flipping through the pages. "I don't recognize—wait!" He jabbed a finger at a page. "Madame Louisa! She's a weakness for fine fabrics. She's a regular customer for me imports." His features darkened. "She has a woman revenant?"

Rasheeda nodded. "Katrina."

He snapped the book closed. "Then she's the one."

Rasheeda pulled her ledger from his hands. "I agree. Now where is my sustaining oil?"

"Not so fast. I'll be needing to confirm it's her. Once we accomplish that, you'll have your oil."

"Damn you!" she cried. "The moon will be full soon. If I don't start anointing on time—"

"If Madame Louisa is the one, you'll have your precious oil in plenty of time."

She could feel her patience slipping away. "What will satisfy you?"

"I want to set up watch on her brothel. After Jesse Timbers ran from the Stone Ox, he returned with a man with a scarred face."

"The one who stabbed Toby."

"The same. If I see him lurking about her premises, that will be proof enough."

"Then let's get to it quickly. You'll need that dress you were wearing."

"Oh, no. I'll not be donning that again."

"Oh, and I suppose you're just going to walk in the front door of her seraglio and inquire after a man with a scarred face?"

"No, but—"

"She knows you're alive. This scarred man you talk about will have told her. If she's guilty—and I've no doubt she is—she'll be watching for you. She killed you once, so she'll have no hesitation about doing it again."

"I can die again?"

"It takes some doing, but a revenant can be killed for good."

For some odd reason he looked relieved.

"All right then. The dress it is. I'll go down there tomorrow—"

"No. *We* will go down there tomorrow. Two, um, ladies will be less conspicuous. Besides, I don't dare let you out of my sight. I don't want anything happening to you before you return what's mine."

"All right then, 'we' it is. And if all goes well, you'll have your heathen oil back before nightfall."

"At what price?"

"I'll already have me price: the name of me murderer."

So he said now. But she'd seen the way he'd been eyeing the tallies in her ledger. He'd want a healthy sum of cash before handing over her missing carafe. She ground her teeth in frustration. He had her over a barrel, and she'd have to pay whatever he demanded.

But after that . . . she thought of her derringer. A .41-caliber bullet through his scheming revenant Irish brain would be sweet revenge. And then into the crematorium with him.

Good-bye and good riddance.

Rasheeda was known at Madame Louisa's, so she wore a veil as well this time. They strolled East Twenty-Seventh Street among the midday pedestrians, feigning animated conversation. Governor Westinghouse's electrification program was in full bloom here.

"As much as I can't wait for electricity to reach Harlem," Rasheeda said, pointing to the utility poles, "I think they're ugly."

And they were. Five stories tall with at least a dozen crosspieces, and wires, wires, wires, running over the sidewalk and angling back and forth in the air above the street.

Liath didn't reply. This close, she could make out his features through the veil draped from his hat; his gaze was fixed on the brownstone that served as Madame Louisa's seraglio.

They slowed as they passed the building. The space to the right of the front steps displayed ferrotypes of the ladies available within.

"Rather fine-looking brassers," Liath muttered.

"She brags that she runs a 'quality establishment.'"

With no sign of activity, they walked on to the corner and turned around.

Liath said, "With that arena over on Madison Avenue, her business must be booming. Why would she want to kill me?"

"I wouldn't take it personally. Some women have a fatal weakness for diamonds."

They crossed Twenty-Seventh Street at Lexington and walked back on the other side. As they came abreast of the seraglio, a steam car pulled to a stop outside. Liath grabbed her arm and they stopped to watch. His grip tightened as a man with a long scar down his right cheek stepped out from behind the wheel and opened the rear door.

Then the lady herself emerged, resplendent in a dress of two-toned velvet, golden at first glance but indigo in the lowlights as the fabric moved. Liath's hand became a vise.

"You're hurting me," Rasheeda whispered.

His grip relaxed, but his voice was tight and cold. "That's the man who stabbed Toby. And the bitch Louisa is wearing the fabric I was carrying to me sister."

He started toward the curb, but Rasheeda pulled him back.

"Don't be a fool. She has a cadre of bouncers inside. A headlong rush will end in disaster. You need to plan your next move."

He nodded. "You're right. Must stay calm. Must approach this with a cool head."

Must stay alive, Rasheeda thought. *At least until I have my oil back.*

RASHEEDA WAS SEATED in her office when Liath, still in the dress, entered without knocking. He placed a dirt-encrusted carafe on her desk.

"There. We're even."

She snatched it up, pulled the stopper, and sniffed. She closed her eyes and sighed at the familiar aroma.

Wait . . . what had he just said?

" 'Even'?"

"You held up your end, I'm holding up mine."

"But . . . aren't you going to demand cash too?"

"That wasn't the deal."

"I know, but I assumed—"

"What? That I'd welsh?"

"Well, yes."

He smiled. "I'm a character from a penny dreadful, remember? I keep me word."

Shock left her almost speechless. "But—"

"I believe we've already had this conversation." He stepped to the door, then turned back to her. "I'll be keeping the dress for a while, if you don't mind."

"Consider it yours. But tell me . . ." She pointed to the carafe. "Where did you hide it?"

He smiled again. "I buried it in your graveyard."

He gave her a little salute, then turned and closed the door behind him.

Still in shock, Rasheeda leaned back and stared at her carafe. What a strange, strange man.

5. UNDER A HUNTER'S MOON

Liath wished he had paid more attention to the brothel itself while they were surveilling Louisa. He'd spent days in this damn dress and bonnet watching the comings and goings and assessing the physical layout of the building. He had spied Louisa numerous times on a top-floor corner room overlooking the street. Unfortunately, the basement windows were barred and the first-floor windows were set high; unless he brought a ladder, the two doors—one front and one rear—were the only points of entry.

On the third day, he decided to make his move. He'd noticed during his two days on watch that Louisa's four bouncers left as a group around noon and returned before two o'clock when the brothel opened its doors to the public. Today was no different. They exited the rear door—the "discreet entrance"—and disappeared down the alley that ran to East Twenty-Sixth.

Now was his chance. Despite his increased strength and diminished sensitivity to pain, Liath held no illusions about his ability to overcome those four burly thugs. So the best time to confront Louisa and retrieve his diamonds was when she was alone.

He dearly would have loved a peek indoors before entering, just to see if he might spot her whereabouts, but the high windows prevented that.

Raising the hem of his dress, he padded up the rear steps, his picks at the ready. But to his delight he found the discreet entrance unlocked. Were he in charge, he would have kept it bolted during the establishment's off-hours; perhaps it was supposed to be locked, but obviously the bouncers had forgotten to do so.

He eased the door open and tiptoed through the back hall that led to some sort of sitting room. And there, reclining on a settee, he found the madam herself. Did his good fortune know no bounds?

He glanced around and saw a table for cards and perhaps meals. A pool table sat nearby, and a dartboard was fixed to the far wall. He wondered at a long rope running through a pulley fastened in the center of the ceiling, then through another near the wall, then down to a boat cleat bolted into the chair rail. Part of some strange deviant sexual contrivance, no doubt.

Pulling off his bonnet as he entered the room, he strode toward her and said, "Surprised, Louisa?"

Instead of the expected cry of shock and alarm, Louisa looked up and gave a serene smile.

"Well, well, well. Mister O'Shea. I was afraid you'd never gather the courage to come inside."

Liath skidded to a halt. "What?"

She seemed to have been expecting him.

She laughed. "I do so love your expression just now." Her features hardened. "Do you really take me for such a fool?"

Why wasn't she afraid?

"And what would you be meaning by that?"

"I've been aware for some time now that you'd been brought back to life. I know who did it, though I don't know why and I don't know how." Her eyes narrowed. "But I will learn."

"Why did you set upon me?"

She ran a hand over her velvet dress. "I love this fabric. I wore it just for you."

They both knew she hadn't done him in for the fabric. Well, never mind all this. He'd lost the element of surprise, but he still had the upper hand. He stepped closer.

"Where are me diamonds?"

She laughed. "My dear man, they're far out of reach, where no man shall go."

Another step. She seemed to be goading him. Did she have a pistol hidden close by? Was that why she was so calm? Not that it would do her any good. He was already dead.

"Hand them over or you'll end up like Jesse Timbers."

She smiled. "Ah, yes, Jesse. He became a little talky trying to impress one of my girls. She mentioned it to me, and soon Jesse and I had a plan."

He gave her a hard stare. "You know damn well—"

A sudden commotion behind him. He turned to face four men charging from the rear hallway. The bouncers had returned, each brandishing a truncheon. They hadn't gone to lunch—they must have been hiding around the corner, waiting for him to make his move.

After an instant of shock and chagrin at how he had waltzed into Louisa's trap, Liath instinctively stepped back into a boxing stance. As the first thug came at him, he ducked the truncheon swing and sent him tumbling back into his mates with a roundhouse right to the jaw. His brass knuckles were in the bodice of his dress, but before he could reach them the bouncers were upon him.

Truncheon blows from all sides rained upon his head and neck, driving him to his knees. As his vision blurred, he heard Louisa's voice echo from increasingly far away.

"You didn't think that dress fooled me, did you? All the while you've been watching me, I've been watching you!"

Her laughter faded into the enveloping darkness.

LIATH OPENED HIS eyes. His vision swam for a few seconds, then cleared. He tried to move his arms, but his hands were bound behind him. He kicked his legs, but they met no resistance. After a moment of confusion, he realized he was hanging in midair. And something was constricting his throat.

"He's alive!" cried a voice from somewhere below him. "Good God, the bloody bastard's still alive!"

He looked down and saw Louisa and her four bully boys staring up at him from the floor of her sitting room. The men looked awestruck, Louisa merely amused. Her blond revenant servant, Katrina, dressed in a short French maid costume, stood to the side and stared into space. Katrina had killed him, but he bore her no malice. She was little more than fleshy clockwork. Liath reserved his wrath for the ones who had plotted his death.

"I warned you it wouldn't kill him," Louisa said. "Now aren't you glad you tied his hands as I told you?" She looked up at him. "I closed my business tonight in honor of your capture. We'll devote the evening to trying to find a way to make you stay dead."

Liath wouldn't mind that terribly—as long as they went first.

"Well, if we can't kill him," said the one he knew, the one with the scarred cheek, "what do we do with him?"

One with long blond hair said, "I know!"

He hurried over to the far wall, plucked all the darts from the dartboard, and returned with them.

"First one hits him in the cock wins," he said, handing two to each of his fellows.

Liath realized with a start then that he was as naked as the day he was born.

"Not much of a target," cried the bearded one, and they all laughed.

Liath would have argued to the contrary but saw no point. He tried to wriggle out of the noose around his neck, but it had been pulled too tight. His wrists were behind him, locked into steel manacles. Here was the use for that rope and pulley: to hang him. His head was brushing the ceiling while the floor waited nine or ten feet below his soles.

"Wins what?" said one with a squinty eye.

"Yeah! We need a bet here!"

"Buck apiece then!" cried Blond.

They all cheered and dropped their coins onto the card table. Then they began tossing their darts. The pain was minimal, even when one of them scored a bull's-eye on his manhood. But the humiliation was almost more than he could bear.

LIATH DIDN'T KNOW how long he hung there, first as the human dartboard, then as a target for billiard balls. The bouncers would fling them as hard as they could; Katrina would retrieve them from wherever they landed and hand them back. Sunlight had faded from the windows, replaced by the pale glow of the full moon.

Full moon!

He stared down at Katrina. He knew she hadn't been anointed this cycle because he'd been watching the brothel and Rasheeda had not made an appearance.

"Louisa," he called, and noticed that his voice sounded harsh and, well, strangled. "Let me be asking you: Has your maid been anointed this month?"

She looked up at him and frowned. "What do you know of that?"

"We are both revenants." Figuring he might as well keep up the fiction Rasheeda had promulgated, he added, "If Miss Basemore doesn't arrive soon with her magic oil, we'll both be going limp as rag dolls."

Though she said nothing, concern darkened Louisa's features.

He added, "And then, what fun will I be?"

He prayed Rasheeda wouldn't show. Tonight was the third night of the full moon. When it set, the unanointed Katrina would go mad, killing everyone in sight. And Liath would witness the deaths of those who successfully carried out his murder while he remained hanging here, safely above her berserker rage.

Wait . . . what about himself? Would he too go mad? Well, why not? He was a revenant just like Katrina. But he would not be able to join in the carnage. His rage would be spent on kicking the air.

Just then the doorman stepped into the room.

"I know you said no visitors, madam, but a Miss Basemore insists on seeing you."

Louisa's grin of triumph was like a knife through Liath's still heart.

"Let her in. Immediately!"

A moment later Rasheeda swept into the room. She paused for a heartbeat when she glanced up at Liath, then continued toward Louisa.

"You're late. The moon has almost set."

"But still in time," Rasheeda said. "I had unforeseen complications."

"Rasheeda, no!" Liath cried. "You mustn't!"

Louisa's mouth twisted. "You know each other, of course."

"Of course." She stared up at Liath and shook her head in dismay. "My assistant brought him back from the dead."

Louisa seemed surprised. "So you admit it."

Rasheeda shrugged. "You've already guessed. Why continue the charade?"

"I wholeheartedly agree," she said with a wicked smile. "But why did you raise him after *I* buried him."

"Need I remind you: in *my* cemetery."

Louisa's turn to shrug. "The grave had been dug, and where better to hide a body?"

"Indeed."

"Don't you dare think of laying claim to him."

"Quite the contrary. He was resurrected without my knowledge and has been nothing but trouble since." She pulled a small glass carafe from her purse. "He even stole my sustaining oil. He's the reason I'm late."

"Let's get this done." Louisa clapped her hands. "Katrina! Here!"

The maid dutifully approached and stopped before her. Rasheeda stepped close, and Liath watched her mumble the chant as she traced the proper designs on the revenant's face and throat with the green oil.

"There." She stepped back. "Good for another month."

Louisa looked from Katrina to Liath. "Why so different? She is a mindless slave, and he still has a will of his own."

"He's one of the willful ones I warned you about—resurrected too soon after death."

"Ah! You did say that makes a difference. This is fascinating. You must share all your secrets with me someday."

"It is not to be taken lightly. Someone must die so that another may live again."

Louisa's eyes glittered. "I have no problem with that." She looked up at Liath. "What about him? Will he go all boneless if not anointed?"

"Of course."

"I have interesting plans for him. Will there be an extra charge to work your magic in him?"

Rasheeda smiled. "You're a loyal client. This one is on the house."

"Rasheeda, no!" Liath cried.

Louisa made a flourish with her hand. "Then by all means."

As the bouncers lowered him to the floor, he pleaded with her. "Please don't be doing this!"

He prayed that this was all a ruse to get them to place him in reach so that she could produce a knife and cut the rope. He watched her hand slip into her shoulder bag, but instead of emerging with gleaming steel, it held that foul green oil.

Her gaze was unwavering as she held up the carafe. "You almost ruined my business for good by stealing this, then you blackmailed me with it, you rotter! And you expect forgiveness? Mercy? From *me*? You should know better."

Yes . . . yes, he should have known better than to expect help from her. A woman without loyalty or conscience—what else should he expect? She cared for only one person in this world: Rasheeda Basemore.

The bouncers pinned his legs and steadied his head as she traced the designs and spoke the words. Then they hauled him back up to the ceiling.

"Now that that's done," Louisa said, handing her an envelope, "tell me: How does one kill one of your revenants?"

"With great difficulty." She pointed up at Liath. "As you have learned, hanging doesn't work."

"How about beheading?"

"That immobilizes the body, but the head lives on."

Liath watched in horror as a slow smile stretched Louisa's lips. "Now *that* could be interesting."

"The only way to cause final death is by destroying the brain—either by piercing or by boiling it within the skull. Burning the whole creature works, of course."

Creature . . . was that all he was?

Louisa leaned closer. "You must have had to dispose of a few revenants in your time. What is your preferred method?"

"I slip them into my crematorium. I'll put it at your disposal if you—"

"No, no." Louisa waved a hand in the air. "I need something more creative, something with more . . . *flair*."

Liath couldn't believe this conversation. "Couldn't you be discussing this somewhere else?"

Scar bounced a billiard ball off his skull. "Shut yer trap! This is interestin'."

"Why don't you take a page from Nero?" Rasheeda said.

Louisa frowned. "I've heard that name. Is he from Five Points?"

Rasheeda laughed. "No, he was a Roman emperor who used to coat Christians with tar, impale them on pikes, and set them ablaze as torches to light his winter garden."

Louisa stared up at Liath with an avid expression. "Oh, I like that. No, I *love* it!"

"Well, I must be off," Rasheeda said. "More stops to make before the moon sets."

"Of course. I'll walk you out. We must get together for lunch sometime. It's so rare that I meet a kindred soul such as you."

Liath watched them go. Rasheeda . . . beyond all reason he'd somehow expected better of her. More the fool he.

LIATH LOST TRACK. He suffered further indignities as a target while enduring gleefully demented discussions between Louisa and her minions on how best to immolate him. The "Nero method"—as they came to call it—was the runaway favorite, but debate raged as to whether to make a torch of his entire body, or just his head.

Then he heard Beard say, "Katrina! Pick up the balls."

Liath looked down and saw the maid standing statue still, arms akimbo.

"Hey, you dumb bitch!" Beard said, stepping close and leaning into her face. "Did you hear what I said? Pick up the fucking balls!"

She cocked her head and swiveled toward him in a herky-jerky way, staring.

"I told you to—"

The rest of whatever he was going to say died in a gurgling crunch as her right hand shot up, gripped his voice box, and ripped it free. Beard fell away, spraying blood as he clutched at his ruined throat.

The room fell silent for an instant as Liath, Louisa, and the three remaining bouncers stared in horrified shock. Then pandemonium broke loose when Katrina shoved the bloody flesh into her mouth and charged. The bouncers recoiled for a heartbeat, then waded in with enthusiastic whoops. They were experts in dealing with unruly male brothel clients and this was just a maid.

Liath watched the melee in wonder. Katrina should have been bowled over by the men, but she fought like a wildcat. Her deadpan expression never changed, but within seconds Scar had a gouged eye hanging from its socket and Blond's right ear had been torn off. Squint swung a billiard cue and broke it across her back. She barely noticed. Instead she snatched the remainder from his grasp and rammed the sharp, broken end deep into his chest.

The lady of the house must not have liked the way this was going for she was squeezing past on her way to the door. Katrina grabbed a huge handful of her hair and yanked back. Louisa screamed as half her scalp ripped from her skull. Then Katrina lifted her and slammed her against Blond. As both toppled to the floor, Katrina leaped atop them and literally tore them open.

The cries of pain that filled the room drew the doorman. When he saw what was happening, he pulled a knife and buried it in Katrina's back. Katrina's eyes widened—she'd felt that. She spun and grabbed him by his head, then lifted him and shook him like a doll. Even from up near the ceiling, Liath could hear vertebrae shattering. The doorman's eyes rolled back and she dropped him.

The room had quieted now except for Scar's moans. He staggered about, cradling his dangling eye against his cheek. Katrina grabbed the other end of the broken cue from the floor and stabbed him through the throat.

As Scar gurgled and choked on his own blood, Katrina looked up at Liath. Was he next? No, she couldn't reach him. And even if she could, she didn't seem interested in a fellow revenant.

Scar finally collapsed in death, and then . . . silence. Well, not exactly. Katrina was kneeling beside Louisa's partially eviscerated body chewing noisily on a bloody handful of her liver. As tempting as that looked, Liath couldn't think about food now. Any hunger was washed away in the flood of questions rushing through his brain.

What had just happened here? Rasheeda had anointed both Katrina and him, yet Katrina had gone berserk and he hadn't. It made no sense. But then, nothing in his life had made sense since the night Katrina drove that blade through his heart.

AFTER SATING HERSELF on Louisa's liver and Blond's pancreas and a variety of other offal, Katrina lowered herself onto a chair near the wall and closed her eyes. Moments later she toppled to the floor like a sack of rice.

Now what? Liath thought as dawn began to pink the windows. *Do I hang here until the harlots show up for work?*

He heard the front door open.

Here comes one now.

But no. A harlot of another sort appeared.

Rasheeda stepped into the room and surveyed the carnage.

"Well," she said, smiling and nodding with satisfaction. "That worked out rather well, didn't it."

" 'Well'? *'Well'?*" He was shouting as best he could with a rope around his neck. "You call this 'well'?"

She looked up at him. "Better than well, I should say. Rather perfect, actually."

It struck him then.

"You *planned* this?"

"Of course. Louisa had guessed what I've been up to. Not that she was threatening to expose me. Quite the contrary. As you heard tonight, she wanted to learn how to do resurrections. Can you believe it? She wanted me to teach her so she could become a competitor. Not likely."

"But you anointed the maid and still she—"

"I anointed her with this," she said, pulling the carafe from her bag.

"Exactly—"

She unstoppered it and poured the contents onto the floor. "Colored olive oil."

Liath closed his eyes and fought a smile. An utterly devious, utterly ruthless, and ultimately amoral woman. And yet . . . somehow wonderful.

She removed another identical carafe from her bag and anointed Katrina. "She'll be able to walk in a few minutes. I—oh, my." She reached around and removed the doorman's knife from the maid's back. "How inconvenient for sitting."

"But what about me?" Liath said.

She looked up at him again. "Yes . . . what about you? You weren't supposed to be here. I had planned on dealing with only Madame Louisa and her thugs, but you managed to complicate matters by getting yourself captured and strung up like a side of beef. I had to alter my plans."

"I meant, why didn't I go berserk?"

"Because I used the genuine sustaining oil on you."

"Why?"

She frowned. "I'm not sure. You look terribly undignified up there, by the way."

Still holding the knife, she walked over to where the rope was cleated to the wall and placed the blade against the cord.

"Ready?" she said, raising her eyebrows.

"More than ready."

She began sawing through the heavy coils. Soon enough they frayed and then parted. With a thump, Liath dropped to the floor and flopped back onto his derriere.

"Now find some clothes," she said as he struggled to stand. "And do remove those darts from your arse. They're . . . unbecoming."

"I'd be delighted to," he said, rattling his manacled wrists behind him. "But there's the small matter of these."

Sighing with annoyance, she said, "Must I do everything?" She waved toward the bloody, ruined corpses. "You search their pockets. They're quite messy and I don't want to stain my dress."

Liath did the best he could with his hands behind his back but fortunately Rasheeda found a key chain in Louisa's purse. Once his hands were free, he appropriated the doorman's clean coat and pants.

Rasheeda began leading a docile Katrina toward the discreet entrance. "We'd better leave before someone shows up."

"Do you have a car?"

"Toby is waiting with the hearse by the alley."

"Good old Toby. You go ahead. I'll be along."

"What are you up to?"

"Like last time, we'll be needing to make it look like a robbery gone terribly wrong, plus I want to clean up any evidence that might be linking us to this carnage."

A frown. "Evidence? What—?"

"Me dress, for one."

Me dress . . . never in his strangest dreams had he imagined that phrase passing his lips.

"And most important, I want to find me diamonds."

"Very well, but be quick about it."

"I'll be but a minute."

As soon as she and the revenant had disappeared around the corner, Liath hurried over to Louisa's eviscerated corpse and grabbed a handful of what Katrina had left of the liver.

God forgive me, he thought as he shoved it into his mouth, *but this is delicious.*

Still chewing, he hurried up to the top floor to the front room where he'd seen Louisa. He rummaged through her drawers until he found a lockbox, then fumbled through the key ring till he found one that would open it.

It held some nice bracelets and two diamond necklaces, which he pocketed. Also a stack of shares in something called Standard Oil. He shrugged and pocketed those too. Who knew? Might be worth something someday. But nowhere could he find his diamonds.

. . . *out of reach, where no man shall go* . . .

A strange thing to say. For all he knew that meant they were somewhere off the premises. Yes, most likely.

Returning to the first-floor abattoir, he found his dress balled in a corner. Before leaving he used it to wrap another piece of Louisa's liver—for later—then hurried out to the waiting hearse. Rasheeda sat on the far side, the bloodied Katrina in the middle. Liath slipped in beside the maid.

"That was a long minute," Rasheeda said as Toby got them moving.

"I couldn't find me diamonds. Louisa said they were hidden 'out of reach, where no man shall go,' but where in hell that might be I've no idea. Odd thing to be saying, don't you think?"

Rasheeda frowned. "Very. 'Where no man shall go . . .' I can't—" Her eyes lit. "Oh, my!"

She lifted Katrina's short, blood-soaked skirt and spread her thighs.

"Aha!" she said. "Look!"

Liath turned to the window. "Really, Ra—"

"I'm quite serious. Look."

So look he did. He saw the revenant's smooth thighs and frilly knickers. What did she—? Wait . . . was that a leather string protruding from the knickers?

"What . . . ?"

"Pull on it. Go ahead—*pull*!"

Hesitantly, Liath grabbed hold of the strip and pulled. Out came a small leather pouch. He pulled it open and found his uncut stones safe within. Sighing with relief, he looked from the pouch to Katrina's knickers, to Rasheeda.

"'Where no man shall go . . .'?"

She dropped Katrina's skirt. "It's complicated."

"Well, thanks for waiting," he said, tucking the pouch away. "I was afraid you'd be leaving without me."

She stared ahead, smiling crookedly. "Oh, I wouldn't do that—not after all the trouble it took to save you."

"*Save* me? You suggested coating me with tar and setting me ablaze to use as a lantern!"

She laughed. "Oh, that. I knew they'd never survive long enough."

"Really . . . why did you come back?"

"For Katrina, of course."

"Of course. As you said before, why let a perfectly good revenant go to waste?"

"Exactly."

He leaned across the docile maid. "Are you *sure* that's all?"

"Well, if you want to know the real truth . . ."

He leaned closer. "Yes?"

She pushed him away . . . gently. "I've decided it might prove useful to have a revenant with a penny-dreadful sense of honor indebted to me."

Was that the reason—the *real* reason? With this woman, yes, it could be that and nothing more. But he sensed it might be only half the story.

Liath leaned back and crossed his arms.

Maybe he'd put off his final dying a wee bit. Just long enough to find out. No worry about running out of time. As long as she kept anointing him with that sustaining oil, he had all the time in the world.

BLIND LOVE

Kasey Lansdale and Joe R. Lansdale

I don't believe in love at first sight. Lust at first sight, maybe, but love? Not so much. It strikes me as a crock, and because of that, I can't believe I let my friend Erin convince me to go to an eye-gazing party with her, a kind of modern-day hippie's answer to speed dating.

What you do is you go into a room with all these other sad, dateless men and women, a timer is set, and you sit down at a table and gaze into each other's eyes for two minutes without speaking. When you've done that with everyone in the room, you're supposed to choose the person you felt a burning eye connection with, go sit with them for a second round, and this time you can talk, having hopefully made a soulful bond by previous connection.

I feared the first two minutes might only involve observing distracting mucus and a bulbous, red sty.

Not Erin. She was all in, high as a kite about the whole thing. It reminded me of the phase she went through when she was into massage therapy applied through psychic power. You're not touched. The masseur or masseuse waves their hands over your body and channels some kind of energy from beyond the veil, or pulls it up from Mother Earth, or some such thing, and sticks it in your back through the enchanted power of healing hands.

I had injured my back once during a sex act with a gymnast. He proved agile but had all the personality of a pommel horse. It was a onetime experience in which I was assured certain positions would bring me unique pleasure, but instead they brought me a bad back and three sleepless nights due to embarrassment and pain. Erin assured me her masseur could pull out the ache, if not the embarrassment. What he pulled out of me was forty-five dollars and an hour of my life. I went home with the pain I came in with.

Bottom line is she's the kind who reads her horoscope for real, believes there are special numbers in her life, and thinks that constipation is a sign of energy clog instead of pizza, tacos, and an abundance of cheese. We even did nude skydiving once—well, there was the parachute. It was supposed to free our inner selves. She swore to me. We ended up with several seconds of fear, skinned knees, scraped asses, and coming down not in the field where we'd planned to, but in a grocery store parking lot in the middle of a busy Saturday afternoon, an episode that led to newspaper prominence, a fine, and overnight jail time.

The problem is she's my best friend and I feel obligated to support her in her quest for the perfect mate, this time via an eye-gazing party.

We were coming off a light, me driving, when Erin said, "I think it sounds romantic."

"With a room full of people doing the same thing? I don't find that romantic so much as creepy. Which celebrity started this trend?"

"I'm just trying to find happiness, Jana."

"I don't think you're all that unhappy. You just think you're supposed to have a man to make you happy. What's that old saying? A woman needs a man like a fish needs a motorcycle."

"Bicycle," Erin said.

"Well, if a fish doesn't need a bicycle, I'm going to bet it doesn't need a motorcycle either. Thing is, you'll find someone, and if you don't, well, we can play cards at your house all day when we're old. You got to stop obsessing about having a relationship. I mean, you got all the tools. You're smart and pretty, have a good job and all your own teeth, so eventually someone who has all their parts working and isn't too scary to look at is going to end up with you."

"Gee, thanks."

"Hey, I'm in the same boat here. My last date spent the whole night talking about his Lego collection. Let me say this without meaning to hurt your feelings, Erin. You're too desperate, and guys can smell desperation the way animals smell fear. Either they feed on it until there's nothing left of you, or it makes them nervous and they run."

"You may have a point," she said as I hit the main highway and honked at a truck that tried to switch into my lane. "Yet, I feel like I'm running out of options. Jordon, girl I work with, she went to one of these events once, met a guy there she's been with ever since. They've even started to dress alike."

Obviously Erin's idea of what's adorable in a relationship is quite different from mine.

"We turn around now, chicken out," she said, "and I end up with a house full of cats and a passion for macramé, you will be to blame."

"I'm more than willing to carry that burden."

"Well, it's too late, because we're here."

We certainly were. It was a long rambling piece of property right in the middle of town. There were hedges around it high enough that you'd have to have a ladder to see over the top, and there was only a gap between them to serve as an opening to a driveway. I wheeled through the gap and along the driveway that wound through a number of tall and well-groomed trees, then parked behind a car in a row with a lot of other cars, all of them so expensive and cool they made my ride look like a hay wagon.

All along the walk were little signs with orange hearts painted on them. Above each heart was a pair of sleepy blue eyes, and at the corner of each sign was a black arrow pointing up the walk.

"This is either the place," I said, "or an elaborate scam to murder us and sell us for body parts."

"You're always negative," Erin said.

"Experience has been a harsh teacher."

At the door Erin knocked, and we were greeted by a small, pretty, dark-skinned woman decked out in traditional East India garb, flowing, bright-colored fabric that always made me think of Tandoori chicken and saffron rice. The woman at the door looked the part, but she moved as if she missed her high heels. Thank goodness she kept her chewing gum. I wouldn't want to have done without all that loud smacking.

Erin showed her a prepaid receipt, and I showed mine, thinking this was two hundred dollars that I might as well have just wiped my ass with.

The place was decorated with photos of exotic spots in India, a few from China. There were shelves containing knickknacks, including a small statue of an elephant with a stick of incense sticking out of its uplifted trunk. The incense smelled like damp earth perfumed lightly with burning silk. Love paid well.

The woman took our coats, put them away in a hall closet, and silently led us down a long hall to a doorway draped with a beaded curtain. When we reached that point, she stopped and said in an accent that had a lot more East Texas in it than India, "Go on in, the swami awaits. Watch that step down though, it's a booger. I've busted my butt there twice today."

She went away, and we took caution on our asses and made the step. The room was huge, but no bigger than Grand Central Station. There was a series of small card tables all about, a chair on either side of each. There were people everywhere. The men were on one side of the room, the women on the other. They were about as diverse as a jury pool, and I was relieved to see there was no one there I knew, though, come to think of it, had there been, they might have been as embarrassed as I was.

At the far end of the room, almost far enough away a pair of binoculars would have been helpful, was another beaded curtain, and out of it came a man who looked like a badly drawn cartoon character. Midsixties, short and thin, white socks with orange stripes and sandals, a ponytail of gray, frizzy hair. He carried a staff, as if he might later in the afternoon have to do a bit of mountain climbing in search of his goat herd.

I said, "Is he really wearing a cape?"

"I believe he is," Erin said. I think even she was thinking she might want to go back to her horoscopes and numerology.

"At least he didn't come in behind a puff of smoke," I said.

Our swami moved to the center of the room and lifted his staff like Moses about to strike the rock and bring forth water. He said, "I am Swami Saul, and tonight, you will bathe in the sweet essence of each other's souls."

I thought, *Oh shit*. But I must admit he had a very nice voice, deep and resonant, just the sort of thing to lull you to sleep when counting sheep fails.

Gently lowering the cane, he smiled and showed us he had some really nice teeth. "The eyes are the windows to the soul. Humans have known this for centuries. Sometimes we forget the obvious. We don't always allow them to do the speaking. We look away. We look down. We don't even make eye contact when we talk. How many men in here really look at women when you speak with them? I mean their eyes, not their bodies. I'm not denying that can also be a treat for the eyes, but think about it, men. How many of you fail to actually concentrate on the eyes, and the soul of the woman?"

There was a bit of a shuffling, and one of the men, an average-looking guy with a comb-over said, "I'm guilty of that."

"No need to comment," said our swami. "It was a rhetorical question."

"Oh," said the man with the comb-over, and he took a seemingly practiced step that placed him behind one of the other men.

"Today's society is too fast paced," said the swami. "Too reliant upon instant gratification. I promise you, after tonight, you will have truly touched each other's souls, and though I cannot make an absolute promise you will match one another with your internal essence, you are more likely to do so here than through traditional dating, and therefore have a real opportunity to meet your proper soul mate. Is that what you would like? Is that why you're here?"

No one said anything.

"That question is not rhetorical," he said.

There were a few murmurs and some words of agreement, but there was still that sensation of being a bunch of cattle trying to decide if we were about to enter the feedlot or a slaughterhouse.

"Erin," I said. "Later, when we're out of here, remind me to beat you to death with my purse."

"Sshhhhh, Jana. Be quiet."

I thought, *Oh hell, now she's into it.*

"Here is how it works," said Swami Saul. "You are not allowed to speak. You sit across from your partner, and you first gaze into the left eye, then move slowly to the right. This is not a staring contest, so do what feels natural."

Nervous laughter from the group.

Swami Saul held up his hand for silence, got it faster than a snake strikes a mouse.

"You must do this as I say, not as you want to do it, if you hope to have the results you desire. It is a far better method than just choosing your mate by appearance."

"He says," I said.

"Shush, Jana," Erin said.

"Your left eye is your receiver, and your right the activator," Swami Saul said. "You do this for a full two minutes. We will tell you when time is up, then you move to the next table and the next person into whose eyes you will gaze. So on and so on until finished with all the tables. When that is done, you will make a note of the number of the person with whom you felt the greatest sensation, and you will then have the opportunity to return to them for conversation. If that works, well, the rest will be up to Mother Nature. But remember, the eyes. The windows to the soul. That is where Mother Nature best reveals herself."

"That makes sense," Erin said.

"Mother Nature is also responsible for what goes on in the bathroom," I said. "And I think this operation has a similar smell about it."

"You're always such an old stick in the mud," Erin said.

We were individually guided to tables by Swami Saul, who I thought had a bit of a heavy hand on my elbow. I was placed in a chair in front of a guy who had had garlic for his last meal and seemed proud of it. The problem was not only the strong aroma, it was the fact my eyes were hazing over with garlic fumes. He was nice-looking enough, though, and

I tried to smile and be nice and look him in the eyes without blinking, which made me feel a little bit like a lizard.

I was gazing like all hell when Swami Saul came by and touched me on the shoulder. "Blondie, blondie," he said. "Relax. Breathe. Let the experience unfold. You are not trying to melt him with your heat vision."

I thought, *Oh, yes I am.*

"You act as if you're facing the sun head-on . . . Oh, sir. Let me offer you a mint. I can smell your lunch from here."

Swami Saul had less tact than I did.

The man was mortified, and I felt sorry for him, but I was glad when he took the mints Swami Saul offered him. By now my time was over, and I moved on to let the next in line deal with his garlic-and-breath-mint aroma.

By the time I was trying to look into my fourth partner's soul, only to find that I was not sinking down into his essence, but was instead bouncing off his retinas, I was starting to slip looks at my watch. I had been there about fifteen hard minutes. Only an hour and forty-five minutes to go.

As we were changing chairs again, Swami Saul was gliding by. I said, "I don't think I'm doing this right. Can you give me some pointers?"

"Believe," he said. "Let faith carry you."

"That's it?"

"Okay. Here's a tip. You're making crazy eyes at everyone. Relax. Think only of his eyes. Only of his eyes. The left, then the right. Each eye has its own soul-felt story."

I tried to focus on Swami Saul's instructions. Focus on one eye, not both, and blink on occasion so as not to appear psychotic. The guy in front of me, mousy in both attitude and appearance, made a jerky head bob, and I couldn't tell if he was seizing, having a chill, or giving me some kind of signal. Turned out he was nodding off a bit, and it was all I could do not to break out laughing. We kept moving around the tables, and behind me I heard Swami Saul offering gentle reassurance in his melodious voice, which reminded me of the narration you hear on crime programs where they're describing some horrible murder with the same calmness you might use to describe good weather.

Glancing at Erin, who was seated to my left, I saw she was deep in gaze with her current partner, who was a good enough looking guy her attention was understandable. He'd done nothing for me in the soul department, but I could see why she would find him attractive. I know that's shallow, but hey, I was at an eye-gazing party, which is the definition of shallow, as well as stupid. Okay, there were a few times when I thought I felt something here and there, though in the end it was more likely a headache from eye strain due to my having astigmatism.

It really didn't take all that much time to go around the tables at two minutes apiece, but it felt to me like it was about the equivalent of the first Ice Age.

"Attention, attention," Swami Saul announced to the room. "If everyone would break gaze and return to your place along the wall, and this time, please use the chairs, no need to stand. Be comfortable."

A beat passed and no one moved.

"Now," Swami Saul said.

This time everyone moved. Chairs squeaked and scraped across the floor as everyone attempted to get seated. I tried to catch Erin's eye—I'd had enough training by this point—but she was as dedicated to finding her chair as a workhorse is to finding the barn. I went over and sat beside her, was about to speak to her when Swami Saul spoke again.

"Under your chair you will find a basket containing papers and pens. Please use these materials to write the number of the person with whom you felt most connected. It is not uncommon to have several choices. Place the number given to you at the top of your notations. We will then tally the numbers, make arrangements for another sitting, this time with timed communications with the person of your choice."

I pulled the basket out from under the chair, trying to think if anyone had really made my eyes twitch, and my heart beat faster, and for the life of me I was having a hard time remembering which man went with which number. I decided garlic breath hadn't been so bad, and the breath mints had helped, a little, and there was the guy in the blue button-down who had a nice air about him, unless you counted his overabundant use of a cologne that smelled like a horse saddle. I wrote down a few numbers so as not to seem odd woman out, folded the page, and tossed it into my basket.

When I looked up, I was surprised to find that everyone else seemed to have finished well ahead of me and were perched in their chairs like seals expecting fish for balancing balls on their noses. Even Erin was staring straight ahead with the same intensity.

Swami Saul collected the baskets, and his assistant, the gum chewer, came into the room and helped him. The baskets ended up on a table at the back of the room with a large dry-erase board on an easel near the wall behind it. The female assistant, smacking her gum like a dog eating peanut butter, went through the baskets and arranged the numbers in separate piles. After going through the goods, she paused and looked at Swami Saul and said something to him. He went over and examined the slips of paper, carefully, then more carefully. He scratched his head hard enough his ponytail wiggled as if it might swat a fly.

I admit that at this point I was curious if anyone I had gazed at tonight had felt a connection to me. This was only a mild concern, but my ego kept me engaged enough I didn't get up with a pee-break excuse and leave Erin to fend for herself.

"Interesting," Swami Saul said. "I don't believe we've ever had it happen quite this way. We have a wide variety on the part of the men, but, except for one woman, all of the women here have chosen the same man. This is a first."

The women in our row against the wall turned and looked first left, then right, except for those on the ends of the row, of course. They just turned and looked. They all had that deep country-fried look that seemed to say, *Was you lookin' at mah man?*

I smiled, wishing to appear neutral, which I was. Even the men I had listed had about as much connection to me as a mollusk, if those things could wear button-down shirts and too much cologne and had a taste for garlic. I was more than willing to forgo my pick in lieu of anyone else's interest, lest I end up with one of my soul-gazing eyes scratched out.

"As all but one woman will know, as she did not choose him, that number is lucky thirteen."

I held my breath tracking the numbers hanging on the bottom of the seats across the way, waiting to see who this stud muffin was, the Adonis that I had somehow overlooked, and then, there he was. Number Thirteen.

I had to rub my eyes and take another look, just in case my pupils had glazed over. But nope. Number Thirteen. I could see him clearly.

"You got to be shitting me," I said without really meaning to.

"What is wrong with you?" Erin said, turning at me in what I can only describe as anger. "Jealous? You want him like everyone else."

"I do?"

"Of course you do."

"I didn't pick him," I said.

"Oh, bull," said Erin, actually good and mad now. "You came here with me and now you want him and you don't want to see me happy with him."

"Say what?" I said.

She turned away from me, her face as red and shiny as a wet tomato.

I gave him another look. He was an uninteresting fellow of indeterminate age, could have been thirty-five or fifty-five. Pudgy, with his few straggly hairs arranged as if by a weed eater. The suit he was wearing was thin and too large for him. It was cuffed unevenly at the sleeves and was either blue or gray; the color seemed undecided. He had on a stained white shirt and a wide tie with palm trees on it. I didn't really remember him, but I remembered that tie. After a few moments of trying to concentrate on his eyes I had decided I liked the tie better, and believe me, I had to split some serious hairs to make that decision.

"This is certainly a first," said Swami Saul. "A real first."

By now all the men had turned to look at Stud Muffin. The looks on their faces were akin to having just been told they were about to be electrocuted for the good of humankind. I didn't blame them. I don't want to be tacky. I mean, I know, it's not about looks when it gets down to what matters. I do know that. But come on. This is the beginning, when it's *supposed* to be superficial and being shallow is all you have. And as conceited as it may sound, Erin and I are something to look at. I know. It's egotistical sounding, but there you have it. I wasn't the kind of girl that upon chance meeting was going to give a damn about a sweet personality. Of course, I was also the kind of girl whose last boyfriend, though handsome and clever, turned out to be married and have two other girlfriends on the side and a website that had something to do with farm animals. I never had the courage to examine it in depth, but one of the sections I saw before I turned off the computer was titled "The Happy Goat."

"I think the women have chosen, gentlemen, sorry. Only one lady here has picked a variety of numbers, and she now has the opportunity to visit with some of you."

"Pass," I said.

"What?" said Swami Saul.

"I'm that woman, and I'm going to pass. If anyone picked me, sorry. I'm passing."

"Oh," he said. "Well, okay."

It was rude, but I really didn't want to spend a lot of time hanging out with people I didn't really want to hang out with and had only written their numbers down so as to not be such an outsider. What I wanted to do was follow all the other women over to see Number Thirteen and decide if I had missed something or if the others would get close up and realize he wasn't really such a hot number.

The throng of giggling women beat me over there, but I was able to peek between the teeming masses and get a closer look at Thirteen. He had looked better from a distance. I went over to Swami Saul and his assistant.

"So, one man, huh? And *that* man? All the women here, except me, are attracted to him? Really?"

"Really," he said.

"What kind of racket is this?"

"Do they look displeased?" he said.

I turned and saw they did not. They were mooning all over him, pawing at him, and shifting in closer and closer. He stood in the middle of them, smiling and still like a pillar of salt.

"I don't get it," I said.

"Me either. And you and I and Mildred here are the only ones that don't."

"You two didn't look into his eyes. I did. There's nothing there. I don't get it."

By now my head was pounding and my eyes were watering. My astigmatism had been given a serious workout, eyeballing all those men, and I felt I needed a new set of contacts, something I'd been putting off getting for a year. Maybe with contacts Thirteen would look a lot more attractive.

"Maybe all them women have brain tumors," Mildred said smacking her gum. "I wouldn't take that little balding fucker to a dogfight if he was the defending champion."

"Now, now," Swami Saul said. "Remember, you are enlightened now."

"Oh, yeah," she said. "Sorry. I forgot."

"So what's the answer?" I said.

"I don't know," Swami Saul said, and his voice had lost that deep down-in-the-well resonance. He sounded now like a regular southern cracker. He shook his head and watched the women clamoring after the little man like he was a rock star.

Standing there, looking first at the women crowding in on the little man, then back at Swami Saul, I got a real sense that he had not rigged a thing and was as confused as me and Mildred. Of course, Mildred struck me as having come into the world confused and having gone through the years without noticeable improvement.

I noticed that the rest of the men had started filing out, dejected and anxious to go.

It took some doing, but I finally got Erin pried loose from the crowd. To facilitate an end to the evening, Swami Saul had started gathering up chairs and carrying them out, and Mildred was gathering the baskets. She stored them away somewhere, came back, and flipped the light switch a couple of times, blinking them in warning.

It took another fifteen minutes to pull Erin out of there, and when she left, she had an address for the little man, but so did every other woman in the room, excluding me and Mildred.

Erin and I didn't talk as I drove her home. It was obvious she had yet to forgive me for my lack of agreement on her pick, and frankly, by the time we were out of there and on the highway, I had begun to feel guilty, but also a little spiteful.

"Look," I told Erin. "I don't see it. But I think I could be wrong."

"Could be?"

"Well, you don't know if something works until it works, do you?"

"Oh, it'll work. He told me so."

"He told you that?"

"With his eyes," she said, "with his eyes."

WHEN ERIN WAS dropped off and I was nearly home, I realized I had forgotten my coat. I wheeled the car around and headed back, hoping Swami Saul and/or Mildred would still be there.

By the time I arrived, it was dark inside and the door was locked, though I kept trying it, tugging like a fool until my arms hurt.

Of course the right thing to do was to go home and find out who owned the place, see if I could get them to let me in tomorrow, because I was pretty sure Swami Saul, who traveled across the country with his little circus act, had rented it for a night and had decamped for parts unknown with his cape, Mildred, and a small crate of chewing gum.

It was a good coat and I wasn't ready to give it up. I went around back and tugged on a door there with the same lack of results. I looked around, felt the place was tucked in tight by hedges, and decided it wouldn't hurt anything if I went around and found a window open. In and out, and no one but me and my coat would be the wiser.

Circling the house, I tried the windows. They were firmly locked. I considered knocking out a pane, undoing the latch, and pushing one up. I liked the coat that much. This was an idea I was floating when the last window I checked moved up with a surprising mouselike squeak.

I hiked my dress and stepped through the opening without breaking the heel off my shoe, then edged around in the dark. My hip found a piece of furniture that hurt bad enough I made a sound like a small dog barking. I waited until the pain subsided and my eyes were accustomed to the dark. There was the desk I had run into, a few chairs folded and leaning against the wall, and a bit of illumination from the streetlights shining through a window near the front door.

Able to navigate now, I made my way to the foyer where we first met Mildred. All the knickknacks that had been on the wall were gone. All that was left of them was a kind of dry stink of incense. The closet where Mildred had hung our coats was empty too, which didn't entirely surprise me. Somewhere tomorrow she would be wearing one of our coats, the pockets full of gum wrappers. I was fit to be tied.

I had started back toward the open window when my foot banged into the trash can. Nothing serious. No toes were lost. But it made me glance into the can. It was full of papers. I recognized them. They were the pages we had all filled out before the event on the Internet. They had been printed and, after serving their purpose, dumped upon Swami Saul's and Mildred's exit.

I pulled them out of the can and tucked them under my arm for no good reason outside of curiosity, then went out of there through the window and walked to my car. Coatless, I drove home.

AT HOME I put on my pouting pajamas, which are large enough that I can jump in a full circle inside of them. I sat at the table and had a bowl of cereal and four chocolate chip cookies. I moped around for about thirty minutes, picking crumbs off my front, then decided it was time for bed.

I tried to go to sleep, but lay in the dark, twisting and turning as if the mattress were made of tacks. I finally went to the kitchen and picked up the stack of papers I had taken from the trash can.

I felt a little guilty, because at the bottom of each we had been asked to tell something about ourselves, our strengths and weaknesses, what we were hoping for in love, and so on, but I didn't feel so guilty that it stopped me from reading.

I found mine near the top. I glanced at it. It read: *I think it's everyone else that is messing up. I'm a real catch. Anyone would be damn lucky to have me. I'm handy with a glue gun, can spell like nobody's business, and some people say I look like that movie star that everyone loves so much right now. Oh, and I got good teeth.*

I always had been proud of my teeth.

I felt mildly conceited for writing such a thing but still considered the comments accurate. I thought about calling Erin, but as it had passed the midnight mark by now and she had work in the morning, I decided not to. I had work too, but I wrote romance novels, which is ironic, and I was able to set my own hours. I wrote under a pen name and was just waiting for that free moment when I could write the great American novel. Susan Sontag didn't have anything on me. Except true success, of course.

I decided I'd keep thumbing through the pages, maybe even get some material for one of my books. The women's pages were on top. I read all the comments at the bottom of each one. Some of them were really sad and desperate. I felt sorry for those women. Only material I was getting was for a suicide letter.

The papers had everyone's address and phone number on them except mine, as I had given a false address and my old boyfriend's work phone number, the one with the animal website. I hoped they'd call. Asking for Jana was bound to make his wife or mistresses unhappy with him.

At the bottom of the stack I came across the forms the men had filled out, and there it was, Number Thirteen. His address was a place well out of town. I didn't know the exact spot, but I knew the area. It was pretty backwoods out there, though still within driving distance. Occupation was listed as MIKE TUTINO'S JUNKYARD. Was junkyard an occupation? I guess so.

Oddly, the man's name was listed as John Roe, not Tutino. The name was not too far off from John Doe. Either he had an unusual last name, or he thought he was way too clever. The rest of the information about him was vague, and there was a notation that he paid for his eye-gazing service with cash.

I thought in circles awhile, finally took a sleeping pill, and went to bed.

WHEN I AWOKE the next morning, I was still irritated about losing my coat. I went to Erin's workplace, a coffeehouse that has a kind of touchy-feely atmosphere about it and a very good Café Americano, as well as books for sale. You could drink and read and buy a book if you took the urge, though some of the books had chocolate biscotti fingerprints in them, and I admit some of them were mine.

Erin wasn't there, and no one knew where she was. She was supposed to have come to work. A friend of hers, another barista I knew a little, said the boss was mad at Erin and she wasn't answering her cell and she had better show up, and with a good excuse or the best damn lie since Bigfoot.

I tried calling Erin on my cell but got nothing. I left a message and drove over to her place. It was a condo, which was essentially an apartment traveling under an assumed name. I had my own key that she had given me to feed the cats when she was out of town, and after knocking and ringing the doorbell and noticing her car wasn't in its spot, I went in.

Funny, but the minute I was inside I could feel the place was empty as a politician's head. I looked around. No Erin. I got a Diet Coke out of her refrigerator, and knowing where she hid the vanilla cookies, I had one of those. All right. I had four or five.

I ate them and drank my drink while sitting on her couch. I tried to figure where she was, and I won't kid you, I was becoming a little scared.

After a bit I had a brainstorm and went to her computer. I used it to examine her search history. And there it was: MIKE TUTINO'S JUNKYARD. I assumed she already had the address from Mr. John Roe, Number Thirteen himself, but she had looked up directions. Could she have gone out there last night and gotten lucky? If you could call bedding down with that little dude lucky. I'd rather have a root canal performed by a drunk chimpanzee.

I searched on the computer a little more and saw the junkyard was no longer in operation, and that struck me as an odd thing unto itself, an abandoned junkyard for a home. I probed around some more but didn't find anything spectacular.

I went home and tried to write, but all I could think about was Erin, and the rerun marathon of *Friends*. I figured that was just the thing to keep me from thinking silly thoughts.

It wasn't. I watched about five minutes of an episode and began to channel surf. I hit a local channel airing a news alert about a missing woman. Then another. And another. I was about to surf on when I thought I recognized one of the photos as a woman at the eye-gazing party, but I could have been mistaken. I hadn't really paid that much attention to everyone, being more interested in myself, which some might say is a failing. But it could have been her.

Calling the police was a consideration, but since what I had going for me was that we had all been at the same place last night, and it was an eye-gazing party, it was hard to believe at this stage I would be taken seriously. Frankly, I was a little embarrassed about asking them to go out and harass a junkyard owner who might have acquired a harem of eye-gazing groupies due to inexplicable optical powers, and that I was immune to his loving gaze because of astigmatism. This was a thought that had started to move about in my brain quite a lot, that I was immune due to a natural malfunction. I wasn't sure how true it was, but I had started to embrace it, started to think maybe Thirteen was something a little different, and for his particular talents nothing could have been more perfectly made for him than such an event.

I mulled around all day, and just before dark I couldn't take it anymore. I decided I'd drive out to the junkyard, just for a look. No big deal.

At least that's what I told myself.

THE JUNKYARD WAS way out in the boonies off the main highway, down a narrow road crowded by pines. As I came to a hilltop—the moon up now and bright as a baby's eye— I could see it. It lay in a low spot, and the junk cars spread wide and far. Fresh moonlight winked off the corroded corpses of all manner of automobiles and the aluminum fence that surrounded them. Behind all those cars was an old house that looked like it needed a sign that said HAUNTS WANTED.

I coasted down the hill until I came to a barred metal gate that made a gap in the aluminum fence. The gate was about twelve feet wide and six feet high, with a padlock no smaller than a beer truck.

I sat there in my car in front of the gate, then decided to back up and turn around, and for a moment I was heading safely back to my house, feeling silly and knowing for sure Erin was probably home now, that she would have some logical explanation, like an alien kidnapping.

I activated the phone on the car dash and called Erin's number, got her answering machine again. I didn't leave a message. I got to the top of the hill, turned around, and went back down, but this time not all the way to the gate. I was dedicated to the mission now.

I parked on a wide spot off the road under a big elm, got out, and took a deep breath. It seemed I had begun a new career in trespassing, and possibly breaking and entering. I hoped I'd find Erin, or the only thing I was going to get was prison time and a close relationship with a tattooed lady with muscles and a name like Molly Sue who liked it twice on Sundays.

I walked slowly, staying close to the side of the road where the tree shadows were thick, glad I had worn comfortable tennis shoes and a warm sweatshirt parka and loose mom jeans. I pulled up the hood on the parka, and for a moment I felt like a ninja.

I went along the fence toward the gate but found a gap in the aluminum wall and decided that would be the way to go. I pulled the aluminum apart, slipped through without snagging anything, then crept along between rows of cars that looked like giant metal doodlebugs. The cars were really old, and if there had been any activity in this junkyard, it was probably about the middle of last century. Grass had grown up between the rows of cars and died, turned the color of rust; it crunched under my feet like broken glass.

Sister, I thought to myself, *what the hell are you doing?*

No dogs with teeth like daggers came out to get me. No alarms went off, and no lights flashed on. There wasn't the loud report of a rifle shot, so I soldiered on.

The cars were like a maze, and at one point I wound myself into the metal labyrinth and came out near the front fence again. I climbed up on the hood of one of the cars and got my bearings, studying my situation carefully. I did everything but break out a sextant and chart the positions of the stars.

Finally, with it all firmly in mind, I tried again, and this time, after more trudging, I broke loose into a straight row that led directly toward the house.

STANDING AT THE foot of the porch steps with only the moon and a dinky key-chain flashlight as my guides, the latter of which would have come in real handy earlier had I remembered it before now, I crept up along the side of the railing, careful of my footing. I had intended only to peek through the windows, where I was sure I would see Erin laughing and sitting on the couch, drinking a soda and having a hell of a time with Thirteen, but before I could, I heard something.

There was a clang, and when I looked, a possum was hustling away from a pile of old hubcaps it had upset among the death camp of vehicles, and that brought my attention to the side of the house. There, its nose poking out from behind the side, was Erin's car. I was certain of it. I went over for a closer look and saw the miniature dream catcher she had made the summer before last hanging from the rearview mirror. That served as a final confirmation.

Glancing around, I saw a number of cars that I had seen at the eye-gazing event. I took some deep breaths to try to calm myself. I could call the police, but it would take them too long. Erin could be in serious trouble right now, and I couldn't afford to wait on the cops to get off their asses and mosey down to this side of the tracks, and the truth was, the cars were here, but that didn't guarantee there was a problem. Maybe Thirteen's appeal had led to an orgy of epic proportions and no one was harmed. I decided I should at least check out the situation a little before throwing myself into a panic.

I fumbled through my pockets, searching for anything I could use as a weapon. I had an old paper clip, a pencil stub, and the keys already in hand, and that was it. Maybe if I found a rubber band somewhere, MacGyver would appear and help a lady out.

Looking through the windows proved useless because upon closer inspection, I realized they had been blacked out with paint. I was left with no other option. It was time to go in.

I pushed at the front door to no avail. It groaned a bit, but it didn't budge. I backed my way down the rickety old steps and shined my light around the base of the house. Near the far left end, behind the overgrown and twisted-up hedges, I spotted a broken window close to the ground that looked just big enough for me to crawl through if I sucked in tight and thought about celery while I shimmied. I pulled back the limb of a bush, gently kicked out the remaining fragments of glass, and in a feet-first motion I slid inside the basement with one swift, effortless move.

Despite the off-putting appearance of the outside, the inside looked pretty normal save for large amounts of a superfine, sparkly dust covering every surface. It looked as though nothing had been moved or cleaned in years and, ironically, could use a woman's touch. Unless it was my touch. All that would get you was a pile of dirty laundry in the corner and enough drain hair to create a rope doll.

I left my tiptoe footprints in the shiny dust like a mouse tracking over a snow-covered hill. After several minutes of searching, I started to feel the churn of my gut lessen. I was pretty sure I was alone in the house. Still, I opened the basement door that led upstairs and connected into the kitchen with the stealth of a hired assassin, just to be sure. I bobbed my light around and once again found nothing but that dust. It was all over the house and where there were cracks and gaps in the old rotten roof, the moonlight shimmered on the dust and made it glitter.

I coasted out of the kitchen and into a large room with bulks of cloth-covered furniture, backed myself against the wall, and leaned there in the shadows. I let the weight of my thumb come off the button of the light, causing it to go black, letting my eyes adjust to the darkness.

I was really nervous now, and since I had not found Erin, or anyone, in the house, but had found her car and recognized the cars of some of the other women from the eye-gazing party, I assumed I had enough material to take to the police. I could leave my suspicions about Thirteen's magic eye and my astigmatism out of the explanation when I spoke to them and would probably be the better for it.

It would certainly be smarter than wandering around a dark house and having the squeaking floor give way and drop me into the basement faster than green grass through a duck's ass to lie in a heap of lumber, broken bones, and if I knew my luck, my mom jeans hanging on a snag above me.

It was then that one of the pieces of furniture that I had taken for an ottoman stood up with a sound like cracking walnuts and a dislocation of sparkly dust that drifted across the room and fastened itself into my nostrils tighter than in-laws at Christmas.

The dust, however, was the least of my concerns. I was more troubled by the fact that the ottoman was not an ottoman but a moving wad of clothes and flesh that, though I couldn't see it clearly, I felt certain was Thirteen. How he had been bundled up like that on the floor, I have no idea, nor did I have the inclination to ask him, but I can assure you, the sight of him coming into human shape that way was enough to make my legs go weak.

I wondered if I had been seen, or if the shadows concealed me, but that was all decided for me when the dust in my nostrils decided to exit by way of a loud sneeze. It was like a starter's pistol being fired, and here came Thirteen, shuffling through the dust, coming right at me. Track had never been my sport, but right then I wished it had, because I broke and ran. Behind me I heard the floorboards squeal and the pitter-patter of feet, and then Thirteen had me.

His hand came down on my shoulder, and I'm ashamed to admit it, but I let out a scream that would have embarrassed a five-year-old girl with its earsplitting intensity. I was yanked back and it caused me to wheel about on my heels, and I was looking right into the shadowy face of the little man.

I clicked on the key-ring light in my hands, lifted it quickly for a look. I can't explain it. It was just a reflex. Thirteen's eyes were still flat and uninteresting, but then something moved in them, and I actually heard a crackling as if a fuse had shorted, and for a moment it seemed as if his eyes had slipped together and become one. I blinked, and then he looked the same, bald and doughy with ugly gray eyes.

We held our places.

I swear I smiled, and once more, the light went off and I dropped it, along with the key ring to my side, said, "Have you seen Erin?"

Really. I did. He didn't respond, just leaned forward giving me the hairy eyeball, and then I got it; he was waiting on me to swoon. He couldn't figure why his evil eye wasn't working, why the hoodoo didn't do whatever it was supposed to do, and that's when I brought my keys up again and raked him across the face, cutting his flesh in the way a knife cuts paper. I shoved him and raced past, into the big room.

Glancing over my shoulder, I was horrified to see he was pursuing me, but on all fours, moving fast and light as a windblown leaf. Now I was in a hallway, and there was moonlight creeping in through a rent in the roof. I had a pretty good view of everything, and one of those things was my reflection in a huge mirror with a small table next to it supporting a pitcher of some sort. I grabbed the pitcher, wheeled, and struck Thirteen on the forehead, causing him to stumble back and fall. It was a short-lived victory. He rose to his feet and came at me with his doughy arms spread wide, making a noise like a cat with its tail caught in a door.

I turned, took hold of the table, and saw in the mirror that his image was contrary to what I had been looking at. Now he was little more than a skeleton topped by a bulbous head centered by one big eye, but when I turned, he looked just the same, a stumpy, balding man in an ill-fitting suit, his mouth open wide and his arms outstretched, ready to nab me.

By now adrenaline was running through me like a pack of cheetahs. I swung the table as he lunged. It was a good shot, resulting in the table coming apart in my hands, but I had caught him upside the head, and it moved farther to the side than I thought a head could move. He did a little backward hop, dropped to the floor, lay there shaking his head like he was collecting his brain cells one by one. On the floor the shards of the mirror winked fragments of my reflection. It was not a happy face.

I darted down the hallway, figuring the jammed or locked front door might be more trouble than I had time for. I came to a stairway, decided on the closest port in a storm, hurried up it silently, pranced along until I saw a hall closet with sliding doors. In my great wisdom as one of the world's worst hide-and-seek players, I carefully opened one of the two wide doors, slipped inside, and snicked the closet shut, plunging myself into total darkness.

IT WAS A choice a two-year-old might make, but until you've been chased by an unknown creature, a supernatural being, an alien from the planet Zippie, or whatever Thirteen was, don't judge me.

I lifted my key-chain light near my face, not yet having released my grip from attacking Thirteen, clicked it on, and flashed it around. There were clothes on a rack, and I pushed in among them. At my feet were piles of shoes, and I must admit I spotted one really nice pair of high heels that I thought I might take with me when I finally decided to depart my hiding place, jump through a second-story window, and hope my legs didn't get driven up through my ass. Most likely I would be found with the high heels clutched tight in my teeth. They were that cute.

The cuteness factor faded, and I made a little noise in my throat when I realized that the clothes hanging in the closet looked familiar, or some of them did. They were outfits the women at the eye-gazing party had been wearing—okay, I'm shallow, I take note of those things—and one of those outfits belonged to Erin. There was something odd about the clothes. They were all pinned there by ancient clothespins, but drooping inside of them were what at first looked like deflated sex dolls (I've seen them in photos), but were in fact the skins of human beings. One of those skins belonged to Erin. I couldn't control myself. I reached out and touched it, but . . . it was not what I first thought. It was her, but all of what should have been inside of her had been sucked out, leaving the droopy remains, like a condom without its master in action.

How I felt at that moment could best be summed up in one word: ill. That's when I heard the squeaking steps of Thirteen on the stairs, then the shuffling sound of feet sliding down the hallway. I pushed back behind the hanging clothes and skins, feeling weak and woozy. I clicked off the light and held my breath.

After what had to have been a world-record time for breath holding, I heard the steps make their way back to the entrance on the hall and heard the squeak of the stairs again.

Flooded with relief, I cautiously let out my breath. At that moment there was a rushing sound in the hallway and the doors slammed open, and there I was, glancing through the skins and clothes, looking Thirteen dead in the eyes once more.

There was no question in my mind he saw me. I did my squeal again, ducked down, grabbed the high-heeled shoe, and came out from under the hanging rod, right at the dumpy, little man. I was thinking about what I had seen downstairs in the mirror, his true image as a bony creature with a big head and a single gooey eye in its center. That's where I struck. I was on target. It was as if his forehead were made of liquid. The heel of the shoe plunged into his skull and went deep. There was a shriek and a movement from Thirteen that defied gravity as he sprang up and backward like a grasshopper, slammed into the wall, and fell rolling along the hallway, the heel still in his forehead. No sooner did he hit the floor than his body shifted and squirmed and took on a variety of shapes, which included a paisley-covered ottoman (nothing I would buy) and finally the shape I had seen in the mirror.

I pushed against the wall, trying to slip along it toward the stairs, taking advantage of his blindness. He staggered upright on his bony legs, weakly clawed at the shoe in what was left of his eye, jerked it loose, and began waving his arms about, slamming into the wall, feeling for me. He stumbled into the open closet, knocked the clothes rack down, scattered the clothes and deflated bodies all over the hallway. When I got to the edge of the stairs, I turned to look back. He lifted his blind head and sniffed the air, then shot toward me. I wished then I had not had the vanity to wear the perfume I was wearing, but I bought it in Paris and had made a pact with myself that I would use it once a week, even if I was merely shopping at Target.

He had smelled me, and now he was springing in my general direction on all fours, and before I could say "Oh shit," he was nearly on top of me. But, smooth as a matador, I stepped aside and he went past me, scratching the air and tumbling down the stairs with a sound like someone breaking a handful of chopsticks over their knee. He hit just about every step on his way down, finally tumbled to the base of the stairs, and came apart in pieces.

The pieces writhed and withered, then turned into piles of blackened soot. No sooner was that done than the house was full of an impossible wind that sucked up the sparkly dust that coated the interior, whirled it in a little tornado, and started up the stairs. Quite clearly, even in the dim light, I could see the faces and shapes of women in that dust. I saw Erin, whipping around and around, her long hair flying like straw.

The black soot piles that had been Thirteen did not move, no matter that the wind went right over them with its dusty passengers. As the dust twirled neared the top of the stairs I stepped back, watched it hit the upper hallway with a howling sound and smash into the closet.

I followed and watched the dust dive into the mouths of the deflated women lying on the floor of the closet. It filled up their bodies, and they filled up their clothes. They tumbled out of that closet and lay in the hallway blinking their eyes, unaware of what had just happened.

"What the hell?" one of them said, and then I saw Erin, rising to her feet from the pile of women, looking blankly around, gathering thoughts slowly, her hair in a knotted clump around her head and shoulders.

I laughed out loud at their confusion, laughed too because I was alive and not an empty skin dangling on a clothes rack by a set of grandma's old clothespins. I began to weep a little with delight, mixing laughter and tears. I grabbed Erin and hugged her tight.

"What happened?" she said. "Where are we?"

"You were eye-gazed by a monster of some kind and all your essence was sucked out and turned to sparkly dust for no reason I can figure and you were a skin hanging in a closet inside your clothes and I rescued you by killing the monster with a shoe to the eye, causing the dust to crawl down your throat and fill you up again."

"Oh," Erin said. "Wait. What?"

"I think this is going to take some time," I said, watching as the women scrounged through the closet looking for their proper shoes, knowing that one would be hobbling her way downstairs, "but I prefer we talk about it somewhere else."

As we descended the stairs, the others following, chattering among themselves, I saw that the black piles of soot, all that remained of Thirteen, had turned gooey and were sinking unceremoniously into the pores of the wood like ink into soft paper.

TRAPPER BOY

Holly Newstein and Rick Hautala

When the shouting started, John knew exactly what was going to happen next.

He crept down the hall and through the kitchen to the back door and let himself out. The rotting floorboard of the narrow porch creaked underfoot as he made his way down to the weed-choked backyard, where Mama's chickens pecked in the grass.

Shep, John's dog, was cowering in his doghouse. He also knew what was coming. He looked at John with a mournful expression in his dark, soft eyes.

The fighting happened whenever Da came home late from the saloon after a hard day's work in the coal mine.

John leaned forward and slapped his thighs with both hands, clicking his tongue and whistling.

"C'mon, boy," he called softly to Shep.

He unhooked the chain that tied Shep to his doghouse, and together they left the yard and started up the hill that rose behind the house. The hillside was so steep that even on summer days daylight didn't hit the house until well after ten o'clock in the morning.

With Shep leading the way, John followed the well-trodden path up the slope. From time to time, he would pause while Shep bolted off into the brush after a rabbit or squirrel. John laughed at the old dog, but his laughter was thin and unconvincing because he was deep in thought . . . and worried about what might happen to Mama.

John took a deep breath of the cool afternoon air, trying to clear his mind as they pressed onward, up the hill until they reached the top. There, in a small clearing, a lone maple tree stood, taller than any of the other nearby trees. Its leaves were brilliant flames of gold and orange in the slanting September sunlight.

John shivered as he sat down under the tree in the shallow depression he had worn in the turf and picked up a twig. Without consciously thinking about it, he began to scratch pictures in the dirt. First, he did a quick sketch of Shep as the dog lay in the shade, panting heavily from the climb and the chases. His tongue lolled out onto the grass, and his eyes were shut. Then, almost absently, John began to sketch other animals, letting his hand—not his head—do the work.

"You know what they're arguing about, right?" John said, addressing Shep.

The dog opened one eye and gazed at him.

"Da wants me to get a job in the mines, but Mama—she wants me to go to school."

John paused and looked down into the valley squeezed on both sides by towering hills. A dark cloud of gray coal dust hung suspended in the air like a pall of smoke over Coalton, with its wooden company houses built along narrow streets, and the big brick company store in the center of town.

As if trying to read his thoughts, Shep made a huffing sound and rolled his eyes to look at John without raising his head.

"I don't wanna go into the mines, that's for sure," he said, scraping the ground with his stick, "but Da says it's about time I started earnin' my keep."

John kept staring at the town below, wishing there was some way he could escape from it all. The late-afternoon light did little to improve his view of his hometown. Far off down the valley, the hulking structure that was the J. C. Harris Mining Company was etched against the silver strip of the Susquehanna River, with the slag pile rising behind it. A train whistle wafted up from the valley, and John shifted his gaze to watch the locomotive pulling a mile-long line of cars filled with anthracite, heading to Pittsburgh or Philadelphia. A funnel of black smoke belched into the sky from the engine, looking like a lopsided tornado.

John sighed. He had never been anywhere outside of Coalton—not even to nearby Scranton, and as he often did, he wished he could hop a train, taking Shep with him, and make his way to the city.

I could be an artist in the Big City . . . Pittsburgh or Philadelphia . . . or maybe even New York, he thought. He had read something a while ago in one of Da's newspapers about a man in Atlantic City who drew charcoal portraits for any passersby on the Boardwalk who had a few pennies to spare.

"I could do that . . . easy," he whispered, staring blankly at the figures he had scratched in the hard-packed earth. Beside the profile of Shep, he had drawn a rabbit, its ears straight up as though hearing a warning, and a large rat. The rat was looking straight ahead, its eyes two deep holes John had drilled into the ground with the tip of the stick. The rat's eyes looked bottomless . . . and evil.

Realizing what he had done, John was surprised. He had been so deep in thought and worry that he was barely conscious of drawing the figures—especially the nasty-looking rat. They all looked so lifelike.

Easing his back against the tree, John looked up at the fluttering leaves. As much as he wanted to, running away meant leaving Mama behind . . . alone . . . with Da. And *that* was something he could never do.

As shadows lengthened, and the sky got dark, John and Shep started back down the scarred hillside toward home. In the yard, he chained the dog and then pumped a bowl of fresh water for him and put it next to the doghouse. John made his way as quietly as he could up the steps to the back porch and then slipped into the house. He listened for his parents.

His father was in the front room that Mama grandly called the "parlor," passed out and snoring drunkenly. His mama was in the kitchen, her back to him as she busied herself putting away the dishes. She was obviously being as quiet as she could so as not to disturb Da and touch off another round.

John came up to her and slid his arms around her waist, burying his face in the soft folds of her dress. Mama flinched at his touch and gently moved away from the pressure of his arms. When she turned to face him, John saw the dark welt below her left eye. Her cheekbone was a small purple ridge with a sickly yellow center.

"Your supper's on the stove," she said. "I saved you some. 'N there are some scraps for Shep in the bucket by the door."

She smiled bravely as she ruffled his thin hair, but he could see that her heart was breaking, if not already broken.

"You need to get to bed early tonight too. Da says he's taking you to the mine tomorrow."

Even though he had known it was inevitable, John was stunned. A cold, bottomless pit opened in his stomach, and his throat tightened.

Mama gazed at him, tears in her eyes as she stroked his hair harder, plastering it to his skull.

"It's so dark and cold in the mine," he said in a small voice. "All the time."

"Yes, it is," Mama replied, "but Da says it's time you started to earn your keep."

John wanted to protest that he had to go to school . . . that he didn't know what, but he was positive there was something better for him outside of Coalton and the mine. His lower lip started to tremble, but he vowed to himself that he would not break down in front of Mama.

"Only nine years old," Mama said softly to herself, and her voice broke into a wrenching sob that brought the tears to John's eyes, too. He turned his back to her and covered his face with his hands so she wouldn't see him cry.

THE NEXT MORNING, shortly before dawn, John and his da marched side by side up to the offices of the J. C. Harris Mining Company. Da was grimly silent, his head bowed, his hat in hand. He kept his other big hand clamped on John's thin shoulder as if he expected that his son would bolt for the hills.

They entered the brick building that housed the offices. After clearing his throat, Da looked down at John and scowled. He licked the palm of his hand and flattened John's hair before knocking on the superintendent's door. The plaque on the door read: MR. HARRY COMSTOCK—MANAGER.

"What d'yah want?" a voice said within.

John shuddered, noticing that the voice was as rough and pitiless as his da's was when he was in his cups.

"It's Otto Schmitz, Mr. Comstock. My boy here wants work, so I brought him to see you."

"Bring him on in, then," said the voice.

Otto opened the door and pushed John in ahead of him, making him stumble. Once the boy caught his balance, he looked around in awe.

Behind a big desk strewn with papers sat a big man with impressive muttonchop whiskers. He was bald on the top of his head, but the hair along the sides was long, reaching to his collar. He was wearing a white shirt and a brocade waistcoat. The collar was greasy and gray, and the vest stained. The golden links of a pocket-watch chain stretched across his bulging belly.

The walls of the room were covered with maps and blueprints that made no sense to John. The air was filled with cigar smoke that hung in dense, blue rafters.

Mr. Comstock looked John up and down as if he were a small horse being put up for auction. His eyes were as blue and cold as chips of ice.

"What's your name, son?" Mr. Comstock asked. His voice made a hollow booming sound that reminded John of thunder echoing off the high hills behind his house.

"John. John Schmitz, if you please. Sir."

A trace of a smile lit the man's face.

"'If you please,' now, is it?" he said, and he shot a curious look at John's da.

John did his best to remain calm as he stared at Mr. Comstock.

The manager's eyes narrowed.

"How old?" he said, addressing Da.

"Twelve, sir," Da said, looking down at the floor as if he knew Mr. Comstock knew he was lying.

"A tad small for twelve, don'tcha think?" He moved closer to John and placed a hand on his shoulder, squeezing it hard.

"Not much meat on him, I'd say."

He looked down at John and smiled thinly.

"So, kiddo, you want to work in the mines like your papa, here. 'S'at it?"

"No, sir," John said. "But my da says I must."

Mr. Comstock guffawed at that.

"You're honest, kid. I'll grant you that." Mr. Comstock laughed a loud, humorless laugh. "And how old did your father say you was? Twelve? Is that right?"

John's gut tightened. He had no idea what to say, so for a moment or two, he said nothing.

"The man asked you a question," his da said, prodding him with a sharp elbow to the shoulder.

"I'm nine, sir. Be ten in February."

"That's what I thought," Mr. Comstock said, casting a sidelong glance at Da.

Satisfied, Mr. Comstock walked back around his desk and sat down, huffing as he did. He picked up the stogie that had been smoldering in the ashtray all this time and gave it a few vicious puffs. Blue clouds erupted, and the end glowed with a bright orange ring that reminded John of how at night a rat's eye will catch the lantern light just right and look like that.

"We're full up in the breakers right now," Mr. Comstock said. John had a momentary flash of hope. Maybe they didn't need him, and he'd go to school after all. "So we'll start you as a trapper." Mr. Comstock eyed him steadily. "Sixty cents a week. Be here tomorrow morning at five o'clock in the A.M. Not one minute late. You'll work till five in the evening every day but Sunday. Got it?"

"Yes . . . Yes, sir," John replied, trying as hard as he could to sound confident and grateful for the job. Sixty cents a week sounded like a lot of money.

"Thank you, Mr. Comstock . . . sir," Da said, bowing so much it looked like he had a coiled spring in his back.

"Now you, Schmitz. Get to work," Mr. Comstock said with a growl that sounded too much like the way his da spoke to Mama. "And you, boy. We'll see you tomorrow morning, five o'clock sharp."

"Yes, sir," John said. "Thank you, sir."

Da shoved John out the office door and cuffed him on the back of his head. John's cheeks flushed with shame and rage.

"That'll teach you to catch me out in a lie," Da said.

John heard Mr. Comstock's mirthless laugh from behind the closed door.

AT FIRST, JOHN had taken comfort that he was working as a trapper and not in the breakers. The boys working there sorted coal all day long under the thin light from the grimy windows, and they got whipped if they didn't do their job fast enough to suit the foreman—and they were never fast enough. John had seen them coughing up thick gobs of coal dust that turned their spit as black as dried blood.

But it wasn't long before he decided that being a trapper might be even worse.

His job was to sit or crouch in the dark for twelve hours straight, with only a small lamp and some candles in case of an emergency, with rats for company, waiting to open the mine shaft doors for the mules as they dragged heavy carts of coal up to the surface and back down again. Opening and shutting big heavy wooden doors. That was it for twelve hours a day, six days a week. John tried not to think about the reason for the doors in the first place—to contain an explosion, if one should happen.

Even on his first day, he was near to freezing in the cold mine shaft, and in twelve hours, he never caught a glimpse of daylight. At least there were windows in the breaker building, and the boys who worked there could go outside for their fifteen-minute lunch break or to take a piss.

John felt sorry for the poor mules that lived their entire lives deep within the mines and rarely saw daylight or took a breath of fresh air. Their eyes and nostrils were coated with a thick black paste of coal dust and mucus.

Within a week on the job, John's pity for the beasts got him into trouble with one of the older boys, Rudy McIntyre. Rudy was a husky, heavy-browed boy who cracked his whip to make the mules move faster as they approached the doors, hoping to catch one of the trappers asleep on the job and make his mules crash through the door. One day, as the cart was passing through the door, Rudy caught John sneaking a bit of carrot from Mama's garden to one of his mules.

"Hey there! You don't touch my mules, boy-o," Rudy yelled.

Before John could back away, Rudy snapped his whip, catching John on the forearm. Even through John's heavy coat, it stung like a wasp bite. John had one last piece of carrot in his pocket, and he shot Rudy a defiant glance before he gave it to the other mule. He enjoyed the soft, warm touch of the mule's lips on his palm. Rudy shot a look of pure hatred at John and would have said—and done—more, but the mules kept trudging ahead and would have left him behind.

"I'll git you, yer bugger," Rudy roared.

After the shift was over, Rudy was good on his word. He waited outside the mine shaft entrance for John to appear.

"I been wantin' to have a talk wi' yer," Rudy said.

Fearing what might come next, John kept walking until Rudy came up behind, grabbed him by the shoulder, and spun him around.

"If you feed my mules again, you little cockchafer, I'll whip the bleedin' daylights outa yer."

John wasn't big enough to fight back, but he didn't have to stand here and take such abuse, either. He turned to go, but Rudy grabbed him by the shoulder again.

"I ain't done talkin' to yer, boy-o," he said, and before John could react, Rudy swung one foot forward and hooked it around John's ankle. Heaving forward, he shoved John backward. A grunt of surprise escaped John as he lost his balance, his arms pinwheeling until he landed in a puddle of mud and coal dust. Several other boys—even a few adults nearby—saw this and laughed. John splashed around, trying to get to his feet, but the ground was slippery. Rudy started for him again, but John somehow found his feet and ran away, weaving and dodging between men, animals, and coal carts. He never looked back to see if Rudy was chasing him until he arrived, breathless, on his own front porch.

When Mama saw what a mess he was, she told him to go take a bath in the rain barrel out back while she cleaned and dried his clothes. Later, before Da came home from the saloon, she mended the tear in the sleeve from the whip. John was both relieved and sad that she didn't ask what had happened. He didn't want to tell her, but he wanted her to hug him and tell him it would be all right. It was becoming obvious that it would never be all right . . . for either of them.

"Go on upstairs. Look on your bed," Mama said when he came back inside, shivering and covered only by a rough towel. His skin was pink and raw from scrubbing, but somehow he still felt dirty and miserable, even as he did as he was told. Upstairs, he found a box of colored chalks resting on his pillow.

Mama had followed him upstairs and was standing in the doorway to his small bedroom.

"I noticed you haven't been making any drawings lately. I thought this would help."

John looked at her, his heart swelling with love and gratitude, but then a soul-crushing thought occurred to him.

"Where . . . where'd you get the money?" he asked.

His mama smiled and shook her head.

"Don't you be asking as to where a gift comes from," she said. "Just accept it with appreciation."

John gazed at his mother with tears in his eyes.

"Thank you, Mama," he said. He was trying not to think how his da would react if he knew she was spending money on something like *this*.

Even as he spoke, he barely stifled a yawn behind his hand. These days it was all he could do to stay awake long enough to eat his supper before tumbling into bed. There had even been a few nights during the first weeks at the mine that he had been sound asleep by the time Da came home. If his parents had argued and fought, he'd slept right through it.

On most Sundays after church, depending on the weather, he would take long walks up into the hills with Shep. Now that he was working, John felt sorry for Shep because he knew the dog was woefully neglected. Gone were the carefree days of running through the woods together or playing baseball with his friends on the empty lot behind the train yards. And it seemed as though fewer of his friends were around. Most of them had taken jobs at the mine, too. Only the lucky ones, the children of the foremen and shopkeepers, went to school. Unless John found a way out of the mine, his fate was sealed, and he would end up just like Da. The thought made his stomach churn.

"DO YOU REMEMBER when we would go to the library and look at the animal and bird pictures in those big books? Your favorites were Mr. Audubon's. Remember?"

It was a rainy Sunday evening, and John was chafing because he had been stuck inside the house all day with nothing to do. His mama had another bruise on her forehead, but it was starting to fade. The purple edges were now a sickly yellow, and the crusty scab above her right eye made her eyebrow appear thicker than normal.

"Why, I remember how we'd come home, and all you'd ever want to do is make copies of the pictures you'd seen. 'Member?"

"Yes, Mama. I remember."

He was looking forlornly out the window as rain pelted the panes. In the dark woods behind the house, thin streams of water gushed down the hillside, looking like shimmering, twisting silver ribbons. Through the rippled smears on the glass, he could see Shep's dark form, huddled as far back in the doghouse as he could get away from the storm. Rainwater pelted the mud puddle in front of the doghouse. The water looked like thick chocolate milk. On days like this, John wished Da would let him bring Shep into the house, but he knew better than to ask.

"You haven't used any of the chalk I gave you," Mama said. "At least I haven't seen any drawings."

"I haven't had time, Mama, with working so hard all day."

"I know . . . I know," she said, lowering her gaze.

Those trips to the library, and drawing birds and animals, now were like memories that belonged to someone else. John felt guilty for not wanting to draw anymore.

"Thanks for the chalk, Mama," he said. "I promise I'll start drawing again real soon."

"I certainly hope so. Those pictures you drew for me back when . . . Why, they looked so real I thought they were 'bout to jump right off the page."

John smiled at that. He'd thought the same thing, but that was when he was younger. Now he was a working man, and maybe he didn't have time for such childish things.

"G'dnight, Mama," he said. He felt exhaustion deep in his bones just thinking about going back to work in the mines in the morning.

"Good night, darlin' boy. I'll be up in a little while."

After John had gone to work in the mine, Mama had taken to sleeping on a pallet in John's little room, leaving Da to sleep in the big bedroom alone.

"Your da snores and keeps me awake," she had said. That was true—Da did snore like a hog—but John suspected there was more to it. He had often heard different, frightening noises coming from the bedroom. He didn't know what they were, but he was glad Mama felt safer in his room. Especially after she put a heavy lock on his door and secured it every night.

John trudged upstairs, put on his nightshirt, and got into bed. Rain pelted the tin roof of the house, but as he drifted off to sleep, an idea popped into his head that made him smile for what seemed like the first time in weeks.

As he hiked up the steep hill to Tunnel Hill Mine Number Two, where he was stationed, John kept a tight grip on the chalk in his coat pocket. He was still smiling at the prospect of what he planned to do. First, though, he had to get past Rudy, who was sure to come at him if he saw him. He moved slowly among the men and machinery, picking his way carefully and keeping a wary eye out for the bully and any of his friends who might also turn on him.

"Get a move on, Schmitz!"

John jumped and, looking up, saw Mr. Kowalchuk, his foreman, glaring at him.

"Teams are already moving. You be late, and I'll fire yer hide."

John hurried into the mine opening and made his way as quickly as he could through the tunnels to his post at Trap Door Number Three. He had no idea how deep underground he was, and he didn't want to think about how many tons of earth were above him and could come crashing down without warning. The surrounding darkness was lit only by the small kerosene lantern he carried. The air was powdery with coal dust that got into his nose and mouth. When he got to his post, he carefully placed his lantern on the hard-packed floor of the mine next to the rough wooden bench where he sat, waiting for the teams to come through.

He smiled when he took a piece of chalk from his pocket and began to draw. On the trapdoor itself, someone had scrawled in large letters: "SHUT THIS DOOR—THAT MEANS YOU," but there was still plenty of flat space for him to draw.

And draw he did.

The first thing he drew was a portrait of Shep that perfectly caught his dog's mournful but loving look. Then he started to create a fantastic menagerie drawn on the wooden planks of the door. His hand moved quickly, and he was barely conscious of looking at what he was drawing. His eyes were unfocused, and he was simply staring inward, into his mind, and tracing onto the wood what he saw there.

As he drew, he had no idea of time passing until from down deep in the tunnel, there came a grinding of cartwheels on the rails, the huffing and snorting of mules pulling the load, and the yipping and shouting as colliers cracked their whips to keep the animals moving.

As he waited for the team to arrive, John looked at what he had drawn on the door. Large areas of it were filled with detailed drawings of various animals. Nearest to the center of the door, where he had started working, was the portrait of Shep. Surrounding him were birds and deer, rabbits and butterflies. Closer to the edges, farthest away from the lantern light, he had drawn rats and wolves, spiders and tigers—vicious animals. He had no clear memory of drawing any of them.

"Open 'er up!" someone shouted from the darkness, and John snapped to. He slid the chalk into his coat pocket, grabbed the latch, and swung the heavy door outward. The creaking wheels and huffing animals drew closer, but John still could only see the glow of their lanterns far down in the dark.

His stomach clenched and his heart starting racing when the team of colliers came into view and he saw Rudy walking alongside the cart. They made eye contact, but neither said a word as the colliers and team pushed past. John's insides felt like jelly as the team moved through the doorway. He thought he was free and clear, but just before the colliers and team disappeared into the darkness ahead, Rudy wheeled around and threw something at John. It missed, but only by inches. John heaved a sigh of relief. He was safe—until the next time.

Taking hold of the lantern, John raised it high so he could see his work. He smiled with satisfaction as he studied the fine detail of the animals and birds. In the dull glow of the lantern, the white chalk lines were stark and vibrant. The colors glowed like sunset. All of the figures stood out with shocking, unnerving dimensionality.

As he admired his work, he gradually became aware of a creepy feeling, like something cold and moist slithering up his back between his shirt and skin. He hunched his shoulders as if expecting to be attacked suddenly from behind. Sucking in and holding his breath, he turned around slowly to see numerous points of red light glowing in the darkness behind him.

Rats! John thought. Dozens of rats . . . all staring at him.

John glanced at his lunch pail, worried that the rodents were going to make off with his food, but they didn't. Faint scuffing sounds filled the mine, and he realized it was the sound of their leathery tails, twitching and brushing across the mine floor.

John quickly realized that the rats were staring . . . not at him, but past him. He turned slowly and looked at his drawings on the wooden door, and then he understood.

The rats were mesmerized by his drawings.

Is this really happening? he wondered.

Feeling a bit self-conscious, he slid his hand into his jacket pocket, took out another piece of chalk, and started drawing again. Before long, he forgot all about his audience as he sketched even more figures of various beasts. He only stopped when other teams of colliers came up the track and needed him to open the door to let them out with the cartloads of coal.

It became a daily routine. Rudy would call John out. John would try to ignore him or escape. Then Rudy, followed by his gang of cronies, would catch up with him—unless John was able to outrun them—and taunt and slap John around until he tripped and fell or was pushed to the ground, sometimes into a mud puddle or a pile of horse dung. Only after he had gotten John to cry would Rudy appear to be satisfied. Once he had proven whatever point he was trying to make, he would smile like a moon-faced idiot through the coal dust that blackened his face and then walk away, strutting like he was cock of the walk.

One day after work, John saw his da up ahead, walking with three other men. They were no doubt heading to the saloon to, as Da said, "lay the dust." After drying his eyes on his coat sleeve, he ran to catch up.

"Are you going home now, Da?" he asked, his voice reed-thin.

Da and his pals stopped, and they all turned to look at him. Their faces were covered by masks of black coal dust that made their eyes stand out, wide and bright. After a heartbeat or two, Da's expression folded into a scowl.

"You been crying like a little baby again, ain't yah?" he said.

John wiped his cheeks with the flats of his hands, smearing the coal dust across his face. He wanted to tell Da about Rudy, about how he was sick and tired of the bullying, but he saw clearly now that he wouldn't get an ounce of sympathy.

"You gotta learn ta' take it 'n not come running to your da for help," Da said. "Stand up and fight back, if you be a man . . . or else take yer punishment like a man."

With that, Da spit onto the ground and turned, walking away with his cohorts falling into step beside him. When they were about thirty feet away, Da said something that John couldn't hear. All the men burst out laughing, and John had little doubt his da had insulted him. His face was burning with embarrassment as he turned and headed for home, knowing—at least—that he was safe from any more punishment for today . . . until later, when Da came home from the saloon.

Arriving home, John couldn't help but notice how pale and fragile his mother had become. She was sad and preoccupied, and she flinched at every little sound. He was sure he was the source of her sorrow and worry. He wished he could talk to her about how bad things were getting, but somehow neither of them could bring it up. It seemed as though

Da was drinking more every week. And if he didn't drink enough to pass out the minute he got in the door, he would be in a towering rage. And he would hurt Mama.

Since John's wages went to Da, John had no money. There was no way for him to escape with Mama and Shep.

Maybe we never talk about anything because there's no way out, thought John.

ONE NIGHT IN late November, John woke up to the sound of Shep yelping and howling in the backyard. He tossed the bedcovers aside and ran downstairs, his heart racing as he flung open the back door and saw Da mercilessly kicking the dog. John leaped off the steps and started toward them, but before he got there, his father kicked Shep so hard the poor dog went flying in the air until he fetched up at the end of his tether. Shep howled once, sharply, in agony as he tried to crawl back to the protection of his doghouse, but there was something wrong with his back. His hind legs kept flopping about on the ground. After a few heartbreaking seconds, the only sounds the dog could make were soft grunting noises as though he was choking back his pain.

"No! . . . Da! . . . Please!" John shouted, tears blurring his vision as he ran over to Shep. He placed himself dangerously between Shep and Da. Tears streamed down his face as he shouted: "*Stop* it! . . . You're *killing* him!"

Da swayed drunkenly as he regarded his son with a wild, unfocused glare. He reeked of whiskey fumes and rancid sweat.

"S' already dead," Da muttered thickly, and then he hawked up a ball of snot and spit it off into the darkness.

Sobbing so hard it hurt his chest, John gathered Shep up into his arms. The dog was shaking and breathing with a deep, watery rattle, but only for a few moments more. With a deep shudder, he let out a long sigh and then was still.

"Useless goddamned cur, if you ask me. You, boy. Get back in the house," Da said, and then he lurched away, weaving from side to side as he tried to make it up the steps to the back door.

John buried his face in his dog's fur and cried for a long time. Shep grew cold in his arms. Snow began to fall, sticking to his hair and Shep's coat. The flakes felt like tiny hot pinpricks when they landed and melted on the back of John's neck.

In the morning, before dawn, Mama made John a bowl of oatmeal for breakfast and slipped an extra potato into his pocket for lunch. Her face was downcast, but she said nothing about Shep, whose snow-covered body lay motionless in the backyard. Da came downstairs and, leaning over the slate sink, stared out the window. John couldn't tell if he was looking at Shep or if he even saw him. Finally, Da hawked up and spit into the sink.

"Damned stupid dog," he said, and then, with a strange, glazed look in his eyes, he turned to John and said, "Hurry up boy. We can't be late."

Days turned into weeks, and weeks turned into months. Toward January, John caught a cold, which settled into his lungs. His thin body was racked by coughing spasms that brought up mucus that was black with coal dust. His eyes glittered with fever. Mama made beef tea from marrow bones to help him regain his strength, but it didn't seem to help much. He knew if he didn't go to work for even one day he would lose his job. And then Da would beat him for the money he wasted on the new boots he got John for work.

His only comfort at work was that he kept drawing, and it wasn't long before the door and walls of the mine were festooned with a wild menagerie of creatures. As the weeks and months passed, he would take handfuls of dirt and scrub some of the figures away, only to replace them with pictures of wilder, more vicious-looking beasts.

The only other constant was Rudy, who continued to torment him. John had long since stopped wondering why Rudy singled him out for such abuse. In a way, it was just like the way Da mistreated Mama, as if she were the cause of all his misery. It never failed that when Rudy passed by in the tunnel, he would shove John if he got close enough or throw something at him—usually a fist-sized lump of coal or a mule turd. Usually, Rudy missed, but the threat of being seriously injured was a daily torment—a torment even worse, John thought, than sitting alone in the mine with only rats for company.

But one day while John was still light-headed from his fever, Rudy hit him full in the face with a lump of mule dung, blinding him. Rudy's laughter was so loud it echoed in the mine shaft while John shook his head wildly and wiped his eyes with his sleeve. The turd had been fresh and left behind a rancid stink than made him gag.

"Good fer yer, yer no good cock-knocker," Rudy said as he hoisted his lamp up high to get a good look at John. And for the first time, Rudy saw—or noticed—the figures John had drawn on the trapdoor and mine walls. He stopped short and gaped at the drawings that seemed to surround him. Even as his mule team lumbered steadily ahead, Rudy looked at John, his eyes narrow with hate.

"Doodlin' on th' walls, eh?"

John was too scared to do anything more than nod.

"You know, I'm goin' ta have ta report yer. Yer'll catch hell for defacin' company prop'ty."

Filled with a sudden surge of rage, John bent down and picked up a jagged piece of coal.

"Yer in some deep shit now, boy-o. The boss finds out, he'll be firin' yer sorry ass."

Without thinking, John cocked his arm back and flung the coal lump at Rudy, hitting him squarely on his cheek. The sharp edge tore a deep gash, and blood began to flow freely down Rudy's face.

"Yer wee piece of shite!" Rudy roared, and he started toward John.

Trembling with fear and rage, John backed away, moving from the trapdoor, deeper into the depths of the mine.

"Get yer ass up here, McIntyre!" one of Rudy's teammates shouted as the cart continued to rumble along the track, but Rudy ignored him. Sputtering like an enraged bull, he strode steadily toward John. His balled-up fists looked as big and hard as sledgehammer heads, swinging at his sides.

As John drew back farther into the tunnel, his pulse was racing so hard that his throat started to ache. His lantern was on the floor by the trapdoor. Its faint glow made Rudy's approaching silhouette appear huge. The coal carts, still rumbling along the track, had long since passed through the door and were out of sight. John heard one of the miners shouting to Rudy, "Never mind the lad, you numb shit! Get back to yer carts!" as they were swallowed by the blackness.

Rudy ignored the warning and rapidly closed the distance between himself and John, who cowered back against the wall.

As Rudy cocked back his fist, a rat darted out of the darkness and ran straight toward him. John had an instant to wonder if his brain might be playing tricks on him because of his fear, but the rat didn't look like any ordinary rat. It was the same shape . . . and the same size—maybe a bit bigger, but its body was outlined with a shimmering white glow that looked like thick chalk marks come to life.

Rudy stopped in his tracks, his eyes following the creature. He shuffled his feet a little, as if afraid the rat was going to crawl up his pants leg. Behind him, in the dim lantern light, shadows stirred and moved with the same eerie glow.

John gasped, noticing distantly that the air in the mine suddenly smelled . . . different . . . peculiar. John suddenly felt like a vise had encircled his chest and he wheezed, trying to draw in air that wasn't there. Rudy apparently took these as whimpers of fear because he started to laugh a deep, cold laugh and moved close again, his fists clenched. John looked past Rudy and saw huge rats and fanged wolves stalking along the floor and eagles soaring through the dusty air. All of them were outlined with white light, and they glowed with bright, vibrant colors as they came swiftly up behind Rudy.

John was frozen with fear and disbelief. He barely noticed the deep, grinding rumble that had started to shake the walls of the mine. The support beams overhead shifted, and rock and grit began to sift down from the ceiling between the rafters. Within seconds, thick black coal dust filled the air, blotting out the faint glow of John's lantern, which he'd left by the trapdoor.

It took John a moment or two to realize what was happening. His worst fears were confirmed seconds later when the deep concussion of an explosion shook the mine. More dirt and rocks fell, and from somewhere deep in the mine, a man's voice shouted "Fire damp! Run for—"

And then the voice was silenced.

The ground kept shaking, knocking both John and Rudy down. As John scrambled to get to his feet, trying to orient himself, dense, choking vapors with a stench of rotten eggs filled the midnight-dark air. The walls closed in.

That was when the screaming began.

Loud and shrill . . . and so close.

At first, he saw nothing through the billow of dust.

And then he did see.

John watched in stunned silence as a wild assortment of creatures—his drawings—swarmed out of the darkness. Beady, wicked eyes glowed green and red in the darkness, and white teeth and claws flashed like lightning. Bright flashes of light hurt his eyes as he watched them swarm over Rudy, whose shrill screams rose high but were all but lost beneath the grumbling roar of the shaking earth.

The ceiling and walls all around John began to crumble. The air was a thick soup of coal dust and poison gases, too thick to breathe. John's lungs felt like they were filled with fire. He had no breath to scream. He could only listen to the sound of tearing flesh.

There was no escape. No matter which direction he ran, John knew he was doomed. The melee of creatures he had drawn were a seething mass over Rudy's still-writhing body, and they were between John and the trapdoor. He couldn't go that way, and if he ran the other way, he'd go deeper into the mine where the damp had exploded. There were dead and dying men down there, he knew, and he was sure the explosion had caused a cave-in.

Rudy's screams were now wet, choking gurgles, and it wasn't long before there came one loud, strangled gargling sound . . . and then silence.

Now that they were done with Rudy, John was sure his creatures would turn on him . . . unless he found a way out of here.

Tears filled his eyes, and he tried to accept the stark truth that he was going to die down here . . . alone . . . and that his mama would find out soon enough that he and, for all he knew, his da had died.

A long, low howl that reminded John of the sound Shep had made the night Da kicked him to death filled the air. Then another flash of white light up ahead caught his attention. His vision blurred, his lungs burning. John wanted to move forward but couldn't. With no strength left to stand, his knees buckled, and he dropped slowly to the floor.

Good-bye, Mama, he thought.

And then, a miracle.

A warm wet nose grazed his cheek. Through narrowed eyes, he looked up and saw that the portrait of Shep he had drawn, the first one he had ever done on the trapdoor and that he had never erased, had also come to life. A wild, flickering white light filled the darkness around him as Shep's big, shaggy head leaned forward. And then jaws closed on John's coat collar, tugging him forward, out of the mine.

"Shep . . . Shep, old fella," John muttered like someone talking in his sleep.

He threw his arms around Shep, and he saw his horde of creatures retreating, their flickering, swirling outlines disappearing into the depths of the mine. A few moments later, distant screams rent the air as the creatures attacked the miners still trapped in the rubble of the cave-in.

Somehow, John fought back the urge to panic. He found a reserve of strength and stumbled to his feet, holding the thick scruff of Shep's neck. Unable to see anything in the dense darkness, he let himself be led up the shaft. The ground was silent now—an eerie silence that John knew was the silence of death.

How many miners are dead down there? he wondered.

Is Da one of them?

He moved his feet mechanically as he walked side by side with Shep. Every now and then, his dog would turn and look at him, eyes glowing unnaturally bright and jowls rising into what John knew had to be a smile.

You came for me, he seemed to be saying with his smile. *And I came for you.*

The dog, his body outlined with vibrating white light, panted heavily as they got closer to the trapdoor. The coal dust had begun to ventilate, and John began to breathe a bit more easily. Blood flowed back into his limbs, but all the while, he was waiting to hear the sound of the other creatures, chasing after him and closing the gap . . . ready to rip him apart.

Up ahead, frantic voices shouted commands. He released his grip on Shep's neck when they were less than fifty feet from the mine entrance. There were lights up ahead—glowing lanterns of the rescue workers charging into the bowels of the mine to try to find and save any survivors. As John and Shep got to the lantern light, Shep's vibrant white evanescence became fainter and fainter until—finally—it winked out like a guttering candle. John realized with a heart-wrenching ache that he was alone.

He tried to run, but his legs were too weak, and he staggered toward the faint, gray glow of daylight and the crowd of men, moving toward him. One man raised his lantern and shone it full into John's face.

"You aw'right, there, young Schmitz?" a voice asked.

John was dazed by the brightness of the lantern light.

"My dog . . . led me out," he said in a choking voice.

"Sure he did, sonny. Get yerself up aboveground. The doc's out there," another voice said, and someone took John by the arm, gripping his arm above the elbow and leading him closer to the entrance. Once he was outside, John collapsed face-first into a snowdrift. The sudden dash of moist coldness was so intense that he almost passed out. Then strong hands picked him up. He took his first true breath of fresh air. When he opened his eyes to see who was carrying him, the brightness of the cloudless sky all but blinded him.

Then he knew no more.

FIFTY-SEVEN MEN HAD died. John was the only one who made it out of the Tunnel Hill Mine that day. Everyone told John how lucky he was to have survived. It all seemed like a nightmare now that he was safely home and in his own bed.

"You could have—you *should* have suffocated, bein' so deep down in the mine like that," the doctor tending him said.

"Or been blown to pieces wi' the others," Mama said.

"Strange thing about that. Some of them must have panicked and just gone crazy. They tore each other apart trying to get out. Never seen anything like it. Bite marks, scratches, limbs torn away . . ." The doctor's voice trailed off, and he shuddered. Then he came back to himself and smiled a little too brightly at John's mama.

"It's a miracle this fella got out, at any rate," said the doctor, and he was touched to see the expression of relief on John's mother's face. He was polite enough not to mention the fresh, swollen bruise that ran the length of her jaw.

Da had been in another part of the mine when the explosion happened, and he had escaped. Mama insisted that John stay home and rest in bed to clear his lungs and cure his fever, no matter how long it took. Da scowled at that and clenched his fists, insisting the boy had to get back to work right away or else lose his job. They needed the money, he insisted, but Mama countered by saying that if John died from pneumonia, it would do nobody any good. The doctor took Mama's side, insisting that John would be permanently weakened and maybe even die if he didn't take a week or more to recover properly. He guaranteed that he would speak to Mr. Comstock personally and make sure John would have his job when he returned, so Mama won that round.

Da went straight back to work the next day. Working day and night, the miners shored up the support beams and, once it was safe enough, started digging down to recover the bodies of the dead. It wasn't long before that section of the mine reopened, and it was back to business as usual.

But not for John.

He was in bed for two days with a raging fever, fading in and out of consciousness, sometimes muttering, sometimes yelling about how "they" had come to life and killed Rudy and how Shep had shown up and saved his life. His thin body convulsed with sobs whenever he talked about Shep.

On the third day, the fever broke, and John lay quietly in his bed.

"You stay right there in bed and sleep for now," Mama said, soothing his brow. She was obviously worried about his delirium. The bits and pieces she'd gathered from what he said terrified her. She feared he might be a bit tetched in the head from his fever.

"This afternoon," she said, "perhaps, we'll set you up on the couch in the parlor. Let you see some sunshine and get some fresh air. You'll be happy to know that your da got a personal note from Mr. Comstock himself, telling him that not only will you have your job, but he'll give you three days' pay, too, for your suffering. So I'll go ta the butcher's 'n get you a nice roast for supper."

John nestled down in his bed, pretending to go to sleep, but it wasn't long after she was gone that he tossed the covers aside and got out of bed. He felt like he was walking on stilts as he crossed his bedroom floor, stepping over Mama's pallet. His coat, still thickly stained with coal dust and mud, was hanging on a peg on the back of the door. He grimaced as he reached into his pocket and felt around until, to his great relief, he found that he had not lost his chalk.

In the miasma of the fever-dreams, he had had an idea. It might not work outside the mine, but he had to try. Otherwise, he and Mama were as doomed as poor Shep. Keeping one clear image in his mind—his da kicking the life out of his beloved dog—he took a piece of chalk and walked down the hallway to Da's bedroom.

I have to make sure Mama locks the door to my room tonight when she comes in, he thought.

Squatting on the floor, his hands trembling with barely repressed rage, he began to draw on the back of the door. First, he drew a finely detailed picture of a bear with its arms raised, its claws exposed, and its jaws wide open. He stepped back to admire his work, and he began to laugh, a low gravelly laugh that racked his whole body. He laughed until the tears poured down his cheeks.

Finally he stopped. "Lion, next," he said, and picked up the chalk.

STEWARD OF THE BLOOD

Nate Kenyon and James A. Moore

Christian Burr watched his son run across the pebbled drive to the foot-high grass. *What a mess,* he thought. Of course, it had been a long time. But for some reason he had imagined the house the same as always, with the sweeping drive, sparkling pond, lawn lining the edge of deep green forest. Wild animals had always been prevalent here, darting out from the thick cover of the trees at dusk and dawn, deer drinking at the water's edge, fox cubs slipping through the twilight. When he was a boy, he'd sworn he had seen a wolf more than once in the mist of early morning.

He couldn't imagine that now. Even the forest looked empty and neglected.

"Sammy!" Susan had stepped out of the passenger side of the car but held on to the open door. "Don't go running off yet! We don't know what's *there*!"

The five-year-old boy continued on his stumbling way, now into even higher grass that reached above his waist. Burr imagined the blades suddenly wrapping around the boy, pulling him down and slithering over his mouth.

When Sammy's mother called his name a second time, he stopped, looked over his shoulder at his parents, and sighed.

"Sometimes I want to tether him," Susan said. "From the looks of this place I probably should."

She was right. Burr stared at the sprawling house. Even after what he'd been told by the executor of his grandfather's estate, he was shocked at its condition.

"It's in bad shape, I'm afraid. But that couldn't be helped. Your

grandfather was a stubborn fellow, and it was his wish that you not be contacted until five years after his death."

"Are you telling me my grandfather died five years *ago? And nobody told me?"*

"I understand this is a shock. I tried to have the court see him as feebleminded, but that didn't work. Believe me, Arthur was anything but, and everyone around here knew it. He left specific instructions. No one was to come here. And no blood relations were to be told of its condition."

Five years, Burr thought. It was hard to imagine that this kind of decay had happened that quickly. The farmer's porch was a weathered claw of wood. The paint was peeling, gutters hanging loosely from the eaves. Brambles grew high and tangled around the back corners and hid whatever cracks might be running through the foundation.

Susan looked at him over the roof of the car. "Are you sure your grandfather didn't leave it to you to punish you for something?"

Burr smiled at her, hiding his own growing sense of dismay. His grandfather had always loved riddles and practical jokes; perhaps this was his last one. Susan smiled back with less enthusiasm, before turning and leaving the safety of the car (somewhat reluctantly, he saw) to rescue Sammy, who had wandered a bit farther away and gotten himself tangled in brush along the edges of what remained of the lawn.

Burr glanced through the open front door into the backseat. Lisa was looking out the window at something only she could see. As they left the house in New York that morning her rage had been like a hurricane. She hadn't spoken to anybody since. He understood her anger at being uprooted; change didn't suit her. A child with her condition needed to be surrounded by a comfortable, well-known environment. Parenting a girl with special needs had proven even harder than he'd imagined. Lisa was often in her own world, governed by rules nobody understood, least of all him.

"Why don't you come and explore with Sammy?"

To his surprise she opened the back door and got out, and he was left staring at her back as she walked away, fifteen-year-old shoulders rigid.

Burr turned back to the house and found himself standing alone. The worst events of the recent past faded away; the loss of his job, their money troubles, the death of close loved ones, all lost in a whirl of memories and time. He felt the house pulling at him, a strangely physical ache.

Glen Ridge.

He was still standing there, ghosts chasing themselves around in his head, when he heard the car making its way up the drive.

* * *

THE DEVIL, AS they say, is in the details. The house was a shambles, with grass high enough that, as he drove toward them, Rodney Talbot could barely make out the child wandering through it, or the attractive woman who chased after the little one. Aside from the new master of the house, the only one he could see clearly was the daughter, a beauty in her own right, and the one who had what his old friend Arthur had always called "the sight."

That left Christian Burr, father, husband, and only surviving heir to Arthur's estate, standing alone by his car.

How long had it been since Talbot had seen Christian? The boy had been a teenager. It was after Arthur had made Talbot his business partner but before he'd become the executor of his estate, and certainly before Talbot knew Arthur was . . . well, that the man he called his best friend was different.

Arthur Burr was not normal. He never had been. But he'd been a good man in his own way. He'd owned this little mountain town once upon a time, supervising the construction of nearly every home and providing protection for generations of families—while receiving valuable things in return, of course.

And where was the money that the man had earned over that very long lifetime? Talbot's lips pulled into a thin, weary smile. He knew, of course, but was not allowed to say. Not yet.

Christian was staring at his Cadillac as Talbot came to a stop, a puzzled expression on his face. Arthur's grandson was older now, but his expression was much the same as always. That was the boy's trouble, really. He was as much a dreamer as his grandfather but without the resources to allow him that sort of mentality. Talbot was familiar with the problem. It was the way of the blood, trickling down through the line until it found a pool in which to gather.

Problems could also present opportunities.

Talbot slid out of his comfortable car and stood on legs that preferred sitting whenever possible. Getting old was never a pleasant notion, and he had done all he could to delay the inevitable, but just lately it was worse. Arthritis guaranteed that. The wind caught his thinning hair and tried to pull it from his scalp. The appropriate level of hair gel made it stay in place, even if it also gave him a slightly greasy look that he disapproved of, not that it mattered anymore. He still dressed himself in finery, but he also knew that no woman was looking at him with an eye toward courtship.

There had been a time when he would have made Christian stand on the other side of his massive oak desk and wait patiently while he sorted through a thick sheaf of papers in his briefcase. That too had changed with age. These days he preferred to be done with theatrics and merely handle matters quickly and efficiently. The time for drama was long past in his eyes. Not so with Arthur. Talbot had every intention of following the rather obscure demands of his best friend—at least at first—but he didn't have to enjoy it.

Very well, Arthur. One last time we shall play your games. Talbot reached into his custom-tailored suit jacket and pulled a thick envelope from the inside pocket.

"Can I help you?" Burr was looking at him with a slightly perplexed expression that would have never been found on his grandfather's face.

Talbot smiled. "I think, my good man, that you have that the other way around. I'm the executor of Arthur's estate, and I'm here to help *you*."

Burr smiled, his face a full decade younger as the expression eased the tension in his features. "Mr. Talbot? We spoke on the phone. I wasn't expecting to see you." Burr offered his hand and Talbot took it, pleased by the firm grip. Damn, but he looked like his grandfather had in his prime: the bright, piercing eyes and a strangely icy tint to his skin, as if he was perpetually cold. It was almost haunting.

Talbot smiled back. "I thought I would give you the keys in person." He patted the envelope in his other hand and the metallic tinkle of the ring of keys sounded dully through the thick paper. "Along with a few final words from your grandfather. Arthur requested that you read it yourself." He paused a moment. "He wanted to make sure that no one else confused the matters he wished you to consider."

"I'm afraid I don't understand." Burr took the envelope and seemed surprised by the weight.

"Well, you know your grandfather, Christian. He was a man who liked to handle things a certain way, with a bit of mystery thrown in."

Burr nodded. "I meant to ask you, Mr. Talbot: what happened to my grandfather's body?"

Rodney Talbot looked away, his eyes moving over the grass and line of trees that stood like motionless soldiers about to march upon the helpless interlopers. "He asked to be buried out there, in the forest he loved," Talbot said. "An unmarked grave. It was his dying wish. I didn't see any reason not to grant it." Talbot motioned to the envelope. "Now, go ahead and open that, if you like. You may be surprised at what you find."

* * *

COLORS SWIRLED BEFORE *her in the air like oil on the surface of a pool. She reached out and dipped her fingers through them, watching streaks of blue and orange trail from her fingertips, mix, and form faces with mouths open in silent screams.*

Sounds assailed her from all sides, the tick of sunshine off pebbles, a hiss of insect legs moving in the tall grass, the squeal of dust dancing beyond the passage of the car that had stopped near her father.

A few more steps and she reached the edge of the abyss. Somewhere beyond her feet was the source of the strangest sensations, wafting up like a cloud. The darkness before her was only a wall, built to protect and conceal; she could see that much clearly. But she could not see all that lay beyond, and it puzzled her.

The rage early in their journey had been about this change, her frustration over her inability to see what was coming. But something *was coming, something important. All her life, she could sense things that others could not. Inanimate objects spoke to her; music played through living creatures; spirits gathered in places of death. There was a world beyond the one that most people knew. She felt it, every day.*

Just as she felt the others gathered within the forest, thousands of them, watching from places that hid them.

Waiting for her to arrive.

CHRISTIAN BURR TOLD Talbot to head home, that he preferred to read the letter later and on his own terms. Looking for privacy, he left Susan to tend to the children outside and found his way into the house.

Once inside, he felt better almost immediately. Past the sagging remains of the porch, the structure appeared to be fairly sound; remarkably so, in spite of its appearance. The interior was in much better shape than the porch. Immediately ahead of him the stairs led up to the second floor. To his left was a study, to his right an archway into the living room. They used to have the Christmas tree in there during the holidays, Burr thought. Memories flooded over him. He could remember them wheeling the piano into this little front room and they would all gather around near the tree and sing carols in his grandfather's native Czechoslovakian tongue. That tree was always a living one; his grandfather had insisted on it. After the opening of presents and the meal, Arthur would take him alone into the forest and they would plant the tree somewhere in a weighty and somber ritual filled with words that Burr did not understand. He had always sensed the ritual was more important to his grandfather than the holiday itself. Arthur Burr filled nearly every other waking moment with jokes and wordplay, winks of an eye, riddles that left everyone stumped for hours on end. But he never joked about the planting of that tree.

Strange. He had forgotten about that until now. Another memory flitted at the edges of his consciousness, something important he couldn't quite remember. Distracted, Burr stepped into the living room, dust swirling in the still air. All the furniture was exactly the same. He could hardly help feeling angry at the state of everything. Why hadn't somebody notified him sooner? His grandfather had loved this house. Perhaps Burr could have seen to it that the place was kept up.

Of course he could never have afforded that, not after being downsized and their recent money problems. Everything had seemed to happen all at once, the bad news rolling in day after day until he'd very nearly broken under the weight. His own parents' death in a terrible car accident six months ago had been the worst of it. He'd tried to reach his grandfather then, without success. Now that made more sense; Arthur was already gone himself, as it turned out. The news of the old man's death had been another blow, and to find out that he had actually died years before had made it even more bizarre and disturbing.

They had had no other choice but to come here, city slickers forced to relocate to this isolated mountain community five hundred miles from home. Driving through the town center had felt like going back a century in time. People had stared at the car as they rolled by. They had stopped for gas at the only station available, and a mention of Arthur Burr had gotten nothing but a shrug and muttered breath from the attendant. Christian's grandfather had practically built Glen Ridge with his own hands, and had been beloved, as far as Christian had ever heard, but apparently the courtesy always shown him did not extend to his descendants.

This is our home now, for better or for worse. Fate had seen to that.

The envelope could not be put off any longer. Burr took a chair and sat down in the sunshine, pulling the contents free with trembling fingers. The letter he set aside for now, drawn to the other papers; at first, genealogy reports that appeared to trace the Burr lineage back to the Czech territories. It appeared that his grandfather had changed the family name from Burian to Burr when he came to America around the time of World War Two. With that came the memory that had eluded him earlier: his grandfather telling him Czechoslovakian legends as bedtime stories. One in particular, about a giant forest creature called a Leshy that could take any shape, had terrified him to the point of sleeping with the light on and the covers pulled up to his chin, quaking at the blackness beyond the bedroom window.

But all that was lost as Christian Burr focused on the bank statements beneath the genealogy reports. For a moment his brain refused to process what he was seeing. The number seemed to be a mistake. *Eight million dollars?* How was that possible? Arthur Burr had been a builder, overseeing construction of a good number of the houses in town, and had certainly been comfortable enough, although Christian had never really bothered to understand the details of his business. He had never imagined that his grandfather had been this successful.

My God. He let out a sigh, then a small whoop. This changed everything. *Everything.*

Only then did he turn to the letter.

My dear boy, where to begin? There are secrets that you must understand. I am gone, and yet I remain, a tree that has lost its leaves but still stands tall and rooted to the ground. Now I must provide Braille for a blind man. So, to begin, riddle number one:

What bends without breaking,
gives shelter without roof and walls,
warms after death,
sighs without breath?

Forgive me for my wordplay, but that is my nature. It is too easy to be handed the answers before you begin. There is power in the journey and the discovery.

I remember your father's awakening after you were born. He was born blind too, much to my chagrin. I could not travel to your home (I never traveled in that way, do you remember this?) and so I met you when your parents came to visit when you were three months old. Your father said the light of stars was held in your eyes, that he saw this when you came from the womb. He was right, and yet he was wrong; it is not just the light of the stars, but the sun and moon and all that is holy about this world. That is what is kept within you, within all of us.

That light is passed, one to the next. And once every few generations, it is allowed to shine forth. It is your job to assist with the transition.

I have rules for you. You must rebuild this home, and once it is rebuilt, you must live here with your family for the rest of your life and never leave. You must allow the children access to the woods at any time, no matter how dangerous that may appear, and accept without hesitation whatever happens as a result.

You must become, my dear boy, a steward of the blood.

Once you have settled here you can never leave Glen Ridge again.

That may seem harsh, but I think you will find everything you need at your fingertips, and more. If you do this, the account I have set up for you is accessible; if you do not, Mr. Talbot will remove that access permanently.

One last riddle for you:

Reaching stiffly for the sky,
I bare my fingers when it's cold.
In warmth I wear an emerald glove,
and in between I dress in gold.

Find the answers, and you will see the light.

BY NOW THE boy had likely seen the details contained within the envelope. Talbot had hoped to watch Christian's reaction and gauge how to proceed from there. But plans change, of course, and Rodney had already decided that it was time to move things along a bit more quickly.

Talbot walked through the woods as the bite of arthritis began to fade away, feet settling exactly where they needed to in order to avoid the thorns and nettles catching on his fine suit, shoes never once falling prey to mud or stones that would have scuffed the polish. He had been trained in the ways of the woods. He had learned many, many things over the long years.

When Arthur Burr had first settled in town as a young man, before everyone's perspectives had changed, he had been ridiculed for being different. Arthur had been much like his lovely great-granddaughter. Back then they'd called a man like Arthur "slow-witted" and "addled." Now they might say "autistic." None of the terms were right, of course.

Things had certainly changed, all right. Talbot smiled. He'd been a child when they met seemingly by chance in these very same woods. Back in those days he had never even dreamed of owning a suit. He'd had exactly two pair of pants and neither had been owned by him the first time around. He let his fingers drift across the leaves of the closest tree, a birch with peeling bark that looked like flaking, mummified flesh. The wind sighed around him and several wasps buzzed nearby. He did not fear the wasps, never had and likely never would. Arthur had shown him a great number of secrets over the years, and he understood the woods better than most could ever comprehend.

Things rustled through the trees, and then came the soft, careful padding of a wolf. He waited patiently for the animal to come closer. The beast was a large one, old and scarred. It looked at him with clear, intelligent eyes, and he looked back. "It's been a while since I saw you, hasn't it?" The wolf brushed itself along his hand, and he rubbed his fingers through the thick fur. The winter coat hadn't completely fallen away yet, but it would soon enough. He tugged a soft tuft of shedding fur from the animal's flank and let it drift away in the wind.

"Arthur knew your name, didn't he? Your real name, I mean. Of course he did." The wolf gave no response save to nuzzle his hand.

Arthur had shared a great number of his secrets, but not all of them. It wasn't a matter of friendship; it was a matter of keeping the trust of others. With the right names, a man could very well make demands of the creatures of the wild. If a man knew the right words, the right way to go about it.

That was why he never feared the wasps. He'd learned the right words to deal with them a very long time ago. Arthur had taught him that and many other things.

He thought of the man's smile, the simple, carefree actions that had caused so many people to think that Arthur was deranged. What was the word that people used that made them both laugh so often? *Bedazzled.* That was the one. As if the world around him was simply too much for him to comprehend.

He closed his eyes and looked at the world the way Arthur had shown him so long ago. It was a very different world indeed. With his eyes closed and his sight open, he stood and walked, and the wolf walked with him.

He covered the distance—almost a mile—with ease. And finally, although it took some time, he found the right spot.

Despite his advanced years, he crouched close to the ground and then leaned back against the coarse bark of the gigantic tree, resting the side of his face against the wood. The wind sighed across him, a gentle caress that made him think of the red-haired beauty both he and Arthur had loved so dearly. In the long run, she had chosen Arthur, had borne him a son. That was all right. There had been a time when the love he felt for her was reciprocated, and he had never held much of a grudge for her choices and couldn't have held a grudge against Arthur had his life depended on it.

Nearly two hours passed before he let himself rise from where he'd been squatting. Most would have been in agony from sitting in one place, in so awkward a pose, for as long as he had. Rodney Talbot was not most people.

The wolf was long gone. Where it had been, the ground was cold to his touch. That was all right. He had not been napping. Nor had he been lost in dreams. He had been doing as Arthur had asked.

He allowed a tight, small smile. There was warmth, and a little sadness too. Soon he would have to depart from Arthur's well-laid plans. It was regretful, but necessary. But not yet.

"Now for the next part of this. Time for awakenings, I think."

The words he whispered were not known to many humans. But those words were heard, and very clearly at that.

Soon the wind picked up, and the clouds began to gather.

Rodney made it back to his car before the storm came in earnest. Of course, he'd planned it that way. It was a storm that he'd designed.

The storm came up through the valley, turning the mountaintop into a shadowy, cloud-shrouded beast and tossing the leaves of trees with a sound like a long, drawn-out hiss. The sky lowered overhead, icy-gray sheets of rain visible in the distance as the old farmhouse seemed to huddle in the foothills.

Christian Burr was still sitting in the dining room and lost in thought, the contents of the envelope strewn across the table and his grandfather's letter in his hands, when he heard shouting.

He went to the front porch. Susan's voice cut through the wind like a knife, high and full of panic. *Sammy.* Money and riddles forgotten for the moment, Burr shoved the letter in his pocket and leaped down the steps. Susan was standing near the edge of the small pond, hands cupped to her face, screaming into the growing wind. But it wasn't Sam she was calling for; the boy stood clutching his mother's leg.

Susan spied Burr, scooped up Sam into her arms, and ran to her husband. "Lisa's gone," she said breathlessly, spots of red on her otherwise pale cheeks. "I got distracted near the water, turned my back, and . . ." She shook her head. "I can't find her anywhere."

Burr scanned the immediate surroundings, his eyes moving over their old Subaru wagon and its empty backseat, the house, the ragged lawn. There weren't many places to hide. Unless . . .

He turned to the wood's edge, a chill creeping over him. The trees ran in a thick line, but a faint, worn path led through the tall grass. Could Lisa have been tempted to explore there? Anything was possible.

"The storm," Susan said. "Chris, please . . . you have to get her back before it hits."

He nodded. "Take Sammy and get in the house," he said. "She couldn't have gone very far."

Burr didn't wait for an answer. The wind grew even fiercer, with a smell like ozone and mud as he ducked his head and ran through the grass, following the path toward the forest. At the edge of the trees he paused; in the soft dirt there he could clearly make out a partial shoeprint.

Lisa had gone into the woods.

Burr glanced back at the house. Susan and Sammy were nowhere to be seen; hopefully they had listened to him and made it inside. The storm seemed to race through the valley, more clouds boiling up and bursting with rain. It had come up so fast. He had only minutes before it would be upon him.

Burr entered the woods.

Inside the first line of trees, the wind was softer, buffeted by the thick canopy of leaves. It was even darker in here, and he moved forward cautiously, calling out Lisa's name with no response. The path appeared to continue on, faint but visible, meandering left and right around trunks and clumps of brambles. The air smelled of rich earth and decay, along with something else he couldn't place. He had a sense of things lurking beyond the edges of his sight, watching him, and he quickly grew claustrophobic and disoriented. He turned, looked behind him, the path suddenly gone; where had he entered the woods? It should only have been twenty or thirty feet away, but instead he saw nothing but branches and leaves.

Burr called out for his daughter again, pushing forward through the gloom. Now he could have sworn he heard whispers, too soft for him to make out any words. Perhaps it was the wind in the treetops.

Your grandfather is buried somewhere in here. Burr stopped short, heart pounding. A notion that had seemed quaint, if a bit odd, now felt more unsettling. He could be walking over Arthur's grave right now.

"Lisa!" Burr shouted. "This isn't funny. Come out, right now!"

No answer. He pushed through heavy branches, feeling blind in the growing dark, a twig snapping back across his face and making him wince. But nothing was there except more branches, more leaves.

Movement came from the left.

He stepped forward again and almost stumbled over something. Burr crouched to find a pair of girl's sneakers, half hidden in old leaves. A few steps farther on he found a shirt, and then a pair of jeans.

Thunder cracked the sky, rumbling through the valley and sounding slightly muffled through the trees. Wetness dripped from above onto Burr's head as the first raindrops began to fall.

Then he heard Lisa scream.

* * *

THE WORLD HAD changed.

Lisa Burr had felt it as soon as she stepped through the forest wall. The barrier that had hidden things from her fell away as if she were shedding an old skin, and she felt everything click into place. She had suddenly awakened from a terrible dream. The forest was still thick, but she could see everything clearly in a way that transcended sight. It was not "sight" as she had known before, but something more, something deeper that incorporated her very essence.

She was still aware of the sounds, colors, smells, and tastes that normally assaulted her senses, and yet she understood each and every one of them and their places in the world around her in a way she never had before. It was like magic, and along with it came a great sense of satisfaction, a purpose that had been denied her for the first fifteen years of her young life.

The forest was speaking a language, one that she finally understood.

The human clothing she wore felt terribly constrictive. She took off her shoes. The soil beneath her feet gave off a rich chocolate hue wherever it was most fertile. Leaves above her head passed knowledge along through a sound like whispers in the dark, and the drops of rain that had begun to patter down sang of their journey from the heavens as they quenched the parched roots below. A fox barked a warning as she moved, a bitter scent from the creature's glands wafting out as a red cloud; without thinking, she responded, soothing the animal's fears with a hum that began low in her belly and sounded like the buzz of bees.

Lisa removed her shirt, then her jeans, repulsed by the toxic, chemical smell of them. The fox came forward and nuzzled her hand. Almost immediately, she sensed movement all around her. Other animals emerged from their hiding places, one by one: three squirrels chattered about her appearance as they darted down a thick pine branch; a deer came picking his way on spindly legs; a porcupine waddled forward, spines down in a gesture of acceptance.

Others came behind them, dozens, hundreds; the woods were full of them, and Lisa could feel them all calling to her, welcoming her to their domain.

She stepped forward into their embrace, her entire body tingling fiercely. The falling rain caressed and nourished her as it sang, roots of plants and trees digging into the soil and drinking deeply, pulsing with new life. Animals that had nuzzled at her suddenly parted as one, and another padded forward silently on giant paws; a wolf, its shoulders nearly taller than her own waist. She sensed both its power and its ac-

ceptance of her, the knowledge that she was completely safe here but also that this creature expected something important from her.

She let the wolf lead her forward through the woods, her feet finding the right path without thought, avoiding sharp objects with ease. At some point she sensed her father pierce the barrier of the trees behind her, heard him calling to her, but she did not hesitate. Several animals slipped away, circling back, but most of them continued along with her, a massive and nearly silent march through the woods like a somber parade, meant to bear testament to something she could not quite grasp. Not yet.

Lisa slipped through undergrowth and branches like a ghost as they went deeper into the forest. Finally the thick trees gave way to a circular clearing. In its center stood a massive tree, its naked branches stretching toward the dark sky. Rain clouds had lowered themselves until they appeared to nearly touch the bony, wooden fingers, and the tree's gnarled, rough bark glistened wetly. There was almost no light, but Lisa had no need of it; she could see everything far beyond the limits of her eyes.

The rain washed away the last of the chemical stink that had permeated her skin, and she stood naked and whole, spreading her arms wide like the tree, embracing the world around her.

She was shocked when another human form stepped out from the shadows. She recognized him as the man who had come to visit her father in the big car, but she had not sensed him standing there, even though she had felt everything else around her.

"K noze," *the old man said.* "Hodnej." *The huge wolf padded across the clearing to stand at his side. "Welcome," he said, smiling at Lisa. He spoke without saying a word aloud, and yet she understood him clearly.* "Blahopřejeme k promoci! *It is time for you to awaken, Lisa Burian."*

Christian Burr stumbled through the thick trees, pushing away the branches that stung his face. The scream had been Lisa's, he was sure of it; who else would be out here in the storm? His heart pounded with fear, body charged with adrenaline as he tried to keep going in the right direction. It was nearly impossible. Everything in the forest served only to confuse him, the sounds of dripping rain, the shadows that seemed to dance and change as he moved, the grasping branches. He could become lost out here very easily, he realized, with the forest stretching on for miles.

With that thought came the memory of his grandfather's stories about the Leshy, the legendary Slavic forest creature that protected the forest and confused travelers who were ignorant enough to trespass on his lands. A Leshy could appear to be an ordinary human but could take any living form, his grandfather had said, from the smallest insect to the largest animal. It could protect crops and livestock in exchange for tribute and worship, and if a human befriended one, he could be taught the secrets of magic.

But a Leshy could also make you disappear forever if you did not obey its wishes.

Why had he thought of that? He hadn't remembered those stories since he was a boy, but now they seemed fresh in his consciousness. Burr pushed on, listening for any signs of his daughter. His mind kept worrying at the details of his grandfather's bizarre letter and set of instructions, and the riddles it had contained:

What bends without breaking,
gives shelter without roof and walls,
warms after death,
sighs without breath?

And the second one:

Reaching stiffly for the sky,
I bare my fingers when it's cold.
In warmth I wear an emerald glove,
and in between I dress in gold.

Trees, Burr thought suddenly. *The answer to both is trees.* He stopped, looking up through the dripping rain at the canopy high above him. The leaves were thick, branches intertwined. Above that the storm raged; he could hear the wind and the rain lashing at the forest, but down here it was calmer, quieter, and he began to get the sense that he was not being led astray at all, that he simply had to get his wits about him and begin to listen more carefully.

Find the answers, his grandfather had written, *and you will see the light.*

With great effort, Burr cleared his mind of the clutter and confusion that had gripped him from the moment he realized Lisa was missing. Almost immediately, he sensed something coming. Flitting through the cover of the treetops came a flock of birds, hundreds moving as one as they passed over his head. He sensed and heard them but did not see a single one until a small sparrow alighted on a branch directly in front of him, cocked its head in the dim light as if studying him before flitting to the next branch, and then the next, leading him on.

Christian Burr slipped forward, following the birds deeper into the forest.

"It's the synthetics." The girl looked at him for a moment, barely seeming to comprehend that he had spoken, and then looked down at herself, as if suddenly realizing that she was unclothed before him. Rain glistened on her glowing flesh. "I did the same thing when I first became aware of how bad they smell, how they feel when they touch the skin." He smiled softly. "These days all I wear are clothes I have specially made. All natural. Cotton fabrics and silk. Even the buttons on my shirt and jacket are custom." He pointed. "Wood and stone and occasionally bone."

The girl frowned slightly. She was a beautiful thing, and he could sense the power starting to build in her, growing like the clouds that were even now rising to greater and greater heights above them. A thrill ran through him, one he tried hard to suppress.

"Your great-grandfather was my best friend. I think he would have liked to meet you under different circumstances, my dear, but it has to be this way."

She looked at the tree. To most people it might merely look like another oak, but he knew better, and judging by her expression she did too.

Talbot smiled and nodded his head. "That's right. He's here." His hand caressed the thick bark of the tree. Five years since he'd buried the acorn inside his best friend's chest, making sure to pierce the meat of the heart as he'd been instructed to do. Five years since he'd buried the body himself, jumping through nearly endless legal loopholes in order to properly guarantee the secrecy of the final resting place. These days secrecy was almost impossible, but he'd managed. There was truth to the old saying about money talking, and even though the majority of Arthur's fortune had been put into trust, he'd left enough to grease the proper legal wheels.

Lisa came closer to the tree, not speaking. Her eyes stared at the powerful, vibrant oak. He knew what she saw. Arthur had taught him over years what came to her instinctively. She could see the raw, magnificent power that was Arthur's spirit locked within its branches.

The woods here were protected. Rodney had seen to it. He had done so much over the years, because he loved Arthur and because he understood his best friend. Trust funds had been established, taxes paid, and more funds set up to guarantee the legal protection in perpetuity. All of this Rodney had willingly done to ensure that the family would be protected and cared for.

And yet when all was said and done, he had been left alone, set adrift, taught so much and yet not enough. Not nearly enough.

Lisa put her hand on the bark of the tree and closed her eyes, communing with her great-grandfather for the first time, truly communing with him as only a few people would ever be able to understand.

She had eyes and she could see. That was her birthright.

It was also Rodney's gift, and he felt a flare of jealousy that he'd tried so very hard to suppress. He felt it—and reveled in it.

The words were uttered very softly, and the trap he'd laid was triggered.

The girl was beautiful, no two ways about that. She had features that were so similar to Magda's, Arthur's wife. To the woman Rodney had willingly surrendered to Arthur when their love was so evident.

And that, too, made his actions easier.

Talbot began to undress. He hated his fleshy, pale white belly, his flaccid, shriveled penis and wrinkled skin. He was ancient, his cells dying one at a time; his body ached now, and he could feel death standing behind him all the time, waiting for the right moment. *Not yet,* Talbot thought. *Not yet.*

He slipped a knife from the pocket of his pants. Lisa's hand tried to pull back from the tree, but nothing happened. Her sweet, innocent eyes flew wide, and her mouth drew down in a frown of unexpected pain.

"Don't fight it, sweet girl." Naked now, Talbot put a hand on her shoulder, but she was too busy struggling to notice. "The more you fight, the more it will hurt; and Arthur never wanted you to feel pain."

Her skin was warm and soft, but the muscles beneath her flesh jumped as if electrified. Her brow was stippled with sweat, and her breaths came out as tiny, frenzied gasps.

"Arthur told me that you were the next Leshy and that I was to bring you to him. And so I have." He spoke softly to her, his voice barely a whisper. "But I have to tell you, I don't think you're quite the right choice for that. I think it might take someone with more experience." He brushed her ear with his lips and she tried to flinch away, but the binding spell was working. His eyes traveled along her arm, looked at where her hand and forearm had already been covered by the same thick bark as that which covered the tree that housed Arthur's spirit. A low groan came from her and she tried to sag, but her legs were held in place by the binding spell, and no matter what she tried, there was no escape for her.

"It's nothing against you, sweet Lisa. I think you are a lovely child and

I've watched your family from afar for a very long time. But I am growing old now, without Arthur's help, and I need to remain vital. I need to remain strong."

His hands ran along her shoulders and down her arms, keeping the knife's edge against her skin. He stopped his progress down the length of her forearm just shy of the bark that was swallowing her flesh.

"I found the ritual. It took a lot of time and research, and believe me, it took a lot of money. You are the Leshy, Lisa. But thanks to the words, the proper care and processes, I can bind you to Arthur. You remain the Leshy and as long as you live, I retain the Stewardship."

He let the blade bite, just enough to draw blood.

Oh, how she fought. Lisa pulled as hard as she could and actually shook him off for a moment, but in the process she offended the power that bound her and it retaliated. A flaring light rippled across her skin and the bark swarmed like a thousand hungry ants, crawling up her arm and covering her shoulder, her breasts, her stomach. Lisa's eyes flew wide and she screamed. Rodney could feel her pain and frowned. The cut should be shallow and not dangerous, just enough to share a few drops. He did not want this. Quite to the contrary, he wanted her happy and healthy.

"Please, child. Don't fight. I never wanted you to suffer." Talbot shook his head as he sliced his own forearm and let the blood drip onto her skin, mixing with her own. "Arthur would not approve."

CHRISTIAN BURR FOLLOWED the sound of the birds.

At some point he had closed his eyes, but it made no difference. The sound led him forward, and he found that his feet knew exactly where to step to avoid roots and sinkholes, rocks and brush. He ducked around branches without a single mishap, and as he did his mind seemed to expand, soaring over the forest and watching from far above. He felt the rain pounding down and the wind shaking the trees, but underneath it all he was sheltered like a fetus in the womb. With the rain his spirit was washed clean, and he found himself listening to the sounds of the forest in a way that seemed intimate.

But it wasn't just sounds, Burr realized; it was scents and other ways the forest connected to him that he had never imagined. He let these lead him deeper, and when he emerged on the edge of a clearing and saw the gigantic tree at its center, he was not surprised.

Nor was he surprised to see the huge wolf watching him from the other side with luminous eyes and lolling tongue, or the countless other creatures of the forest creeping forward from its edges.

But what did surprise him was the image of Rodney Talbot, stripped naked, caressing the nude form of his fifteen-year-old daughter as she stood fused to the tree, her hands and arms all but disappearing into the thick bark.

Revulsion washed over him, and rage flew fast on its heels. He stepped out, into the clearing. "Get away from her," he said.

For a moment, he thought Talbot didn't hear him. And then the man turned his head, and Burr saw the forest reflected in his face. His eyes were tinted green, his lips blue. His skin had begun to take on the texture of the bark that was absorbing Burr's daughter, one cell at a time.

Talbot looked at the wolf and made a guttural sound, like a river rushing and tumbling over rocks, and the beast took a step toward Burr, then another, growling deep in its throat as Talbot turned back again and focused his attention on the girl.

THE SOUNDS OF *the forest had changed.*

Before they had been lilting, sweet, beckoning her forward; but as she touched her great-grandfather's shell, the sounds had begun to nip at her like playful dogs. The man had spoken and the song had changed again. Its bite had teeth and it hurt. It meant to catch her now, to bind her and never let her go.

She tried to pull away, but it was no use. The living bark had begun to flow over her flesh. Somewhere deep within the beat of the tree she felt another presence, one with a powerful, deep and ancient voice. But it would not come to help her, not anymore. It was too far gone and bound to the roots that had buried themselves so deep in the soil.

Just a short time ago, she had finally understood herself fully for the first time; her disability, as her school counselors had described it, wasn't a limitation at all, but a gift. She had felt herself emerging like a butterfly from a cocoon.

But now that gift had become her prison, and the same power that drove it was being used against her.

Lisa screamed, a very human sound, and felt the man come up behind her, violating her with his hands as they moved across her shoulders, pulling something from her that hurt worse than anything else. He spoke the ancient words and the feeling intensified, a drawing out like blood being sucked from a wound.

The pain was too much to bear. The man's voice had gotten louder now, a rhythmic chanting that tore at her again and again. She tried to yank her feet free, but it was as if someone had driven spikes through her heels; when she looked down she saw that roots had sprouted from her flesh, wriggling like snakes as they found the soil and dug in.

The giant tree shivered, once, twice, three times. Talbot shrieked in triumph as the bark enveloped Lisa's face and the world began to fade away.

CHRISTIAN BURR STOOD his ground as the wolf approached. The warning growl left his legs weak and his heart racing ever faster, and he felt himself beginning to lose control. He still wasn't sure what was happening, but it seemed impossible. What he had seen didn't make any sense. His daughter was being *absorbed* . . .

Burr felt the familiar panic that always overtook him when the stress got to be too much, and the detachment that went along with it was close behind. He had never been good at dealing with intense situations; he had wondered, after Lisa had been diagnosed, whether he had just a little bit of what she was born with and had passed it along in a more concentrated form.

She is a Leshy.

There is no such thing. And yet he could feel the truth like some monstrous wild creature bursting through the forest. His grandfather had been one too. Now it was time for another to take over, but it would not be him.

He was simply a steward of the blood.

The wolf was close enough to touch. Burr could smell its wet, sulfur smell, see the glint of its long, sharp teeth. Unbidden, words sprang to his lips: a phrase his grandfather had taught him as a young child while they planted the Christmas tree, words that sounded like gibberish but that he had been made to repeat, over and over.

"Klid je les, poslouchat stormy."

The wolf paused. *"Steal život od cizince, a dej mi to,"* Burr said. The wolf took another step forward, panting, and stopped, cocking its head as if listening.

There was more to the ritual, but Burr couldn't remember it. He looked at Talbot. The man had continued to change. He was swelling in size like a bloated tick, his hands still on Lisa's shoulders, his head thrown back at a grotesque angle. His hair had changed from silver to a thick brown, and his flesh had lost the barklike pattern and begun to take on a bluish tone. His eyes were the color of summer grass.

Burr considered trying to run past the wolf, but it was already too late. Lisa was almost completely shrouded in bark, a cocoon of living armor that turned her arms to branches and absorbed her legs and feet until they appeared rooted to the ground. Burr could barely make out his daughter's features, but what he saw was frozen in horror.

Talbot screamed again in triumph, a look of ecstasy on a face that had turned thirty years younger. At that moment, the wolf gave a snarl and leaped at the man with bared teeth.

The weight of the huge animal knocked Talbot's hands away from Lisa and the two bodies tumbled to the ground, one human, one animal, with the animal quickly gaining the upper hand before Talbot slipped a knife free from beneath him and plunged it deep into the wolf's side.

The huge beast howled, and Burr felt a white-hot flare of pain in his chest. Above them the clouds seemed to open up, a great crash of thunder shaking the forest floor and lightning cracking across the sky. Burr felt the other animals in the forest cry out in wordless agony, thousands of them, along with the trees that seemed to shiver as wind whipped through the valley.

Burr thought he saw something move in the center of the clearing as a sound like the ancient moan of a shifting mountainside rose up to envelop them all. He stepped toward his daughter, the final phrases of the tree-planting ritual finally bursting forth from his throat like a cascade: "*Ať máte kořeny dlouho a tvůj duch žije dál! Může lesa a chránit vás a krev svázat ducha!*"

RODNEY TALBOT WAS on fire.

The blood of the Leshy had mixed with his, and it felt as if a million insects crawled beneath his skin. His mind expanded to fill the clearing and then the entire forest, and he felt the connection of every single creature, every tree. After all these years, the remainder of Arthur's secrets and knowledge were being passed along to him.

The feeling was glorious. He reveled in it, throwing his head back as his body began to change, feeling the rain course down his face. His howl was without words, an animalistic sound of triumph and awakening.

Dimly, he heard someone else speaking aloud in the ancient tongue. And then something knocked him to the ground, breaking his connection with the Leshy. Rage filled his mind as he felt the rough fur of the wolf above him, its hot breath at his throat. "*Zvíře,*" Talbot growled. "*Tvá krev rozlije!*"

He fumbled for the knife and stuck it deep into the beast's side, feeling its blood pump in a hot gush across his chest. He struggled with the weight of the body across his own as the wolf's life ran out of it and seeped into the forest floor.

Rain poured down in buckets when Christian Burr spoke once more.

Thunder shook the ground as Talbot looked up in shock. Arthur was moving, his huge, grizzled branches reaching toward the sky, as if to embrace the lightning bolt that streaked down to earth to strike.

The bolt sizzled with energy as it hit the largest outstretched branch with a tremendous cracking sound. The branch broke in half, tumbling toward where Talbot lay helplessly pinned beneath the body of the wolf. He had the time to see the rough spears of wood protruding from its broken end racing toward him.

No, he thought. *Not this, not now . . .*

Christian Burr watched as the huge branch tumbled down. It was nearly twice the size around of a man's chest, and its jagged end hit Rodney Talbot square in the face.

The man's head disappeared in a cloud of red pulp, driven cleanly from his shoulders and crushed into the ground beneath the branch's weight. The headless body jerked, then lay still as the branch tumbled onto its side with a crash that shook the forest.

Another moan rose up from somewhere deep within the ground, a sound like a whale in the ocean depths. The fierce storm began to subside, rain fading to a steady patter, lightning and thunder receding into the distance.

One by one, the animals emerged from the trees around the clearing, picking their way forward to where Lisa Burr still stood rooted in place. The forest hummed with energy as she shook once, then twice, the bark cracking from her skin and falling to the ground.

Lisa opened her eyes and spread her arms wide, drinking in the rain and the animals' presence, a light smile on her face.

Christian Burr ran toward his daughter.

Around them the animals waited, watching. The wind continued to howl, and the trees shivered with the wind's demands.

And on the ground the body of Rodney Talbot was taken by the forest. The rough bark that covered his skin was almost identical to that of the great tree nearby and where his blood had flowed a moment before there were now roots, fine filaments reaching into the ground.

Christian held Lisa in his arms and spoke softly to her, small nonsensical sounds of comfort that she responded to as she held on to him in return. But Lisa wasn't crying. She was smiling, her eyes wide with a primal joy.

As twilight fell three days later, and the darkness grew deep and the sounds of the waking forest drifted across the old farmhouse, the people of Glen Ridge came calling.

It began with a trickle at first; a knock on the door announced the arrival of James Footer and his two young children with a wax-topped jar of fresh honey, the children gaping at Lisa from behind their father's legs. Ten minutes later, elderly widow Joan Sunland came with a wrapped box filled with linens for their table, placed a wrinkled hand on Lisa's head, and then left without a single word. Five minutes after that came Terri and Steve and Giles, neighbors from Old Farm Road, along with their families, bearing fresh vegetables from their gardens. Terri ran a specialty clothing shop in town and brought organic blouses and pants for Lisa to make her more comfortable. She had served Lisa's great-grandfather, Terri said proudly, and was happy to be able to continue the tradition now.

That seemed to be the end of it, and Susan had put away the produce in the fridge and they had already gone up to bed when the sounds of vehicles could be heard below. Susan went to the window and stood motionless for a long moment.

"Come here," she said to Burr, her voice little more than a whisper. "You won't believe it."

He went and peered through the glass. The road that wound up toward the house was full of cars, a long line of them and more coming, twinkling headlights snaking all the way up to their front steps.

Burr went down to greet them, but it was soon apparent that they hadn't come for him. He got out of the way as the people laid their gifts at Lisa's feet. She stood radiant before them in a way he'd never seen before, the power in her seeming to thrum so that every person who set foot near her could feel it.

There was no point in trying to refuse the gifts, and no one would accept payment for anything. Susan began to help move them to other rooms, and while she did, Christian Burr slipped out the back. He walked through the moist grass, under the moonlight sky to the forest's edge, and followed the path inside.

He could remember how often the neighbors and friends of the family had come by to see his grandfather. It had never seemed particularly unusual when he was a child, and now, in hindsight, he remembered his grandfather's stories and understood better why they came. *The Leshy can be kind. The Leshy can be cruel. That is the way of Nature and that is the way of the Leshy. When the Leshy is kind, it is best to say thank you.*

It wasn't bribery, not really. It was simply the tradition that had grown in the old country and that was now carried onward in Glen Ridge, a town that had always prospered since Arthur Burr came along.

Burr followed the path deeper into the woods, moving through darkness without a single misstep. Earlier that day he had found the rest of his grandfather's papers in the basement. These papers were now a tool for reaching Lisa and teaching her. She would never be like other children; he knew that and he understood it better now. But she needed to be reminded that she was part of two worlds, and Christian suspected that was where he came in.

The Leshy was the protector of the woods, and in turn, he would serve as her steward, to keep her safe from a changing world that failed to understand the old ways.

Your father said the light of stars was held in your eyes, that he saw this when you came from the womb, his grandfather had written. *That light is passed, one to the next. And once every few generations, it is allowed to shine forth. It is your job to assist with the transition.*

It was the natural order of things, really.

Sometime later Burr reached the clearing. The huge tree, now missing a limb, reached upward toward the pregnant moon. There was no sign of the old man Talbot's body. He was gone, absorbed by the forest he had sought to control. The oddly shaped tree where he had been reached toward the greater tree as a child reaches toward its father.

The great oak did not seem interested in reaching back.

CALCULATING ROUTE

Michael Koryta and Jeffrey David Greene

The GPS was exactly the type of birthday present you could expect from David—cheap, thoughtless, and sans gift receipt.

Robin had gone overboard in her gratitude, because while the USS *Relationship* was sinking she still wanted to pretend they could carry on, or at least turn around, but even as she kissed him she thought, *What yard sale is this thing from?*

It didn't have instructions, didn't even have a box. Just the display unit and the power adapter that plugged into your cigarette lighter, the thing so obviously secondhand that it should have had someone else's name written on it. In fact, she discovered when she turned it on, it as good as *did* have someone else's name on it: the home address was already programmed in, and it wasn't hers, and she couldn't figure out how to change it. Lovely.

Hardly a splurge from David, then, but she didn't *need* a splurge; all she needed was at least the imitation of compassion and caring. They'd been together five months, and anyone who'd been with Robin for five months should have known a few things about her, one being that she didn't venture outside of her comfort zone much. Her daily routes—work, grocery store, gym, dog groomer, rinse and repeat—were well trod. The more thoughtful gift would have been a blindfold to make the trips challenging, not a GPS to keep her from getting lost driving the same damn roads she drove every day. With her birthday falling just ahead of Valentine's Day, he had another chance, though. Maybe she'd get the blindfold next.

Even the name was generic: StreetDreams2000. No Garmin or Magellan or even TomTom, nothing anyone had ever heard of, and with a number affixed that made it seem dated, more than a decade behind the times.

She loathed it not because it was pointless but because it was a perfect symbol of their relationship, and it became an even more perfect symbol when she actually went so far as to hang the dumb thing up in her car just to please him. There was no point to pleasing him, she knew this, and yet here she was, still trying. Now *that* was a symbol, and not one she wanted to consider too deeply, though it was hard not to when it stared her in the face on every drive.

The idea was simply to have it visible, she had no intention of using it, but the device turned on every time she started the car. In this way, at least, it was ahead of other models she'd seen, because it didn't even have to be plugged into the cigarette lighter to function. That fascinated her. Turn the key, and the screen came on, as if they were linked, but she'd never attached it to the car in any fashion beyond the suction cup that held the mount to the windshield. It should have no way of knowing that it was even inside of a vehicle, as far as she could tell, but, to be fair, Robin wasn't a gadget girl, and she was used to marveling at things other people understood, like the way her iPhone would upload photographs to her computer without instruction. One of her friends had sighed with exasperation while trying to explain the concept of "cloud" file storage. Robin figured the StreetDreams2000 must run on something similar.

Still, she didn't need it on, and so if it had just shown her the map in silence while she drove, fine, she could deal, but instead the thing talked. A chipper British voice asked her over and over again if she'd like help finding her destination. Finally she told it yes, just to shut it up, and the voice activation was remarkable, much better than those customer service robots that made you wish you'd been born in the day of the rotary telephone. She gave the address of her insurance office just one time, and it was a tongue twister, so she was sure the device would never understand, but immediately the British voice came back with: "Calculating route to Twenty-three Thirty-two Coriander Courtyard, Marietta, Georgia."

It took her a few miles to realize its flaw: the voice activation might have been top of the line, but once it was talking to her, she'd mindlessly followed the instructions, as if *she* was the robot, and made a left turn three miles ahead of where she needed to turn. She was swearing at the GPS, and at David, and considering a U-turn, when she realized she was on a one-way street. Nothing to do now but follow through.

The street kicked her out into a small subdivision that had sprung up in recent years where once there had simply been fields and For Sale signs. She'd never driven out to see the place, and once she got there she was curious, so she followed the GPS instructions through the winding streets, eyeing the look-alike brick homes, and suddenly found herself at a stop sign facing the back of the business park that included her company. She looked at the clock and said, "I'll be damned."

Robin knew *exactly* how long it took her to drive to the office, and, even if she'd caught nothing but green lights on the way, she was four minutes early. The shortcut through the neighborhood was a true timesaver. It might not sound like much, four minutes, but it *felt* like plenty. And if you did the math, that was eight minutes each day, and forty minutes per week, and *two hours* each month. Which meant it was exactly one day of free time added onto her life each year.

A day of your life back? She smiled at the StreetDreams2000. The gift that kept on giving, indeed.

THE MAGIC DIDN'T work everywhere, of course. The grocery store run was the same as always, and the gym, but on Saturday she saved six minutes on the trip to the dog groomer, twelve minutes round-trip. It was funny how you never considered a change in route once you've determined the best way. Or at least she didn't. Maybe more creative types did. But once Robin locked on to something that worked, she didn't change it up without a good reason. The neighborhood that was saving one day of her life each year in four-minute increments had been behind her office complex for years and she'd never even thought to consider the driving possibilities it offered. The idea of a computer telling you where to turn seemed like anti-independence, but it didn't feel that way. Robin had always had an irrational fear of getting lost—perhaps one of the reasons she didn't explore alternative routes—and the GPS gave her confidence to try. After it saved her thirty minutes at least cutting through Atlanta rush-hour traffic to meet David for dinner downtown on Monday night, she began to think that perhaps it had been a very thoughtful gift, after all. Maybe he recognized some shortcomings in her that he didn't want to say out loud, and this was a gesture. It was an awful lot to assume about a used GPS, but, still, they had their best night together since the early weeks, and she couldn't help but feel a connection to the gift.

She wanted to go home with him after dinner, in fact, wanted to have sex. No, check that—she wanted to *fuck*. And that wasn't a word she liked hearing for lovemaking; even in the movies, it gave her an involuntary sour face. The word belonged as an insult, not tied up with romance. But on Monday night, it was exactly what she wanted, and it was exactly what they did, even though he was working the late shift, which meant he was tying his shoes at midnight when she was pouring an unprecedented third glass of wine, watching him get dressed while she lay still tangled in the sheets.

"You wanna just . . . stay here?" he asked. "I mean, you can." He looked at her and then around the house with unease, as if she might take to prowling through the drawers and closets. She'd never been alone in his house before.

"No, I'll go home," she said. "It would be weird without you here. And lonely."

The last part she never would have said, but she managed to not only get the words out, but to do so coquettishly, and somehow it led to one more round of sex and a spilled glass of wine and David running out the door already twenty minutes late for work while she stood barefoot on the sidewalk and laughed.

What a night. What an odd, wonderful night. It had taken on an amusing fog to her, the wine good-natured as it settled into her bloodstream, and she was sleepy, and for just a moment, one long lonely hesitation, she thought about staying. She could be asleep within minutes, and maybe this was just the sort of thing they needed.

In the end, though, she couldn't do it. Got dressed and found her keys and left despite the alcohol buzz. It was no doubt a product of the buzz that she thought the GPS turned on before she turned the key in the ignition. She wasn't used to being drunk, or anywhere in the neighborhood of drunk, but hand to God she felt she'd barely slammed the car door before the screen lit up. Maybe not, though. Surely not. As the engine warmed, the polite British voice asked for her destination, same as always, trustworthy, and she said, "Home" before remembering that it wasn't programmed right for that.

"Taking you home," the British voice said, and she corrected it.

"Thirty-seven Thirty Collins Drive," she said. "New destination. Thirty-seven Thirty Collins Drive."

"Calculating route."

No bold ideas from the GPS this time, just out to the freeway, same as always. She was enjoying the haze of wine and sex and her mind was on David as the dark road rolled by, thinking that maybe she'd made a mistake, maybe they did work, maybe she should finally break down and suggest a trip out of town, to that place in the mountains, the one where—

"In 10.6 miles, take Exit 29E—Sandy Plains Road," the GPS intoned.

"Yes, sir," she murmured, and for the first time she really felt sad about her decision. Maybe she'd imagined the uneasiness on David's face, maybe he *wanted* her to stay. God, could she get through one day of her life without so many *maybes*?

"Take exit ahead."

Maybe, she thought as she exited the highway, the problem wasn't him, or even them, but her. She was set in her ways, she knew this, and his gift of the GPS had proven that it wasn't always a good thing. She'd benefited from some changes. And now, being set her in ways had her going home alone to an empty bed. No, it wasn't always a good thing.

"In one mile, turn right onto Hiram Avenue."

She wouldn't have taken Hiram. She glanced at the map, trying to see how this was a good idea, but it was zoomed in tight. When she tried to adjust it, the British voice chastised her.

"We ask that you refrain from operating the GPS keypad while your vehicle is in motion. Thank you."

Well, the hell with it, then. She'd take Hiram and see if this shortcut was as good as all the others.

What Hiram was—long and dark. What Hiram wasn't—a shortcut, not that she could see. The pleasant wine fog was fading, and she was suddenly aware of how late it was and remembering all the reasons she didn't like to be out alone at this hour. Robin hated being scared, and these situations were ripe for fear. Just when she was about to make a U-turn and return to the highway, the StreetDreams2000 interrupted her fear with a reassurance:

"In three-tenths of a mile, turn right onto Sterling Street."

Progress. She knew Sterling Street, or at least knew one end of it. She imagined she had to be at the far opposite end now, but her internal navigation wasn't great, so she trusted the GPS and turned right. The darkness ahead and lights in the rearview mirror made her second-guess this immediately, but the GPS voice told her "Continue to follow the road" and she figured the only thing you could do to make a bad short-cut worse was to deviate from the new plan.

She made a left turn on South Ballanger, and then another right, and she had the idea that the GPS was doing the same thing it had done to shave four minutes off her drive to work—cheat by cutting through residential neighborhoods. That relaxed her, as it was already a proven technique.

"Turn right onto Sampson's Ferry Road."

She'd been driving for twenty minutes now on a trip that should take no more than that, and she no longer recognized anything. Maybe it was time to give up on the genius of the StreetDreams and double back to Sterling Road. The only problem with that was that she was no longer certain *how* to double back. The route to get here had been convoluted. The iPhone had a GPS option but she didn't like the idea of driving and using her phone, and she certainly didn't want to pull over in this dark stretch of desolate road to play with her phone. It looked like she was driving down the streets of a neighborhood that hadn't been built yet, the pavement fresh but the lots on either side empty. Not a streetlight in sight.

"In five hundred feet, bear left."

Bear left? There was no place to go. The road dead-ended, and now she saw that it was exactly what she'd suspected—an unrealized residential development carved into what had once been farmland. Her headlights were shining on a large lot map and a sign that boasted DREAM HOMES STARTING AT $400,000, COMING NEXT YEAR!

They were still selling lots, but no construction had taken place. The sign looked old and dirty, too, and she wondered whether next year had really meant *this* year or even *last* year and the development plan collapsed beneath the real estate market and the economy. Regardless, she needed to figure her way back out of these winding roads.

She pulled onto the hard-packed dirt and gravel to turn around. Ahead of her a weathered, decrepit barn loomed against the night sky like a discarded set item from a B-movie horror flick, and the British voice said, "You have arrived at your destination. Welcome home."

"This is not *home,*" she snapped as she put the car into reverse, and then she paused before pressing down on the accelerator, struck by a sudden, alarming realization: this had never been home for anyone. Even if the GPS was a secondhand gift, as she'd suspected, no one would have programmed an empty lot in an undeveloped neighborhood into it as their home address.

Something moved in the rearview mirror then. A ripple of shadow, and Robin screamed, a sound so loud and high and hysterical that she couldn't believe it had come from her.

And all for nothing, too. Because the shadow was gone. She stared in the mirror and saw nothing but empty black fields, and ahead nothing but that weathered sign boasting of unbuilt dream homes, and she knew that it was time to get the hell out of here because she was starting to get scared, really scared, and Robin had led an overly cautious life for many years rooted in one simple principle: she hated to be scared.

Now the time had come to admit two things—she was scared to stay here, and, for a completely irrational reason, she was scared of the GPS. She didn't like the way she blindly, dumbly trusted it, and four minutes saved going to and from work each day wouldn't mean much if it led her down the wrong street sometime. An empty, dark street.

A street like this.

She put the car in park, grabbed the GPS, and—after one careful glance in the mirror and then out the window to her left, making sure that the moving shadow had indeed been her imagination, she stepped out of the vehicle, walked to the back of the car, and heaved the GPS as far as she could into the darkness. She got some distance on it, more than she'd expected—fear was fuel, evidently.

"I'll find my own way from now on, thanks," she said when it landed in the distant weeds, and then she turned back to her car for the last time in her life.

Police found the car in the same position the next day—door open, engine still running, though the low-fuel light was on by then. Robin's body, what was left of it, lay some six feet away.

Her boyfriend told police he had no idea what she was doing in that empty maze of streets at midnight, so far from her home, and everyone they interviewed assured them that Robin was not one to take shortcuts or try new routes home. She'd been driven there, they insisted, kidnapped and forced into the abandoned area; there was absolutely no other explanation.

Motives were hard to come by. Her purse remained in the car, untouched. The only thing they could say was missing for sure was a GPS unit, but the boyfriend confessed that it couldn't have been worth much, as he'd picked it up for $40 on the afternoon of her birthday, a panic gift because he'd forgotten that it *was* her birthday. If it had been a botched robbery attempt, they'd have been better off with the car or the purse.

For a time there was some hope that her final movements could be tracked using the GPS, and possibly the killer even located through it, if it was still on and putting out a signal. But David, the boyfriend, had no corresponding paperwork or serial numbers and couldn't even recall the brand. It wasn't one of the common names, he said. Just some generic rip-off. A pawnshop special.

Two weeks later, David having been cleared through witness accounts and autopsy time of death, the police had no suspects in the homicide.

At first Riley didn't even recognize it as a GPS.

It just looked like the corner of a black plastic rectangle that someone had wedged between a busty Power Girl action figure and a Cthulhu plushy doll on the toy rack in the back of the comic book shop.

Could be Star Trek memorabilia that somebody left behind, he thought with idle disinterest as he moved through the shelves. *A replica phaser or something.* He was too busy to investigate at the moment and figured it belonged to Carmen—Riley's sole employee. Carmen was the weekend guy, and he was always messing up back orders and leaving Jolt Cola cans and other crap all over the place. Riley liked Carmen though, particularly because Carmen took most of his paycheck in store credit.

Only after a lunch of jalapeño-flavored ramen did Riley find time to give the imposter item a second look. This time he shoveled the Power Girl figure—in her glossy clamshell packaging—aside and reached for the suspicious black square.

Strangely, it wasn't a toy, or a statuette, or anything else related to *Star Trek, Firefly,* or *Battlestar Galactica.*

It was a GPS.

Wonder who left this here? Riley thought, pushing the only visible button on the device. The GPS powered on and its screen flickered before showing a cartoony image of a moon with a human face gazing down at a long cobblestone street below.

The moon's face smiled and winked, as if it was holding some secret knowledge, and a moment later the text scrolled by:

The StreetDreams2000.

Riley knew the onslaught of new-comic-release-day customers would be in any moment, demanding their comic books, so he headed back behind the counter and placed the device next to the register. As the afternoon regulars filed in to pick up their issue pulls, Riley questioned each one about the GPS, but no one seemed to know anything about it. He was pleased—for once—when Carmen finally pushed his way into the shop seeking out his pulls for the week.

"My comics in yet?" Carmen asked, flipping a long shank of greasy black hair out of his eyes. Just a few years ago, Carmen had been a bassist for a number of speed-metal bands, including FightZombies, an infamous group that went on to minor fame (sans Carmen) by touring various dives, barns, and house parties all the way from north Georgia to West Virginia.

"Yes," Riley said, gathering up Carmen's pulls and sliding them across the counter. Carmen's selection of comics was rather eclectic: on top was his run-of-the-mill Marvel stuff, but underneath, carefully hidden inside a paper bag, were his hentai manga, Japanese comics that featured busty women having sex with large penis-shaped robots and tentacle beasts with hundreds of eyes. Riley never understood the fetish and rarely asked about it. "Here you go."

Carmen nodded, thumped his fist flat on the counter, and turned to leave. "Thanks, chief."

"Wait, before you go, I've got to ask you something." Riley pulled the

GPS from behind the counter and offered it to Carmen for inspection. "This yours? Or do you know if someone left it here over the weekend?"

Carmen squinted, and his eyes became ferrety slits. "Naw." He shook his head slowly. "Definitely ain't mine. Don't think anybody left it here either."

"Not even one of the guys from the Yu-Gi-Oh tournament?"

"Uh-uh."

"You sure?"

"Positive." Carmen leaned heavily on the glass counter—a habit that annoyed Riley to no end. All he needed was for Carmen to shatter the glass and impale himself upon the upraised sword of the Red Sonja statuette below—

"What did I tell you about leaning on the counter?"

"Sorry." Carmen stepped back and leaned against a shelf of newly arrived comics instead. "It doesn't look like a normal GPS to me."

"You know anything about them?"

Carmen seemed to think about that, his eyes going wide as he scratched at a crusty brown stain on the *Dr. Who* T-shirt underneath his biker jacket. "I don't know. I mean, I read about them in *Consumer Reports*—"

"Really?"

"Yeah, *really*. I was looking for a dashboard-mounted GPS for the van a while back. You know, for touring and whatnot. Read a bunch of reviews for TomTom and Magellan and shit." Carmen pointed at the StreetDreams2000. "Never seen that one before. Must be some flea market brand."

Riley glanced down at the sleek unit and its bright screensaver, which continued to flash the StreetDreams logo over a digitized background of plump clouds. "I don't know. Seems like it's pretty high quality to me."

"Whatever." Carmen shrugged and peeked into his paper bag, the one containing his X-rated import comics. For a fleeting moment one of the covers was visible and Riley saw a bright red nipple being tweaked by suction-cupped fingertips. Carmen interrupted Riley's gaze with a question: "What are you going to do with it?"

"Keep it behind the desk and see if anyone asks for it, I guess."

"Well, somebody obviously left the thing here; you don't just *accidentally* carry that thing in from your car and drop it behind some comics. Nobody is coming back for it. Just keep the thing. Or better yet, sell it to a pawnshop."

"I'm not selling it."

"Give it to someone special, then," Carmen said. "Free gift. And with Valentine's Day on the way."

"Yeah, right."

Riley didn't have a girlfriend, but neither did Carmen, so why it bothered him so much, he couldn't say. It just did.

"One of our best shopping weeks," Carmen continued. "Every hopeless sad sack will come in here and blow money on comics because they sure as shit can't blow it on roses or lingerie, am I right? Hell, it's like Christmas in this business, it's like—"

"Shut up," Riley said. "Carmen, just shut the hell up."

"Suit yourself," Carmen said, indifferent to his anger, now staring blankly at the GPS again. "I would dump that thing, though. It's almost like someone was *trying* to get rid of it."

Riley finished up his evening close-out ritual by counting the till, boxing up a modest pile of old role-playing game books, and then pulling down the window shutters. Just before heading out for good, he stopped and looked at the StreetDreams2000, which was still flashing its hypnotic screensaver.

Incredible battery life that thing has, he thought.

He knew that the right thing to do would be to hold the GPS in the shop for a few days at least. See if a customer maybe came back in to reclaim it. Riley knew what it was like to lose something important and then feel that immense rush of calm when you recognized it was in the hands of a Good Samaritan all along. It was the righteous thing. A heroic thing. The kind of noble action that builds a customer base.

Still, he'd always wanted a GPS, but never truly felt the need to buy one. His life didn't warrant such a device. He barely ever went anywhere that required directions, and everywhere important in his world was within a fifty-mile radius of his house. His stirring social life consisted of driving to and from his shop, visiting his mother in Norcross on the weekends, and maybe catching a LAN party with the guys over at the Strategist.

It wasn't a new, adult monotony. The monotony of his youth had been similar—unless punctured by bullying or rejection. He'd always been the weirdo, and mostly that settled on his looks. In middle school, his peers had nicknamed him "Pug" because of his flat, sloping cranium, bulging eyes, and pert, upturned nose.

Things didn't change much in high school, not until he fell deeper into his love of superheroes, Hammer Horror flicks, and *Star Trek*. Eventually he found friends—fellow geeks with equally interesting nicknames—and they spent every waking hour together in the camaraderie of shared fanboy obsessions. This allowed them to block out the rest of the social universe. Their geeky interests became a fortress of solitude, a self-governing civilization complete with its own lexicon, social cues, and inside jokes.

Everyone else moved on after high school, going on to Georgia Tech or schools out of state. Riley had never been a stellar student and so he didn't follow his friends to college. The next year was hard. With his universe of fellow geeks moved on he wasn't sure what to do with himself. The nearest comic book shop was twenty miles away, and it mostly catered to little kids playing Pokémon. He'd lost his friends, lost his wonderful cocoon made up of back issues of Alan Moore's *Swamp Thing* and piles of twenty-sided dice.

Then he figured out a way to stay a fanboy forever: he looked at a map of comic book stores around Georgia and found an underserviced area. Then he scraped together enough family money to move to Winder and open Kingdom Comics. That was ten years ago.

At first it worked. Kingdom Comics made him feel vindicated.

I'm not Pug anymore, he would think. *I've built my own world. I can live out the rest of my days surrounded by people just like me.*

But now, as he edged toward thirty-two, he recognized the chief limitations of his chosen profession: money. Over the years he watched as his high school friends' lives grew with new families and bigger houses. For Riley, every last dollar went to keeping Kingdom Comics alive. He felt like he didn't even have enough money to take a girl on a date (if she would've gone in the first place), and his lack of funds certainly removed the possibility of any vacations, new cars, or pricey gadgets.

Riley gritted his teeth and snatched the StreetDreams2000 off the counter.

Fuck it, he thought. *Maybe this one is for me.*

THAT NIGHT, IN his ancient Nissan Sentra, he played with his new toy. The StreetDreams2000 was shedding LED light, illuminating the dangling, tentlike felt ceiling of Riley's disheveled car. Usually the shabby interior would've bothered him. It was a visceral reminder of just one more thing in his life that was mediocre, imperfect, or just plain crappy. But for once, he didn't care, because today he had the StreetDreams2000. He was staring intently down at the GPS, playing with the settings, changing its voice to that of a Finnish man with a deep baritone, then a throaty woman speaking Magyar, and finally he settled upon the voice of a pixielike British woman who sounded part secret agent, part phone sex worker.

The voice controls were remarkable. It seemed to pick up on every word you said, no matter how rushed they came, or what accent you used on them. One setting option said: LET ME GET TO KNOW YOU. Riley grinned at that. Getting to know a GPS? Whatever.

"Get to know me," he said.

A moment later the British voice uttered back to him: "Hello, User1. What is your name?"

"Riley."

"Good to meet you, Riley," the StreetDreams2000 said. "What would you like to do today?"

He sat in silence for a moment, unsure of how to answer. *It seemed like an odd question,* he thought. *Almost open-ended, at least from the tone.*

"Are you asking for an address?"

"An address or a location of your desire." The GPS seemed to pause for a moment, before adding—he swore with a slight flirtation: "If you can dream it, we can get you there."

Riley grinned a bit and decided to play along. He had had a lot of fun messing around with a customer's iPhone Siri, and the StreetDreams2000 seemed like yet another opportunity to mix it up with a feisty artificial intelligence.

"I'm hungry," Riley said.

"Hungry for *what,* Riley?"

It was better than Siri. Better than anything of that kind. He decided to screw with it a bit more, see how much it *really* understood.

"The best fucking fish tacos in Georgia," he said.

"The best fucking fish tacos in Georgia," the StreetDreams2000 repeated, not missing a beat. "That would be Restaurante Del Mundo, 16778 Akers Boulevard, Atlanta. Would you like me to ready your directions?"

AFTER ROUGHLY AN hour of following the StreetDreams2000's sweet, dulcet-toned commands, he found himself at Restaurante Del Mundo, a small pueblo-styled building out on I-20. When he went inside, the restaurant looked barely open: unfinished drywall, a few tables and chairs, a counter, and a register. Not even a posted menu. The grand opening was a few weeks away. How in the hell had the GPS determined *this* was the place for fish tacos?

The owners, a stocky husband and wife duo, stomped out from in back and seemed perplexed but genuinely glad to see Riley. He tried to leave, but they insisted that since he'd gone out of his way to find them, they'd cook for him. After a bit, they came back from the kitchen with a big plate of fish tacos. The food was unbelievable. The fish tasted fresh and lightly seasoned, and the tortillas were warm and soft without being overly doughy.

Yup, he thought, licking fresh pico de gallo from his fingers. *These are the best fish tacos I've ever tasted.*

After he'd finished what easily might have been the best meal of his entire life, the owners asked Riley how he'd found about them.

"Honestly?" Riley said, smiling crookedly and fidgeting with his napkin. The truth felt embarrassing. "My GPS brought me here."

The owners seemed shocked. According to them, Restaurante Del Mundo hadn't even officially opened yet and wasn't in any phone book.

"We want to get a, what do you call it? MyFace page. And on the Google. But we have not yet."

"Well," Riley said, "maybe somebody is giving you a hand with that, and you just don't know it."

When he hopped back in the car, he grinned wryly at the GPS perched on his dashboard.

"So you've got magic powers, right?" he said. "How else would you know about this place?"

The GPS didn't answer him. Instead, the screen flashed back to a current road map and that sexy voice chirped: "Next destination, please."

"Take me to the best comic book shop in Georgia," he said and then immediately regretted asking the question. He didn't want to hear the truth—would rather hear a lie: that it was Kingdom Comics. But he knew that wasn't the truth. He had worked incredibly hard on his store, kept it well stocked and solidly organized, but it wasn't the best. He knew that. But part of him just wanted to feel like he'd really accomplished something.

Pug from high school might've gone out and started a mediocre comic shop, he always thought. *But not me. I built something great.*

The GPS was about to pass judgment on that, though, and Riley knew he shouldn't have asked.

"The best comic book shop in Georgia," the StreetDreams2000 said. "That would be Oxford Comics, 2855 Piedmont Road NE, Atlanta. Would you like me to ready your directions?"

"No. And Oxford Comics can kiss my ass."

Silence lingered in the air, but then there was a faint whining sound, coming from somewhere unidentifiable. He wondered if maybe it was the GPS or perhaps just his worsening tinnitus from all that Pantera played in his youth.

Oxford fucking Comics, he thought. It wasn't just that Kingdom

Comics wasn't the best—rather it was the fact that despite Riley's best efforts it still wasn't the best. He was a loser. Couldn't succeed at anything. Couldn't build a successful comic book shop. Couldn't find a woman to love. Was still Pug, after all these years. Still the kid from countless confrontations with jocks in the hallway who pushed him up against lockers or spilled his backpack over, dumping his character sheets, *Dungeon Master's Guide* and *Monstrous Compendiums* all over the ground. "Fetch it, Pug!" they'd say, laughing and shoving him to the linoleum floor. "Fetch!"

Pug was a loser. Pug hadn't achieved anything, hadn't built something important with Kingdom Comics. Instead he'd forged a prison from which he could never escape—

"I'm not Pug anymore," he said, aloud, feeling stupid as soon as the words hit the air.

"Pug is not a known address or location," the StreetDreams2000 said. "Please repeat."

He didn't respond to the request. His temples were starting to hurt—aching from grinding his teeth. It grew uncomfortably quiet in the car again, but the StreetDreams2000 broke the silence with a single question: "Where would you like to go, Riley?"

"I don't know. Okay?" He squeezed the faded steering wheel until his knuckles ached. "Stop fucking asking."

"'I don't know' is not a known address or location," the StreetDreams2000 said. "Please repeat."

"Stop fucking asking me!"

"'Stop fucking asking me' is not a known address or location," it said, but this time the tone sounded different. Almost annoyed. "Please offer a valid destination request."

"I don't—whatever—" Riley sighed loudly, frustrated. "Just take me home."

The GPS didn't answer. Not immediately. Instead it seemed to pause, as if thinking, before saying softly: "If you can dream it, we can take you there."

Riley's eyes welled with tears, and he couldn't even explain why. Maybe it was the way the StreetDreams2000 was talking now, as if this cold A.I. really cared about him and wanted to deliver him to the location of his dreams. Maybe it was because no voice so kind had reached him from a human face in years. Fuck years, *hadn't reached him from a human voice in his whole goddamn life*. He was crying now, how pathetic was that, sobbing into his palms, the tears dripping between his fingertips.

"Take me home," Riley said, before whispering: "Take me to someone who loves me."

"Calculating your route, Riley. Calculating your route."

Thirty minutes later he was driving through a downpour, listening to bad wipers squeak across the windshield.

Need to get those replaced, he thought, brain still foggy with tears and emotion. *They're a driving hazard.*

"In 10.6 miles, take Exit 29E—Sandy Plains Road."

Part of him recognized how crazy this all felt. He was following the soft, cooing directions of a GPS that seemed able to magically find any location that he desired. Now it was taking him to someone who would love him? What in the hell was he following this thing for?

Because if it's half as good as those tacos . . . he thought, and managed a laugh. What the fuck did it matter? He had a full tank of gas and, as usual, nobody was waiting on him.

The StreetDreams2000 clearly didn't share his mirth. Her voice was hard now. All business: "In one mile, turn right onto Hiram Avenue."

He was thankful that Hiram still looked like civilization to him, albeit a civilization wreathed in a thick Scottish fog. Riley leaned forward and squinted, trying desperately to see anything beyond his windshield. He couldn't help but imagine misshapen creatures hiding in the shadows. One too many comic books. Or ten thousand too many.

"In three-tenths of a mile, turn right onto Sterling Street."

He followed the orders and the fog gradually broke, and Riley was relieved to see a series of housing developments—the expensive kind that he'd never be able to buy into. But the next set of directions gradually took him deeper and deeper into territory devoid of streetlights or finished construction.

"Turn right onto Sampson's Ferry Road."

This next turn brought him over a hill and onto a gravel road that shook his Nissan's ailing suspension. Riley gazed around and realized that he was deep in the middle of nowhere. Time to give up on the StreetDreams.

He was just about to turn around when the GPS barked another order at him:

"In five hundred feet, bear left."

From what he could tell, the gravel path seemed to cut out here, stopping at the end of the field.

"Bear left," the StreetDreams2000 said, its polite British voice suddenly sounding a bit petulant.

He paused, considering what to do next, and his headlights illuminated the empty fields and a sign promising dream homes to come.

That was it? The GPS thought this was funny? Riley wanted to find someone who loved him, and in answer the GPS took him to a place where nobody lived?

"You're a prick," he told the device.

"Riley, please bear left." A pause, then, "Trust me, Riley. Bear left."

To the left he saw a gravel track leading into the empty lots, mounds of dirt pushed to the side from back when they'd hoped to break ground on a neighborhood that had never come to life.

You can still turn around, he thought. *There's nothing here for you.*

"Riley." The StreetDreams2000's voice sounded soft and forgiving again. "Riley. Bear left."

He spun the wheel and his tires sputtered over the grass as he pulled onto the dirt road. The next stretch took him a few hundred feet, around one of those dirt mounds, toward sharp hills that were cradled with dense woods. There was an ancient barn practically clinging to the side of a steep hill; contorted tree limbs had grown through holes in the walls, and the wooden branches cradled the building like wretched hands. Riley pumped the brakes and his car rolled to a stop, engine sputtering.

"Some GeekSquad programmer is going to pay for this shit," he said. "Somebody thinks this is funny? I'm going to get my money back tomorrow."

But of course he wasn't. He had no receipt, nor even an idea of where the crazy GPS came from. Nobody to blame. So he'd go home and *find* someone to blame.

I wonder if some dickhead customer thought this was funny, and actually meant it for me, he considered for the first time. *If they're listening to me and laughing right now—I swear to God, if I find out someone has been listening to me sit in my car and cry, they are going to see a new version of me, a side they can't even imagine. I will tear their arms right off their smartass bodies . . .*

That required getting home, though. And how in the hell did he get home from here?

Maybe the GPS still would do *that* much for him. Maybe if he just put in the address, the obnoxious piece of shit on the dashboard would get him out of this downpour and back into his basement with some Chinese food on the way. Even if it was laughing at him.

"New destination," he said, trying to make his voice hard, badass even, no more of the teary-eyed shit.

"You've arrived at your destination, Riley."

"Like hell I have. Address. New address. New destination. *Now.*"

"Where would you like to go?"

"Home! I want to go *home*!"

The StreetDreams2000 spoke again, the last words Riley ever heard: "You *are* home, Pug."

Deputy David Watts had been in Harvest Moon Farms three times in his first five years with the sheriff's department—once to break up a keg party, once at the report of someone setting off fireworks, and once following a drunk driver who'd turned into the hopeless swirl of circular lanes in an attempt to evade police, unaware that there was only one entrance and exit. The squad cars had parked there and waited for him to complete a high-speed series of turns, delighting himself by losing their lights, only to be hit with them again when he emerged back at the front. That had been some pretty funny shit.

Now Watts had been in the unfinished neighborhood twice in a month, both for homicide victims.

The place had never struck him as spooky before. Just sad. All those roads leading to nowhere and nothing. They had names and signs, they had parcels on file with the county, they had everything except a reason for existing. The developer had gone bankrupt at the start of the recession, and in this housing market, nobody was eager to absorb the project. It was too big, too expensive, and too pointless—houses were cheap in Atlanta right now, you could get into decent areas for a decent price, and the planned development was simply a poor location, an extra five minutes from anywhere you'd possibly want to be. Five minutes didn't sound like much, but they added up over time.

Now, though, it was A Big Fucking Deal Crime Scene, and that meant, as it always did, that Deputy Watts was on the bench. He'd found the first body, and now they were up to two, and the fun thing about that was they'd put his boss on the bench, too. Chief Deputy Swanson, aka Fish Sticks, always so happy to take the glory, was a forgotten memory of the investigation now, and that pleased Watts to no end. The Georgia State Police and the FBI were both at the scene, the big-dick contest was swinging between them now, and Fish Sticks couldn't do a damn thing about it but watch and pout. At least Watts had no delusions of grandeur; he was used to this shit and, frankly, preferred to be out of the spotlight, because the only time the spotlight found him, it tended to be when he'd fucked something up, like getting caught running his lights and siren just to go to Arby's.

Today's assignment, then, was right up his alley: wander around the neighborhood while the hotshots worked the scene, pretending to be on the search for evidence. As if there would be evidence a half mile away, hiding out in the weeds. Well, maybe there could be, but it was a safe bet that Watts wouldn't recognize it if he saw it. The only place that looked halfway interesting was the creepy old barn, but of course the evidence techs had claimed that, and the local deputies were supposed to conduct a "field search of the perimeter." Which meant, of course, that they were instructed to go wandering around aimlessly.

They sent him away from the main scene, out to search though they didn't tell him what he was searching for. It had rained two nights in a row and the place was a mud bog. They'd moved a hell of a lot of earth out here without ever so much as digging a basement—mounds of dirt stood at the back of most of the lots, beaten down by rain and wind and time. It must have been hilly, once, and they'd cleared the hills in order to make each boring, flat yard look exactly alike. Didn't want any neighborhood jealousy. *Why do they get a hill next door?!*

The place made great sense as a body dump—isolated, hidden, but close enough to the freeway to get out of town fast—but what was strange was the forensics experts kept insisting that the bodies hadn't been dumped here. They hadn't been dead on arrival, just dead *after* arrival. And there was no connection between the victims, one a prim-and-proper office girl, the other a comic book store owner. They'd never met, had no mutual acquaintances, and were so wildly far apart in profile that any theories were hard to come by. Not only that, neither of them had the slightest reason to drive through Harvest Moon Farms, which implied that they'd been coerced there, forced somehow. That had been the prevailing theory, but Watts had just heard that the forensics team was coming up empty—and emphatic—with that research. They were convinced that nobody else had been in the vehicles, that both the man and the woman had driven themselves to the dead end of their own volition.

It was, in Deputy Watts's professional opinion, pretty weird shit.

He would have liked to hang around and listen to the big shots toss their theories about, because this story was getting good play in the newspapers, and pretending he was key to the investigation might get him laid if he talked loud enough in front of that bartender at Chili's who always seemed to give him extra salsa, but instead they had thrown him out here on the search. It was a shitty way to kill a shift, plodding around the empty lots, poking through knee-high weeds and grass, searching for—what? He had no idea. All he found were old beer cans and weathered fast-food bags. And the plastic pipes, of course. Each parcel had been marked off with plastic PVC pipe, orange tape wrapped around it. More heavy duty than the traditional surveyor's stakes, and that was good, someone had really been thinking, because nobody was breaking ground at Harvest Moon Farms.

He stopped at the far corner of the westernmost lot and took a piss and, while in midstream, decided to make it interesting. The empty pipes were there, after all, and why not test your aim? Watts wasn't much good with his duty sidearm, but he was one hell of a piss shot.

SOMEONE WAS PISSING in Odie's living room.

This was a new grievance.

All day long he'd watched the silent computer monitors that showed the activities at the murder scene, and all day long he'd seen that the idiots remained fixated on the wrong place: the barn, the barn, the barn—all the attention went to that pointless old barn, and not once had anyone so much as given a look at the plastic pipes. That was, of course, the point of a lot of tedious work. Odie had placed exactly 320 sawed-off pieces of pipe in the muddy lots of Harvest Moon Farms, each one emblazoned with orange surveyor's tape, and of the 320, only 7 served an actual purpose, bringing air into the bunker. Now someone was taking a piss in one of them. Odie's hand drifted to the Bushmaster AR-15 closest to him—one of sixty-three weapons (sixty-five if you counted the grenades) that he had with him in case the police ever reached the right destination.

No point, though. No need. Years ago, the government had no idea who they were pissing off when they fired Odie from his computer engineering job designing military-grade rescue beacons, similar to the kind that were sold to civilians for use on mountain-climbing expeditions and solo ocean crossings, the kind that would report *exactly* where you were and route emergency messages directly to a bunker in Texas that had been built to outlast anything up to and including a nuclear strike. Now, almost five years later, the government had no idea who they were pissing *on,* and Odie was hardly about to let his grand experiment fall apart in a burst of automatic gunfire directed at the cock of some moronic local cop.

He watched the yellow stream splatter down and then come to a jerking, halting end—prostate trouble?—and finally there was nothing left but a few slow drips on the concrete floor.

He looked at the puddle with distaste, sighed, and shook his head. In time maybe he'd find it funny, but right now it seemed pretty offensive.

It must be growing dark, because on the monitors he could see the evidence technicians setting up spotlights. Pointing the wrong way, of course. Behind them, the entrance to Odie's bunker lay in shadows and beneath thirty feet of compacted soil.

He'd had fun watching them for a time, but it was growing old now, and he was anxious for new visitors. That was the real fun. Harvest Moon Farms was quickly growing a reputation as a body dump, but that wasn't the truth at all. No corpse had ever been brought there and dumped. They'd all come home.

There were two thousand StreetDreams GPS units out there in the world, circulating at first from where he'd left them, eventually making their way through pawnshops and discount electronic stores and online auction sites.

His grand database with its monitoring scripts and sophisticated digital readout told him that nine hundred and ninety-seven units offered current potential. Many were sitting on car dashboards right now, shooting footage through fingernail-sized cameras, capturing audio through tiny microphones, and beaming it all back to Odie's bunker by way of satellite.

He had built each StreetDreams2000 with his bare hands. Odie felt proud of every one of them too. They were his surrogates—sent out into the world to hunt and gather. Over hundreds of hours watching hundreds of potential visitors through his GPS units, he was enormously pleased with the response. Sure, some rejected the StreetDreams2000 right away. They either left it where they found it, sold it, or gave it away. Odie's calculations had suggested that a large number would do exactly that. But many people kept the device—not knowing that Odie's remote eyes and ears were on them the whole time.

Out of this blessed group, Odie could hope for only a small number of candidates to make it here. He was surprised, though, at how easily some would come. Some people apparently were happy to trust the directions that the StreetDreams2000 offered. Others needed more direct coaxing, though, so Odie would get involved remotely, speaking to them through the device, talking them home. Personal attention, after all, was among the most desired qualities in customer service. There was no navigational aid in the world that offered more personal attention than StreetDreams.

But he wanted more visitors. He wondered how many he might see before it was all over. Right now his computers showed four quality candidates—one was a couple driving from Florida back to Indiana, arguing the whole way, the man *insisting* that his wife trust the GPS commands and put away that damned road atlas; Odie thought they could be very intriguing, and he hoped the police were gone before any of them arrived. The police could slow things down, certainly. Put cars out on the road, keep surveillance at the end of Sterling Street, watch and wait.

All of this could have been avoided, of course, if he just hid the bodies, moved the cars, that sort of thing. He'd considered it briefly, but he saw no fun in that sort of game. There was nothing new about it, nothing fresh, nothing that people would remember after he was gone. Now a man sitting comfortably beneath the murder scenes the whole time, watching the dumb-ass cops scour the surface of the earth while the body count continued to climb thanks to the source directly below them? *That* was fresh. That was going to make Odie one of the immortals.

He had enough military-grade MREs (meals ready to eat) for a year and, with all this spring rain, more than enough freshwater filling the cistern to match it. He had his guns, and his computers, and his batteries, and his books. He was in no hurry to go anywhere. Why would he be?

Odie was home.

WHEN WATTS FINISHED with his piss, he zipped up and looked over his shoulder at the team working by the barn. None of them had so much as glanced his way. They didn't give a damn what he was doing out here, as long as he wasn't in their way. He could strip naked and sit in the grass and it would probably be four hours before anybody noticed.

"Taxpayer dollars at work," he said, and laughed though it wasn't funny. He was tired and he was bored and he had hours ahead of him in the cold rain.

He'd wandered about fifty feet before he saw some more junk in the weeds, this time a piece of scrap plastic instead of a fast-food bag. He walked over to it, as if there was some point in studying every bit of trash in the area, and then stopped and frowned. Not scrap plastic at all. It was an electronic gadget of some sort.

He knelt, moisture soaking the knee of his pants immediately, and picked it up and turned it over.

StreetDreams2000.

A GPS unit. Shit. This actually mattered. This actually might matter. The girl who'd been killed, her boyfriend had insisted that she'd been robbed of a GPS unit, and they'd never found the thing.

"Probably not the same one," Watts said, but he wasn't confident. It damn well might be the same one, and that meant he could go back to those assholes at the barn and show them that he was the only one out here who'd achieved anything, show them that . . .

"*Shit,*" he said, and stopped walking abruptly. He was holding the device in both hands, had turned it over to inspect it and then started carrying it along, held by all ten of his ungloved fingers. "You dumbass," he whispered.

This was going to piss them off. He would hear holy hell about this, and even old Fish Sticks himself would get in the mix, because bitching at Watts remained within his jurisdiction, even if nothing else did. They'd all pile on him for tainting evidence, and, hell, he'd probably end up in the papers. Probably put a picture of him up, with some sort of headline announcing what a dumbass he was, and what if his girl at Chili's saw that?

Drop it, then. Just drop it back down and pretend he'd done it right, go over to the barn and tell them he'd found something of possible evidentiary value. That was the term. He'd say it all casual and cool and they'd expect nothing until he led them over here and showed them what exactly it was. Nobody would need to know how stupid he'd been.

Until they ran the fingerprints. He was a dumbass squared now, his fix-it plan even worse than the first mistake.

What to do, then? Hide it again? Someone would find it eventually, and if they got a print off it and it came back to him, he'd not only be in trouble, he might be mistaken for a suspect.

That sent an uneasy chill down his spine. He'd been the first officer out here the day the woman was killed. They *could* look at him as a suspect.

He stared down at the device and pressed the power button, as if it would somehow provide him with an answer. The screen lit up and a moon winked at him. He powered it down immediately—for some crazy reason he didn't like the way the moon had winked like that. Almost as if it knew he was in trouble.

"I need to get rid of this thing," he muttered. That was the only option that didn't end with him getting his ass reamed.

It was small enough to fit in his pocket. He walked back to his cruiser and opened the door and shoved it under the seat. When he got off shift, he'd smash it up and toss it in a Dumpster somewhere.

IT WAS THREE more hours in the rain before they let him go, and he intended to get rid of the GPS right away, but Chili's was on his route home, and he swung in just to see if the cute bartender was there.

She was. Not only was she there, but she wanted to talk, and the bar was basically empty, just the two of them in conversation as the waiters came and went.

"Why so quiet tonight?" he said.

"Not many people want to sit at the bar at Chili's on Valentine's Day."

"Shit, I didn't even realize."

She gave him a sad smile, and she looked even prettier because it was sad, somehow. "Not many people want to work at the bar, either. Everyone else has a date, right? Well, not me. No roses, no chocolates. Not even a card." She gave a little laugh and said, "It's a dumb holiday, anyway, but it would be nice to get something on it. From someone."

"That's why I'm here," Watts said.

"Oh, yeah? So where's my gift?" She was teasing him, obviously joking around, but still it was the closest to true flirtation he'd gotten from her, and it was then that he had his epiphany. He had a gift for her, and he could even be slick giving it to her. He could say something cool, by God, and slick, cool lines were scarce for Watts.

"I'll go get it," he said, trying to sound nonchalant.

He jogged out in the rain and grabbed the GPS from his cruiser and carried it back in. She looked at it with one eyebrow raised.

"Um, not even wrapped. You seriously just pulled that thing off your dashboard and carried it in here and expected me to believe it was a gift?"

And here it was, the opportunity for the slick line, please, please, let it work.

"If it's wrapped," he said, "you can't use it to find my place very well, can you?"

She smiled. Hesitantly, maybe, but she *smiled,* and then she reached out and took the GPS.

"You're serious?"

"Of course. Will you come by?"

She was eyeing the GPS warily.

"If you don't like it," he said, "I can write out directions. Or just give you my number. Maybe it was a dumb idea. Sorry. Maybe—"

Backfired, he thought, reaching for the GPS now and feeling like an idiot, realizing all the ways in which this was wrong, but she pulled back from him.

"I love it," she said. "That's a sweet way to ask."

Holy shit.

He'd scored. He sat back on his stool and hoped his grin wasn't too goofy.

"I just might." She pressed the power button with one red-polished fingernail, and the screen filled with its winking moon face. Now it didn't seem hostile to Watts at all. It was a buddy to him, a lifeline. "That was a totally sweet way to give a girl a Valentine."

"Welcome to the StreetDreams2000," the device said in a British accent. "And Happy Valentine's Day. Where would you like to go today?"

For a moment they were both frozen, and then she started to laugh, so he did, too.

"How did you program it to say that?"

"I'm slick like that," Watts said, and he had a feeling he was going to be getting more than a little extra salsa tonight. Tonight was going his way. To think of the trouble he'd be in right now if he'd handed that thing over to the evidence techs, and instead, look at him now. It felt like there'd been someone watching over him today, and right now, whoever it was? He had to be smiling.

No question about that.

SISTERS BEFORE MISTERS

Sarah Rees Brennan, Cassandra Clare, and Holly Black

In the midst of a wild forest, at the edge of what had once been a town and was now ivy-bound ruins, there was a cave. In that cave lived three witches.

They were witches bound to the service of a dark god and the relentless pursuit of evil. They sat from glowing dawn until deepest dusk, gloating over their past evils as they had once gloated over old bones of victims, until the bones had all worn away.

They were sisters, though they could not remember their parents or the days of their childhood. It had been many ages since they made their offerings and bound their souls to the Dark Lord in exchange for power.

The three sisters were called Hibiscus, Clytemnestra, and Scylla.

On any day a traveler might wander into the forest and find them in their accustomed places. Hibiscus sat on a throne of stone and surveyed the ruins with endless satisfaction. Clytemnestra sat in a bower made of evil blooming flowers; her preference was for nightshade.

Scylla liked to sit in a seat she had made of tree roots and the leg bones of long-dead deer, dreaming of romances she had read in books that had long since crumbled away and magazines with hot-pink covers that were no longer produced in their land. Scylla was the silliest of the witches, though her heart was just as black. When she was crossed, she never forgot, and she never forgave, and she never failed to find her victim and visit a hideous punishment on him. It was Scylla who invented boiling people in oil, and she was bitter she had not received any credit for it.

"She's silly because she is the youngest," said Hibiscus of the raven hair and darkest imaginings. She was the eldest and the wisest, and the one who devised all their evil schemes. Hibiscus had toppled kingdoms and turned seas to blood in her time.

"You might think after two thousand years such differentiations would be meaningless," Scylla pointed out, sullenly.

"She sulks because she is the youngest, too," said Hibiscus. "It is the right of the youngest to sulk and the oldest to bully, while the middle sister is left only to complain."

Clytemnestra was not listening. Clytemnestra's special power was over the minds of living things. Once she had made princes dance to their deaths for her amusement, and countless young maidens drown in their own tears.

Now she had a large family of squirrels that she tormented. Currently she was forcing them to produce a play. It was awful torture, as squirrels are not naturally given to dramatics.

"Please, O cruel and glorious mistress," said one squirrel, whom she had gifted with the power of human speech for her own dark purposes. "Might I know what my motivation is in this scene?"

Clytemnestra pointed to a tiny, squirrel-shaped Iron Maiden.

The squirrel bowed his little, furry head. "Understood."

Clytemnestra had not spoken much in the last hundred years, but she always managed to get her point across.

Scylla turned her single eye into the light, making the blue of its iris gleam. It was a part of the bargain with the Dark Lord that the sisters had but one eye between them, though that eye could see into the future and also shoot death rays from its slit pupil.

"One day my prince will come," she mumbled.

"Good," said Hibiscus. "I'm getting awfully tired of squirrel."

The thing about ruins is—as everyone knows—they are often excellent real estate opportunities. And lo, so it was that builders came to the ruins of the old town and began, slowly but surely, to construct a new town on top of it. First came men and women in suits who pointed at things and had servants running before them. Then came the trucks with supplies, the cement mixers and Dumpsters and Porta-Potties. And men, lots of men, who were healthy and loud and who appeared willing to take off their shirts at the slightest provocation.

"They are so very loud," said Hibiscus, playing idly with a vial of a poison so deadly that it not only killed whosoever drank it, but raised them from the dead just to kill them all over again. She sighed. "I miss the quiet. I suppose I will have to do something about that."

"Yes," agreed a squirrel. "The sound of the jackhammer compromises the integrity of our performances." Then, realizing he'd spoken out of turn, he ducked back into the knothole of a tree.

"No, please," said Scylla, who enjoyed sneaking to the edges of the forest and watching the workers. "Please let them be. I like to hear them. And soon we will have a whole town to toy with."

It seemed to Hibiscus, though, that Scylla was less interested in a whole town than one of the workers. He was slender and young, with a mop of corn-yellow hair and eyes the color of a fern and the annoying habit of singing under his breath while he worked. He also appeared to be the son of one of the suited men, although he worked as hard as anyone else. Scylla liked to take the eye all afternoon and peer down at him in the manner of someone who was about to take a captive and torture him until he couldn't remember his own name, but only that he loved her. Which did promise to be amusing.

"Very well," promised Hibiscus, "but I can't speak for Clytemnestra."

"I don't see why not, since she won't speak for herself," groused Scylla, crossing her arms over her chest.

Clytemnestra snorted, then went back to forcing a quartet of foxes to try their paws at acrobatics. It was going about as well as expected.

"Nothing ever changes," Scylla continued. "We never travel. I want to see the great cities and the oceans and the mountains. I want to wear big, sparkly dresses and go to the movies and eat popcorn until my fingers are greasy with butter. I want to be in love, real love, the kind where the boy is conscious."

That seemed ridiculous to Hibiscus, and she complained about it, as oldest sisters are wont to do, but Scylla was not listening. The next day she put on a dress made of silvery spiderwebs woven tightly together, and a sparkling eye patch over the hollow of her right eye, and climbed down from her throne to the forest floor.

When the blond young worker, whose name was Marcus, saw her approach, he thought she was the most beautiful thing he had ever seen. She seemed to glide above the ground, and when she took his hand and led him away from the other workers, he was happy to go. She guided him to a copse in the forest where black flowers grew, and they sat in the grass and exchanged conversation. It had been years since Scylla had talked to anyone but her sisters, but fortunately Marcus was bedazzled by her golden hair and slender figure and seemed to think that her stories of squirrel torture and boiling oil were hilarious fables.

"I have never met anyone like you," he said, taking her hand. "The girls of the village are as dull in comparison as caterpillars to butterflies."

They kissed, and Scylla found his mouth soft and sweet. She wondered if the rest of him would be sweet as well if she cooked him, perhaps in a pot with vegetables.

"Marry me," he breathed.

"I cannot," she said. "For I am bound in service to a dark god, along with my sisters, and I cannot leave them. Without me, they would be blind."

"I know what it is like to have an overly dependent family," Marcus said. "But surely you deserve freedom for yourself?"

She gazed into his green eyes, and her heart melted. "Where would we run to?"

Marcus seemed vague on that topic, but he was clear that they would be very happy there. He wove a wonderful tale of love, and flowers, and more love. Wherever they went, apparently, there would be an excess of beds. Scylla allowed herself to be convinced.

It was clear to her, however, that if she was to venture into pastures new, she would need the eye. Scylla told herself that her sisters would hardly miss it, that they would want her to be happy, that it would be quite funny to take it.

She told herself many things, and they all added up to her stealing away in the middle of the night, away from her sleeping sisters and into her lover's arms.

She did leave a note, but of course her sisters could not read it.

Nevertheless, they soon gathered what Scylla had done.

"I am going to boil that brat until she is nothing but bones and broth, and then I will drink the broth and crunch the bones!" Hibiscus exclaimed.

"What will come of my production?" Clytemnestra asked. "Without my guiding eye, who will see to the costumes? And who will beat the foxes when they miss a step? Everything will be ruined!"

"Not to worry, I rather fancy myself a director," said one of the squirrels, and Clytemnestra gave a low moan of distress.

She was clearly becoming hysterical. This meant Hibiscus had to pull herself together and think. Hibiscus had known her sisters a long time. She did not need to peer into a dark future to know how this latest escapade would end.

"Hush," she said and passed Clytemnestra a live rattlesnake so she could suck on its head. "How does it usually end, when mortals are in our company?"

"Death, pain, madness," said Clytemnestra, her voice slightly muffled around the snake. "More pain. That rash of beheadings. The rain of mad chickens. Oh, and plague, of course. I can't believe I almost forgot plague!"

"Exactly. Patience, my sister," said Hibiscus. "Patience, and then terrible bloody vengeance."

Meanwhile, Marcus and Scylla were walking hand in hand down the street of the next village over. They had not been able to travel far, because Scylla had turned the coachman into a beetle for insolence and stepped on him. Marcus had missed this, being in the privy at the time.

"What a shame the fellow ran off," said Marcus.

Scylla coughed. "Indeed."

Scylla told herself that the course of true love never did run smooth, but she was beginning to think that perhaps her oldest sister was right—as she so often and so irritatingly was—and that men who were conscious were more trouble than they were worth.

Just then, a small and charming tot raced down the street toward them.

"Do you like children?" Marcus asked, sighing a gusty, soppy sigh, like a wet bedsheet hanging in the wind.

"I do," said Scylla, brightening at this evidence of a common interest. "They're very handy for potions, of course, and very juicy and tender after a long day when all you want is a snack."

Marcus looked appalled.

"I also," Scylla offered, after some thought, "enjoy sucking out their youth and innocence and consigning them to eternity as imps in the service of my dark master."

This did not please Marcus any better, and Scylla's black heart sank down to her cruelly pointed shoes. How long can any love last, if the man involved will not accept your true self?

As it turned out, not long.

She could make him forget her misdeeds with a little magic, but she couldn't forget the way he looked at her each time she disappointed him, the fresh horror and the ridiculous shock—as though he'd never seen anyone pull wings off a butterfly before! Or attach them to a mouse! As though it wasn't funny to watch the creature try to get off the ground! It was absurd, the way she had to act around him to make him happy.

And where were they supposed to live? Scylla could get them plenty of money, but Marcus seemed against all her suggestions regarding how she might go about doing that. And when she described her dream of a cottage with a nice little garden of mandrake, deadly nightshade, opium poppies, and a few other necessities, he got very distressed. In fact, Marcus, despite his great beauty, was becoming a bit of a bore.

But the final straw came when she caught him chatting up a shopgirl. She had been in the back, selecting a very fine length of black cloth that she thought would make an adequate wedding dress if she trimmed it out in bat fur, when she spotted Marcus holding a ladder for a blushing girl in the process of shelving soap. The girl told him that her name was Honey. He told her that such a pretty name suited her, being so pretty herself. Scylla was furious—both that she hadn't previously noticed how criminally terrible he was at flirtation and also that he was directing those criminally terrible flirtations toward another girl.

She left with him, pretending that she didn't notice the longing look he shot back toward the shop.

That night, while he slept beside her in their hotel room bed, she plotted her revenge. Perhaps she should change him into a lizard and feed him to a cat. Or maybe she'd curse him to have a limb fall off every six months until he was just a talking head. Or enchant him so that each of his lovers died the moment he kissed her.

In the morning, Marcus was looking glum. "I do not think this thing between us is working out," he said.

"No, it isn't," she agreed. He looked very beautiful in the morning sunlight, very noble and square jawed, and she still admired his cheekbones. "I am so glad you agree."

And she turned him into a pale yellow rabbit. At first the rabbit ran around the courtyard of the hotel a bit, but he was soon calmed with carrots. She tucked him in the bodice of her dress, where his ears hung out a bit, and set off with all speed toward the forest.

When she arrived at her sisters' dwelling place, they were not nearly as agreeable as Marcus had been. They were quite angry, in fact. Furious, even. They explained that after she had gone away and taken their single eye, leaving them to crash blindly around the forest, they had not been able to find food and had been eating rocks and grass, rendering them very unwell. Clytemnestra's play had fallen into ruins—most of the rodent actors had run away, except for a few squirrels and a chipmunk. The chipmunk was directing, but since he did not understand basic plot elements such as foreshadowing and denouement, the play no longer made sense.

Clytemnestra was lying upon the ground.

"Ruined, ruined," she moaned. "It's all ruined. My vision is ruined! And why is it ruined? Because I can't *see*!"

"I don't see why you're complaining," said Hibiscus sadly. "You're not the one who bit into a rock and broke your last tooth."

"I have explained, over and over again," said Clytemnestra, "that actors should be suitable for their roles, that it can't all be about the tortoise action scene, and that removing the climax is a bad idea because stories should have endings!"

"I liked that tooth," muttered Hibiscus.

"Er," said Scylla. "Hi?"

The two sisters, as elder sisters will when faced with the youngest, forgot their differences and began to converge menacingly on the sound of Scylla's voice.

"Sisters," said Scylla. "I am truly sorry. I have learned the error of my ways and I grieve if my actions have caused you any inconvenience! But I have learned a life lesson: that I was dreaming my life away when what I truly wanted was what I had all along: not romance, but being true to myself, being with you, serving our evil master and delighting in the suffering of the innocent. Until now I did not know myself. So you see it was all for the best."

She hastily thrust Marcus into the hands of Clytemnestra. There was an uneasy moment while Clytemnestra looked as if she might be about to eat him, but then she petted his ears and set him among the squirrels, where the chipmunk began to order him to learn lines.

"The eye?" Hibiscus said, warningly.

"Oh, er, yes!" Scylla replied brightly and plucked it from her eye socket. She had never worn it for so long before and felt the darkness descend on her ominously as she stretched out her hand. "Here it is. And I am willing to give up my turn at it for—"

"Your turn? Your turn!" Clytemnestra roared, snatching the eye. "You'll be lucky if you ever have a turn again!"

"That's not fair!" Scylla began. It wasn't like she hadn't brought it back!

"Eminently fair, eminently fair," muttered Hibiscus. "But your punishment must be even more fair than that. I thought about taking your voice, but I do like to hear you prattle on. And I thought about taking your hands, but you can be so useful with them. And I thought about taking your heart before I remembered you'd lost it to that rabbit, so you clearly wouldn't miss it much. But then, then I realized what we must take from you—your feet!"

"My feet?" Scylla shrunk back. "No. They're *my* feet. They're not for sharing." But she felt the sharp bright line of pain across one ankle. She winced. This was going to *hurt*. "Ow!"

"Without feet, you can't run away," said Hibiscus.

"Oh, don't whine, we'll let you have them back sometimes," Clytemnestra told her. "Or bird claws. Or hooves. That is, if you're very, very, very good."

The sisters placed Scylla gently in her accustomed seat of bones and roots. Scylla squawked and sulkily kicked Clytemnestra in the shin with her protruding ankle bone. But even as angry and unhappy as she was to be footless, she had to admit that she had been even more unhappy in town. And once Marcus the rabbit had been placed in her arms, she buried her face in his fur and found she preferred him this way too.

In the end, Scylla stopped missing her feet and learned a valuable lesson about what she truly wanted as compared to what she'd thought and dreamed she wanted, and Hibiscus and Clytemnestra learned how they valued their young sister, by missing her. Also family discipline was upheld through mutilation, which was harsh but fair. The town remained a ruin of ashes and bones brought down by evil, but it had been too late for the townsfolk before this story began.

Even Clytemnestra's play was a success. To the surprise of all, Marcus turned out to be a sensational leading rabbit and was much beloved by all the squirrels.

SINS LIKE SCARLET

Mark Morris and Rio Youers

It began its miserable purple existence nine and a half years ago, a growth in the inner layer of his colon, which—untreated—metastasized into his lymphatic system, internal chest wall, and liver. It was doubtless other places by now. His bones. Maybe his lungs. He'd skipped his last two rounds of chemo, because it was cruel, cold, and pointless: a shot of ugly that left him whimpering at hell's door. The doctors hadn't been hopeful before his few treatments began and told him now that his life expectancy was down to months. He believed them. No reason not to. The blood in the toilet bowl, and in his saliva, delivered a similar prognosis. And his body—once firm and powerful—was now a rawboned rack of hurt. But what the doctors didn't know was that there was an older pain, a *deeper* pain, that he had suffered for many years. He'd lain in machines that had scanned his body, but as far as he knew there was nothing for the soul. Should such a machine exist, the doctors would find his malady: a shadow, worse than any cancer, and shaped like grief.

Allan Strand closed his eyes and fumbled for the hip flask in his pocket. Antique silver, dulled and dented with use, filled with liquid morphine. He unscrewed the cap with buckled fingers and raised the flask to his lips. A single swallow, raspy throat clenching like a fist. Allan groaned and his thin body trembled. He didn't feel relief so much as numbness—the physical pain encased in ice that would melt all too soon. And that deeper, emotional pain . . . still there, but the morphine had lifted hands for him to hide behind.

He smeared blood from his lips and screwed the cap back on the hip flask.

"Though your sins are like scarlet, they shall be as white as snow."

He opened his eyes. The boy was gone.

HE HADN'T SPOKEN to Holly for twenty-five years. Their marriage—once, like him, firm and powerful—had withered to nothing following the murder of their only son. There had been eleven subsequent months of togetherness, each as fragile as eggshells. No lovemaking. No comfort or assurances. They finally separated in the winter of 1987, whereupon Allan's wings had stretched far and wide. He flew his crippled coop to begin a new life in Canada. He'd hoped thirty-five hundred miles would nullify his woes and responsibilities. He was wrong. His pain had spread its wings, too. Some things refused to be left behind.

"Hello."

Holly, it's Allan . . .

He breathed his sickness into the mouthpiece and rubbed a tear from his eye with the heel of his free hand. Her voice awoke memories, both dark and light. So easy to envision the girl he had fallen in love with. Nineteen years old. Green eyes and a line of freckles across her nose, as distinctive as the markings on a cat. The bow in her hair had come untied, and Allan had pulled it free and handed it to her before she lost it. That was how they'd met. She'd taken the ribbon from his hand and twelve years later they stood beside the too-small coffin of their one child with a valley of emptiness between them. Allan would never have believed that silence could be so deep.

"Hello . . . ?"

Holly . . . I have something to tell you.

He opened his sandpaper mouth, not sure that he could speak at all. To utter a single word—even one as innocuous as *hello*—demanded vast courage. He gripped the phone tighter. His throat clicked. He considered hanging up, and in the end didn't have to; Holly beat him to it. The empty line was a different kind of morphine. Old pain slipped sweetly away—temporarily, at least.

There was a copy of yesterday's *Daily Mirror* on the table in front of him. He'd found a convenience store downtown that sold a few British tabloids. They were always a day or two late, but for Allan—who was unfamiliar with the Internet—it was the best way to keep up with the news back home. The paper was open on page seven, where a black-and-white picture and two-column story wavered like smoke, and which he'd inhaled, inducing waves of nausea and despair. It had prompted him to call Holly, even if he hadn't mustered the courage to talk to her. Now he inhaled the story again, the headline: MEADINGHAM MONSTER DIES IN

BROADMOOR, and the picture of a thin man with close-set features and a small, dark mouth. The caption beneath read: *Desmond Grayson—termed the "Meadingham Monster" after killing twelve children in the 1980s—suffered a fatal heart attack in his Broadmoor Hospital room on Thursday. He was sixty-two.* The killer's eyes regarded Allan impassively, as if his sins were unformed, and the blood on his hands could so easily be washed away.

The image unsettled Allan. It always had, and he had seen it thousands of times. It had been splashed across the news throughout Grayson's trial, so synonymous with evil that it had attained cult status. Allan had even seen it printed on posters and T-shirts. Desmond Grayson may have been a diminutive, psychologically frail individual . . . but the media had made him famous.

His victims were aged between six and eleven. He lured them by asking for directions or pretending to look for something he'd dropped, and the moment the children lowered their guards, he grabbed them. He took them to his house, where he raped, tortured, and killed them. Then he dumped their bodies in secluded locations in and around Meadingham. It was a wave of terror that lasted six years, ending on a frosty night just after Christmas of 1989, when Grayson was pulled over for speeding. One of the two officers who spoke to him was sufficiently alerted by his odd behavior to ask him to open his trunk. The bloodstains they found on the upholstery prompted them to take Grayson in for questioning, and twenty-four hours later he had confessed to all twelve murders.

Allan remembered Holly's shock when she first saw Grayson. She had expected a person both imposing and demonic—the stuff of horror movies. But in reality he was well groomed and courteous, and he sat throughout the trial with his hands folded primly in his lap, his voice—on the occasions he spoke—soft and controlled. Holly regarded the child killer with as much disbelief in her heart as hate. *How can someone so normal-looking commit such ungodly crimes?* she had asked. But it wasn't Grayson's appearance that unsettled Allan, so much as the emptiness in his eyes. Did he really feel *nothing*? Was he indifferent to all the blood he had spilled . . . to the small, broken bodies piled behind him?

Thomas—their son—was seven years old. His body was discovered in a dilapidated barn two miles outside Meadingham. Although he had not been raped, he had been stabbed thirty-eight times. His body had been covered in abrasions and bruises. His right arm and neck had been broken. The officer in charge of the murder inquiry, Detective Inspector Lomax, had informed them that it was the broken neck that had killed their son, and that the knife wounds had been inflicted postmortem. The thinking was that Thomas had died from falling down Grayson's basement steps, thus denying the killer his sadistic pleasure. Lomax's tone had been one almost of satisfaction, as if the little boy had bravely and resourcefully outwitted his abductor, but for Allan and Holly, it was the end of everything.

Their togetherness fractured, along with their happiness. Holly's kind and loving heart shattered, and she strayed all too often into a vortex of depression and delirium. She once drove to London with the intention of attacking Grayson as he was ushered from the Old Bailey. Unable to get close, she hurled abuse and pushed ineffectually at the crowd, and in a frenzy she attacked the young PC who tried to restrain her, gouging his cleanly shaven cheek. In the end it took four policemen to wrestle her into a Black Maria, after which she was detained in a cell overnight and issued with a caution, despite the extenuating circumstances. Shortly afterward, she downed a cocktail of lorazepam and vodka and spent the night in Meadingham General having her stomach pumped. Allan wanted to care, but he didn't . . . *couldn't*. The distance between them had grown too vast, and he had problems of his own—this new and terrible illness: a cancer of the soul that struck long before the disease touched his body.

Running a hand down his sunken face, Allan closed the newspaper. He reached for the phone again, dialed the first three numbers, then hung up. Pain rolled through his stomach. His right leg twitched. He coughed—sprayed blood against his bunched fist—and fumbled for his morphine. The hip flask's curves and dents were so familiar that he took comfort from simply holding it. Alas, not enough; he had a callus on his lower lip where he'd so often pressed the collar.

When the pain subsided, he picked up the phone again, dialed Holly's number, then cut the call before the connection could be made. He wept for a long time, albeit silently, the tears rolling down his face and dripping off his chin. Then he tried calling her again . . . still couldn't. Perhaps it would be easier to catch a flight to England and talk to her in person.

His tears had made an impressive puddle on the table. He used the newspaper to mop them up, then turned to page seven and scrawled black X's on the monster's impassive eyes.

TWO DAYS LATER he made the call, not to Holly, but to British Airways reservations. He was going back to England. He was going home.

There was peace in his decision, yet no reprieve from the pain. If anything, the shadow on his soul only grew. He battled through the hours, his fragile body twisted out of shape, cold with sweat. Exhausted, he collapsed on his bed and fell asleep. It was like falling into a box of broken glass. He awoke with a start to the insipid gloom of evening, a half-packed suitcase on the bed next to him, and his dead son, Thomas, standing in the corner.

Seeing him was nothing new. Allan often spotted him in the shadows, or in the corner of his eye, but his visits had become more frequent since the cancer took hold. His son was as fair and beautiful as he had been in life, but disturbingly, uncharacteristically, the little boy was always silent, his staring eyes shining like cold moonlight reflecting off glass. Allan had tried speaking to him, even reaching out to him, but had never received even the merest flicker of a response.

There was only one way to make him disappear.

Allan's hip flask—never far away—was on the bedside table. The dying man snatched it up with a spavined, bird's-claw hand and unscrewed the cap. He pressed the collar to the hard spot on his lip and took a full hit as Thomas stared at him.

He closed his eyes . . . waited.

"Though they are red like crimson, they shall be like wool."

There was a time when Allan had been afraid of flying. Back when life meant something, when it seemed too precious to risk. Now the thought of crashing in flames, of being snuffed out as easily as a bug on a windshield, was almost too much to hope for. It was odd how he clung so tenaciously to the grinding misery of his existence, even while constantly wishing that Fate would intervene and absolve him of all responsibility. He had contemplated suicide, of course, but it was precisely that warped sense of *responsibility* that kept him here. He simply couldn't allow himself the blessed release of ending it all, not when so much remained unfinished. Allan found a bizarre sense of pride in the idea that, whatever he'd been reduced to, he still retained a shred of . . . what? Decency? Humanity?

He barked a laugh, which quickly became a series of rasping coughs that felt as though every tube and passage from his esophagus to his bowel was being dredged with meat hooks. Cupping one hand over his mouth, he used the other to scrabble in his trouser and jacket pockets, hoping to unearth an old tissue or screwed-up handkerchief. He knew that to the hale and hearty his sickness was an affront, a crime against life's optimism and vitality. Knew too that the mucus-clotted blood spattering his palm was the incriminating evidence that would excite a level of attention he could do without. Oh, there would be a ripple of concern shown by his fellow passengers and the air crew, but mostly there would be revulsion, alarm, fear. Post-9/11, a man coughing up blood in an airplane was not merely ill, he was *infected*. Over the past year, Allan had grown weary of telling people that he wasn't contagious; even wearier of their dewy-eyed pity when they found out what was really wrong with him—especially when that pity barely masked their relief that the cancer was devouring *him*, and not *them*.

He was still rooting through his pockets when he spotted the sick bag between his knees, poking out from the pouch affixed to the back of the seat in front. He snatched it out as the young man beside him—whose bronzed skin and sun-bleached hair gave him the illusion of immortality—asked, "You all right, mate?"

Allan barely nodded before half turning away, his scrawny body shielding his actions from the man's curious gaze. He smeared blood from his palm on the stiff paper, then folded it over and dabbed telltale flecks of red from his lips before scrunching the bag into a ball. His bones felt full of ground glass as he pushed himself to his feet, but he managed to scurry down the aisle toward the back of the plane without attracting undue attention. Indeed, the majority of his fellow passengers were too distracted by trivialities—computer games, in-flight movies, banal interviews with soap stars in gossip magazines—to even afford him a second glance. In recent weeks, as mortality had homed in on him, its great black wings beating ever closer, Allan had felt increasingly like an alien observing the pointless actions of another species from afar. He resented and reviled the way so many people passed the time without effect, wiling away their precious lives in increments. But although he felt an urge to rail against their wastefulness, he was aware too of the great tragedy of human existence, which was that death made a mockery of achievement, and that the more a person accumulated in life, the more he or she was set to lose when their once seemingly endless days were scattered like dust.

Relieved to find one of the four toilet cubicles unoccupied, he pushed open the door and slipped inside. Locking the door behind him was like sealing himself into his very own fortress of solitude, in which he was gloriously immune from all interference and contact. The soft roar of the airplane engines lulled him. Indeed, it was comforting to think of himself as a minute, insignificant speck high above the planet, his pain-racked body both perfectly still and hurtling through the sky at hundreds of miles an hour. Still clutching the ball of blood-smeared paper, he lowered the toilet seat and sank slowly down on to it, his joints grinding with hurt as his knees and hips bent at right angles. He closed his eyes and allowed his mind to detach itself from its surroundings. At first it was like tumbling slowly and luxuriously into sleep, and then he became aware that his mind was drifting back through his memories, like a balloon snatched from a child's hand by a capricious wind. Somewhat randomly, the balloon became snagged on the spiny branch of a specific memory in which Allan was fourteen or fifteen. It was a blustery autumn day, and Allan, a keen footballer, had decided to try his luck at the after-school team trials.

There was a girl he liked. Melody? Melanie? His memory of her was vague. She was nothing but a smudged recollection of dark hair, a pretty face. Allan thought she might have been in the year below his.

He wanted to impress this girl—*that* he remembered. And she must have liked him too, because she was prepared to stand huddled in the cold at the side of the pitch on his behalf, hair blowing in the wind, watching the largely disorganized efforts of twenty-two teenage boys with muddy boots and red-raw legs.

Her presence inspired Allan that day. It lent him the energy, dominance, and determination that he too often lacked. He was a decent footballer, but his dad, who'd been a better one, always maintained that his son was too lazy to achieve his full potential.

Allan wasn't lazy this day, though. For these ninety minutes, he was glorious. He bossed the game from midfield. He ran rings around boys who were generally considered stronger and faster and more skillful than he. Although his memories of Melody/Melanie were a blur, he recalled with utter clarity that his team won 6–2 that day, and that he scored two of the goals. He scored one of them from the halfway line. Looking up as the ball was passed wide to him, he saw that the opposing keeper had advanced to the edge of his penalty area. Striking the ball sweetly, he watched it loop over the hapless keeper's head, bounce on the edge of the six-yard box, and nestle in the back of the net.

Although he didn't know it then, this proved to be the pinnacle of his football career. He made the team, but once there he didn't particularly shine. The other boys in the squad—cool, athletic, cliquey—didn't *actively* dislike him, but neither did they welcome him into their ranks with open arms. In the end he either stopped getting picked or drifted away of his own accord—he couldn't remember which. As for Melody/Melanie . . . he had no idea what happened to her. Despite his heroics, he didn't think they had ever dated, though he couldn't remember why. He wondered where she was now, how her life had panned out. Was she happy? Was she still alive? He hoped so.

When he opened his eyes, he was shocked to find tears running down his cheeks. He felt a sense of loss so profound it was like a twist of hot pain at the base of his ribs. When someone tapped lightly on the door, he raised his head slowly, his neck seeming to creak like a rusty hinge.

A woman's voice. "Hello? Are you all right in there?"

Allan cleared his throat, but his voice was still a rasp. "Fine."

"Only you've been in there for quite a while."

"Sorry. I'll be out in a minute."

He pushed the balled-up sick bag into the slot for used paper towels, and then slowly washed his hands, watching as the water in the circular steel basin turned briefly pink before running clear again. He rinsed out his mouth and splashed his face, dabbing at his eyes and wet cheeks with a clean paper towel. He dried his hands and then, as an afterthought, slipped a number of folded paper towels into the inside pocket of his jacket, next to his hip flask. Finally, he flushed the toilet, unlocked the cubicle door, and pulled it open. Two stewardesses stood in the kitchen area sipping water from paper cups. One of them smirked as she glanced at him, as though trying to conceal a laugh, her eyes as blue and glassy as a doll's in her immaculately made-up face.

"Sorry," Allan muttered. "I wasn't feeling too well."

The girl's candy red lips curved in a smile. "That's quite all right, sir. We'll be serving dinner soon. I didn't want you to miss it."

Allan gave a curt nod and turned toward the rows of identical seats, above which the backs of heads roosted like variously hued wigs. He looked down the central aisle, and his scrawny body clenched like a fist.

Thomas was standing beside his empty seat.

Allan could see him quite clearly. His son was no illusion, no accumulation of shadows given wispy form. He was as solid as his surroundings, a small boy in a striped T-shirt and blue shorts, his blond hair reflecting the shine of the reading lights overhead.

He stared blankly at his father, his eyes glazed, his mouth set in a stubborn line. Allan began to tremble. His hand groped in his jacket pocket even as his mind groped for the mantra in his head.

"Though your sins are like scarlet . . ."

His fingers closed around the cold steel of the flask.

" . . . they shall be as white as snow."

He tugged out the flask, fumbling with the cap.

"Though they are red like crimson . . ."

The cap, dislodged, tumbled from his fingers and bounced beneath the seat of a dozing fat woman in a flowery dress, a broken-spined paperback open in her lap.

" . . . they shall be like wool."

As he raised the flask to his calloused lips, trying to hold it steady, he sensed a presence behind him, and heard the gentle clearing of a throat. A soft voice, reasonable, almost apologetic, murmured, "Excuse me, sir, is that alcohol? Because I'm afraid—"

Allan's fear and pain and misery seemed to coalesce, and to transform as they did so into a red flare of anger. Momentarily defying his infirmity, he swung around to confront the air stewardess who had smirked at him seconds before.

"It's morphine, you stupid woman. I have terminal cancer. I've been given special permission to bring this on board. You should have been *informed*."

He hissed out the words, keeping his voice low, but such was his fury that he was peripherally aware of several heads in the nearest rows of seats swiveling to regard him. The stewardess took a step back, her cheeks reddening, her previously immobile face twisting into a moue of dismayed apology.

"Of course, sir, we *were* told. My mistake, I . . . I . . ."

"So you don't *mind* if I make a vain attempt to ease my pain?"

"No, of course not. Please . . . go ahead."

His eyes still fixed on the girl, partly out of anger, though mostly to avoid looking at Thomas, Allan once again raised the flask to his lips. He swallowed, grimaced, felt the morphine shuddering through him, numbing as it went. Without another word to the stewardess he turned and looked along the aisle.

Thomas had gone. But for how long this time? His visits were becoming more frequent.

"Excuse me."

Allan looked to his left. The fat woman was now awake, and looking at him with something like trepidation. She held the cap of his flask between two chubby fingers and a thumb.

"Is this yours?"

Allan took the cap and screwed it back on. The gritty sound it made was like the rasp of his lungs in the silence of night.

"Thank you," he said.

THIS ANCIENT REALM, Allan thought. *This Albion.*

On the surface, England was drab and crumbling. Gray stone, gray clouds. But beneath its skin he sensed a strangeness, a wildness. He felt it as a vibration in the air, pulsing up from the earth itself and tingling in his veins. It was the deep-rooted energy of battles raged and blood spilled. It was witchcraft and paganism, sacrifice and sorcery, dark secrets and forbidden lore. This haunted island was full of ghosts, and Allan felt more attuned to them than he ever had before. They were all around him—in the way people talked, in the smell of the railway carriage, in the undulating fields and woodland that scrolled past the rain-streaked windows.

Allan felt like a husk after his flight—desiccated, cadaverous, so lacking in substance that if it wasn't for the pain holding him together, he thought he might evaporate. He sat in the window seat of a train rattling toward Meadingham, beside a bearded man in a Queens of the Stone Age T-shirt, whose iPod leaked music that sounded like the frantic scratching of a trapped insect. Across from him, a delicately beautiful girl with strawberry-colored hair scowled at a copy of Graham Greene's *The End of the Affair,* as if every word offended her.

A dark shape in a field snagged Allan's attention. When his eyes jerked instinctively toward the window, it felt as if nerves were being tweaked in the sockets of his skull, causing him to bite back a hiss of pain. He couldn't even make sudden movements now without it hurting. He thought again of the carefree boy who had scored a goal from the halfway line and felt a profound sadness wash over him. He was like a stranger, someone who knew the future but couldn't change it. He fought an urge to cry for that boy, for what he would become, and focused instead on the dark shape in the field. Dusk seeped across the land, so the shape was mostly in silhouette, but he could see that it was a boy, standing there alone, out in the cold.

I'm sorry, he thought and reached for his flask, but even as he did so he realized his mistake.

It wasn't a boy at all, it was a standing stone. Yet as the train sped by and the stone receded into the distance, Allan couldn't shake the notion that it really *was* a boy—one who was fractured and alone, and rapidly filling with darkness.

He found a moment of blessed calm after alighting from the train—ten seconds, no more, where the world stopped revolving. Nobody else on the platform. Not a bird in the sky or a leaf skittering along the tracks. Even the train had shuddered out of earshot. Everything was suspended between then and now. He was alone, and it was divine. He breathed air that was only his and cast his gaze on things only he could see. The platform clock was frozen at 13:36, and maybe it would never tick again. His pain, too, had disappeared—a thing of the past, like every other shadow. Allan looked along the platform, at the slightly crooked sign—MEADINGHAM—affixed to the railings.

Home, he thought, and the first half of his life whirled through his mind like dead flowers in the wind. He looked at the tracks stretching into the distance and felt like taking to them himself . . . riding this static, painless moment until the rails faded from beneath his feet. He took a single step toward the edge of the platform, then the world found its motion: all chatter and agitation, impatience and pain. An automated voice announced over the Tannoy that the next train on platform one was the 13:47 to Liverpool. People spilled around Allan too suddenly. He was bumped and barged without apology, almost knocked to the ground by a youth playing with his smartphone. The pain returned, too, as wide and fast as the 13:47 to Liverpool. It journeyed through Allan to all destinations, a rattling thing. He felt the reassuring shape of the flask in his pocket and hastened from the platform, rolling his luggage behind him.

Three taxis idled outside the station. Allan chose the nearest and slumped across the backseat. He breathed hard and smeared pink spittle from his lips. The driver tossed his luggage into the trunk and slammed it closed. Allan thought of Grayson's victims. Faces in the darkness. Thomas stood at the curb and looked at him. His face was pale and beautiful.

Unscrew. Swallow. Gasp.

" . . . shall be like wool."

Gone.

The driver pushed his belly behind the wheel and wheezed. His bloodshot eyes flicked into the rearview mirror.

"Where you going, mate?"

Allan put the flask away—patted his pocket as if it were his heart. He wiped his mouth and sighed. He had planned to go straight to his old house, where Holly still lived. They'd had discussions, prior to their separation, about moving. A new home, a new beginning, without the weight of memories. But it was these memories that Holly clung to—strands of their former, happy life bunched in her fists, and the reason why she lived there to this day. Twenty-six years since Thomas's death, and Allan wondered if she had changed his bedroom at all. Were his little gray socks still balled up in the top drawer? The same box of toys in the corner? The same posters—*Back to the Future* and *Bananaman*—stuck to the walls with the same little blobs of Blu-Tack? Allan shook his head. *This is going to be more difficult than I ever feared,* he thought.

"The meter's running, mate," the taxi driver said. His eyes, reflected in the mirror, were narrow pink slits. Perhaps he'd noticed, only now, just how sick Allan was.

"Colvin Road," Allan croaked, and wondered if his own eyes were black X's. The taxi pulled away from the station with a jerk, and Allan heard his luggage shift in the trunk—thud against the upholstery. He turned from the mirror and viewed this ancient realm through the rain-blurred window.

HOW COULD HE hope to confront Holly without first confronting himself? Allan had spent the first eighteen years of his life on Colvin Road, in a semidetached council house with cold walls and blind windows. He got out of the taxi, wincing at the pain, and looked at the place he had called home for so long. The windows had been double glazed and its pebble-dash façade covered with a skin of clean brickwork. There was more color in the garden, too—chrysanthemums and peonies that never would have survived in Allan's era. He felt, again, the importance of nurture, and the darkness that can seep in without it.

How dark are you now?

He considered the cancer running through his body, like a thousand children flying a thousand black kites. He closed his eyes and felt the shadow on his soul. It had claws, but no hands. It had teeth, but no mouth. Sometimes he felt it shift inside him, like an eel in dirty water.

The memories were here. Some had never been forgotten, while others were like echoes in a void. He felt again his mother's strong arms, could see the nicotine stains between her fingers and hear the rhythmic tone of her voice. His father, a wiry man with flaming red hair and brown, broken teeth, his hands so work sore he could strike a match off his knuckles. His sisters, Mary and Gail, teaching him to lie and smoke and cheat. Three pets buried in the garden. Eighteen summers. Eighteen birthdays.

How dark are you now?

The rain hitting his bedroom window. The smell of Airfix glue. The damp-stains on the walls. The leering faces in the patterns of the brown-and-yellow curtains. Allan connected each memory to the next, like stars in a constellation, in the hope of determining some shape, however vague.

He recalled a boy and his father. The boy in tears, holding in his palm a watch with a broken strap. Such a small thing, and so easily repaired.

I broke it, Daddy, he said, a dimple set deep in his chin and his little hands shaking. *I'm sorry . . .*

Rage like a bullet. The father roared, and his hand came down, connecting with the side of the boy's face. The sound was thunder. The boy staggered backward and fell . . . fell forever, it seemed, and still with the watch clasped in his hand.

"How dark?" Allan wheezed.

The house he had grown up in had changed—several cosmetic improvements—but it was nothing compared to his old school, which had fallen in the opposite direction. Its redbrick walls were cracked and sagging, smeared with vulgar graffiti. The doorways were cluttered with empty beer cans, flattened cigarette butts, spent condoms. Yellowed sheets of newspaper gathered in the corners, blown there by the wind, glued to the brick by damp and piss. The windows were boarded over with plywood, each tattooed with obscenities. Allan crossed the litter-strewn playground, weeds forcing their way through fissures in the cement, and found a gap between the boards. He peered into a dusky classroom—couldn't see much, except a bead of light across the floor, and his dead son standing in the corner. Thomas had never attended Meadingham Secondary; had been killed before he was old enough . . . but here he was anyway.

Allan reeled from the gap in the boards, hand to pocket. He took a shot of morphine and repeated his mantra until the pain had been masked.

Back across the playground, bent against the drizzling rain, wondering what had happened to this place. He'd heard that many schools across England had closed down because of funding cuts, but Meadingham Secondary wasn't just closed—it was infected. No more children. No vigor, or future. It hunched in the rain with its wounds revealed, a pitiful husk.

Allan stopped at the edge of the football field. Just a muddy expanse now. No goalposts or corner flags. It was here, over forty years ago, that he had played the game of his life. Here where, for ninety vibrant minutes, he had been everything he wanted to be: admired, applauded, a healthy teenage boy with the arc of his life ahead of him. He searched for that child now, but saw only a mist of rain. Melody/Melanie was there, though, standing a short distance away. Her dark hair flew in the autumn wind.

"Hello," he managed.

She turned his way but looked right through him.

"Where are you now?" Allan wiped drips from his nose. His cracked lips trembled in something like a smile. "What did you become? Are you happy?"

All at once he saw a different destiny: a life with this pretty girl, who grew into a strong and beautiful woman. His ever-loving wife and the mother of his children. Four wonderful boys with broad shoulders and names that began with the same letter. He saw it all in a moment—a flash. This destiny. This *could-have-been*. And Allan could smile without it hurting. He could *exist* without the hip flask in his pocket. There was no cancer in this alternate life. No shadows.

He walked back toward the school, wondering if the butterfly fluttered its wings in such a fashion. Could one decision—or *in*decision—cause the ripples to spread in a completely different way? Or was he destined, no matter what, to tread the path he now walked? Was fate so unyielding?

Allan's legs trembled with all the walking, and the rats in his stomach whipped their ropy tails. He sat down on a wall, fished one of the airline's paper towels from his inside jacket pocket, and spat a wad of blood into it. He thought about balling it up and tossing it into a doorway with the old newspapers and crushed beer cans—adding his cancer to its own—but instead folded the towel and pushed it into another pocket. He wiped rain from his eyes and looked toward the football field. No sign of the girl now. No reminder of that possible destiny. He was alone.

Late afternoon, and the daylight—if you could call it that—was quickly fading. Allan thought of Holly. Only three miles separated them now, although the emotional distance was beyond measure. He had come here hoping to build a bridge but was afraid his soul might be lacking the raw materials.

Still, in the time he had left . . . he had to try.

He recalled her voice on the phone, one word—*hello*—that had set his mind spinning. He hadn't been able to speak to her. Everything inside him had clenched. Would it be any different in person? Would he stutter and walk away, carrying his burden, a coward until the end?

Would she slam the door in his face, or fall into his arms?

Would her hair smell the same?

How dark are you now?

Was her soul filled with the light he needed?

HE COULDN'T FIND a pay phone anywhere; the classic red telephone box, which adorned every street when he lived here, appeared to have become a thing of the past. Allan ended up dragging his luggage into a pub, ordering half a bitter (one thing that, blessedly, hadn't changed at all), and having the barman call a taxi on his mobile phone.

The taxi driver was an elderly man who'd lived in Meadingham all his life. He pointed out the many changes as they drove through the town: the Wetherspoon's bar where Woolworths used to be; the multistory car park built on the spot of the old library; a shimmering office block that had replaced several small stores. So many changes—too many for Allan to keep up with. He sat in the back and watched the ghosts whisper along High Street and grunted in agreement every time the driver remarked that the country was going to the dogs.

They followed Cattlestock Lane out of town, the gray buildings and bleak streets giving way to rolling hills and farmland. The driver stopped talking and turned on the radio. The Beatles sang "Yesterday." The windshield wipers left streaks on the glass.

The barn appeared from behind a clutch of black trees on the left side of the road. With its collapsed roof and blistered boards, it looked exactly—*hauntingly*—as it had when Thomas's body was discovered there twenty-six years ago. Allan thought it was mental residue—a trick of the memory, attached to his pain. Maybe a sip of morphine would make it disappear. He pulled the flask from his pocket and asked the driver to stop.

"The barn," he croaked, unscrewing the cap.

"What about it?"

"You . . . you see it?"

"Yeah."

Allan sipped anyway. He wiped his eyes and blinked and sipped again. The barn wavered in his vision. He stifled a cough. The morphine touched him with many hands, and each felt like ice.

"It's been there for years," the driver said.

"Yes."

"I always get a chill when I drive past it. You know that Meadingham Monster, right?"

"Yes."

"They found one of his victims there. Little boy. Seven years old."

A slight shift in the scene, and this *was* mental residue: the barn cordoned off with barrier tape, policemen with dogs searching the area for evidence while television and newspaper reporters squabbled for the best positions. A white van was parked in the field beside the barn, with Thomas's shattered body inside, wrapped in a sheet.

"Tell me something," Allan said, sliding the flask back into his pocket. He blinked and the white van disappeared. "How can everything else around here change so much, when that hideous old barn looks exactly the same?"

"God only knows," the driver said. He shrugged, then looked over his shoulder at Allan. "Seems to me that, sometimes . . . it's the bad things that stick around."

THE OLD HOUSE hadn't changed much, either. The front door and windows had been painted, and there was a newer car in the driveway, but other than that, Allan could have been stepping into 1987. He paid the taxi driver and wheeled his luggage down the garden path to the front door.

A thousand doubts crept in. An ocean of fear and anxiety. He knocked on the door (an enfeebled tap of the knuckles) before he could change his mind. The sweat and rain trickled down his face as he waited. His heart had been pounding hard all afternoon, but now it grew wings and flew furiously around his body, banging off every surface like a fly in a bottle.

He saw her soft silhouette through the frosted window set in the front door and suddenly wished he were back in Toronto, calling her on the telephone—this would *surely* have been easier over the phone. He clutched the flask in his pocket and wiped his eyes, then the door opened and she was there. The breath creaked from his withered lungs, and for what seemed like an age he couldn't draw another. The first thing he noticed—before he saw how terribly she had aged, and that the coldness in her eyes was still there—was that the bow in her hair had come untied. A wild coincidence, almost certainly, but for one second he was twenty years old again, and the future was theirs to write.

She didn't recognize him, of course. He was stooped and skeletal, the illness had drawn all the character from his face, and he had claws instead of hands. She looked at him questioningly, and it was only when he reached out with one of those claws and pulled the ribbon from her hair that she realized who he was.

Her mouth dropped open. Her cold green eyes fluttered.

"Hello, Holly," he said.

For a moment she said nothing. Just stared at him like he was something new, something that disquieted her. She was skinny and haggard, her flesh the color of the gray skies under which she lived, her once-laughing mouth set in a thin, straight line from which a myriad of tiny wrinkles radiated outward. Her hair, once so lustrous, was now gray and brittle. Allan wondered whether she too was ill. She certainly didn't look healthy.

They might have stood there all day, a tableau of bitterness—of dashed hopes and lost lives—if he hadn't raised his hand and offered her the ribbon.

She looked at it but didn't take it. Instead she asked, "What do you want?"

Allan tried to smile but could only grimace. "I've come to see you."

"What for?"

"It's been a long time, Holly. Too long." The arm holding the ribbon ached and he lowered it. He blinked rain from his eyes. "There's something I need to tell you."

"So tell me and have done with it."

He felt battered not only by the rain but by the vehemence of her words. Weakly, he said, "Aren't you going to invite me in?"

"Why should I?"

He hesitated, then played his trump card. It felt oddly triumphant to do so. "I'm dying, Holly."

He hadn't expected compassion, and he didn't get it. Holly flinched ever so slightly, as if he had raised a hand to her, and then her face hardened again. "What's that got to do with me?"

"I just . . . well, I wanted to see you before I . . . I just wanted to make amends."

The sound she made startled him. A harsh bark that it took him a moment to realize was a laugh. Then she said, "Isn't it a bit late for that?"

He was shivering now. The rain seemed to be getting inside him, worming into his skin. "I hope not. Won't you at least let me try?"

She remained silent, her face as hard as ever.

"Please, Holly. I haven't much time. I flew halfway around the world for this."

"I didn't invite you here."

"I know that, but . . ." All at once the strength went out of him. He felt like a sponge, his clothes and flesh saturated, too heavy to support him any longer. The handle of his suitcase slipped from his numb fingers and clattered to the path. The wet ribbon dropped from his other hand like a dead bird. Allan felt his vision narrowing, the world receding from him, but he didn't realize he'd stumbled until his shoulder crashed against the wall beside the door. He cried out as jagged forks of pain tore through him, and then he felt himself gripped by hands like twisted wire, felt his body supported as he stumbled over the threshold, out of the rain, into the house.

The pain from the blow to his shoulder was raging, gathering pace inside him, echoing and radiating from its point of origin into his bones and his soft tissues. He groped for his flask but couldn't get his hand to work properly.

"What are you doing?"

"Pocket," he gasped, and even that was like coughing out nails. "Flask."

"You mean this?"

He squinted. Through the grayness he saw the flask being offered to him. He took it, and with Holly's help twisted off the cap and tilted it toward his mouth. The callus on his bottom lip burned when he pressed the metal edge against it, but after a moment the pain faded and he began to revive.

Holly helped him along a corridor, through a door, and into the welcoming softness of an armchair. "Here," she said and dumped a towel on his head. He dried his hair and face, then wrapped the towel around himself and sat shivering. Holly knelt on the floor, her back to him, twisting the knob on a gas fire. The "real-effect" flames flared, then settled. He felt heat lapping toward him, though it couldn't penetrate the cold at his core.

Holly turned and stood, scowling at him. Her eyes jerked to the flask and she asked, "What is that? It doesn't smell like brandy."

"Oramorph—liquid morphine." He shrugged. "It's for the pain."

"And what happens when it runs out?"

He felt a spike of alarm at the prospect. It was a reminder that he needed to organize a continuing supply while he was over here, and sooner rather than later. Perhaps Holly would help him. He had the necessary documentation.

"It won't," he said. "I won't let it."

"How often do you take it?"

"As often as I need to."

She eyed the flask with suspicion, as if it contained something dangerous—salmonella or anthrax—that she was afraid he might release into the atmosphere.

Allan clutched it tighter. He lowered his eyes.

"Do you want tea?" She asked the question aggressively, as if it were a challenge she defied him to refuse.

"Please."

"Anything to eat?"

"No. Thank you."

While she was away he looked around the room, his head turning slowly from within the folds of the towel, like a tortoise waking from hibernation. The carpet was a warm coral color, the upholstery, cushions, and curtains emblazoned with bright floral patterns. It should have been a cheerful room, and yet it seemed to Allan that there was something desperate about it. In the corner was a sideboard on which were propped two framed photographs of Thomas, both of which Allan recognized. One was of him standing on a Cornish beach, squinting into the sun, wearing a yellow-and-black T-shirt and red swimming trunks. The other was of him blowing out the candles on a cake with a big number 5 on it. There were no photographs of Allan.

Holly returned with the tea. He'd half expected a tray with a pot and china cups, but instead she shoved a mug unceremoniously into his hand. The tea was pale, insipid. He sipped, grimaced.

"Not to your liking?"

He shook his head, then winced; even this small movement caused him pain now. "No, it's fine. It's my throat and stomach. Ulcers. Tumors. I don't know."

She regarded him dispassionately. "Where have you got it? The cancer."

"It started in my colon. A long time ago. I had no idea, of course, and it just ran wild. I think it's everywhere now. I stopped the chemo . . . the treatments."

"Why would you do that?"

"Because they can't help me. They only prolong the pain." Allan sipped his tea and held up the flask. "This is my only relief."

Her eyes flickered briefly to the sideboard, the photographs of Thomas. "Well, it's no more than you deserve."

He sighed. "You're probably right."

Then she put her mug down, hard, on the small table by her side. He expected to see anger on her face, but instead her eyes teared up, and suddenly she looked ashamed. "No," she said, "that's a horrible thing to say. You *don't* deserve it. It's just . . . I've hated you for so many years. You *abandoned* me, Allan. When I needed you most, you . . . abandoned me."

"I know. I'm sorry."

"Why did you go?"

"Because I was hurting, too. Because I couldn't reach you. You were lost to me."

"I was grieving."

"I know. And so was I. But we weren't grieving together. What should have halved our burden only . . . doubled it."

"So you ran away."

"I didn't run; I just left. I thought it would be best for both of us."

"You were wrong. I needed you, Allan. I was reaching out for you. Couldn't you see?"

"No, I couldn't." Her claim astonished him. "You had a wall around you that I couldn't penetrate. I tried, but . . ."

"You didn't try hard enough."

The bitterness was back in her voice. Allan wondered whether it was justified, whether he *hadn't* tried hard enough. It was possible, he supposed. Maybe he had failed to recognize and respond to Holly's need because to have comforted her, to have shared and absorbed her grief, would have felt like a betrayal, like lying to them both. There was so much that Holly still didn't know. And if there was ever going to be honesty between them again, then she *had* to know, however hard that might be.

"Haven't you got anything to say?" she said.

Despite her anger, despite her antipathy toward him, he could see that her need had never really gone away, that she was reaching out to him even now. It was as if the years of distance between them suddenly meant nothing at all, as if time was a flimsy curtain that could simply be swept aside.

Allan nodded, then finished his tea and placed the empty mug on the table beside the armchair. He kept hold of the hip flask, though—clutched it tighter than ever. "This is so difficult. You won't like what I have to say." He wiped his trembling mouth. "But it's the reason I'm here."

"Just say it."

He'd rehearsed this moment, but now that he was here, in front of her, he didn't know where to start. He gasped and stammered . . . used the towel to mop his damp brow. Eventually, he managed, "My sin . . . it's . . ."

Red like crimson.

" . . . It's buried deep inside me. A *part* of me now. I can't eradicate it, but maybe I can soften its edges . . . go to my maker with just a shred of peace . . . and maybe I can eliminate some of your pain, too."

"Your sin?" Holly narrowed her eyes.

"The Monster," Allan said. "Grayson—"

"Dead," Holly snarled. Her green eyes blazed. "The fucker's dead."

"Yes, I read it in the newspaper." He ran the towel across his brow again. He smelled rain and sweat in the fabric. "I saw it as a sign . . . to come here, to see you . . . before it was too late."

"It's not right, though, is it?" Holly snapped, as if she hadn't heard him. "A heart attack. He deserved to suffer for killing Thomas . . . for what he did to *all* those children."

Allan was silent for a moment, then he said, "You don't have to worry about Grayson anymore. Because the thing about Thomas . . . what I wanted to tell you is . . . *he* didn't suffer."

She scowled. "What do you mean?"

"He was never scared. Never alone. Not like you thought. Grayson didn't kill him, Holly."

Her eyes widened, as if the lid were being pulled back on something she didn't want to see. Something terrible. "What are you talking about, Allan?"

He was shaking again. Tears gathered in his eyes. "That day. The day Thomas died. It was a Saturday. You were in town. Buying a new frock."

"With Verity," she said, her voice breathless, as though she needed to cement the facts into place. "I was with Verity, and you were at home, repairing something—"

"The radiator," he said. "We had air trapped in the bathroom radiator. It was banging and shuddering like there was something trying to get out. I was bleeding the system—"

"And Thomas was out playing with his friends."

"No."

She stared at him, eyes wide with panic. "No? What do you mean, no?"

He took a deep breath. It hurt; fish hooks and barbed wire. "Thomas *wasn't* out playing with his friends. I told the police he was, but he wasn't. He was in the house all morning. Part of the time he was watching me—*helping* me, as he called it. Then he got bored and went downstairs to watch TV. I was struggling with the valve, the radiator was leaking, and my temper was fraying at the edges. I heard a crash from downstairs, and Thomas let out a squeal. I was furious and worried at the same time. I yelled his name but didn't get a reply, so I packed a few towels around the leak and rushed onto the landing."

Allan's throat crackled. He gasped and took a quick shot of morphine. The pain, this time, was harder to displace. It lodged somewhere in his heart. A cold and jagged thing.

"Thomas came up the stairs. He was crying . . . holding something in his hand. He held it out, and I saw that it was my grandfather's watch."

Allan stopped again. He screwed the cap on the flask as the boy bloomed in his mind. Beautiful Thomas, wearing his striped T-shirt and blue shorts. He had tears in his eyes . . . a dimple set deep in his chin.

I broke it, Daddy.

"The strap was broken. That was all. He'd been playing a game—James Bond, or something—and had fallen off a chair. It was the original strap, and very delicate. It didn't take much to break it."

I'm sorry . . .

"I could have had it repaired, but at that moment, with my patience so thin, that didn't seem to matter."

Allan paused again. It was the longest speech he'd made in some time and he felt exhausted, breathless. He wasn't cold now. His insides, all the way from his gullet to his belly, were hot, pulsing, inflamed. With shaking hands he unscrewed the flask's cap and took yet another hit of morphine. Holly sat perfectly still, staring at him.

"Then what happened?" she rasped.

He swallowed, winced. "I saw red. I lashed out. It was supposed to be a clip around the ear, like my dad used to give me, but I was just so angry . . ." He wheezed for air. A tear rolled down his withered cheek. "I caught the side of his face—harder than I expected. He fell. Thomas fell. He went backward down the stairs. He hit his head and I heard his neck crack. He was like a broken doll, tumbling over and over . . ."

His voice faded. He sat, huddled and shrunken.

Holly said nothing for a long time. Her eyes were small green stones set in her marble face. Her thin chest barely moved. This silence was nothing that Allan had expected, and he sat through it with pain all around. He recalled stepping off the train earlier that day, and that brief moment of nothingness. He longed for it again—to be trapped in a world where everything had stopped.

Holly opened her mouth, then closed it again. She looked at him. Her eyes flooded with venom. She looked away.

"You killed him," she said at last, her voice cold and yet filled with a kind of wonder. "You *killed* our son."

It was Allan's turn to open his mouth . . . close it again.

Holly stood up, wobbled a little—had to clutch the back of the armchair to keep from losing her balance. She teetered unsurely to the window, then back again, as if she didn't really know what she was doing.

"I've had to live with this for twenty-six years," Allan continued. "It's done nothing but grow inside me. A shadow. A *darkness*. But you, Holly . . . your shadow can be lifted. You don't have to think about Grayson anymore. You no longer have to torture yourself with thoughts of Thomas alone and terrified. Because he never met Grayson. He was never locked in the trunk of Grayson's car, never exposed to his evil. It's a shock, yes, but please try to see the positive in this."

Holly's mouth dropped open. She gaped at him. "The positive? How can there possibly be a *positive*?"

"Thomas didn't suffer," Allan replied. "He wasn't . . . corrupted in the way you thought he was."

Her eyes flickered wildly; she looked as though she was having difficulty assimilating his words. When she spoke, her voice was distant, detached.

"But you *allowed* me to think he was. I've been in hell for the last quarter of a century, Allan. No mother should endure what I've had to. And you left me there. You went away and . . . *left* me there."

"I had no choice. You see that, don't you? If I'd told the police the truth, I would have been sent to prison for killing my own son. And Thomas would still be dead. It wouldn't have made any difference—"

"*It would have made ALL the difference!*" Suddenly she was screeching, spitting at him. Her body was rigid, her hands curled into claws. Allan thought she was going to fly at him, tear at him. Then she froze.

"The wounds. On Thomas's body. The knife wounds."

"I had no choice, Holly."

"*You* did that?"

"I had to make the police believe he was another of Grayson's victims." Allan wiped his face with a trembling hand, his voice wheedling, begging her to understand. "No words can explain what I was going through. I just told myself that he was already dead . . . that he couldn't feel anything."

"And you dumped his body?" she asked. "In the barn?"

"Yes."

"That horrid place?"

"Yes."

She turned away from him and wobbled again, then lowered her face into her hands. Her narrow back trembled, shoulders like ridges of ice.

"This isn't happening," she hissed, trying to readjust to these new revelations, to get the facts straight in her head. "It can't be real."

"I'm so sorry."

"But he confessed." She looked at him again, but Allan doubted she really saw anything but the fog of her own anguish. "Grayson confessed to Thomas's murder—to *all* the murders."

"That was . . ." He had been about to say "a stroke of luck," but stopped himself at the last moment, wondering whether it might sound more callous than he'd intended. He stammered again, his mind struggling for the right words—if such words even existed.

She stepped closer. Her eyes were still wild, her body taut with painful emotion.

"I was surprised," he said finally, "when Grayson confessed. I figured it was some sick sense of pride—that he was only too happy to claim as many victims as possible. Or maybe he had simply lost count. Maybe the children he killed meant nothing to him. Who knows what goes through a killer's mind?"

"*You* do."

"No . . . I'm not the same as Grayson." He considered his sins, and how they had haunted him over the years. They had metastasized inside him, spreading from his heart and soul, into his mind, into his *body.*

Maybe they had caused the cancer, a seed of darkness and loathing, allowed to grow. He then considered Grayson, who had brutalized—terrorized—all those children. He had an ocean of blood on his hands, a mountain of darkness in his soul. Yet his eyes were always so impassive . . . unaffected.

"We're nothing alike," Allan gasped. "I'm a man who made a terrible mistake. He's just an evil bastard."

Holly raised a hand as if to slap him, but instead she pointed a trembling finger at his face. Allan flinched. The pain was unreal.

"Don't you dare sit there and pass judgment on others." She spoke through gritted teeth. Her haggard skin blazed. "You killed our son. You violated his body. You put me through years of hell. And then you come back here and expect me to . . . to be *grateful* to you for finally telling the truth."

"I expect no such thing." Allan licked his papery lips. "You deserve to know what happened. That's why I'm here . . . to remove your shadow, and to partly remove mine."

"Clearing your conscience before you die?" She leaned closer. Her eyes were in flames. "It doesn't work like that. You're going straight to hell."

"I'm already there." He coughed and sprayed blood against the back of one hand.

"You're the most cowardly man I've ever met." Her voice bubbled with rage. "At least Grayson confessed to his crimes. *You're* the real monster."

"Don't say that."

"You sicken me."

He wiped the back of his hand on the towel, leaving a bright red smear.

"What I said before, about you deserving it . . ." She looked at him avidly, hatefully. "I've never meant anything more in my life."

"Your anger is equaled only by my guilt." Allan looked past Holly, toward the corner, where the photographs of their son adorned the sideboard. "I see Thomas everywhere I go. Just standing there. Staring at me. A constant reminder of what I did."

"And *that*?" She pointed at the morphine. "That makes it all so much easier, I assume."

"It's all I have," Allan said. "It's the only thing that eases the pain and makes Thomas go away."

"I hate you."

"I know."

Suddenly she darted forward, snatched the flask from his hands. He tried to react, to stop her, but his limbs were so unresponsive he might as well have tried to snatch a fly from midair.

"No, Holly," he pleaded. "I need it."

"I needed my son," she said. "I needed my life. But you took them from me."

Her rage erupted, as he knew it would. She screamed—a long and terrible sound, which seemed to pour not only from her mouth, but from her eyes, her flared nostrils, her fingertips. She lunged at Allan, lifting the flask above her head and bringing it down with savage force. He saw only a flash of silver before the base slammed against his forehead. His frail skin split and blood spattered the towel. She hit him again, cracking his cheekbone. He half lifted one arm, but it was no defense at all. A third blow broke his nose. He felt it pop. His head flopped to one side. She struck him again, and a crimson world opened below him. He started to fall, but not before the flask came down yet again, splitting his upper lip and knocking out two of his teeth. He spat one of them out. Swallowed the other. His eyes flicked to the back of the room. Thomas was there, watching without expression.

HE OPENED HIS eyes.

You're going straight to hell, Holly had said, and he'd replied that he was already there. But he was wrong. So wrong. He'd been nowhere near hell at that point.

Now, however . . .

The rope binding him to the radiator was too thick to break, and the knot too tight for his weak fingers to loosen. It was tied around his ankle. The coarse fibers chafed his skin. He looked around the room for something that might help, but there was no help here.

Thomas's bedroom was—as he had expected—exactly the same. The curtains. The bedding. The posters tacked to the walls. Allan saw his son everywhere. Five years old, curled up on the bed. Six years old, racing his Matchbox cars across the carpet. Three years old, proudly dressing himself in the morning, his shoes the wrong way around. The memories were as unbreakable as the rope that bound him. Allan tried to scream but managed only a feeble hiss. He clawed at his eyes with blunt, trembling fingers. The shadow inside him roared.

Holly stood in the doorway. Her eyes were green ice, filled with hate. The ribbon in her hair was mottled with his blood.

"Does it hurt?" she asked.

He nodded and wept. "Terribly."

"You'll be wanting this, then?" She held out the hip flask. More dents in it now, and smeared with his blood.

He made a low, longing sound in his throat and started to crawl toward her. Such slow and painful progress, with every wasted muscle screaming, every brittle bone like straw. His ragged mouth hung open, dripping red.

"Almost there," she said.

The rope around his ankle pulled taut. He could crawl no farther. He whimpered, then reached out, hand trembling. Holly held the flask only inches away. He stretched his fingers.

"Please, Holly . . . *please*."

She swirled the contents. He heard the glorious morphine lapping against the inside of the flask.

"Not much left," she said.

"I'll take what there is." The rope—stretched so tight—cut into his ankle. His fingertips grazed the flask's worn surface. "I *need* it."

"So do I," Holly said. She smiled wickedly, unscrewed the cap, and emptied the flask's contents onto the floor. Allan collapsed and made pathetic lunging motions with his upper body. The morphine seeped into the carpet.

Gone.

"It's my pain relief now," Holly said. Still smiling, she stepped out of the room and closed the door behind her.

Allan retreated to the wall, crawling through the memories. He tried again to loosen the rope around his ankle. His fingertips bled with the effort.

Thomas watched him from the corner. He appeared more solid than before. More *permanent*. Allan turned away from him, to where three-year-old Thomas tied his laces. Away again, and five-year-old Thomas murmured in his sleep, gathered the sheets a little closer.

Allan sobbed. He wiped the blood from his face and looked at the window. The rain had stopped. The clouds had cleared. A rich sunset bled into nothingness.

Wonderful, endless nothingness.

Like scarlet, Allan thought.

ABOUT THE AUTHORS

Kevin J. Anderson has written more than 120 novels, more than 50 of which were national or international bestsellers. He is the author of the Dan Shamble, Zombie PI humorous horror series; fantasy epic *Terra Incognita*; and SF epic *Saga of Seven Suns;* as well as *Hellhole* and the new *Dune* novels with Brian Herbert. He edited the *Blood Lite* anthology series and is the publisher of WordFire Press. He is also known for his work in the universes of Star Wars, X-Files, Batman, Superman, StarCraft, and other popular franchises.

Robert Jackson Bennett's 2010 debut, *Mr. Shivers,* won the Shirley Jackson Award as well as the Sydney J. Bounds Newcomer Award. His second novel, *The Company Man,* won a Special Citation of Excellence from the Philip K. Dick Award, as well as an Edgar Award for Best Paperback Original. His third novel, *The Troupe,* has topped many "Best of 2012" lists, including that of *Publishers Weekly.* His fourth novel, *American Elsewhere,* was published in 2013 to wide acclaim.

Amber Benson is a writer, director, and actor. She currently writes the Calliope Reaper-Jones series for Ace/Roc, and her middle-grade book, *Among the Ghosts,* came out in paperback in 2011 from Simon and Schuster. She codirected the Slamdance feature *Drones* and cocreated (and directed) the BBC animated series *Ghosts of Albion* with Christopher Golden. She spent three years as Tara Maclay on the television series *Buffy the Vampire Slayer.*

Holly Black is the author of bestselling contemporary fantasy books for kids and teens. Some of her titles include the Spiderwick Chronicles (with Tony DiTerlizzi), the Modern Faerie Tale series, the Good Neighbors graphic novel trilogy (with Ted Naifeh), the Curse Workers series, *Doll Bones,* and her dark fantasy novel, *The Coldest Girl in Coldtown.* She has been a finalist for the Mythopoeic Award, a finalist for an Eisner Award, and the recipient of the Andre Norton Award. She currently lives in New England with her husband, Theo, in a house with a secret door.

Sarah Rees Brennan is the author of the Demon's Lexicon trilogy, the first book of which was an ALA Top Ten Best Book of 2009, and the coauthor of *Team Human* with Justine Larbalestier. Her newest book is *Unspoken,* a romantic gothic mystery about a girl who discovers her imaginary friend is a real boy. *Unspoken* is an ALA Best Book 2013 and on the Tayshas list. Sarah writes from her homeland of Ireland but likes to travel the world collecting inspiration.

Chelsea Cain is the author of the *New York Times* bestselling Archie Sheridan thriller series, including *Heartsick, Sweetheart, Evil at Heart, The Night Season, Kill You Twice,* and *Let Me Go* (August 2013). The series has been published in over thirty languages and recommended on *The Today Show,* and appeared in episodes of HBO's *True Blood* and ABC's *Castle.* Stephen King included two of her books in his top ten favorite books of the year, and NPR named *Heartsick* one of the best 100 thrillers ever written.

Rachel Caine is the *New York Times* and *USA Today* bestselling author of more than forty books, including the Morganville Vampires series. She lives in Fort Worth, Texas, with her husband, fantasy artist R. Cat Conrad. You can visit her website at www.rachelcaine.com.

Cassandra Clare was born to American parents in Tehran, Iran, and spent much of her childhood traveling the world with her family, including one trek through the Himalayas as a toddler where she spent a month living in her father's backpack. She lived in France, England, and Switzerland before she was ten years old. Since her family moved around so much she found familiarity in books and went everywhere with a book. She started working on her YA novel, *City of Bones,* the first book of the Mortal Instruments series, in 2004, inspired by the urban landscape of Manhattan, her favorite city. The Mortal Instruments books went on to be *New York Times, Wall Street Journal,* and *USA Today* bestsellers, as did the companion series, the Infernal Devices. Cassandra lives in western Massachusetts with her husband and three cats.

Gregory Frost is a writer of dark fantasy, SF, young adult, and historical thriller fiction. He has been a finalist for every major fantasy genre award. His latest novel-length work is the YA-crossover *Shadowbridge* duology, voted in 2008 "one of the four best fantasy novels of the year" by the ALA. His historical thriller, *Fitcher's Brides*, was a Best Novel finalist for both World Fantasy and International Horror Guild Awards. Other Frost short stories appear in Ellen Datlow's *Supernatural Noir* anthology, and in *V-Wars,* edited by Jonathan Maberry. He directs the fiction writing program at Swarthmore College.

Jeffrey David Greene writes his fiction at a small desk covered in action figures. Sometimes he discusses his story ideas with a chorus of noisy and opinionated Chihuahuas. He lives in Smyrna, Georgia, with his wife and teaches at Southern Polytechnic State University. Currently, he is at work on a YA urban fantasy novel.

Allan Guthrie is an award-winning Scottish crime writer. His latest novella, *Bye Bye Baby,* was a Top Ten Kindle Bestseller. He's also co-founder of digital publishing company Blasted Heath and a literary agent with Jenny Brown Associates.

Charlaine Harris, a native of the Mississippi Delta, has lived her whole life in various Southern states. Her first book, a mystery, was published in 1981. After that promising debut, her career meandered along until the success of the Sookie Stackhouse novels. Now all her books are in print, and she is a very happy camper. She is married and has three children.

Rick Hautala wrote close to thirty novels. His recent books include *The Demon's Wife,* from JournalStone; *Chills* and *Waiting,* from Cemetery Dance Publications; *Star Road,* cowritten with Matthew Costello, from Thomas Dunne/St. Martin's; and *Glimpses,* a short story collection from Dark Regions Press. Born and raised in Rockport, Massachusetts, Rick was a graduate of the University of Maine in Orono with an MA in English Literature. He lived in southern Maine with his wife, author Holly Newstein, until his death in March of 2013. In 2012, he was awarded the Lifetime Achievement Award from the Horror Writers' Association. For more information, check out his website, www.rickhautala.com.

Rhodi Hawk has been fascinated by storytelling since her earliest memory, when her grandmother read to her from *Peter Pan in Kensington Gardens.* Rhodi has been reading or writing ever since and began her career as a transcription linguist in U.S. Army intelligence. She won the International Thriller Writers Scholarship for her first work of fiction, *A Twisted Ladder.* A compulsive traveler, she lives in Magnolia, Texas, with a host of critters, including her husband, Hank.

Nate Kenyon is the author of seven novels and dozens of short stories in the horror, thriller, and sci-fi genres. His first novel, *Bloodstone,* was a Bram Stoker Award finalist and won the P&E Horror Novel of the Year. *The Reach,* also a Stoker Award finalist, received a starred review from *Publishers Weekly* and was optioned for film. Kenyon's novels *StarCraft Ghost: Spectres* and *Diablo: The Order* were based on Blizzard's bestselling video-game franchises, and his next *Diablo* novel will be released in 2014. Kenyon's latest novel is the thriller *Day One* from Thomas Dunne Books.

Sherrilyn Kenyon is a *New York Times* bestselling author who has claimed the number one spot sixteen times from 2010 to 2013. This extraordinary bestseller continues to top every genre she writes. With more than twenty-five million copies of her books in print in over one hundred countries, her current series include: The Dark-Hunters, The League, Chronicles of Nick, and Belador. Since 2004 she has placed more than fifty novels on the *New York Times* list in all formats, including manga.

Michael Koryta is the *New York Times* bestselling author of nine novels, including *The Prophet, The Ridge,* and *The Cypress House.* His prizewinning work has been translated into more than twenty languages and praised by writers such as Stephen King, Dean Koontz, Scott Smith, and Michael Connelly. A former private investigator and newspaper reporter, he lives in Bloomington, Indiana, and St. Petersburg, Florida.

Joe R. Lansdale is the author of over thirty novels and numerous short stories. He has received nine Bram Stoker Awards, an Edgar Award, and numerous other awards and recognitions. He lives in Nacogdoches, Texas, with his wife, Karen.

Kasey Lansdale was born into the world of writing. Daughter of renowned horror author Joe R. Lansdale, she was first published by Random House at the tender age of eight for the short story, "The Companion." Her nonfiction article "Growing Up Lansdale Style" was published in 2012 by *Horror Zine*'s online anthology and later in *Horror Zine*'s print anthology, *A Feast of Frights.* She is the editor of the forthcoming horror anthology *Impossible Monsters,* published by Subterranean Press in 2013. Lansdale is also known for her work as a singer/songwriter and has just completed her first novel.

Tim Lebbon is a *New York Times* bestselling writer with almost thirty novels published to date, as well as dozens of novellas and hundreds of short stories. Recent releases include *Coldbrook*, *Reaper's Legacy,* and *The Sea Wolves* (with Christopher Golden). Future novels include *Into the Void: Dawn of the Jedi (Star Wars)* and *The Silence.* He has won four British Fantasy Awards, a Bram Stoker Award, and a Scribe Award. Fox2000 acquired film rights to his Secret Journeys of Jack London series, and his Toxic City trilogy is in development with ABC Studios. Find out more at www.timlebbon.net.

David Liss is the author of seven novels, most recently *The Twelfth Enchantment*. His previous books include *A Conspiracy of Paper*, which was named a *New York Times* Notable Book and won the 2001 Barry, MacAvity, and Edgar Awards for Best First Novel. *The Coffee Trader* was also named a *New York Times* Notable Book. *A Spectacle of Corruption* was a national bestseller, and *The Devil's Company* has been optioned for film by Warner Brothers. Liss is the author of the graphic novel *Mystery Men,* has written *Black Panther* for Marvel Comics, and currently writes *The Spider* for Dynamite Comics.

Jonathan Maberry is a *New York Times* bestselling author, multiple Bram Stoker Award winner, and freelancer for Marvel Comics. His novels include *Extinction Machine, Fire & Ash, Patient Zero,* and many others. His award-winning teen novel *Rot & Ruin* is now in development for film. He is the editor of *V-Wars,* an award-winning vampire anthology. Since 1978 he's sold more than twelve hundred magazine feature articles, three thousand columns, plays, greeting cards, song lyrics, and poetry. He is the founder of the Writers Coffeehouse and cofounder of the Liars Club. Jonathan lives in Bucks County, Pennsylvania, with his wife, Sara Jo.

Stuart MacBride is the number one bestselling author of the Logan McRae series, set in Aberdeen; the standalone *Birthdays for the Dead;* and the near-future thriller *Halfhead.* He's won an award or three, been inducted into the International Crime Writing Hall of Fame, and in 2010 he chaired the Theakstons Old Peculier Crime Writing Festival. He lives in the northeast of Scotland with his wife, Fiona, and a small fuzzy serial-killer cat called Grendel.

Sarah MacLean is a *New York Times* and *USA Today* bestselling author of historical romance. Her love of all things historical earned her degrees from Smith College and Harvard University before she set pen to paper and wrote her first book. She lives in New York City.

Jeffrey J. Mariotte's fifty-plus books include supernatural thrillers *Season of the Wolf, River Runs Red, Missing White Girl,* and *Cold Black Hearts;* horror epic *The Slab;* thriller *The Devil's Bait*; and many more. He also writes comic books and graphic novels, including the long-running horror/Western series *Desperadoes, Fade to Black, Zombie Cop,* and others. He's a co-owner of specialty bookstore Mysterious Galaxy with locations in San Diego and Redondo Beach, California. With his wife, Maryelizabeth Hart, he lives on the Flying M Ranch in rural southeastern Arizona, far away from almost everything. Find him online at http://jeffmariotte.com.

James A. Moore is an award-winning author of over twenty novels in different genres, including the critically acclaimed Serenity Falls trilogy and the young adult Subject Seven series. His latest novel is the sword and sorcery fantasy *Seven Forges.* His recurring antihero, Jonathan Crowley, has appeared in half a dozen novels, with more to come. You can find out more about him at http://jamesamoorebooks.com.

Mark Morris is the author of over twenty novels, among which are *Toady, Stitch, The Immaculate, The Secret of Anatomy, Fiddleback, The*

Deluge, and four books in the popular *Doctor Who* range. His short stories, novellas, articles, and reviews have appeared in a wide variety of anthologies and magazines, and he is editor of both *Cinema Macabre,* a book of horror movie essays by genre luminaries for which he won the 2007 British Fantasy Award, and its follow-up *Cinema Futura.* His recently published or forthcoming work includes the official tie-in novel for zombie apocalypse computer game *Dead Island*, a novelization of the 1971 Hammer movie *Vampire Circus,* and *The Wolves of London,* book one of the Obsidian Heart trilogy, which will be published by Titan Books in 2014.

Holly Newstein's short fiction has appeared in *Cemetery Dance* magazine and the anthologies *Borderlands 5, The New Dead, In Laymon's Terms,* and *Epitaphs: The Journal of the New England Horror Writers Association.* She is the coauthor of the novels *Ashes* and *The Epicure* with Ralph W. Bieber, originally published under the pen name H. R. Howland. She lives in Maine with her fur kids, Keira, Remy, and Cielo.

Tom Piccirilli is the author of more than twenty-five novels, including *Shadow Season, The Cold Spot,* and *A Choir of Ill Children.* He has won two International Thriller Awards and four Bram Stoker Awards, as well as having been nominated for the Edgar Award, the World Fantasy Award, the Macavity Award, and Le Grand Prix de l'Imaginaire.

Carrie Ryan is the *New York Times* bestselling author of the critically acclaimed Forest of Hands and Teeth series, which has been translated into more than eighteen languages and is in development as a major motion picture. She is also the editor of the anthology *Foretold: 14 Tales of Prophecy and Prediction,* as well as author of *Divide and Conquer,* the second book in Scholastic's multiauthor/multiplatform series, Infinity Ring. A former litigator, Carrie now writes full-time and lives with her husband, two fat cats, and one large dog in Charlotte, North Carolina. You can find her online at www.carrieryan.com.

Michael Marshall Smith is a novelist and screenwriter. Under this name he has published more than eighty short stories and three novels—*Only Forward, Spares,* and *One of Us*—winning the Philip K. Dick, International Horror Guild, and August Derleth Awards, along with the Prix Bob Morane in France. He has been awarded the British Fantasy Award for Best Short Fiction four times, more than any other author. Writing as **Michael Marshall,** he has published six internationally bestselling thrillers, including *The Straw Men, The Intruders,* and *Killer Move.* His latest novel, *We Are Here,* was published in 2013. He lives in Santa Cruz with his wife, son, and two cats. See more at www.michaelmarshallsmith.com.

F. Paul Wilson is the award-winning *New York Times* bestselling author of nearly fifty books and many short stories spanning horror, adventure, medical thrillers, science fiction, and virtually everything in between. More than nine million copies of his books are in print in the United States, and his work has been translated into twenty-four foreign languages. He also has written for the stage, screen, and interactive media. His latest thrillers, *Cold City* and *Dark City,* feature his urban mercenary, Repairman Jack. Paul resides at the Jersey Shore. Visit www.repairmanjack.com.

T. M. Wright is in his forty-third year as a writer (in training). Author of twenty-three novels (in and out of print) in various languages, a few short stories (he finds the novel easier to write), and lots of poetry, Wright is convinced that the quest for exactly the right word or phrase can hobble any writer. A father, grandfather, woodworker, and artist, Wright loves Boston terriers, Maine Coon cats, and vegetarian cuisine.

Rio Youers is a multiplatform writer, working in books and comics. He is the British Fantasy Award–nominated author of *End Times* and *Westlake Soul.* His short fiction has been published by, among others, Cemetery Dance, St. Martin's Griffin, and IDW Publishing. Rio lives in southwestern Ontario with his wife, Emily, and their daughter, Lily Maye.

Lidia Yuknavitch is the author of the antimemoir *The Chronology of Water* and the novel *Dora: A Headcase*, as well as three books of short stories. She thrives on moss and water in Portland, Oregon.

COPYRIGHT NOTICES